REALIZING THERE WAS NOTHING ELSE TO DO, T.J. BRACED HERSELF FOR THE CONFRONTATION AND LOOKED DIRECTLY TOWARD THE DOOR.

It opened.

"And to what do I owe this surprise?" Chance drawled. He stood framed within the doorway, making no move or attempt to ease the strained silence that hung between them as he waited for her answer.

Suddenly unable to move or utter a sound in defense of being caught in his room, T.J. stood motionless, frozen to the spot. Every inch of her body was acutely aware of him, every nerve ready to jump at his slightest movement, every muscle primed to flash into action if he approached.

Finally, Chance stepped into the room and, without taking his eyes off her, kicked the door shut behind him.

Sweeping the Stetson from his head and tossing it onto the bed, Chance halted before her, their bodies only a few inches apart. His gaze moved over her from top to bottom and back up again, flagrantly assessing her, instilling her with yet more unease as it paused upon the rapid rise and fall of her breasts. An imperious little smile tugged at one corner of his mouth as his gaze rose once more to meet hers.

"Why are you in my room?" he asked softly, letting the words roll off his tongue like smooth, hot honey.

TODAY'S HOTTEST READS
ARE TOMORROW'S SUPERSTARS

VICTORY'S WOMAN   (4484, $4.50)
by Gretchen Genet
Andrew—the carefree soldier who sought glory on the battlefield, and returned a shattered man . . . Niall—the legendary frontiersman and a former Shawnee captive, tormented by his past . . . Roger—the troubled youth, who would rise up to claim a shocking legacy . . . and Clarice—the passionate beauty bound by one man, and hopelessly in love with another. Set against the backdrop of the American revolution, three men fight for their heritage—and one woman is destined to change all their lives forever!

FORBIDDEN   (4488, $4.99)
by Jo Beverley
While fleeing from her brothers, who are attempting to sell her into a loveless marriage, Serena Riverton accepts a carriage ride from a stranger—who is the handsomest man she has ever seen. Lord Middlethorpe, himself, is actually contemplating marriage to a dull daughter of the aristocracy, when he encounters the breathtaking Serena. She arouses him as no woman ever has. And after a night of thrilling intimacy—a forbidden liaison—Serena must choose between a lady's place and a woman's passion!

WINDS OF DESTINY   (4489, $4.99)
by Victoria Thompson
Becky Tate is a half-breed outcast—branded by her Comanche heritage. Then she meets a rugged stranger who awakens her heart to the magic and mystery of passion. Hiding a desperate past, Texas Ranger Clint Masterson has ridden into cattle country to bring peace to a divided land. But a greater battle rages inside him when he dares to desire the beautiful Becky!

WILDEST HEART   (4456, $4.99)
by Virginia Brown
Maggie Malone had come to cattle country to forge her future as a healer. Now she was faced by Devon Conrad, an outlaw wounded body and soul by his shadowy past . . . whose eyes blazed with fury even as his burning caress sent her spiraling with desire. They came together in a Texas town about to explode in sin and scandal. Danger was their destiny—and there was nothing they wouldn't dare for love!

Available wherever paperbacks are sold, or order direct from the Publisher. Send cover price plus 50¢ per copy for mailing and handling to Penguin USA, P.O. Box 999, c/o Dept. 17109, Bergenfield, NJ 07621. Residents of New York and Tennessee must include sales tax. DO NOT SEND CASH.

TIMESWEPT LOVE

Cheryln Jac

ZEBRA BOOKS
KENSINGTON PUBLISHING CORP.

ZEBRA BOOKS are published by

Kensington Publishing Corp.
850 Third Avenue
New York, NY 10022

First Printing: September, 1996
10 9 8 7 6 5 4 3 2 1

Printed in the United States of America

This book is dedicated to my husband, Jack, and my mom and dad, in thanks for traipsing around Arizona with me while I "soaked up" the atmosphere for this story, and reveled in the history of the Old West.

To Ken and Stacy for taking care of my animals and home, and Chantel, for lending me the infamous camera and hats.

And also to everyone I met along the way who helped; especially the librarians in Tucson who dragged out book after book for me.

And to Margot and Tom Beeston of the Triangle L Ranch in Oracle, Arizona, where we "set up camp."

Chapter One

Tuesday, July 12, 1996
Tucson, Arizona

T.J. gripped her gun in her left hand and held the barrel pointed toward the sky. Her other hand clutched at the sheer rock at her back, but failed to find a handhold. If she took one wrong step there was nothing to prevent her fall into the sprawling canyon below.

She closed her eyes, just for a second, in an effort to calm her nerves. The warmth of the sunbaked rock at her back penetrated the starched fabric of her police uniform. She felt the rock's rough surface scratch at her skin, even through her shirt. A thin veil of perspiration covered her forehead. She chanced a look down and cursed herself for doing so. It was a long drop, more than five hundred feet. A deadly drop. Every nerve cell in her body was trembling. She hated heights. She'd always hated heights. Even standing near a window, if she was above the first floor, gave her the willies. Her knees had begun to shake.

She slid her right foot along the ledge, slowly, cautiously, pressing down on it carefully, waiting for the ledge to crumble beneath her weight. She sighed with relief when it didn't. Her stomach churned nervously at the thought of taking another step.

Why in heaven's name had she followed Calder out here? And why hadn't she called for backup?

She took a deep breath and reminded herself she was a police officer, a well-trained professional. At the moment she had no doubt her captain would argue that last point. Still, she had a job to do. T.J. inched her way carefully along the narrow ledge, the fingers of her right hand, stretched out and flattened on the wall, feeling their way over every inch of rock, every crevice and crack in its surface. She wouldn't look down again. If she did, she knew she'd fall. T.J. stared up at the vast blue sky and tried to think only of catching the man she was chasing.

Jake Calder was a convicted thief who'd escaped from an Oklahoma prison a year ago. He'd obviously decided to make Tucson, Arizona his new home, and upon his arrival he'd immediately taken up his old profession. But this time his old profession had taken a nasty new turn. His last robbery had gone bad, very bad. A clerk at the bank had managed to press the silent alarm button. Working alone, Jake had stayed in the bank too long, trying to stuff as much cash as he could into the bag he'd carried. He'd heard the police sirens nearing and, in a panic, had taken a hostage to insure his escape. The woman ended up dead.

T.J.'s hatred of the man she was chasing flared. The hostage Jake Calder had killed that day was T.J.'s little sister, Lisa McAllister, fresh out of college and cashing her first paycheck at the bank Jake had chosen as his target.

A large bird swept low into the canyon, catching T.J.'s attention as it flew past the sun.

T.J. heard a scraping noise and paused, forcing the painful memories of Lisa away and focusing on the matter at hand. Calder, several feet ahead of her, was making his way along the rock ledge. He was moving fast, widening the distance between them.

She quickened her pace, becoming a little less cautious. She didn't want to lose him now. She took another step, wider than the last. Dammit. She wouldn't lose him. Her foot hit a piece of raised rock on the ledge. Her head swung downward instinctively, her eyes searching for the object that had nearly caused her to trip. Instead her eyes focused on the canyon floor far below. This was where they'd found Lisa's body, down there in the tall Saquaro and Cholla cacti, broken and scarred.

T.J.'s foot slipped from the rock and thudded onto the floor of the ledge. Fear gripped her as she felt her balance waver at the unexpected movement. Her body swayed slightly to the left as she fought to regain her step. She felt the edge of the ledge crumble beneath the sole of her black running shoe. Her foot frantically searched for a secure foothold, the fingers of her left hand clutched at the sheer rock at her back, and her hips protruded forward as she struggled to press her shoulders into the cliff.

Her foot found solid ledge and her shoulders pressed into the rough, red cliff. A rivulet of perspiration trickled down one temple and over her cheek. She had regained her balance. Relief swept through her body like a tidal wave, leaving her momentarily limp. She slumped against the rock wall, unable to move. T.J. closed her eyes and said a silent prayer of thanks.

"Get a hold of yourself, T.J.," she mumbled to herself a moment later in an effort to boost her failing nerves. "It's not over yet, and you can do this. You have to do this—for Lisa."

She took a deep breath and ordered her heart to calm its mad thumping, her pulses to slow their headlong race. If she didn't regain control of herself, she wouldn't have to trip and fall, she'd most likely just faint and end up meeting the desert floor in a way she didn't really want to meet it. And she had no desire to visit the city morgue, at least not as a customer.

T.J. stood still and forced herself to count to ten, twenty, thirty. It wouldn't do to rush Jake either. He had a bad temper, she knew, and a trigger finger that had become real itchy since he'd killed Lisa. No doubt he figured he had nothing to lose by committing a second murder, or even a third and fourth, if the need arose. T.J. extended her count to forty. There were several squad cars in the precinct that had accumulated evidence of Jake's itchy trigger finger when their officers had spotted him and he'd in turn spotted them.

Forty-one, forty-two, forty-three . . .

She couldn't cause him to panic or lose his temper and start firing at her. Free-falling from a Tucson-Santa Rita mountain cliff with a bullet in her was not how she planned to end the day. Also, she couldn't take the chance that one of Jake's bullets might whiz past her, smash through the window of a car passing over Gates Pass nearby, and kill an innocent tourist on his way for a day of fun and games at the Old Tucson Movie Studios.

Forty-four, forty-five, forty-six . . .

It would be nice, she thought, if one of those tourists would use his cellular phone to call the precinct and get her some help. But then, she wasn't really that close to the snaking curve of Speedway Avenue that anyone not really looking for her might see her. Of course, if someone did call the precinct she'd not only get help, she'd also get suspended, since she wasn't supposed to be working on this case in the first place.

Forty-seven, forty-eight, forty-nine, fifty.

T.J. concentrated her gaze on the huge, fluffy white clouds that drifted by, offering only momentary shadows rather than rain to the arid Arizona desert. She dropped her gaze and looked out at the endless vista of rock, red earth and tall cacti. Jagged buttes rose here and there to break the flat monotony of the landscape, creating plateaus that left the land at alternating levels of height, and the dazzling tones and odd shapes of nature's wild plants lent color and beauty to the harsh red-brown land.

She felt the unmerciless heat of the summer sun beat down on her, the dark blue threads of her uniform attracting the hot rays, soaking them up, pulling them toward her like a magnet. Several small beads of perspiration formed on her forehead and tickled her skin as they slowly descended toward her brows. She felt still more slip from her chest to trickle down between her breasts.

She knew she had to move again, but she didn't want to. Following Jake Calder out of town, into the mountains, and up onto this ledge had been a mistake—a foolish mistake. Her mind told her to move, but her body failed to obey. She wanted to remain right here, in this one spot, where, for the moment at least, she felt safe.

Unable to help herself she peeked down again.

"Lord, please let me get off this ledge alive and in one piece," she whispered. "I'll never do anything stupid again, I promise."

She wiped her forehead with the back of the hand that held her gun, then returned hand and gun to a ready position, pointed skyward. Her index finger flexed, stretched, then rewrapped itself around the thin trigger.

T.J. took a deep breath and felt the metal of the police badge pinned above her left breast touch her wrist. It was hot from reflecting the sun, and its presence was of little comfort at the moment. Jake Calder didn't care if she was a cop, he'd shoot her just the same, maybe even quicker because she was a cop. She tightened her grip on the police issue .38, flexing her trigger finger again, and felt the sweat on her palm rub onto the carved handle of the gun.

She shifted the weapon to her right hand, rubbed her

left palm against her thigh until it felt dry again, and transferred the gun back to her left hand.

She began to move, inching her right foot along the ledge, pressing down, securing her weight, and following with the left foot. Up ahead the cliff followed the curve of the mountain. T.J. moved slowly around it, praying with each step, clinging to the rock at her back.

She heard a scuffle of movement and turned her head. Jake Calder was just a few dozen feet ahead of her. She paused and watched him move away. He was a big man, well over six feet tall, with massive shoulders and a chest that looked more like a brick wall than part of a man's body. She remembered from seeing his mug shot that his eyes were as cold as a winter night in Alaska, and as black as his heart. His size should have been a hindrance on the narrow ledge, but it wasn't, because he had one big advantage over her, one she'd read on his rap sheet but hadn't remembered until it was too late to do her any good. Jake Calder had been a window washer for two years on some of Oklahoma City's highrise buildings. He was experienced at moving along narrow ledges and around sharp corners. He wasn't afraid of heights as she was. Jake Calder felt comfortable up here among the clouds, with nothing to hang onto but a sheer wall of rock.

He disappeared around the side of the mountain and then suddenly, she heard him laugh.

Damn, she was going to lose him. She had to move fast. Fighting down her fears, T.J. hurried after him. T.J. transferred her gun to her right hand, turned her head to look at Calder, and took aim. "Hold it, Calder."

Jake paused, already having climbed several feet up the cliff toward the plateau above. He looked down over his shoulder at her. A leering grin curved his thin lips, and his black eyes, cold and unyielding, mocked her.

"Maybe another time, sweetheart," he said.

A second later he disappeared over the top of the ridge.

"No way, Calder," T.J. called back. She swore beneath her breath and rushed toward the jagged outcropping of rocks he'd used as steps. Her heart pounded madly. Damn, he was getting away.

She rammed her gun into its holster, carefully turned to face the cliff wall and reached up to grab a small ledge of rock. T.J. placed one foot on the first jagged piece Calder had used as a step. She pushed upward off of the ledge and raising her other leg, grappled about until her foot found the next jagged step.

"Hey, sweetheart." He laughed—the sound an ugly, deep rumble. "Ever thought of flying?"

T.J. felt a shudder of fear trip up her spine and froze. Dear Lord, he hadn't left. She looked up.

Jake Calder grinned down at her, long strands of oily black hair hanging about his face, a face whose features, in spite of the smile, were hard and stony. As she stared up at him, his hand appeared and T.J. saw his gun, pointing directly down at her.

T.J. cringed away from the bullet she knew would slam into her body any second. Her right foot slipped from the small ledge of rock and her fingers lost their hold. She felt her weight shift outward, following the wayward foot, pulling her body away from the cliff and toward thin air. Fear seized her. It welled up in her throat, strangled the scream struggling for escape, swept through her body, and turned her flesh cold. She made a desperate grab at the cliff face with her left hand while her right clung tenaciously to the small outcrop of rock. Her fingers brushed over craggy cracks and crevices, searching vainly for something to grab. A shower of pebbles and dirt flew out about her, raining down on her head, but her hands found no grasp.

Jake Calder's laugh echoed through the still afternoon air.

T.J. closed her eyes, and felt another scream struggle to escape her lips. The fingers of her right hand dug into the dirt and rock, but it began to crumble and disintegrate beneath her desperate grip. Her hat flew from her head, and her hair broke free of the pins that had secured it. Long, chestnut tendrils flew around her face and whipped wildly in the wind, momentarily blinding her. Her right foot smashed against the cliff. Her left slipped from the ledge.

Her body plunged backward into nothingness. Dear God, she was going to die.

Blackness swirled about her, closing in on her mind as her body tumbled through the air at breakneck speed, hurtling toward the ground far below. An endless chasm of shadow engulfed her, shades of black and gray that surrounded her and offered a warm blanket of unconsciousness in which she could hide from the horrors of the moment's reality.

But T.J. fought the darkness, fought to stay awake, conscious and alert. She would meet death as she'd met life, head on.

She felt herself hit the ground, hard. First her tailbone, then the rest of her body. Her legs flew upward, but her head snapped back and slammed against the earth. Her jaws clamped together, jarring her teeth and slicing off a shred of skin on the side of her tongue.

Pain instantly encircled her rib cage, throbbed at the back of her head, struck her tailbone and burned the side of her tongue. Did you still hurt after you died? T.J. opened her eyes, expecting to see the pearly gates. Instead she saw that whatever world she was in was nothing more than a crazy blur whirling out of control in a blaze of blinding colors. Heaven was not what she'd expected it to be. What had happened to the tunnel so many talked about with the white light at its end? She closed her eyes again. Her life hadn't passed before her. Another myth disspelled. Nausea filled her and rolled up into her throat. She gagged and fought it down. A soft moan escaped her lips.

Damn, was this really how it happened? She tried to open her eyes again. Cymbals crashed in her head. Angels had headaches? She groaned. Maybe she wasn't an angel. She ignored the pain and forced her lids to part. The spinning blur began to subside and the world slowly came into focus. T.J. raised her head slightly off the ground, pushed up onto her elbows and startled, looked up into the most beautiful pair of blue eyes she'd ever seen.

T.J. closed her eyes and reopened them, expecting him to be gone. He was still there.

Chapter Two

Tuesday, July 12, 1881
Tucson, Arizona

Chance Burkette looked down at the woman who had just lost consciousness, then back up at the cliff she'd obviously fallen from. It was a wonder she was alive, but after a fall like that, it would probably only be a matter of minutes.

She moaned then, and he turned his gaze back to her.

"You're okay, lady," he said softly, figuring it was a lie, but what else was someone supposed to say to a dying person? Chance hunkered down beside her.

She stirred again, this time moving a leg. Chance stared in shock. He would have thought that impossible. With a fall from that cliff, every bone in her body should be shattered into a thousand pieces.

Curious, he ran a hand over her limbs. She had some nasty scratches on her hands, but nothing seemed to be broken. He looked at her head, touched her chin gingerly

and tilted it first to one side and then the other. She had
a gash on one temple, but that appeared to be all. He felt
around her rib cage with his fingertips. Everything seemed
intact. Chance frowned and looked back up at the sheer
cliff. She had to have fallen at least 500 feet. He shook his
head. She was either superhuman, or extremely lucky—
unless she had injuries inside. He couldn't tell about that.
He'd have to take her to Doc's, if she lived long enough
for him to get her there.

"Damn," he muttered softly, "I didn't need this." A
string of pithy oaths slipped from his lips. He'd been
tracking some of Gil Calder's men, hoping they'd lead him
to the outlaw's hideout. Now he'd have to turn back, and
returning to pick up the trail would be useless. Between
the desert animals, weather, and other riders trampling
over it, the trail would be long gone by the time he got
back to it. Then again, he had a hunch they'd been leading
him in circles since the trail had doubled back twice and
was again within little more than a dozen miles from Tucson, where he'd started from.

Slipping his arms beneath her, Chance lifted T.J. against
his chest and rose. Before walking to his horse he stood
still and looked down at the woman cradled in his arms.
Maybe she hadn't fallen from the top of the cliff. That
could be why she didn't seem to have any broken bones.
Maybe she had been climbing up the cliff and fell only a
short distance.

She was dressed in mens clothing of a type and material
he'd never seen before. Obviously the lady was from back
east. He didn't know about the big cities there, but in
Tucson, if a woman dressed in mens clothing, she wasn't
called a lady. His gaze raked over her blatantly, assessingly,
and he released a long, slow sigh of appreciation. The
trousers and shirt weren't flattering, but their straight lines
and bagginess weren't enough to conceal the enticing
curves that made up her body either, assuming conceal-

ment was what she was trying to accomplish. Had she been trying to pass for a man? Chance scoffed at the idea. Some women would have been able to pull that off. Like Calamity, up in Deadwood. He looked at the woman's face. Its beauty matched the lithe frame beneath the baggy clothes. This one definitely would have a hard time passing for a man, even if she'd bound her breasts, which she hadn't, and tucked her hair up under a slouch hat. He looked around but saw no hat.

Her features were soft, delicate and graceful, yet he sensed a steeliness about her, a hidden strength or determination. A man didn't meet too many woman who possessed both breathtaking beauty and strength, and Chance sensed this woman had both in abundance. At least he was certain she had the beauty. He felt a warmth of desire stir deep down inside of him and purposely fought against it.

Obviously it had been too long since he'd visited Maeve's Place.

His attention turned to the gun that lay beside her on the ground. It was just about the strangest looking thing he'd ever seen. Its polished handle was slender and seemed to have finger grooves carved into it, and its black barrel was extremely short. But it was definitely a gun, evidently another newfangled design from back east. Bending carefully so as not to drop the woman, Chance picked up the gun and shoved it beneath his own gunbelt, then straightened again.

He stared at the unconscious woman, mulling over a dozen questions about her in his mind, none of which he was going to get answers to at the moment. He should get her to Doc's. She didn't look hurt, but maybe she was touched in the head. Had to be. No sane person jumped off a cliff. And even if she'd fallen, what the hell had she been doing scaling a cliff anyway?

Chance softly blew a wayward tendril of silky chestnut hair from her cheek. She was a pretty little thing, even if

she did dress like a man. He shifted her weight against his
chest so that her head was cradled against his shoulder. It
had been a long time since he'd held a woman with any
degree of tenderness. When his body ached for release,
he went to Maeve's Place. The girls there were friendly
and always happy to see him, including Maeve. He didn't
need any other kind of woman. Not now.

He turned and whistled for Diablo. The big bay stallion
moved toward him instantly, the whiteness of the star on
his forehead intensified by the brilliance of the afternoon
sun.

"Kneel for me, boy," Chance ordered. He nodded his
head toward the ground to emphasize the demand.
"Down, Diablo."

The horse immediately dropped to his front knees and
Chance swung one leg over the animal's back, settling
easily onto his well-worn saddle. He situated T.J. in front
of him, her legs draped over one of his, her body still
pressed close, picked up the reins in one hand and nudged
the stallion's ribs with his heels.

"Let's go, boy."

The huge horse rose to his feet. Distancewise it was not
a long ride back to town. But the fact that he had to keep
Diablo at a slow walk in case the woman had internal
injuries, stretched it into a seemingly endless journey.
Chance silently cursed every foot of it.

The woman remained unconscious during the trek, but
she moved around almost constantly; moaning and twisting. The twisting is what got to him. She snuggled close,
her breasts crushed against his chest. Her hip pressed up
against him, and with each step Diablo took, she swayed
in his lap, rubbing against Chance until he thought he
would go mad. His body turned hard, aching with desire,
burning with passion, and all for a woman who was not
only a complete stranger, but was unconscious to boot. It

had definitely been too long since he'd visited Maeve's Place.

Chance reined up in front of the jail house. Swinging his right leg over Diablo's neck and slipping his left from the stirrup, he slid to the ground, holding T.J. securely within the circle of his arms. It was nearly a blessed relief to get her off his lap.

He stepped up onto the boardwalk, then realized he was standing in front of the jail house and had meant to ride directly to Doc's place.

"Damn," he muttered under his breath. His body was so weary, and his bones so saddle sore from riding half the night and all day, he felt he was going to drop.

"I'm too danged tired to even think straight." He looked at Diablo. "Go on to bed, boy." The horse whinnied and headed for the livery stable that was only a few doors down the street from the jail house. Chance looked down at T.J. and found himself thinking he wouldn't mind going to bed for a few hours himself, but if she were sharing that bed he knew he wouldn't be sleeping. The thought was a delicious one and brought a smile to his mind, if not to his lips, followed immediately by a wash of guilt. The poor woman was dying and here he was lusting after her body.

Chance turned abruptly and began to walk toward Doc's. If there had been even a shred of doubt in his mind that it was long past time for him to visit Maeve's, it was gone now. He glanced down at T.J. again. He'd go directly after he dropped the woman off at Doc's.

It was nearing sundown, and not many people were out on the streets. The sky would soon be black. Several shopowners were closing up for the day. They stared as Chance passed. A couple of them inquired about the woman in his arms, but none pressed the issue when he kept walking and didn't answer.

His gaze studied her clothes again. They were dark blue and stiff looking, like an army uniform. Yet he knew she

wasn't wearing an army uniform, unless she was some kind
of foreigner.

He'd never seen shoes like the ones she wore either.
They were black, smooth, and soft looking. They laced up
the front but both shoe and laces stopped below the ankle.
The soles were made of some kind of mushy stuff lapped
over the top of the toe and up the heel part of the shoe.
Except there were no heels. The entire sole of the shoe
was flat. His gaze moved up the line of her slender legs.
The holster she had strapped around her waist was the
oddest looking thing he'd ever seen. He wouldn't even
have known it was a holster if it weren't for the gun sheath.
The belt itself had little box like things, metal loops and
some type of hook hanging off it.

She moved in his arms, twisting slightly to one side and
moaning. Her breast pushed against his chest. Chance
looked down and realized that her shirt front was slightly
open. The top two buttons had ripped off and left it unse-
cured. White lace peeked from the opening, along with
the golden swell of one breast. Chance felt his already
aroused and frustrated body heat up more, which only
served to inflame both his anger and disgust with himself.
The inseam of his pants was getting threateningly tight.
Her hand moved to press at his shoulder. "Calder . . . stop
. . . Calder. . . ."

Chance froze. Calder? The heat of passion that had
invaded his veins turned to ice at the name she'd muttered.
He felt his muscles tense.

"Hey, Marshal, what happened?" Henry Witherspoon
stepped down from the boardwalk that ran along the front
of his general store and peered over Chance's shoulder.
"Who's that you got there?" The storekeeper's bald pate
reflected the sun.

Chance heard the man's inquiry and met his curious
gaze, but he didn't answer.

His eyes moved back to rest on T.J.'s face as she shifted

position against him again. It was probably just a coincidence, her knowing someone named Calder. Then again,
there weren't that many Calders in the area that he knew
of other than the outlaws. In fact, there was only one,
Millie Calder, and she was all the way up in Camp Verde,
several days ride from Tucson. Nevertheless, the Calder
this woman knew was most likely someone other than Gil.
Still, it was a hell of a coincidence—him chasing a Calder,
coming across her on the trail, and her calling out the
name Calder. When she came around he'd find out for
sure.

He began to walk again, slowly, studying her as they
moved down the street. Her hair was the same rich color
as that of the desert floor at sunset, brown with deep
shadows of red, and just a hint of gold. Her skin had a
golden hue to it, not all white and pasty looking like most
women liked to keep it.

They thought pale skin made them look delicate.

He thought it made them look ill.

Chance remembered his late wife, Caroline. Whenever
she'd gotten one little ray of sunshine on her face, she'd
closed herself up in the house for days afterward with all
the curtains drawn and a pound of rice powder plastered
to her cheeks. But then, that's how she'd been raised,
instilled with all the old southern traditions by a mother
who'd grown up with them.

Chance pushed the memory of Caroline aside and
returned his attention to the woman in his arms. Finely
arched chestnut brows curved over her closed eyes, eyes
edged with the longest, silkiest red-gold lashes he'd ever
seen. Her cheekbones were high, and her nose . . . sassy,
he decided. It turned up just enough at the tip to be
termed sassy.

He'd known a woman once who'd had a nose just like
that. The memory brought a smile to his lips. It had been

long before his marriage, but he remembered her well. All fire and spit, she'd been. A real handful for any man.

Chance sighed. But that was a long time ago. He looked down at the woman in his arms. Her lips were full, sensuous, and rosy, though unpainted or rouged.

Her eyelashes fluttered and her lids parted, briefly, then closed again. "Calder, no, stop," she murmured.

There it was again, that name, Calder. Damn, what if those two outlaws he'd been tracking had been going to meet up with her? What if . . . ? A dark suspicion took form in his mind, but he instantly denied it as probable.

"Ma'am, can you hear me?" he asked, his tone harsher than he'd meant it to be. "Can you hear me?"

"Ummmm . . ." T.J. pushed a hand against him again and moved her head slightly back and forth, as if denying something.

A frown creased Chance's brow. She was a stranger in these parts, he knew that much. But what had happened to her? Why had she jumped off that cliff? Or had she fallen? Maybe someone had pushed her—was that it? Was that why she was calling Calder, because he'd pushed her off the cliff? The frown deepened. He hadn't seen anyone else, but that didn't mean someone hadn't been there. With a whirl of questions filling his mind, he began to walk toward Doc's again. What reason would Calder have for pushing a woman off a cliff? No, that wasn't the answer. But what if his earlier suspicion wasn't as improbable as he'd thought?

Chance puzzled over the situation. He usually knew when a stranger wandered into or even came near his territory, and Tucson was part of his territory. So why didn't he know about her?

He cursed softly beneath his breath. It wasn't as if he didn't have enough damned trouble, what with Billy the Kid's cohorts spilling over into Arizona after their leader got himself killed in New Mexico. Marshal Garrett could have done a neater job on that one, like arrest everyone before they got away. And then there were the Indians. A few had left the reservation and started attacking some of the settlers.

It was Chance's job to know everything that went on in the territory, and he didn't know about her. That made him uneasy, real uneasy. His earlier suspicion began to take root. He'd heard that the Calder gang was in the area somewhere, and he knew that the outlaw leader, Gil, had a wife who rode with him and sometimes traveled ahead to towns, alone, to scout them out for her husband and his men to rob. Was this her? Were the Calders scouting Tucson?

He crossed the street and passed by the Wakes & Lyle Saloon.

"You can bring her up to my room, Chance, honey," one of the saloon girls drawled from her second-story window. "I'll take care of both of you."

Deep in contemplation, Chance failed to hear the invitation. He stared at the face of the woman whose head rested against his arm. Could this be Gil Calder's wife, Sue Ann? And if so, had she been heading into Tucson? To scout out the bank, see if the pickings were good enough for them? Maybe she'd been sent to size up the local authority? They'd done that a few months ago when the gang had held up a bank in Telluride, Colorado. It made sense. Perhaps those two outlaws he'd been following were supposed to meet up with her out there.

Still, if she was Calder's wife, why the hell had she jumped off that cliff?

Maybe it was a diversion. The thought screamed in his brain. Chance spun around and stared at the bank cater-cornered across the street. There was no unusual movement about it, and only one horse was tied to the hitching post out front. He breathed a sigh of relief. It had been a crazy thought anyway. No one could have known he was going to ride out in that direction today, or even that he was going to ride out of town at all. Unless Calder had figured he'd ride out after his men, attempt to trail them to their hideout.

Even if all that were so, what was she doing on that cliff? No one would be foolish enough to jump off a cliff and risk breaking her neck just to create a diversion. And if Calder had been there, he'd have helped her. Chance's showing up wouldn't have stopped him. Calder would have been delighted to shoot Chance dead without any witnesses and be done with it.

Chance continued on his way toward the doctor's office, the roweled silver spurs attached to the rear of his wedge-heeled boots tinkling merrily with each step he took.

A reflection of the setting sun sparkled on the silver and gold badge pinned to the woman's shirtfront, and drew Chance's eye. He stared at it in puzzlement. McAllister. Number 3164. TPD. What the blazes did that mean? It looked like a badge, but what kind was it? And what was a woman doing wearing a badge anyway? He tried not to let his gaze stray to her breasts, but he failed. Another button of her shirt had slipped from its hole.

"Damn it, Burkette," he whispered harshly, "keep your mind where it belongs."

If she was Sue Ann Calder, he reasoned, forcing his mind back on business, she could be in disguise, maybe posing as one of those Pinkerton detectives from back east. He'd heard they sometimes wore uniforms, and even hired women on occasion. Then again, maybe she wasn't Sue Ann Calder but really was a Pinkerton agent. Maybe she was a Pinkerton after the Calders. But again, if she was an agent, what was she doing out there on that cliff all alone? Without even a horse?

Chance shrugged and shifted her about in his arms. He'd get answers to his questions soon enough once he got her to Doc's and the old man put some smelling salts under her nose. That is, if she hadn't injured herself inside so badly that she wasn't going to wake up at all. But somehow, though it had to be a miracle, he didn't think she was that hurt. She didn't seem to be in severe physical pain.

Her face flinched slightly and her eyelids fluttered open, closed, and open again. She looked up at him.

Chance stared into her eyes and felt himself get lost in the emerald depths that looked back up at him. Golden specks danced within her eyes, like spots of fire, and her face was alive with emotions. Shock drew her delicate features tight, confusion pulled her brows together, and fear left her eyes wide and full of alarm. At first she tried to pull away from him, cringing without really physically moving. Then, as if sensing he meant her no harm, she relaxed slightly. He could feel her tension, the tautness still in her limbs, the stiffness of her back and shoulders.

"It's okay, ma'am," he said softly, trying to reassure her. If she was crazy he didn't want her going hysterical while he was holding her pressed to his chest.

"What happened?" T.J. stared up at him. "What's going on?"

"You fell, I think."

He shifted her weight a little and kept walking. "I found you and brought you into town. I'll have you at Doc's in a minute."

"Fell?" T.J. echoed. She tried to look over her shoulder, but the movement caused a sharp pain to pierce her neck and brought her up short. "Oh, damn."

Chance frowned at her cursing. Obviously she wasn't a lady, at least not a well-behaved one.

T.J. tried, to lift a hand to her neck and felt another stab of pain shoot up her arm.

"Geez and damn." She grimaced and looked back at the cowboy who held her, straight into the same blue eyes she'd seen upon waking after her fall. A flash of warmth spread through her and she had absolutely no idea why. But she did know that it made her uncomfortable.

"Okay, you can put me down now, cowboy. I hurt like hell but I'm not going to fall apart."

"I'm not a cowboy," Chance growled, instantly irked by the insult. The newspapers had labeled Calder's followers cowboys. And he was definitely not one of Calder's followers.

"Please?"

He dropped the arm that had been beneath her legs, but maintained the grip of the arm wrapped around her back. Her body instantly swung downward, brushing against the length of his. The movement sent a surge of desire coursing through him and nearly brought a groan to his lips. Only the stoutest effort of self-control kept him silent and still. Her feet met the ground, or rather, the tip of her toes touched the ground, barely.

His arm slipped to encircle her waist and he held her solidly pressed up against his own body, her breasts crushed to his broad chest. The front of her holster, with all its accessories, pushed against her waist and into the flat of his stomach. To keep his mind from wandering to more dangerous ground, he forced himself to think about the holster's odd design. If it was supposed to be the latest fashion in some eastern manufacturer's line, then he was going to remain old fashioned, because he wasn't wearing one of those things.

T.J. wriggled against him, trying to slip from his grasp. "Let me go, damn it!"

He sensed, as well as felt the rapid beat of her heart, thumping against her breast, against his chest, attesting to her fear. Though why she should be afraid of him, he didn't understand unless. . . . The idea that she was Sue Ann Calder again flashed into his mind. Was it possible? Could it really be possible that Sue Ann Calder had fallen smack into his arms? He looked down at her and felt a conflict of excitement and disappointment within himself. Something in him didn't want her to be Sue Ann, but he couldn't deny that she did fit the description he had of the outlaw's wife.

His hand at her waist felt the tiny breadth of that span, and he experienced a sense of surprise at her lack of a corset. But then, her whole outfit was strange and very improper. Of course Sue Ann Calder probably wouldn't be concerned about what was proper or not, considering her life-style and choice of a husband. He let his hand fall away from her.

T.J. took a step back.

"Who are you?" she said, her voice high-pitched and strained.

Chance took a deep breath and inhaled the faint fragrance of jasmine that surrounded her. Caroline had hated the scent of jasmine. He'd given her a bottle of jasmine perfume once for her birthday and she'd thrown it away, saying it reminded her too much of her home in Louisiana, which her family had lost to the Yankees.

Chance's frown deepened as he studied T.J. and saw her bottom lip begin to quiver slightly as she defiantly returned his stare. Her momentary bravado was slipping. He recognized the hint of fear that had returned to her eyes—eyes that were as deep and green as a mountain pine, that captivated him and made him think of things he'd never wanted to think of again.

His gaze remained riveted on her and the urge to kiss her almost overwhelmed him. Forcing himself to break eye contact, Chance pulled his gaze from hers. This was not the time or the place for such thoughts or actions, and she definitely was not the woman, especially if she was Sue Ann Calder.

He needed answers to the Calder gang's movements and he needed them fast or people would die, people he cared about very much. But if he got answers from her at all, it wasn't going to be now. She looked about ready to faint again or start weeping.

He wasn't sure which, and he didn't much welcome the prospect of either.

Chapter Three

T.J. stared up at the cowboy in almost as much disbelief as emanated from his eyes as he stared down at her. His look, she was certain, also held a bit of disdain. Maybe he didn't like cops. But then, why come to her rescue? And who the hell was he, anyway?

Her gaze strayed to their surroundings. She had kept her eyes closed most of the time they'd ridden on his horse because her head was throbbing horribly. When she'd felt the horse stop, and the two of them slide to the ground, she'd tried to open her eyes to look around and the world had tilted crazily. Since then she'd either kept her lids closed, or her gaze riveted to her rescuer, but now she felt better, stable. She looked around, past him, and felt a sense of surprise.

"What the—?"

"You all right, ma'am? You're not going to swoon again, are you?"

She looked back up at the buildings that lined the street. They were, T.J. searched for a word, ancient. They were. . . .

Suddenly she knew exactly what they were: Old Tucson, the city that the moviemakers had built years ago to film western movies. The Old Tucson Movie Studios. They still filmed here, and operated the place as a tourist attraction. Just last year her sister Lisa had been an extra in a movie shot here about Wyatt Earp. A sigh of relief escaped T.J's lips at recognition of where she was, but the emotion was a fleeting one. She still felt confused and filled with questions.

What was she doing in Old Tucson? How had she survived that fall off the cliff? How had she gotten here? And where was Jake Calder? But that last question was the least of her worries at the moment. And so was the dime store cowboy standing in front of her. He was staring at her as if she'd just appeared out of thin air, she knew, but she didn't care. She had to have some answers as to what had happened. She peered around him. A sign over the building directly behind him read "Tucson Land and Assay Company."

She was right. She was in Old Tucson. One and two-story wood and adobe structures lined both sides of the street, and a wooden walkway made of rough planks ran along the front of each building. The streets were quickly becoming dark. T.J. squinted slightly to better see the identifying marks of the buildings on the other side of the assay company. One looked as if it was supposed to be a post office, and the building next to that had "Express" painted in huge yellow letters across its false, second-story front. A stagecoach sat at the hitching rack in front of the building. A grizzled man dressed in buckskins, who T.J. assumed was the driver of the stage, was helping a woman into the coach.

T.J. frowned. She hadn't been to the studio lot in a while but she could swear that the stagecoach ride and the Express depot were located at the west end of town near the mock railroad station. T.J. shrugged mentally. It really didn't matter. At least now she knew where she was, if not how she'd gotten there.

She looked back at the woman boarding the stagecoach. It seemed odd that she was also dressed in costume, her gown reminiscent of the late 1800s. Unless they were actually shooting a film today. T.J. smiled to herself. That had to be it. The woman was one of the actors that worked in Old Tucson, like the stagecoach driver and the cowboy whose arms had just released her.

To her left were several horses tied to a hitching rack. She turned around and saw, directly behind her, a wooden step leading up to a raised plank walkway, and a pair of louvered swinging doors. The tinkling sounds of a piano, accompanied by loud laughter, wafted out from beyond the doors. T.J.'s gaze strayed to a large window set beside the doors and framed with yellow and red stained glass squares. The words, "Red Garter Saloon" were painted in bright red letters and outlined in white across the glass.

But what was happening in the saloon, or whether she was standing in the middle of a movie lot wasn't her biggest concern at the moment. She was more interested in the fact that she was alive, though she couldn't understand how.

Nothing was making any sense. She scrunched her eyes closed for a second, shook her head, and tried to come up with a logical explanation of what had happened to her. A short while ago she had fallen off an outcropping of ledge halfway up the Tucson Mountains. She'd been hurtling through the air toward the canyon floor hundreds of feet below and certain death. That she was alive now was absolutely wonderful, but unbelievable. She opened her eyes and looked at her rescuer. Light from the saloon window filtered into the street to penetrate the dimness of dusk and allow her a partial view of him. A well-worn, black Stetson rode low on his forehead, but it didn't obscure his hard-cut features.

His face was a contrast of darkness and light, the sharp curves of high cheekbones, granite like jaw and black brows creating a plethora of shadows, while the chiseled planes of his broad forehead, the bridge of his straight, aquiline nose and the hollows of his cheeks were valleys and plateaus of taut, bronzed flesh. Each line was square and purposeful. Strong was the word that came immediately to T.J.'s mind. She sensed his strength was not merely physical.

He sported a black mustache, thick, drooping at the corners of his lips, and the same color as the ragged curls of hair that tickled the tops of his ears beneath the hat, and edged the rear of his shirt collar. His actions had been those of an angel, but his dark, devastating looks were more those of Lucifer.

She felt her breath catch in her throat and deliciously hot shivers raced up her spine—definitely an inappropriate reaction for the situation. She was suddenly assailed by a wave of dizziness. A small moan escaped her lips and she swayed.

Chance reached out quickly. His arm encircled her waist and he pulled her toward him.

T.J. lifted her hands to his shoulders and pushed against him.

"No, let me go." Her voice wasn't as steady as she would have liked. In fact, the words came out more as a breathy plea than an order.

His arm remained securely clamped around her waist.

"Why don't you just settle down, ma'am? You already caused one ruckus with everyone in town wondering about you. There's no reason to go causing another by being hysterical."

His tone was rich and seductive, like warm, sweet honey and black velvet.

The dizziness passed and T.J. cleared her throat and tried again. "I am not hysterical, and I asked you to release me." She pushed against him. "Please." This time she spoke with authority, making the words an order rather than a request.

He let his grasp loosen again and T.J.'s feet settled firmly back on the ground.

"Thank you."

She took a hesitant step away from him and her legs wobbled unsteadily. She paused until the trembling stopped. She kept her eyes riveted on the man who said he had saved her life. If he'd rescued her after her fall, as he claimed, it would have been just as easy to drive her to the hospital in Tucson as to the old studios. Then she recalled having been on a horse, not in a car. She'd deal with that later. Right now she had to cope with this cowboy, and find out why she wasn't dead.

His dazzling blue eyes held her momentarily spellbound, a sensation she tried to shake off but couldn't. They were the blue of the ocean, deep, dark, and mysterious, innocently revealing nothing, purposely hiding everything. Finally she let her glance travel slowly over his body, sensing the almost overpowering aura of masculinity and virility, of reined-in power and strength that surrounded him.

She was of the immediate impression that he was like a thunderstorm trapped in a bottle; wild and savage, and fiercely lethal if unleashed.

He wore a pale-gray cambric shirt, with a dark-brown leather vest. Both stretched taut across his broad, muscular, shoulders. His chest was wide, his waist slender. A holster of plain but well-oiled leather was strapped about his hips and rode low over the right one. A leather thong attached to the tip of the gun sheath was tied about his thigh. Leather shotgun chaps encased his long legs—legs which were obviously lean and well-honed to a saddle.

Her gaze rose from the scuffed cowboy boots that showed from beneath the ground-dragging hem of the chaps and followed the line of quarter-sized silver conchos that made their way up the side of each fringed legging. Sunlight glistened off each concho, as it did off of the badge pinned to his vest. Her gaze moved toward it. The design was simple; a five pointed star within a silver circle, the words U.S. Marshal engraved across the star's face and painted black. T.J. frowned. She looked back at his face and found that he had removed his hat.

"Ma'am, I think we'd better go on over to Doc's and let him have a look at you. That was a pretty bad fall you took."

A rebellious lock of black hair had fallen forward and given him a rakish air that suddenly seemed dangerous.

Like a flash of lightning, reason kicked in and T.J. remembered the situation. They were in the studios. He was an actor, that was all. But if he was an actor, what had he been doing up in the mountains below that cliff? That area was well away from the studio site. And how in blazes had she survived that fall?

"Who?" She stopped. Her voice had gone squeaky again. She cleared her throat. "Who are you?"

One dark brow rose, just slightly, and Chance tipped his head in acknowledgment.

"Chance Burkette, ma'am." He jabbed a thumb at the badge on his chest. "Territory Marshal."

"Territory Marshal," T.J. repeated absently. "Yeah, right. And I'm the governor."

One corner of Chance's lips curved upward. He shook his head. "No, I don't think so, ma'am. Some folks might think it a nice change, at least on the eyes, but our governor's a crusty old coot. Ugly too. And you certainly aren't that."

T.J. didn't hear him. Her attention had been drawn by a young boy going into the building across the street. Her gaze moved from Chance, to the boy, to the squat wooden buildings only a few dozen feet away and which lined the dirt street behind him. They looked like Old Tucson, yet at the same time they didn't, and she couldn't explain why.

She turned back to the cowboy.

"Thanks for your help, cowboy. I'm okay now."

Except I don't know how I got here, she thought to herself. Or even why I'm still alive.

"You said you saw me fall off of a cliff?"

"Nope," Chance said. "I said I saw you land. But I didn't see you fall from the top." He looked at her quizzically. "Did you?"

T.J. nodded. Somehow she'd survived the fall from the cliff . . . probably landed on another outcropping of rock that had broken her fall and knocked her unconscious. Then, maybe not immediately, she evidently rolled, and fell again. She looked down to take stock of her physical status. Everything seemed intact, though she couldn't deny that her body felt like one big horrendous ache. So how come she didn't remember the fall? Or, if her theory was right, the first landing? She glanced up and around at the old buildings again. "Why did you bring me here—?"

A cowboy came crashing through the doors of a nearby saloon and landed face down on the boardwalk.

Startled, T.J. jerked around. Realizing it was a stuntman and they were most likely filming inside of the saloon, she relaxed and turned back to the man who stood in front of her.

"I don't understand what happened. I mean out there in the mountains. How did I survive that fall? Did you catch me?"

He didn't answer.

The tall, silent type, T.J. thought.

With a wary glance toward the saloon, Chance settled the Stetson back on his head.

She ignored her throbbing head and aching limbs and smiled up at him in an attempt to look friendlier.

"Well, I guess if they're filming here, I should move out of the way, huh?"

He still didn't answer.

She looked around.

"I don't recognize this street. Where's the entrance from here?"

The furrow between Chance's brows deepened and he continued to stare at her in puzzlement but remained silent.

T.J. gave a mental shrug and looked around again. Maybe she should label him rude rather than the tall, silent type. Her gaze moved over the town, what she could see of it now that the sun had settled behind the mountains. There weren't any streetlights. She was in the studios, that was evident. So how come it still didn't feel right? There was an oddness to it all, as if she had woken from a deep sleep only to find herself still enmeshed in a dream.

A hint of fear threatened her enforced calm as her gaze moved over the buildings again. They looked real, almost too real. A cold chill swept up her spine.

But she had to be in the Old Tucson Studios, it was the only explanation wasn't it? There was nothing else in or around Tucson that looked like this.

"Ma'am, I think I'd best get you over to Doc's place and have him look you over," Chance said, afraid that any minute she was going to go crazy on him. He didn't like the way her eyes kept darting around, first at him, then around the town, as if she didn't know what she was looking at. "You seem a bit dazed-like. We ought to make sure you didn't bust nothing, too, when you fell off that cliff."

His eyes darted toward the saloon. Something was going on in there. He could hear scuffling and had a feeling any minute a bad fight was going to break out. The sheriff might need his help, but he had to get this woman to Doc's first.

"Ma'am, I think we're going to have some trouble here."

He nodded toward the saloon. "So let's go on to Doc's, while I can escort you."

T.J. turned back to the cowboy and the swift movement caused the world to spin around her. She clenched her fists and stiffened, waiting for her equilibrium to return. Why did she keep getting dizzy?

"You can cut the script, cowboy," she said, smiling to soften her words. "I'm okay. Really," she added at his skeptical look.

"I don't think so."

She felt an instant flash of irritation. Whenever she was in uniform most men reacted to her in one of two ways: either they treated her like some brain-dead little cutie who did nothing more than drive a golf cart and give out parking tickets, or like an Amazon they thought could chew nails and wrestle King Kong. She didn't much care for either treatment.

"Well, I know so," she retorted coolly, making no effort this time to soften her words. She rested a hand on her holster and realized it was empty. A stab of panic pierced her heart. Where was her gun? Her gaze shot back up to meet his, and the world began to spin again. Faster this time. She fought the dizzying sensation. "Where's my gun?" T.J. asked, her voice barely above a whisper.

Chance handed her the strange looking gun he'd picked up from the ground, but emptied of bullets.

T.J. slid it easily into her holster, but left the leather safety flap unsnapped. She didn't feel in danger exactly, but she didn't feel safe either. The hair on the back of her neck was standing on end and she didn't know why. She had her gun back. She wasn't hurt, really. No one was threatening her. Yet something was wrong, she knew it. But what?

She looked at the surrounding buildings, at the street, at the sidewalks. This time she really looked. The street was too wide, not narrow like the movie lot. There was

nothing modern to be seen: no advertisements, no souvenir T-shirts hanging in shop windows, no signs pointing
the way to public restrooms, and no hum of engines behind
an ice-cream parlor or restaurant. Hell, there was no ice-
cream parlor. And no restaurant. But the most notable of
all was that there were no lights on the streets and no
tourists, not a one.

She'd been to Old Tucson lots of times, had even drawn
duty there. She knew, without a doubt, that there were
always tourists. Always. And the place stayed open every
night until nine. She whirled around to look in every direction. Even when the stunt shows were going on at one end
of town, even in the worst of weather, there were always
some tourists loitering about, right up to closing time.
Her head whipped about again, her eyes searching for
something familiar.

A buckboard rumbled down the middle of the street, a
young man and woman settled on the high seat. They
pulled to a stop in front of a building that had the word
hotel painted across its false roof front. To T.J.'s left, a
couple of men on horseback, their dusters covered with
dirt and grime, as if they'd been riding for days, reined
up before a hitching rack. They slid from their saddles
and stomped their way across the plank sidewalk toward
a saloon. One paused halfway there, turned and spit a wad
of tobacco chew onto the ground. He saw her look of
astonishment and laughed. A second later he and his partner disappeared beyond the swinging doors.

She turned her attention back to the man beside her.
He was at least two or three inches over six feet tall. She
was forced to look up, her own five foot four coming
nowhere close enough to look at him eye to eye.

For the second time, she let her gaze travel up and down
his long, sinewy body, but this time her scrutiny was more
intense, more focused. A holster was slung low over his
right hip. An old fashioned Peacemaker protruded from

the sheath that was tied to his thigh. T.J. had to admit the gun looked real. A bowie knife, sheathed in leather, hung from the front of the holster belt, just to the left of its silver buckle. Her gaze moved upward and paused once again on the old-fashioned U.S. Marshal's badge pinned to his leather vest.

He looked authentic, as if everything he wore had been purchased out of a museum rather than from a reproduction manufacturer or movie costumer. T.J. smiled to herself. Either he'd just stepped off of a movie set, or he was one of the permanent actors in Old Tucson, kept around to give the tourists their money's worth. Either way, he looked damned good. T.J.'s shoulders stiffened against the thoughts that suddenly, and traitorously, tripped through her head. She was on duty, and this was not the time for such things.

She looked back up into those dark blue eyes, around at her surroundings, and then met his gaze again. Midnight blue melded with mountain green, unflinching, revealing nothing, revealing everything. Suddenly, T.J. had a sinking feeling in the pit of her stomach. Fear once again and unreasonably filled her breast. Her fingers dug into the soft flesh of her palms. "This is Old Tucson," the words almost stuck in her throat as she stared at him. "Isn't it?"

Chance chuckled. "Well, ma'am, it's Tucson all right, but I never heard anyone call it old before."

Chapter Four

"And you're one of the actors here, right?" T.J. persisted.

Chance Burkette's brow creased in a deep frown. First she'd insulted him by calling him a cowboy, now an actor. His temper flared. He wasn't a cowboy, and he didn't look like any damned actor. Buffalo Bill Cody, now he looked like an actor, with his yellow hair hanging over his shoulders, that greased mustache, and those fancy fringed and beaded buckskins he wore. All primped and pretty, that was an actor. Chance glanced down at his dust-covered chaps and the scuffed toes of his boots. He sure as hell was not primped and pretty. He settled his gaze back on T.J. and, raising a hand to lift his hat an inch over his head, said, "I'm the Territory Marshal, ma'am. Chance Burkette."

He reset the hat on his head and waited for a reaction. When no reaction came at all, Chance said, "Listen, lady, I realize you took a pretty good knock on the head in that fall, but that wasn't my fault, and there's no reason to be nasty about it. Now, we really ought to get you on over to Doc's place and let him take a look at you."

"I'm not being nasty," she snapped, "I just want to know what's going on." She felt tears sting her eyes, and fought to control them. What had happened? Was she suffering from amnesia? How much time had passed since she'd been chasing Calder? She assumed it had been only a few hours. Was she wrong? Or had she even been chasing Calder? Had it all been a dream?

She struggled to remain calm.

"Look, I'm sorry, cowboy, okay? I didn't mean to bite your head off. I'm just a little confused about things."

"I told you, I'm not a cowboy," Chance said, his own tone gruff. "I'm the Marshal."

"Okay, you're the Marshal." She'd heard that actors were temperamental, but this one was ridiculous.

A wave of nausea suddenly hit her and T.J. swayed. It passed instantly and she straightened her shoulders and smiled.

He looked worried.

She extended her hand toward him in an effort to emphasize the fact that she was fine.

"I'm T.J. McAllister," she said, as if trying to convince herself as well as him. "I'm an officer of the Tucson Police Department. Badge Number 3164. Thank you very much for your assistance, Marshal Burkette." She emphasized the title he seemed so intent on bearing, just to make him happy, then looked down at her uniform as if to reassure herself that what she'd said was the truth.

"I really am all right." At his look of skepticism, she continued. "I'll prove it. I have a cat named Dooby and a dog named Duchess. I drive a 1992 black Trans-am, and I live at 2904 Palm Desert Drive with my sister, Lisa." She felt a sudden ache in her heart, followed by a gnawing sense of emptiness at remembering that Lisa was dead. She closed her eyes for a brief moment, holding back the tears that threatened to flow over her lids, and then looked back up at Chance. "See?" She forced herself to smile. "I'm fine."

He lifted the Stetson, smoothed his hair back with his other hand, and resettled the hat on his head, pulling it low on his forehead.

"Ma'am, half of what you just said doesn't make a whole lot of sense to me, so . . ." he shrugged, "I think I'd best get you to Doc's."

He tried to take her arm but T.J. jerked away.

"Everything I said makes perfect sense, cowboy, and I'm not going anywhere with you until you tell me where the hell I am."

A crooked smile pulled at one corner of his lips. She could tell because his mustache rose upward on one side.

He pushed the brim of the Stetson with the thumb of his right hand, moving it a little higher on his forehead, then rested that same hand on the wooden handle of his gun. His left thumb was hooked over his gunbelt. "Just where do you think you are, little lady?"

T.J. fumed. He was obviously one of those guys who took his acting roles too seriously and played them to the hilt. But she wasn't in the mood. "I am not a little lady, Mr. Burkette. I am Officer Theresa Jane McAllister, and I asked you a simple question. Where am I?"

The grin widened. "Well, Officer Theresa Jane McAllister," he mocked, "you're in the city of Tucson, which is in Arizona Territory, like I told you a few minutes ago. Now, I'd really like you to see Doc and let him make sure you're okay. Then we can talk."

He pointed past her. "This way."

T.J. glanced over her shoulder, and then back at the man.

"Did you see me fall off that cliff?"

"I told you, I saw you hit the ground."

"Did you see anyone else up there? At the top?"

"Nope. But it's a good thing I was out there and found you or you'd most likely have lain there and died." Chance smiled. "And that sure would have been a waste."

T.J. ignored his attempt at flirtation. She wasn't in the mood for it, though she knew she'd probably kick herself around the block a few times later for not flirting back. It wasn't often, especially in her line of work, that a woman met a man who looked this good and wasn't put off by her uniform and choice of a career. Her tone softened when she spoke again.

"Look, I need to use a telephone, cowboy. Is there a pay phone around here someplace?"

"A what?"

"A phone." She was starting to get a little tired of his act. "You know, hello world, is anyone out there?"

Chance caught the sarcasm in her voice. He didn't know what it was about, and he didn't care. All he knew was that he didn't like it. His shoulders stiffened, his eyes narrowed and his tone hardened.

"I don't know what you're talking about lady, but we've got a telegraph if you want to tell the world something."

T.J. stared at him in disbelief. "There's no phone? Anywhere?"

Chance thought for a moment before answering. She was pulling something, he could feel it, he just didn't know what it was, but he decided to play along with her until he did. "Well, ma'am, since I don't know what the hell this phone thing is you're asking for, I'm kind of inclined to say we don't have one hereabouts. But like I told you before, if you've got a yen to tell the world something, there's a telegraph office down the street a bit."

"Listen, cowboy," T.J. snapped angrily. "Maybe you think lying to a cop is funny, and maybe you think acting as if you're some macho gunslinger in the old west is sexy and will get you a bunch of women drooling all over you and vying for your bed, but I want—"

A loud crash sounded from inside of the saloon behind her.

Startled, T.J. spun around.

Chance muttered a curse under his breath and made to rush past her. Trouble was starting, just as he'd known it would. He felt his arm brush against her as he lunged toward the saloon.

The sound of several gunshots pierced the still air.

A bullet tore through the painted window of the Red Garter Saloon, shattering it and sending pieces of red, yellow and clear glass spilling onto the boardwalk.

But the bullet didn't stop there.

"Get down!" Chance called. He glanced back over his shoulder toward T.J. as he ran up the steps that led to the saloon. The Peacemaker was already out of its sheath and in his hand. He froze in his tracks and his heart nearly stopped when he saw her jerk backward and fall to the ground.

"Son of a . . ." He let the words die on his lips.

Sheriff Elijah Perkins appeared from around the corner, eyes wide, gun drawn, fear etched in every pore of his twenty-three-year-old face. He ran toward Chance, the spurs on his boots jingling.

"Lord Almighty, what happened, Marshal?"

"The saloon. A fight," Chance said, sparing no words of explanation. His full attention was riveted on T.J. now, lying limp and unmoving in the dirt street. "Get in there, Perkins, and stop that damned fight."

Chance reholstered his gun as he leapt back to the ground and the sheriff ran past him. He heard the swinging doors of the Red Garter slam open and crash against the inner wall, heard the young sheriff, whom none of the rowdies in town respected because of his youth and inexperience, yell for order. Chance ignored it all. He hurried over to kneel beside T.J., slipped an arm under her shoulders and pulled her up so that her head came to rest against his chest.

He brushed a thick tangle of golden chestnut hair from her face and felt his stomach knot at the sight that met his eyes. Blood covered her right temple, seeping steadily from the jagged, ugly gash the bullet had left in her flesh when it creased her forehead. Rivulets of blood trickled down the side of her face, tiny streams of glistening burgundy that snaked their way over her cheek, lips and chin.

Billy Higgins, the blacksmith's ten-year-old son ran up to stand beside Chance. His brown eyes grew huge as he stared down at T.J. "She dead, Marshal?"

Chance slid his other hand under T.J.'s knees and hefted her weight up and into his arms as easily as some people would pick up a loaf of bread, then rose to his feet. For the second time in less than ten minutes he stood with the woman who seemed to have appeared from nowhere cradled against his chest.

"Go tell your pa the sheriff needs some help, Billy. And hurry."

"Yes sir," Billy said. He turned and ran down the street, brown hair flying about his head, his bare feet kicking up dust with each step.

Damn, he should have taken her to Doc's when he'd first wanted to. He should have just hauled her off by the collar and forced her to go, instead of standing there arguing with her. Then she wouldn't have been standing there in the street and gotten herself shot.

Chance turned and began to walk hastily toward Zachary Burkette's clapboard house. With each step he took, the roweled spurs attached to the back of his wedge-heeled boots jingled, the leather fringe on his chaps danced and swayed, and the polished silver conchos that lined the outer seam of each legging caught the light streaming out from the windows of the saloons he passed and reflected it back in a myriad of blinding color. Several men sitting on a bench in front of Warden's Saloon, a half block from the Red Garter, stared at Chance as he passed, some curious about the woman in his arms, some with respect for the man himself, and a few in hatred of everything he and the badge pinned to his chest represented.

He met no one's gaze, but he was well aware of every man's movement, no matter how slight. His pace was quick, and he was at the corner within seconds. He turned it, moved past two buildings and paused before the third. It was a two-story clapboard house that had recently received a new coat of yellow paint. White shutters were attached to each tall window and two scraggly rose bushes had been planted in the front yard, one on each side of the shallow steps that led up to the oak and glass front door. The soft glow of an oil lamp streamed out from the two first floor windows and into the yard. A waist high white picket fence enclosed the entire property.

Chance kicked open the gate on which Doc's sign hung, and moved up the rock bordered dirt path to the porch. At the door he paused, then lifting a leg, banged against the door's base with the toe of one boot.

"Come on, Doc, hurry up. It's me, Chance. I got a patient for you."

He moved to ram his foot against the door again and nearly fell when it abruptly opened just as his leg swung forward.

"Land's sake, Chance, what's going on?" Doc said, as he yanked the door open. A cloud of neatly trimmed white hair surrounded the old man's head, chin, and upper lip. In his hurry to get to the door, he'd shoved his little square spectacles on so quickly that they sat crooked on his short, bulbous nose. "A body could hear you thundering all the way to Texas and maybe even down Mexi. . . ." His words trailed off when he finally noticed the woman in Chance's arms and the blood on her face. "Lord'a mercy, what happened?"

"She got shot, Doc."

"I'm a doctor, I can see that, Chance." Zachary Burkette stepped back from the door and motioned his nephew past. "Take her into my office and put her on the table."

Chance moved through the narrow foyer with its wall hugging oak staircase, past an overcrowded but comfortably furnished parlor and into the large, high ceilinged room Doc had set up as his office. He lay T.J. on the sheet-covered table the old man used for operating and examining his patients, and stepped back. "A bullet grazed her head. Split the skin open." He looked at the old man anxiously. "She going to be all right, Doc?"

Doc shook his head and lit an oil lamp. "Well, I don't know. Give me a minute to look her over." He handed the lamp to Chance. "Here, hold this close so I can see." He brushed a few strands of hair from T.J.'s forehead and carefully fingered the wound, righting his spectacles and bending down close to get a better look.

"Well, Doc?"

The old man straightened and waved a dismissing hand at Chance. He lifted first one of T.J.'s eyelids, peered at her eyeball, and then repeated the process with the other eye.

"She'll be fine, Chance, fine. Just a flesh wound, that's all. Though if that bullet had gone another half inch or so to the right we'd definitely be having us a funeral instead of a patient."

Moving to a cabinet that stood against one wall where he kept his medical supplies, he retrieved an amber colored glass bottle and a piece of cloth, which he began to soak with the contents of the bottle. He turned back to T.J. and dabbed it against her temple.

"What happened to her?" The old man glanced over his shoulder at Chance. "And don't just tell me she got shot. I've figured that out on my own."

"A ruckus broke out over at the Red Garter. Bullets

started flying and one of them hit her. She was standing in the middle of the street.''

The doctor taped a bandage to T.J.'s forehead and returned the medicine bottle to the cabinet. He moved to stand beside T.J. again and looked down at her face for a long moment, as if studying her. ''Getting to be so's a body can't even walk down the street anymore and feel safe. Hate to think what it'll be like in a few years if the law doesn't get a handle on those cowboys.'' He shook his head.

''We're trying, Doc.''

Doc waved a hand at him. ''I know you are, son. But you need more men. The governor ought to realize that. One man can't do it all.''

''I can get help if I need it.''

''Who is she, Chance? I don't think I've seen her around these parts before.''

Chance shook his head. ''Me neither. I was out tracking a couple of cowboys and saw her falling off a cliff out near the pass.''

Doc looked up in surprise. ''What?''

Chance nodded. ''I caught sight of her just before she hit the ground. Can't for the life of me figure how come she's not dead. But when I got to her she seemed fine, except she was unconscious. I checked her over for broken bones and didn't find any, but I thought I'd bring her to you. Unfortunately she got shot first.''

Doc nodded. ''Well, at least you inherited a fair share of good sense from my sister before her time was up, God rest her soul.''

Chance felt the familiar hurt that always came when he remembered his mother and father.

''Her time wasn't up, Doc, and you know it. Calder and his gang just pushed the clock forward, that's all.''

''Chance, I know how much hate you've got stored up inside of you at Calder and his cowboys for what they did, but you've got to let it go, son. Get on with your life. Look at your brothers, Morgan and Nick, off to California to try their hand at ranching out there. They're getting on with things, Chance, with living, not still trying to track down the Calders and get revenge.''

"Justice, Doc," Chance said. "Justice, not revenge." He felt a pang of guilt at not having told Doc the truth about Morgan and Nick, but it was better this way. The old man would only fret, and lambast him about it every chance he got. It was better he didn't know.

"As far as you're concerned, Chance, revenge, justice, they're one and the same. At least when it comes to the Calders."

Chance drew T.J.'s gun from his waistband and held it up in front of the old man. "She had this on her."

Doc frowned. "Never seen one like that before."

"Me neither." Chance pointed to the badge pinned to T.J.'s shirt. "And look at that badge."

Doc nodded. "3164. Tucson PD." He looked at Chance. "What's that mean?"

Chance was in the process of pulling a thin wallet from T.J.'s pocket. He shrugged at Doc's question, mumbling, "I don't know," and flipped open the wallet. "Look at this," he said, and held it out.

"Says her name is Theresa Jane McAllister and she's an officer of the Tucson Police Department." He turned questioning eyes to Chance. "I don't get it."

"Neither do I." Chance drew several plastic cards from the flap opposite the one that held T.J.'s identification card. "And what are these?"

"Chevron," Doc read off of one. "1990 dash 1996. American Express. 1989 dash 1997."

"Yeah, but what are they? What are they made out of?"

Chance flicked the corner of one card with his thumb. "And what do those numbers mean?"

T.J. moaned and both men turned back toward her.

Chance moved to stand beside her, an anxious look in his eyes, which didn't escape Doc's notice.

"She all right, Doc? She's not hurting, is she?"

"She's fine, I told you." He looked at Chance pointedly. "But why are you so worried? She's a stranger in these parts, isn't she?" Doc fingered the fabric of T.J.'s shirt. "What kind of outfit is this she has on anyway? Some kind of newfangled uniform?" He looked up at his dead sister's middle son. "What'd this gal do, Chance, steal it from the army?"

"I don't know about her clothes, Doc, but I think she's Sue Ann Calder."

"Calder? Gil Calder's wife?"

Chance nodded. "I heard he sometimes likes to send his wife into a town ahead of the gang, to kind of scout things out for them when they're thinking of pulling a robbery. I also heard he's in the area or coming this way. I been expecting something to happen for a while now."

"Pop, is that you?" T.J. mumbled. She lifted her hand and tried to open her eyes, found the light blinding even when she squinted, and gave up the effort. Her head throbbed from a piercing pain that enveloped her skull and centered, with crashing intensity, in her right temple.

Despite his suspicions of her, Chance couldn't stop himself from reaching out and grasping her flailing hand. "It's all right, ma'am. I brought you to the Doc's office."

T.J. heard the vaguely familiar voice and her mind registered the words, but she still didn't understand.

"What happened?"

She forced her eyes open. The world was fuzzy and blinding. The light hurt and made her headache worse. Her eyes drifted closed and she struggled to open them again. She didn't like feeling helpless and out of control. Her lids fluttered open. This time the scene before her was a bit clearer. The cowboy she'd been talking to in the street earlier stood over her.

"A bullet got you in the forehead," the doctor said.

"A bullet?" she echoed weakly.

"Don't worry," Doc added hurriedly, "You'll be all right. It only grazed your temple. But you're going to have to take it easy for a few days, young lady." He bent down over her face so that she could see him. "You came about as near to getting yourself killed as a body could."

T.J. tried to sit up.

"Whoa there girl," Doc said. "Just where do you think you're going?" He placed a gnarled, old hand on her shoulder to prevent her from rising farther. "You got one nasty cut on your head. You lie still."

"Got to . . ." T.J. sank back down. The world spun around her like a toy top gone crazy. She closed her eyes. "I've got to get back to the station." She took a deep breath and flinched from the pain. T.J. touched her head and the doctor pushed her hand away.

"Don't do that," he snapped.

"But I've got to report in to the captain."

"Captain?" Chance asked, instantly more alert and suspicious. He edged Doc aside and looked down at her. "What captain?" he demanded. "What kind of captain? Are you in the Pinkertons?"

T.J. gasped as a new wave of pain filled her head.

"Got to tell him . . ." she gasped again. "Got to tell . . ." Her hand fell to her side. "Tell Calder."

T.J. passed out and Chance's gaze, cold and hard, met Doc's across the table.

"Calder," he repeated, the one word confirming the suspicions he had about her.

Chapter Five

Two days later, T.J. finally woke up. She opened her eyes to sunlight, yawned, and stretched her arms wide. Her shoulder and back muscles felt stiff and sore, and her head hurt, especially her right temple. The cuffs of the nightgown she had on caught her attention and filled her with surprise. She bent one arm and looked more closely at the cuffs double ruche of ivory lace trimming.

"Pretty snazzy for hospital attire," she mumbled to herself.

Her gaze moved to take in the room and as she did, she became confused and uneasy. This was no hospital room, not like any she'd ever seen anyway. Was she in some kind of private clinic, a convalescent hospital, maybe? She studied the room. The ceiling was high, maybe fourteen feet, and in one spot it was waterstained. The walls were papered with an alternating pale yellow ribbon and rose pattern that was badly faded, and a shade was drawn over the room's lone tall, narrow window.

Memory totally escaped her. Where in blazes was she?

The door to the room opened just then and Doc entered

carrying a tray laden with steaming vegetable soup, a huge chunk of freshly baked bread, a dish of strawberry preserves, and a glass of milk.

Though she'd passed in and out of consciousness for the past two days, T.J. remembered the old man. He had usually been there when she'd woken. He'd taken care of her. He was a doctor. The thought was instantly comforting and she relaxed.

The smell of the soup momentarily pushed all concern and worry from her mind as her stomach growled and took over her attention. Anyway, she didn't feel threatened any longer. So what if she wasn't in a hospital? She didn't like them anyway. Maybe she was in some sort of hospice, or outpatient home.

"That smells good," she said, as the old man placed the tray on her lap.

She was still a little weak and woozy, but her strength seemed to have returned, and the world wasn't spinning around her anymore, thank heavens. She'd woken up a few times the day before and had gone right back to sleep, unwilling to endure the blur of color that appeared, and the pain in her head that went along with it, each time she'd opened her eyes.

"Well, good morning, missy. I didn't know you were already awake, but I was hoping you'd open your eyes soon. Kind of hard to feed someone who won't wake up."

"Good morning," she said, her voice raspy from disuse.

"Umm, you seem pretty lucid."

"And hungry," she croaked.

"Good. You've got your appetite back, and your head's healing right along, so I'd say you're doing all right," Doc said with a chuckle. "This here was my lunch, but since you're awake, we'll make it yours." He laughed again when she started to refuse. "It'll give me an excuse to go on over to Mrs. Reilly's later and have some of her chicken pie." He settled the tray onto T.J.'s lap.

She smiled and tasted a spoonful of soup.

"Umm, Campbell's never tasted so good."

Doc's bushy white brows drew together and he looked at T.J. in confusion. "Campbell's?"

"The soup. It's great."

"Mrs. Reilly sent it over." He chuckled again. "Better than your Mrs. Campbell's, huh?" He continued without waiting for her reply. "Well, Mrs. Reilly would be right pleased to hear that, I'm sure. She runs the boarding house next door. Reilly's Rooms. I eat at her place most meals." He laughed. "Can't stand my own cooking."

T.J. stared at the doctor, seeing him as if for the first time. His pants and vest seemed antiquated, but it wasn't the fabric that looked old, it was the style, the cut of the garments. And his white shirt had no real collar, merely a strip of thin white fabric, almost like the collars of the Nehru shirts that had been popular in the sixties. T.J. had seen an old picture of her father, taken before she was born, in which he'd been wearing one.

Doc sat in a rocker that was placed next to her bed, crossed one leg over the other, and began to read a newspaper he'd brought in with him. T.J. noticed his shoes, laced up the front and over the ankles. The tie at his neck was nothing more than a thin black ribbon, and a watch chain looped from the right pocket of his vest across his waist, and disappeared within the left pocket of the vest. He looked so. . . . she searched for a way to describe him. . . . old-fashioned.

The eerie sense that something wasn't quite right assailed her again. She didn't know what it was she didn't feel was right, and she didn't know why she felt that way, she just knew something was wrong and the feeling was beginning to give her the willies.

She glanced around the room, and the sensation grew steadily stronger as her gaze moved from one unfamiliar object to another. Everything in the room looked as if it had come straight out of a museum or antique shop. The tall head and footboards of the bed she lay in were nothing more than simple coils of iron entwined together and painted white, and the quilt that covered her was definitely handmade. The lamp that sat on the marble-topped cherrywood table next to the bed had no electrical cord, and when T.J. glanced beneath its amber colored glass shade, she saw that where a socket and bulb should be was instead a wick, its tip burned black.

A white porcelain pitcher and bowl, the side of the pitcher painted with yellow roses and pale green leaves, sat on a high bureau directly opposite the foot of the bed. It was an old-fashioned bureau, with plain brass pulls and an oval mirror that tilted and was held up by two curving wooden arms.

On the floor and next to the door was a brass spittoon, and sitting on a cane-backed chair next to the bed was a chamber pot, decorated with the same gold roses and pale green leaves as the bowl and pitcher on the dresser.

Was she still in the Old Tucson Studios on some movie set? Was this man a retired doctor, spending his golden years acting out a role for tourists, who had taken care of her when she'd gotten hurt?

She closed her eyes. None of it made any sense. Not the room, not the doctor, not how she'd gotten here. None of it. Then again, if this was a movie set, then it all made perfect sense, at least all the antique furniture and the man's old-fashioned clothes. But, if she'd really been struck by a bullet, why hadn't they taken her to a hospital? Why have her stay here? And for that matter, where was here? Then another thought struck her. How long had she been here?

She set the tray aside.

"Doc?"

The old man folded his paper and looked up.

"Yes, missy? You want more soup?"

"How long have I been here?"

"Two days. Well, three if you count the day Chance brought you here."

"Chance?"

Doc began to move back and forth in the rocking chair.

"Chance Burkette, the marshal. He carried you here after you got shot." Doc frowned. "Don't you remember?"

T.J. nodded.

"I remember. Kind of. He's tall, right? Black hair and deep blue eyes. And handsome."

"That's him." Doc chuckled. "Leastways, the ladies always call him handsome. I call him ornery. But what I meant was, do you remember getting shot?"

"Sort of. But, Doc, I really need to use the telephone. I have to call my captain."

The old man shook his head.

"I heard about them things, telly phones, I mean. Saw one, too, when I was back in New York last year visiting my niece, Katherine. That's Chance's sister. They had one of them telly phone contraptions set up at the hotel I was staying at." He shook his head again, as if in disbelief, and chuckled. "Damndest thing I ever saw. People talking to each other through a wire. Who'd have believed it?" He stood up, tossed his paper back onto the chair, and took the tray from beside her on the bed where she'd set it. "Don't expect them to be around much, though. Leastways, not out here. Ain't practical. Nope, not practical at all." He left the still half-full glass of milk on the table beside the bed. "Finish your milk, missy."

T.J. sighed in frustration. These people in Old Tucson really took their roles seriously, but enough was enough.

"Doc, really now, come on, I need to use the phone. It's important. Please, where is it?"

He paused at the door and looked back.

"I told you, missy, I ain't got one. Don't expect I ever will either. No one in the territory does, far as I know. Not even the governor. Jonesy's Telegraph works just fine though. I'll send a message for you if you like. You want more soup?"

T.J. shook her head. Had something horrible happened that her mind was trying to block out by refusing to remember anything at all? T.J. tried to reconstruct the last minutes of what her memory allowed her to recall. She'd been chasing Jake Calder and she'd fallen from a cliff. Somehow she'd survived the fall, but when she'd woken up. . . .

T.J. sighed. She felt as if the world had shifted gears and she'd gotten caught in a chipped cog. The sense that something was out of wack hung over her like a black thunder cloud. She tried to shrug the feeling away. What was wrong was that she'd been close to catching Jake Calder, and she'd lost him. Then she'd fallen off a cliff, been shot at and hit. That thought stopped her. Shot at. She had been on a movie set. What were they doing using real bullets on a movie set?

She'd look into that once she got back to work. T.J. frowned. Could that be what was going on here? Could they be trying to make up to her for their accident of using a real bullet? Or maybe cover it up?

The minute Doc shut the door behind him, T.J. moved to throw back the covers. According to the old man she'd been in bed for the past two and a half days. She had to get back to the station. There might be a missing persons report filed on her if that crazy cowboy and the old doctor hadn't notified the police about what had happened down here. And if they were as crazy as they seemed, they probably hadn't. It wouldn't be in the script.

Pain instantly crashed to life within her head as her arm dragged the coverlet from her legs. T.J. paused, frozen in place, and waited for it to subside. Her next movement was more cautious. She slid her legs to the edge of the mattress slowly, carefully, then inched her way off the bed and stood up. The room swirled crazily around her for an instant. She grabbed hold of the headboard and everything settled to a stop and righted itself.

T.J. released a sigh of relief. At least she could stand up. She hoped she could also walk. She looked around the room. Where were her clothes?

An old wardrobe stood in the corner. It was plain, basically just a wooden box with doors, no fancy carved woodwork adorning it. Her clothes had to be in there. She walked slowly toward it, holding the foot rail of the bed for support and stability. A full-length cheval mirror stood to one side of the closet. She watched her reflection as she neared it. Her forehead was hidden beneath a swatch of bandage that wrapped entirely around her skull, which was in turn half hidden by the long, loose tendrils of her hair as they cascaded in waves around her face and over her shoulders. The nightgown she wore was ankle length, ivory in color, and a little too thick in weave to be considered sheer, though it was very feminine. Its neck was high and trimmed with lace, as were the long sleeves, and its voluminous folds swayed about her legs with each step.

She grasped the two wooden knobs that protruded from the face of the closet and swung the doors open. Several shirts, exactly like the one the doctor wore, hung from hooks inside, as well as an old-fashioned suit and a pair of trousers. Her running shoes sat on the floor board.

"Shoes, great. But where are my clothes?" T.J. mumbled to herself.

"Mrs. Reilly's mending them."

T.J. whirled around, startled. She hadn't heard the old man come back into the room. The quick action brought on a brief spate of dizziness.

"Blood from your head wound got on that shirt you were wearing, and several buttons were torn off of it. Oh, and the seat of your trousers was ripped open. Probably happened when you fell off that cliff. They also got dirty when you fell in the street."

"Guess I've been doing a lot of falling lately," she said.

There were a hundred other things she could have said
or done, but her head had begun to throb again.

"Yes, well you're about to do it again if you don't get
yourself back into that bed, missy. You might think you're
all well, but that was a nasty bash you got on the head
from that bullet passing by." He took her by the arm and
helped her back to the bed. "Fool Jenkins, shooting off a
gun like that over a dumb card game. The man ought to
know better than to play with them slicks, anyway."

T.J. practically fell back onto the bed. Her body was
nearly exhausted from its stroll across the room, and there
was a series of maddening thumps going off in her head
that felt more like small explosions.

"Go on back to sleep, missy. Best thing for you." He
took a bottle and spoon from his pocket. "You need something to help you sleep? I can give you some laudanum."

T.J. shook her head on the pillow. "No, Doc, thanks.
I'll be all right."

"I'll check on you again in a little while. Chance'll be
by then, too, I'm sure." He chuckled softly. "He's been
coming by every couple of hours, checking on you."

T.J. lay her head back on the pillow, wondering why
Chance Burkette's concern struck the old doctor as amusing, but too tired to ask. She closed her eyes and lay still
for a long time, but as weary as she felt, sleep wouldn't
come. After half an hour, she sat up slowly and reached
toward the rocker for the paper Doc had left there. Maybe
if she read for a while, she'd get drowsy. That's what usually
happened when she tried to read a book in bed. One page,
two at the most, and she was out like a light.

Her outstretched fingers curled around the newspaper
and she lifted it from the chair. With a sigh she propped
the pillow up behind her back, retrieved the glass of milk
from the table, and lay the unfolded newspaper against
her raised knees.

The headline nearly jumped off the page at her.

Chapter Six

Dumbfounded, T.J. stared at the newspaper headline, unable to believe what her eyes were seeing.

BILLY THE KID KILLED
in Lincoln County shootout with Sheriff Pat Garrett

T.J. nearly choked on her milk. She sputtered, coughed, and wiped a little white stream from her chin. Her gaze remained riveted to the black type as her heart pounded against her breast in hard, shock filled, and racing beats. It couldn't be. This was some kind of joke. Her gaze moved hastily over the headlines of the other articles on the newspaper's front page.

Luther King Arrested for Benson Stage Robbery
and Murder of driver, Budd Philpot.
Giuseppi Esposito, Italian Mafia Leader, Capture
in New Orleans and taken back to Italy.

Big Minnie—230 lbs. of Loveliness to Play Tombstone's Birdcage.

Yellow Fever Attacks New Orleans.

Black Bart Robs Nineteenth Wells Fargo Stage
Near Sacramento, California.

T.J.'s gaze darted to the top of the page in search of the
date. Friday, July 15, 1881. She stared at it for a long
moment, then shook her head. "This isn't funny anymore." She lay the paper on her lap and looked at the
door. Were these movie props? Or were they actually trying
to make her think it was 1881? Was this some perverse
trick of Jake Calder's? No, now she was starting to think
too weirdly. The stuff had to be movie props.

She looked toward the door. "Doc?"

He didn't come.

"Doc?" she called again.

Nothing but silence met her ears.

"Damn." She threw the covers aside and swung her legs
over the side of the bed. Pain filled her head and threatened to send her falling back onto the pillow, but she
fought it.

"Someone's got a lot of answering to do," T.J. mumbled
angrily.

She rose, walked across the room toward the door and
grasped the handle. Another wave of pain assaulted her
at the rapid movements she'd made and she leaned her
forehead against the papered wall beside the doorframe.
A moment later the hurt subsided, somewhat. T.J. opened
the door and stepped across the threshold.

The table Chance had lain her on the day she'd gotten
shot was in the center of the room, and an antique cabinet
sat against one wall. An assemblage of old, brown medicine
bottles was neatly lined in rows behind the cabinet's glass
doors.

"Very authentic," she murmured.

An oak rolltop desk was set against another wall. A mound of papers littered the desk's writing surface, and a small, black leather bag, like an old-fashioned doctors bag, sat atop the seat of a tall leather wing chair set in one corner of the room, near the desk.

T.J. moved toward a door set into the wall on the opposite side of the room. Since it was the only other door in the room except for the one she'd just come through, it obviously led to the main part of the house. She took a deep breath, steeling herself to endure the pain that would again assault both her still sore limbs and her injured head when she walked. Halfway to the door she froze, her gaze pinioned to a narrow space of wall between the door and another cabinet.

"This is just too much," she whispered angrily, but the trace of fear in her voice was evident even to her own ears. She moved toward the door again, the pain in both her limbs and head having subsided to more of an overall dull ache. But once to the door, instead of opening it, she reached toward the calendar that was tacked to the wall beside it. Her fingers brushed over the large printed numbers of the year as she stared at them. 1881. The same as the newspaper.

T.J. jerked her hand back and shook her head. A nervous laugh escaped her throat. Of course they'd match. Wasn't everything in Old Tucson supposed to seem authentic? That's what the tourists paid for. That's what the movie prop people were supposed to do, make everything seem authentic to that time.

She entered the next room, and found herself in an old-fashioned parlor, its furnishings of simple oak wood frame, the padded cushions covered in a plain brown fabric. T.J. moved toward the foyer, and the front door. The top half of the entry door framed a large piece of oval glass which was covered by a sheer lace curtain. She opened the door and stepped onto the wide veranda that fronted the house.

The sounds of leather harnesses brushing and slapping against one another, metal fastenings grating against metal hooks and hinges, and hooves pounding against solid-packed earth met T.J.'s ears seconds before a stagecoach lumbered past the house. Several men on horseback also passed, as well as a young woman in long skirts, her face hidden by the ruffled parasol she held over her shoulder. A small boy, laughing happily, chased a mangy mutt of a dog past the woman.

T.J.'s gaze scanned the scene, searching for some sign of a tourist, and found none. She was smack in the middle of a movie. That had to be it. She looked up at the roofs, down to the end of the streets, and into the small alleyway that separated two of the buildings across the street. There was no movie camera in sight. She stepped quickly back into the house and slammed the door shut behind her. Maybe it was too early for tourists. Maybe the cameras were hidden behind a wall somewhere, camouflaged, so they could shoot from different angles and wouldn't film one another. Her hands trembled and her legs felt weak. She held onto the wall with one hand and raised the other to glance at her wrist, but her watch was gone. Doc had probably removed it. Then she remembered she'd dropped it off at the repair shop that morning on her way to work. T.J. looked back through the lace curtain at the now quiet street.

If it wasn't a movie set, then what was going on? Was some kind of show going on down on the main street, or at the other end of town, where the tourists had gathered to watch? But they wouldn't all go to the show. T.J. smiled. The answer was so simple she felt stupid. There was probably a show going on, they were filming a movie today. That would draw just about everyone off the streets. And that's most likely where Doc was, too, wherever they were filming.

She moved back to the bedroom and noticed for the first time that although her muscles were still sore, most of the pain in her head had eased considerably since she'd begun moving about. It wasn't gone, but it was at least tolerable now. Unwilling to wait any longer to get to a phone, T.J. struggled her way out of the nightgown and into a pair of the trousers she'd found in the wardrobe. She pulled on what she assumed was one of Doc's shirts, or another prop, and tied its long front ends in a knot at her waist. She looked in the mirror. The pants were a bit snug, but then Doc was pretty skinny. Their length was almost perfect. She rolled up the cuffs of the shirt and put on her running shoes. Spying a beautiful silver handled brush lying on the bureau, T.J. quickly ran its soft white bristles through her long hair and looked into the mirror. Obviously lipstick and mascara were out of the question for now, but at least she felt half human again. She made her way back to the front door.

She pulled it open, made to step over the threshold, and ran smack into a brick wall. Or at least what felt like a brick wall, except that it was a bit softer—and warm. She looked up and straight into the dazzling blue eyes of Chance Burkette.

"And just where do you think you're going?" he demanded, making no effort to move out of her way.

T.J. took a step back. "First to a phone. Then back to my own apartment."

"Doc say you could leave?"

"I'll send him a check to cover the bill. Now, if you'll excuse me?" She made an attempt to move around him and felt like screaming when he sidestepped and blocked her way.

"I don't think so, Mrs. Calder."

She had been preparing to ram an elbow into his ribs, but his words left her suddenly speechless. Mrs. Calder? She stared up at him, her eyes wide, mouth agape.

Chance moved forward, effectively forcing T.J. to back into the house.

"What did you call me?"

"Mrs. Calder. Sue Ann, I believe your first name is. Now, why don't you just have a seat over there," he pointed past her and into the parlor, "and let's have us a little talk about where your husband is and what he's up to."

"Calder?" His words had managed to knock the bravado out of her. T.J. walked into the parlor and sank into a chair. She stared up at Chance. The entire situation was becoming more macabre by the minute. Why in heaven's name would this man think she was married to Jake Calder? Indignation burned within her and her stare turned to a glare. "My name is not Calder, Mr. Whoever-you-are. Or Sue Ann. It's Theresa. Theresa Jane McAllister. But most people call me T.J. Officer T.J. McAllister." She took a deep breath. "I don't have a husband. And even if I did, it sure as hell would not be Jake Calder!"

He remained standing and eyed her suspiciously. "Didn't say Jake. I said Gil."

"I don't know of a Gil Calder."

Chance remained silent and T.J. bristled at his look of obvious disbelief. Her composure returned as quickly as it had disappeared.

"Look, I told you, I'm not married, okay? Especially to a Calder. And this whole charade is not funny." She shot to her feet. A momentary blur of dizziness enveloped her, but passed almost immediately. "I've been after Jake Calder for over six months. I'm not a—"

"Never heard of a Jake Calder."

"Well then we're even. You've never heard of Jake and I've never heard of Gil."

"He's your husband."

"No, he's not. I'm after Jake Calder, for bank robbery and murder."

"Never heard of him," Chance repeated.

T.J.'s patience felt strained to breaking.

"I don't care if you've never heard of him," she snapped. "I've never heard of your Gil Calder, so there."

"I expected you to insist on something like that, but I'd hoped you wouldn't. You seem like a decent sort, Mrs. Calder," Chance continued, "why not get away from him while you can still make a proper life for yourself?"

T.J. felt like screaming, except she knew her head couldn't handle the sound.

"Look," she growled from between clenched teeth, "I am not this. . . . this. . . . Sue Ann Calder person. My name is T.J. McAllister, and I'm a cop, okay?"

"A what?"

T.J. felt her blood begin to boil.

"A cop. A cop." She clenched both hands into tight fists. "You know, police officer. Law enforcement agent. Cop!"

He continued to stare at her.

"I'm Officer T.J. McAllister, badge number 3164, of the Tucson Police Department. I was chasing Jake Calder and in the process I fell off that cliff."

"Are you saying you're a deputy sheriff?"

"No, dammit," T.J. snipped. "I'm saying I'm a cop. A City of Tucson police officer. Are you deaf?"

"And you fell from where?"

"You know from where. You were there."

"Tell me," Chance insisted.

She felt slightly weak and sat back down. "A cliff in the Tucson Mountains. A couple of miles in from Gates Pass. I was chasing Jake Calder and was halfway up the cliff after him when—"

T.J. snapped her mouth closed, suddenly remembering she didn't really know this man, didn't know what he and the old man who was supposedly a doctor were trying to pull, or why. But it was definitely time to go. She stood up abruptly, and nearly fell back into the chair when the

cymbals in her head began to crash together again at the
sudden movement.

Chance reached out and grabbed her by the arms, concern suddenly sparking in his eyes at her sudden paleness.
The hard tone of his voice dropped to a soft drawl. "What's
the matter? Are you all right?"

An unexplainable surge of warmth enveloped the flesh
beneath his touch. The imprint of his fingers seemed to
burn through the thin fabric of the shirt she'd borrowed
and brand her skin. A tingling sensation swept up her
arms. Her gaze jerked upward, met his, felt its pull, and
shot away again. She shrugged away from him.

"I'm fine. I just need some fresh air to clear my head."
She moved slowly toward the front door. "And a little
reasonable, and maybe truthful, conversation with a sane
person," she added.

Chance followed, unwilling to let her out of his sight.
If she really was Sue Ann Calder, he couldn't afford to let
her go, not now that she knew he was on to her. He didn't
know about her story, what a cop was, or who Jake Calder
was, and he didn't know what those cards in her wallet
meant, but he definitely wasn't letting her out of his sight
until he found out. And her insinuation that he was crazy
and had been lying to her left him puzzled. She hadn't
asked him anything. At least not anything that made any
sense.

T.J. ignored Chance and moved out onto the veranda.
She descended the three wooden porch steps to the
ground, then walked, slowly and carefully, toward the white
picket fence, and its entry gate.

"Where you going, missy?" Doc said, suddenly
appearing on the opposite side of the gate.

T.J. nearly groaned. Were these men taking care of her
or holding her prisoner?

The old man swung the gate open and approached. A
black bowler sat on his white hair like a dark saucer on a

snow bank. In his left hand he carried a medical bag, a very old-fashioned medical bag, identical to the one she'd seen in his office. He looked past her.

"Chance, you know I said she needed rest." Without waiting for a response from his nephew, Doc turned his attention back to T.J.

"The Zimmer baby decided to make its debut today, but I thought I ordered you to stay in bed a mite longer."

"I need some air, Doc," T.J. smiled, "and a phone. I thought I'd take a walk and find one."

"Well," he chuckled and took her hand in his, "we got plenty of air and places to walk, but I don't reckon you're going to find that tellyphone. But you can look. Come to think of it, fresh air might do you some good. Put a little color back into those pretty cheeks of yours." He released her hand and moved past her to stand beside Chance. "Just don't overdo it." He lowered his voice to a whisper. "Keep close to her, son. She's a spunky one, but she ain't got all her strength back yet. She's weak. Don't let her get away from you."

"I don't intend to, Uncle Zack," Chance answered in a low voice. "You can count on that."

T.J. moved slowly past the open gate, past the two neighboring houses, and around the corner and onto what appeared to be the town's main street. The buildings looked the same as she remembered from when she'd arrived. Another stage was stopped before the Express office, a group of young boys were huddled together in an alley across the street playing some sort of game. Tied here and there along the hitching racks, mainly in front of the saloons, were saddled horses.

Again, she saw no sign of a tourist. She should have asked Doc where the movie crew was filming so that she wouldn't blunder onto their set.

T.J. paused and looked at the sign over the door of the

building she stood in front of. DuMont Hotel. Its windows were covered with fancy lace curtains.

Several women came out of a store a few buildings down and their chatter drew T.J.'s attention. They were dressed in long gowns made of gingham and calico. The women wore lace and ruffle trimmed bonnets to shade their faces from the bright sunlight, the hats held in place by ribbons tied beneath their chins. A wave of weakness overtook T.J. and she reached out to grip one of the poles that supported the overhanging roof of the DuMont Hotel's front veranda.

She looked back at the women who were walking down the street away from her. Several cowboys came out of a saloon down the street. Another was riding a horse down the middle of the street, coming in her direction. It was a movie set. It had to be. She looked around. But where were the cameras? The directors?

For the next hour she wandered the streets, ignoring the painful throbbing in her temple, forcing her weary legs to keep moving. She searched for generators hidden behind buildings, for electrical wires strung overhead yet purposely out of sight, or hidden within woodwork or flooring, for some sign of water pipes and indoor plumbing, for parked cars, or evidence of tire marks in the dirt. She searched for electrical outlets and water spigots, for drain pipes and sewer lines, for fake buildings, PA systems, dressing rooms, and public restrooms. She searched for souvenir shops, hot dog stands, a place to buy a Coke— all the things one would find in the Old Tucson Movie Studios. She found none.

"Just exactly what does Gil have you looking for, Sue Ann?" Chance asked finally, moving up to stand beside her.

"I'm not Sue Ann," T.J. said, her tone hard. Her nerves were strung tighter than a rubber band. She paused in the shadow of a building and leaned against its clapboard wall to rest. "I told you, my name is—"

He held up a hand. "I know; Theresa Jane McAllister."

"T.J.," she corrected. "And why have you been following me?"

"T.J.," he said. "Doc wanted me to make sure you were all right."

"Well, I am, and since you know my name now, Mr. . . . ."

"Burkette."

T.J. nodded. "Since you know my name now, Mr. Burkette, if you're going to talk to me, please use it."

"T.J.," Chance repeated.

"Yes. What?"

"What are you looking for?"

"A phone."

He shook his head.

"Look, could we stop playing these games now? They're not funny anymore, and I'm tired. I just want a phone."

"Can't give you what I don't have," Chance drawled easily.

She pushed away from the wall, murder in her eyes. The man just didn't know when to quit. T.J. moved around the corner of the building and saw the sign of a livery hanging from the front of the next building. It was the only building she hadn't checked, except for one, a saloon. But there had been so many men dressed as cowboys inside, she was certain they were filming and hadn't wanted to interrupt. She moved toward the livery. Maybe it was the headquarters office for Old Tucson, the tourist information center. Hope swelled in her chest.

"Where are you going now, Sue Ann?" Chance asked, shadowing her steps.

She didn't answer. She couldn't, because if she did, it would be with a scream for him to stop calling her Sue Ann, and she didn't think her throbbing head could stand what a scream would do to it. The sun had already given her a headache to go along with the ache of her injury. She slipped past the tall green entry doors of the livery and into the shadows of its interior. The sweet smell of hay immediately assailed her nostrils.

"Hello? Is anyone here?"

A huge man suddenly appeared from one of the stalls, his massive chest and arms bare of a shirt but smudged black with dirt and soot. The leather bib apron he wore was scarred with burn marks. He wiped a meaty forearm over his bald head and moved toward her.

"Yeah, I'm here. What do you want?"

As he neared he stared at T.J.'s trousers as if he'd never seen a pair before, then he noticed Chance standing back by the door. "Oh, hey, Marshal. I didn't see you there for a minute." The man's gaze bounced from Chance to T.J., back and forth, as he tried to determine if they were together, the woman a prisoner, lady friend, or a stranger to both men.

"Hello, Markus," Chance answered.

"Do you have a phone?" T.J. asked haltingly, already certain she knew the answer. The moment she'd stepped into the barn, her hopes had died. It was not the tourist information building, it really was a livery stable. Horses filled almost every stall, and where there wasn't shavings on the floor, there was hay. Several buggies were lined up in the rear of the barn, and a huge anvil was set only a few feet from the door, a bed of hot coals burning in a rock pit just beside it.

"A what? Is that some newfangled kind of buggy?"

She shook her head. There had to be an explanation for this. There had to be. She just had to remain calm and find it. She fought down the panic that bubbled within her breast. They were pretending, that was all, T.J. told herself. Acting, and for some reason not about to break character, even for a cop. What had she done, tripped into the twilight zone? T.J. sighed. She'd have to go about this another way. She smiled at the man. "Can I . . . uh. . . . can I rent a horse here?"

Chance straightened, tensed, and watched her.

Henry Markus, the livery owner, frowned and glanced over T.J.'s shoulder toward Chance.

He nodded and the man turned his attention back to T.J.

"Sure, you can rent a horse, Miss. But I ain't got no lady's sidesaddle. You want a buggy?"

T.J. shook her head. "No, just a horse. And a saddle."

"A saddle?" Marcus repeated, obviously shocked. "You mean, a regular saddle?"

"Yes."

The livery owner's eyes widened. "You gonna ride astride like a man?"

"Yes."

He shook his head and eyed her trousers again.

"How long you gonna be?"

T.J. opened her mouth to respond but Chance answered before she could.

"Couple of hours, Hank, that's all. The lady just wants to go for a ride and get some air. She's been cooped up sick for a few days over at Doc's. I'll be going with her. Saddle Diablo for me, would you?"

"Sure thing, Marshal."

T.J. turned around to face Chance.

"I don't need you to go with me. And I didn't invite you."

He just stared at her without answering.

"Damn," T.J. snapped in frustrated anger. She whirled back around and nearly fell on her face as a wave of dizziness swept over her.

Chance bolted forward. His arms wrapped around her and pulled her to his chest. "That was a fool thing to do, Sue Ann, moving fast like that," he said, the gruff words softened by the rush of unexpected emotion that filled his chest as he held her. It felt good, holding her like that. Desire erupted and coiled, hot and demanding, with his groin. The moment the realization registered, he rejected the newborn feelings. This was not just any woman. This was Sue Ann Calder, the wife of the man who had murdered his family; his parents, his wife and his child. He let his arms drop away from around her and stepped back.

"You're still weak from getting your head split open. Maybe you shouldn't be sitting a horse just yet."

T.J. stared at him as if hypnotized, the breath still caught in her throat, her pulse racing. She should be outraged at his overbearing, chauvinistic attitude. But she wasn't. For some unexplainable and crazy reason, she liked his concern, but mostly she'd liked the feel of his strong arms around her, the sense of his strength embracing her, protecting her. She wanted to feel it again.

"Here's the horses, Marshal," Hank said, walking up behind T.J.

"I think we've changed our minds, Hank," Chance said.

His words broke the spell that had come over her at his touch. T.J. tore her gaze away from Chance and turned to the livery owner.

"No, I'm going." She smiled sweetly toward Chance. "But you don't have to come, Marshal. I'm sure you have other things to do."

Chance grabbed Diablo's reins.

"They'll keep," he said.

"If I ain't here when you get back," the livery owner said, "just put the horses in the corral outside and one of my boys will tend to them."

He turned around and went back to whatever he'd been doing in the rear of the barn when they'd entered and interrupted him.

Chance turned to T.J. Her green eyes sparked with tiny glints of gold, like fire among the pines, and long tendrils of her chestnut hair flowed down over her shoulders, one lock curling close to the open vee of her shirt collar. She looked like an angel, more so than any woman he'd ever seen. But looks, he knew only too well, could be deceiving.

Chapter Seven

Chance let T.J. lead the way, set the pace, and choose the direction they took. He hoped she wasn't going to lead him straight to the Calder gang or he'd be outnumbered, outgunned, and outsmarted. But he didn't think she'd do that. He was pretty certain she was leading him on a wild goose chase, maybe even giving the gang some kind of signal he wasn't aware of, but not taking him near their hideout. Or maybe she was getting him out of town so he wouldn't see several of them arriving.

They rode west, skirting the Tucson Mountain Range. They rode east toward the Rincons, and north toward the bluffs. Finally he followed her south, over the open flat landscape that seemed to go on forever, and down into a small valley. Not until they approached the majestic walls of the San Xavier Mission did she pause.

T.J. reined up several hundred yards from the mission and stared at it. Her gaze moved over every line of the walled-in old building: its twin towers, the right one missing its steeple; the simple balustrade that surrounded the third

story gallery, and the elaborate frontal piece with its columns, swirls and insets of various saints that surrounded
both the entry door and a second story balcony over the
main entry.

"Well, at least something is the same," T.J. said, staring
at the mission. But even as she said the words, the feeling
that they were false assailed her.

Chance remained silent, watching her.

T.J. frowned. Something was wrong, she knew it, felt it.
But what? Her gaze moved once more, this time more
slowly, over the old building. Then she saw it.

"The outbuildings aren't there." She twisted about in
her saddle and looked back over her shoulder. "Neither
is the street sign, or the souvenir shop that should be
right there." She pointed to her left, across the road, then
twisted around to look in the opposite direction at a small
hill to the right of the mission. "The cemetery's there,
but," she looked past the hill to the river they'd just
crossed, "but not the overpass. And where are the Indians?
The Papagos who live here? Where are their homes?"

Chance still didn't answer.

She kicked her horse and he lurched into an easy lope.
She urged him to the top of the hill that served as the
mission cemetery. T.J.'s eyes scanned the northern horizon. Far off in the distance, across the valley, were the
Rincon Mountains to the east, just as they should be. And
to her other side were the Tucson Mountains. Her gaze
dropped to the valley floor. So where was the sprawling
city of Tucson, Arizona?

"It should be right there," T.J. mumbled to herself.

Her eyes darted from right to left, up to the Santa Catalina Mountains that bordered the northern side of Tucson,
and back to the valley floor. But the only thing that sat on
the valley floor was the town she had just left; the small,
antiquated cowboy town she had thought was a movie set.

Panic, confusion and fear began to swell in her breast.

She fought to keep the unwelcome feelings from over-whelming her. What she was seeing couldn't be real, yet when she blinked her eyes and refocused on the scene, it was the same. She took note of her position again, and knew her bearings were right. The city should be right there, with its high rise downtown buildings, its sprawling ranch houses within the canyons on the city's outskirts, and its lone Highway Ten skirting the city's western border. But it wasn't there.

"There's a logical explanation for this," T.J. mumbled under her breath. Her gaze darted about again, looking in every direction. "There's a reasonable answer. I just have to find it."

It took almost two hours to get to Gates Pass, since she couldn't find the road and had to locate it by memory of the cuts and slopes of the mountains. She could have asked Chance to take her back to where he'd found her, but she didn't want to do that. He would ask her why and expect an answer, and the only one she could offer at the moment was not one he would accept. She hardly believed she was even considering it herself.

It took her another half an hour to find the cliff.

"Why'd you come here?" he asked, his tone begrudging.

T.J. ignored the question and, dismounting, went to stand at the edge of the cliff. She leaned forward and looked over its edge. Five or six feet below, a small out-cropping of rock, like a natural ledge, protruded from the sheer cliff. That's where she'd fallen from. T.J. straight-ened. If it really was 1881, if she really had been thrown back in time when she'd fallen off this cliff, then if she plummeted from it again she should return to her own time, to 1996. She looked down at the canyon floor. And if she was wrong she'd be skipping along the trail to the pearly gates.

She inhaled deeply, trying to summon the courage to

jump. It didn't come. Her eyes kept veering to the canyon floor, so far away.

No, it was crazy. It was 1996. Time travel was impossible, a fantasy of authors and movie makers, and Einstein. This was 1996. It had to be.

Six hours later, after what seemed to Chance nothing but an aimless ride that had taken them in one circle after another, T.J. reined in and turned to him. Night had replaced the light of day. Pale moonlight lit the landscape, instilling it with a myriad of shadows, and with the passing of the sun the air had begun to chill. The mountains surrounding Tucson had turned to black monoliths rising against the star dotted sky, and the near endless valley floor to an unfathomable stygian sea.

But T.J. had refused to give up, refused to stop searching, until now. There was nothing else to do. She was exhausted and frustrated. Her entire body felt like one big ache, her head was throbbing, and she was scared silly. Only the strong will she exerted over herself, and her police training, kept T.J.'s hands from shaking and her mind from plunging into complete hysteria. Nothing was as it should be. The only thing she'd recognized was the mission, and it wasn't really quite right either.

There were only two possibilities left to her now, and she was too weary to deny them any longer. Either the fall from the cliff had left her certifiably crazy, or she'd somehow been thrown back in time. There was no other answer to what she'd been experiencing. A movie company couldn't make the town of Tucson, with its several hundred thousand citizens, just disappear. It couldn't camouflage roads and highways so well that there was no trace of them, or dismantle an overpass. And it couldn't have torn down the outbuildings at the mission. That would never have been allowed, even for a movie company, no matter how much they paid.

T.J. sighed deeply. There was no other answer. Crazy or

thrown back in time, those were her two choices. Neither felt very appealing. She wasn't at all eager to admit to herself she was crazy, and if she was, would she be sane enough to admit it? And time travel? She nearly laughed, except it wasn't funny. Was she really in 1881? And if so, why?

For the first time in T.J.'s life, she knew what absolute terror was.

Chance watched her, as he'd been doing all day, his own emotions in total turmoil. She was beautiful, mysterious, alluring, more than any woman he'd ever met. He had known he was attracted to her the first moment he'd laid eyes on her, and he'd been fighting it like hell ever since. He didn't need a woman in his life right now. He didn't want one, especially not one that might turn out to be Sue Ann Calder, or at the very least, a Pinkerton agent.

But the logic of his mind was having a hard time convincing the stirrings she caused within his body. Never had he been affected like this by a woman, so hard and so quickly. Not even when he'd fallen in love with Caroline.

His gaze swept over her, outwardly cold, assessing, and scrutinizing, inwardly hot, hungry, and yearning. He felt the stirrings of passion in his blood intensify, found himself hard pressed to thwart the vision of her that invaded his mind, her body entwined with his, her arms holding him, her lithe form hot, naked, and welcoming his every touch. He had spent several good years with a wife, he had known the pleasures of ladies and whores alike, but none had ever affected him like this woman.

His eyes moved to meet hers. The things she had been saying, the story of who she was didn't make sense, yet when he looked at her face he saw no guile etched in the delicately beautiful features, no spark of deceit in those infinitely lucid green eyes.

T.J. raised a hand to cover her eyes, and a long sigh slipped from her lips. When she lowered the hand, Chance saw that tears shone in her eyes, glistening silver as they picked up the last rays of the setting sun. In that same moment, he noticed that her shoulders had sagged, as if in defeat, and her hands had begun to tremble.

"I don't understand," she said finally, staring at Chance. "Nothing's right. Nothing's as it should be."

He heard the note of panic in her tone.

"What happened? Where is everything?" She shook her head again and looked at him, fear plain in her eyes. "What's going on?"

She was about to collapse. He sensed it. Acting quickly, Chance swung his right leg over Diablo's neck and slid from his saddle. He was moving across the ground toward her almost before the soles of his boots touched the hard earth. He saw a shiver shake her body, but knew instinctively it wasn't from cold. The sun had disappeared beyond the horizon over an hour and a half ago and the air was cooling rapidly, but had not yet reached the point of being uncomfortable. She was frightened, deeply frightened, but of what he didn't know. He denied the possibility that she was scared of him. They'd been riding together for hours, alone in the desert and mountains. Why would she suddenly, this minute, become afraid of him? Unless she had recognized something was wrong, unless they had passed some sign, some marking that perhaps meant Gil had deserted her.

Chance refused to consider that she wasn't Sue Ann Calder. He couldn't. Everything pointed to her being the outlaw's wife. He knew Calder was still in Arizona and heading toward Tucson, if not already somewhere near. And Sue Ann Calder had a habit of arriving in a town before her husband and his gang. This time she'd obviously run into a little trouble on the trail first. Maybe she'd met up with a rival outlaw gang or a bounty hunter. Chance reached up and grasped T.J. by her waist, his strong hands almost enveloping its narrow breadth.

"Come on," he said, and pulled her toward him a little more roughly than he'd meant to. She came readily, willingly, her own hands seeking his shoulders. Her feet touched the ground, but she didn't move away from him, didn't remove her hands from his shoulders or her gaze from his.

For one fleeting moment all the doubts and suspicions he felt about her disappeared. Chance wanted nothing more than to press his lips to hers, to know the taste of her kiss and the sweet feel of her body crushed against his. Passion with this woman would be like no other. He sensed it, knew it, as sure as he knew his own name, and his body demanded he pay heed. Instead, he fought against the feeling, and regained his self-control. He won the battle, but Chance wasn't so certain he hadn't just lost the war.

Ignoring the raging fires that flamed within him, the desperate ache to drag her into his arms and ravish her lips with his, he gripped her wrists in his hands and pulled them from his shoulders.

An image of his daughter flitted into his memory. He'd been teaching her to ride only a few days before she'd been killed. The pain of loss the memory brought was just as stabbing to his heart as the day he had discovered her lifeless little body, only hours after Gil Calder and his cowboys had ridden away from the Burkette ranch.

He instantly released T.J.'s hands. She was Sue Ann Calder, he reminded himself coldly, Gil Calder's wife, a murderer's wife.

"It's late."

His words hung in the air, curt, hard, and cold.

Chance walked back around his horse, threw one stirrup up over the saddle and pulled on the cinch to release its buckle. He avoided looking at T.J. Instead he unhooked Diablo's chest strap and slid the saddle from his back. Looking at her was trouble. He had never had this experience with a woman before, his body aching with hunger from just looking. It annoyed him as much as it puzzled and troubled him.

"We've run out of daylight," he said needlessly. "We'll have to camp here for the night and return to town in the morning."

T.J. stared up at him. She didn't answer. What was there to say? What could she say? She didn't know where she was, didn't know where anything was. T.J. fought to control the panic rising in her again. She didn't even know this man, and yet for some reason she felt as if he was her link to sanity, her anchor in a world that had gone crazy. She wanted so desperately for him to draw her into his arms and hold her. When he'd carried her down off the mountain she'd felt safe. She wanted, needed, to feel that way again.

The thought left her totally unnerved. She had always been self-reliant, self-sufficient, willing to lean on no one. Why did she suddenly want so badly to be able to count on him, to be held by him, comforted by him—a total stranger?

T.J. forced her mind away from these emotionally dangerous thoughts and back onto her situation. What had happened to her? What had happened to the world? The sprawling, modern city of Tucson was not where it should be. Highway Ten, the only major highway that led to and from Tucson, was not there. Neither was the Desert Museum with its animals and plants, or the Pima Air Museum with its hundreds of old planes. The Titan Missile Museum was gone, and Sabino Canyon was little more than a primitive forest area rather than the beautiful park she and Lisa had lunched in so often. No houses dotted the landscape.

Fear had a death grip on her heart.

She had ridden toward the small city of Oracle on a path that should have been a paved two lane highway, and wasn't, and found the spot where the Biosphere should be, but the huge environmental testing dome had not been there. What she'd found instead was nothing but rolling desert hills. And Gates Pass didn't seem to exist at all, yet it was the road that led through the Tucson Mountains to the cliff she'd chased Jake Calder to, the cliff she'd fallen off. It was also the road that led to the Old Tucson Movie Studios. Except now they weren't there. The place she thought she had been all this time, wasn't there at all!

Panic once again threatened to overwhelm and consume her, and it took every ounce of self-control she had to fight it off. It wouldn't do her any good to get hysterical and start screaming or sobbing, which was what she felt like doing. T.J. folded her arms in front of her and grasped her upper arms tightly. She turned away from Chance and stared out at the darkening landscape, at the flat, sprawling desert floor that seemed to go on forever.

Chance threw his saddle on the ground, followed by the blanket and saddle bags, then led Diablo to a nearby scrub of brush on which he could munch. T.J. watched him secure the horse's reins to the ground by placing a heavy stone on their ends, then repeat the entire process with her horse. Minutes later he had a fire going only a few feet from where she stood, with a small pot of coffee brewing over it.

The tangy aroma wafted across the night air to tease her senses. T.J. felt a ripple of comfort at the smell. Coffee. She recognized the aroma. Did that mean she hadn't gone completely crazy yet? She turned to look at Chance.

He had hunkered down beside the fire and poured the steaming dark liquid into two tin cups he'd pulled from his saddlebag. Without glancing up at her he said, "Come on and have a cup of coffee, Sue Ann. It'll make you feel better."

T.J. sighed and moved to stand across the fire from him.

"Please, I've told you, my name's not Sue Ann. It's T.J."

Her voice sounded strained, tired, and weak. "Theresa Jane McAllister."

Chance looked up, surprised at the resignation he heard in her tone. He saw the glimmer of tears that she was trying to hold back. He relented.

"All right, T.J."

He handed her a cup of coffee.

T.J. reached out for it. As she grasped the small curl of the handle, her fingers brushed against the tips of his.

She felt as if she'd touched a live electrical wire. A shock of tingling warmth erupted in her fingertips, just beneath the flesh that had touched his, then raced up her arm and spread throughout her body. She looked up at him and saw in his eyes that he had also felt it.

Chance stared down at her for several moments, desire and the need for vengeance fiercely battling each other within him. For one split second, when he saw the need in her eyes, he didn't care anymore, he didn't want to deny the passion boiling in his blood, the need to take her. And why should he deny it? He could have some of his revenge now with her. He'd take Gil Calder's wife to his bed and use her body to satisfy the hunger gnawing at him, and later he would let Gil Calder and everyone else know what he'd done.

It was an ugly thought, a cruel, cold thought, and one that would have surprised anyone who knew him. But she was only an outlaw's wife, he told himself, a murderer's wife. And he was a U.S. Marshal, the widower of a woman her husband had murdered, the father of a child her husband had brutally killed.

And she had made him feel something he didn't want to feel.

A frown suddenly pulled at his brow and he jerked both his gaze and his hand away from her, then rose and moved to where he'd put their saddlebags. He could take her easily, by force if necessary, but he wouldn't. He wasn't a savage. A minute later he returned to her side, holding two blankets in his arms. With a shake of his right hand he unfurled one blanket and dropped it across her shoulders.

"You'll need this." The words were spoken abruptly, his tone harsh. "Nights can get cold out here on the desert, as I'm sure you know."

T.J. pulled the wool blanket around her and sat down beside the fire.

"You came pretty prepared on this ride." She smiled weakly.

"I'm always prepared," Chance said over his shoulder, as he lay his own blanket on the ground. "It keeps me alive."

T.J. had the distinct impression that he wasn't talking about the blankets and coffee. He was referring to being on guard, to being alert and ready for danger. But what did he have to be on guard against now? Her? She looked at him, her mind working feverishly to find answers to the questions swirling in her thoughts. She'd fallen off a cliff while chasing Jake Calder, she remembered that. But the next thing she'd been aware of, the next thing she remembered, she was looking up into Chance Burkette's blue eyes. What had happened in between?

A nervous shiver ran up her spine as she remembered the newspaper and calendar in Doc's house. Both had put the year at 1881. She sat down and stared into the fire, the cup of coffee cradled in her hands. Could it really be true? She closed her eyes and wondered again if she was crazy.

"More coffee?" Chance said, breaking into her thoughts.

T.J. opened her eyes and shook her head, but kept her gaze downcast. 1881. She tried to reason out the implication of it, of everything she'd seen and encountered in the last few hours, but couldn't. As improbable as it seemed, as impossible as the mere idea was, what other explanation was there? She sighed. The notion was absurd. So absurd she felt like laughing, except she couldn't think of any other way to explain what was happening, and that wasn't funny. T.J. frowned.

The logical side of her mind still wanted to dismiss the idea as preposterous. People didn't get thrown back in time. It was impossible. Absolutely impossible. What happened yesterday, last week, last year, is over—gone—finished. The past is gone, dead. And yet . . . She looked over at Chance.

He caught her gaze. The glow of the campfire's crackling flames reflected on his face and gave his skin a bronze cast, turned his high cheekbones and square jaw to planes of gold, the curve beneath his brow and the hollows of his cheeks to vistas of cimmerian shadows. Slowly, almost insolently, he reached up with one hand and pushed a thumb against the brim of his hat, forcing it off of his forehead. Firelight glistened a reflection in the blackness of his brows and transformed them to arched wings. The usual lock of black hair fell forward to curl rakishly over his forehead.

Fear swelled inside of T.J. like a balloon about to explode. Her hands trembled and her mouth went completely dry. Butterflys beat at the inside of her stomach. She could not accept that it was 1881. The idea of time travel was science fiction fantasy. She looked around, her gaze darting from one dark shape beyond the fire to the next. The night was so peaceful, the air so sweet, yet she could not quell the panic rising within her. They had ridden for hours and she had found no sign of life as she knew it, no sign of Tucson, of home. The mountains, the hills, the river were the same, yet they weren't. There were no paved roads traversing the terrain, and each hill and plateau only gave way to more desert, rather than the things she knew should be there: the museums, the buildings, the airport.

Everything she'd encountered since Chance Burkette had found her three days ago at the base of that cliff attested that it was 1881. But how could it be? She had been born in 1970. She'd graduated from high school in 1988, from the University of Arizona in 1992 from the police academy in 1994. How in heaven's name could it be 1881? Because if it was, she wouldn't even be born.

Chapter Eight

T.J. felt her teeth begin to chatter and clamped them together. She wanted to deny the possibility that it was 1881, yet somehow she knew it was true. She looked at Chance. He was staring down into his coffee, then, without lifting his eyes, he brought the cup to his lips and took a long swallow of the steaming liquid.

It wasn't a movie set, it wasn't a trick, and she wasn't crazy. It was 1881. Wasn't it?

T.J. felt an urge to throw herself into his arms, to seek the warmth and security she sensed his strength could offer, but she refrained. She had been trained to handle difficult situations on her own.

But not situations like this, a little voice in her head yelled.

She ignored it. If it was true, if. . . . T.J. sighed and blinked back the tears of frustration and fear that suddenly filled her eyes. If she had somehow fallen through a time warp, then she would just have to . . .

To what? She had no answer.

If she really was in 1881, no one would believe how she'd gotten there. No one. A laugh of hysteria bubbled its way into her throat and she quickly swallowed it back down. She was having a hard enough time believing it herself!

T.J. gripped the tin cup tightly in an effort to still her trembling hands, and sipped at the coffee. If it was true, what was she going to do? She certainly couldn't tell anyone.

T.J.'s imagination and sense of humor popped into gear: *Listen Chance, the reason I've been acting so weird is, well, you see, when I fell off that cliff, and I did fall, I didn't jump, it was 1996. And well, I guess I must have dropped through some kind of time warp because here I am in 1881, and well, it just took me awhile to figure it out, that's all. Sorry.*

T.J. nearly groaned, then another thought struck her. If it was true, if she had fallen through some kind of window in time, was she stuck here forever? The thought sent a chill racing through her body. She'd never see her parents again. A sudden feeling of emptiness, of loneliness and insecurity overwhelmed her. Tears, unbidden and unwanted, ran down her cheeks.

Chance finished off the last of his coffee and, with a deep sigh, lay down. He stretched his long legs out before him, and bent his arms so as to tuck his hands beneath his head.

T.J. looked past the fire at him. The flames crackled softly and leapt into the night between them. He was using his saddle as a headrest and had pulled his hat down over his eyes.

If it was true, if she was really in 1881, he and Doc were her only friends, if you could call a man who thought you were someone else a friend. He believed she was someone named Sue Ann Calder. Ironic, since it was because she'd been chasing a Calder that she was in this mess—whatever this mess was.

T.J. felt hot tears fill her eyes again and turned her face

away, not wanting to take the risk of Chance seeing her lose control. That had only happened once since she'd been a little girl, when they'd told her Lisa was dead. She'd broken down completely then, and it had taken endless days before she could go through an eight-hour shift without breaking into tears. Losing control wasn't a feeling she liked, and was one she always tried to avoid. She wiped the tears from her cheek. Her fingertips brushed against the bandage just above her brow. On impulse she slid it off and threw it in the fire, feeling, just for a moment, as if that just might change everything—but when she looked up from the crackling flames—nothing had changed.

The hat hid his eyes from her view, but he could see her. From beneath barely lowered lashes Chance had been watching her. Guilt for his earlier thoughts nagged at him, and he pushed it to the back of his mind. He tried to tell himself he was waiting for her to make a run for it, try to grab his gun, or signal someone. But he knew that wasn't the only reason. There was something about her that like it or not, drew him. He felt it in his blood, and he'd been fighting it all day. All he had to do was look at her, drop the guard on his thoughts for a moment, and he found himself wondering what it would be like to hold her in his arms and kiss her.

He had seen her turn away, and noticed the stream of tears on her cheeks, but he hadn't moved, unsure of what to do. Caroline had only cried when she'd wanted something, or when she couldn't get her way. There hadn't really been much left of their marriage at the end, but she'd deserved better than to be brutally murdered. Chance felt the heat of outrage warm his blood as the memory of what had happened invaded his thoughts. It had been three years since the Calder gang had ridden onto the Burkette ranch, chased by a posse and seeking fresh horses and food. Three years, but to Chance it might as well have been yesterday.

When his father had refused to cooperate with the outlaws, Gil Calder had shot him, one bullet straight through
the heart. By the time Gil and his gang left the Burkette
spread and headed for Mexico, they'd killed not only Benjamin and Sarah Burkette, but also Morgan's new bride,
and Chance's wife and child. They'd run the animals off
and torched the house and outbuildings. There had been
little left when Chance and his brothers, Morgan and Rick,
members of the posse chasing the Calders, had ridden up
the next morning.

He closed his eyes against the burn of tears that always
came at the thought of his five-year-old daughter being
murdered by Calder or one of his gang. The vow of vengeance he'd sworn against Gil Calder while standing over
Krissy's grave, still burned bright in Chance's memory.

He should have been there to help his family, to defend
his daughter and save her life. A lone tear escaped the
outer corner of Chance's eye and slid down the side of his
face. Peace was something neither his heart nor mind
could accept, not until Gil Calder was brought to justice.

T.J.'s sobs grew deeper, and the sound pulled Chance
from the sorrowful and guilt-ridden memories that always
turned his mood dark.

She sniffed and as another sob broke from her throat,
she raised a trembling hand to stifle it. The small tin coffee
cup fell from her other hand and the dark liquid flew up
and sprayed the crackling flames of the fire, making a
hissing noise.

Chance sat up. He wanted to dislike her for who she
was, knew it was the safest, most logical thing to do, but
something inside of him wouldn't let him. That angered
him all the more. Cursing himself for being a fool and a
weakling, knowing he was courting danger, perhaps deadly
danger, he moved to sit beside her but remained silent,
not certain what to say.

T.J. turned toward him then. Thin rivers of silver moisture glistened on her cheeks and, cradled in small pools along the rim of her eyelids, a fresh onslaught of tears hovered just above the ruche of dark lashes, waiting to fall.

Instinctively, almost involuntarily, he drew her into his arms, offering what comfort he could, and all the while he staunchly tried to ignore the little voice in the back of his mind that kept whispering the word fool, over and over. Chance pulled her against him so that she leaned on his chest and her head rested against his shoulder. What he was doing was wrong, and he knew it. He should stay as far away from her as he could get. She could be purposely playing on his emotions, leading him into a trap, setting him up. He knew any or all of these possibilities were conceivable, even probable, but right here and now he didn't care. Maybe she was Sue Ann Calder, and maybe she wasn't. He could be right, he could be wrong. He didn't know, and at the moment the consideration was the furthest thing from his mind.

He lay his chin lightly on the crown of her head, tightened his embrace around her as she cried, and began to rock slowly back and forth.

T.J.'s arms crept up to his shoulders and she clung to him, her sobs harder now, each wracking her body with a deep shudder. Finally her tears began to dry and her panic subsided somewhat.

"What am I going to do?" she muttered, the words muffled as her face remained half buried against his shirt front. "Nothing's right. Nothing's like it should be, and I don't know what to do. I don't know what's happening."

Chance felt T.J.'s lips move against the fabric of his shirt as she talked, a movement that was as light as the ruffling of a blue lupine's delicate star shaped leaves, and as devastating to his psyche as if the innocent caress had been intentionally seductive. His embrace tightened around her, his heart giving no heed to the dire warnings against this action emanating from his mind. Desire burned hot and hungry within his veins and coiled in a knot deep in his groin, demanding, aching, gnawing for release.

Her arms slipped around his neck, and he felt her fingers entwine themselves in the thick strands of hair that curled over the collar of his shirt. Another shudder shook her body and she pressed herself tighter against him.

"I'm sc . . . scared, Chance," T.J. whispered, calling him by his given name for the first time. Her voice cracked on the words. Fear was not something she gave into easily, but she had used up all her resources to fight it off, and she'd lost. She wasn't just afraid, she was terrified; of the unbelieveable prospect of what had happened, of the possibility that it really hadn't and she was merely losing her mind. "I'm scared," she repeated, "and I don't know what's happening." She raised her face to look at him and cascading waves of chestnut hair swirled over her shoulders, caught the glow of the nearby fire and turned to strands of flaming red and gold silk.

He raised a hand toward her face and with the tip of one finger, gently traced the path of a tear as it slid over her cheek, the touch of his flesh to hers little more than that of a feather.

"There's nothing to be afraid of, darlin'," Chance drawled softly. "No one's going to hurt you."

He could feel the thudding beat of his heart pound against his chest, ready to explode with the emotion that filled it. All day he had been trying to deny the feelings she aroused in him, feelings he had determined long ago never to allow himself to experience again. At least not until he finished the task he'd set for himself. And maybe not even then.

His heart had been locked away, sealed against the world, against caring for a woman, any woman. He had a job to do now—a promise to keep, revenge to take.

Yet in spite of this he'd thought of little else all day except the woman he now held in his arms. He'd watched her ride ahead of him, the subtle sway of her hips on the saddle causing the ache of need inside him to burn all the hotter. He'd ridden beside her, and found it hard to look anywhere but at her face, and into those green eyes that nearly mesmerized him with their sparks of flame and fathomless depths. And he'd ridden ahead of her, trying to redirect his thoughts by removing her from his sight, and blot out the ache of desire consuming him. But it hadn't worked, and now none of his misgivings about her mattered, nothing mattered but that he have her for his own, that he taste her lips, feel her kiss, and love her body.

Reality, with its frightening prospects, suddenly slipped away and T.J. found herself aware of nothing other than the man who held her in his embrace, of his hands pressing against her back, the heat of his flesh burning through the thin shirt she wore and searing her skin. She felt his breath gently stir the wisp of curled hair at her temple, saw his blue eyes turn to dark chasms of passion, and felt that same emotion begin to stir within her own blood.

His head lowered toward hers, slowly, steadily.

T.J. closed her eyes, waiting, her body shivering with anticipation, her fear momentarily forgotten. Fire leapt in her veins as his lips touched hers, gentle at first, seeking, caressing, warm, and finally, demanding. He kissed her for a long time and in his kiss T.J. felt the agony of his need, the loneliness that he kept so well hidden within him, and a hint of what warmth and caring this man could offer.

She had been kissed before, many times, but none had ever stirred or touched her as his kiss did. He was a stranger and yet, at this moment, he was exactly what she needed. He was her strength, her support, her anchor in the world, whatever world it was. He was her worst nightmare, and he was her knight in shining armor.

She opened her mouth to his kiss and his tongue delved forward, urgently seeking the inner softness she offered, the sweetness he craved. He crushed her body up against his so that she was molded to him, curve to curve, plane to plane. Somewhere in the back of her mind, in some tiny, conscious part of conscience, T.J. knew she should pull away from him, knew she should stop him, but she also knew she couldn't. From the first moment she had seen Chance Burkette, she had known this would come eventually, and now that it had she was oblivious to everything else: to reason, to logic, even to their surroundings. Nothing mattered to her now but the tall, dark cowboy who held her cradled in his arms, whose strength lent her comfort, whose mere presence gave her a sense of security, and whose mouth was inciting a passion deep within her like none she'd ever known.

His tongue was a flickering arc of fire within her mouth, burning wherever it touched as his hands roamed over her back and held her to him. She strained to get closer, pressing her body against his, her arms holding tight around his shoulders, her hands at the back of his neck, her fingers hiding within the dark curls of his hair.

T.J. clung to him, her body aching with need of every kind.

Chance pulled slightly away from her and his mouth moved to kiss her neck. He gave a groan of pleasure, intense and deep, when she threw her head back, inviting his touch. His hands moved to her buttocks, pulling her closer, and half onto his lap.

She felt the hardness of his need press against her thigh as his lips moved to nuzzle the hollow of her throat. A moan of ecstasy slipped from her lips, drifting away on the still air of the silent desert night. Lost in a world of unchartered passion, of need so great that it caused her to ache with want, T.J. pressed against him.

His hands slid upward to encircle her waist and then up to her neck, his fingers slipping within the fiery tendrils of her hair, burying themselves in its silkiness.

For one brief second, a flash of time that seemed forever, Chance caught her gaze, and in that second he knew, for better or worse, that he had met his destiny. His thumbs moved to frame her jaw and he tilted her head to receive his kiss again.

Chapter Nine

In the distance the mournful howl of a coyote echoed on the still night air, drifted over the land, and slowly penetrated Chance's subconscious. He abruptly jerked away from T.J. and stared down at her, aghast at what he'd just done, at what he'd intended to do.

He had been about to make love to Gil Calder's wife! Disgust with himself melded with the passion still hot and burning in his body. He had been about to make love to the wife of the man who had cold bloodedly murdered Caroline and Krissy, who had shot his father over a few horses, and then savagely killed his mother and sister-in-law and torched their home. Vivid memories, and the still painful physical and emotional ache they brought, filled his mind and heart.

His eyes narrowed as they turned hard and cold, and his jaw clenched tight to resemble a cut of granite.

"I shouldn't have done that," Chance said, his tone an icy rapier that cut through T.J.'s passion and brought her senses hurtling headlong back to reality.

She immediately stiffened and scrambled back away from him, her own gaze purposely meeting his. What had she been thinking, to let him, a complete stranger do that? T.J. felt her face burn with heat and knew it had nothing to do with the warmth of the flames beside her.

Chance stood and walked around the fire. "Why?" he said suddenly.

T.J.'s brow instantly drew together in puzzlement at the question. "Why?" she echoed. Did he mean why did she kiss him? Why did she let him kiss her? "Why what?" she asked him back.

"Why would a beautiful and intelligent woman like you marry someone like Gil Calder?"

Exasperation filled her.

"Look, I'm not—" T.J. abruptly clamped her mouth shut. No. She couldn't deny what he was saying. If she did, then she had to come up with an explanation of who and what she was, and she couldn't, at least not one he would believe or understand. Then she had a brainstorm. Amnesia! That was her best bet. She'd continue to insist her name was T.J. McAllister, but she'd pretend to have amnesia about everything else, then she wouldn't have to explain anything. She met Chance's gaze again. "Look Mr. Burkette, I don't really know who you think I am, and admittedly, I don't remember much, but I do know my name's T.J.—T.J. McAllister. It's about all I seem capable of remembering, but I'm definite on that point."

"Yeah," Chance answered, the lone word sheathed in sarcasm. "I know."

T.J. felt a flash of temper. "It's true."

"Yeah," Chance said again, and sat down. He busied himself stretching out, laying his head on his saddle, and situating his hat over his eyes.

"Look, I don't really remember anything. Honest," T.J. said. "Not since I—"

Chance folded his hands together atop his chest. "Good night, Sue Ann."

T.J's temper nearly overwhelmed her. She wanted to scream at him, to hit him with her fists. Instead, she fought to regain some semblance of composure. Clasping her hands into fists on her thighs she glared at him across the fire. If this really was 1881, then she had to start coping with the situation, and it might help if she knew who this Sue Ann Calder person was he kept insisting was her.

"Okay, just who is this Sue Ann Calder you think I am?"

He shoved the hat off of his nose slightly and peeked out at her. His expression was sardonic and reflected total skepticism about her words. "Now you're trying to tell me you don't know who you are?"

"No," T.J. snapped. "I told you, I know who I am, but you obviously don't." Her hands trembled in her lap. "I'm T.J. McAllister, but you think I'm someone named Sue Ann Calder. So the least you can do, if you insist on believing that, is to tell me who she is."

"Lady, I've had one hell of a week, and I'm too tired to play games tonight. So, if you'll just excuse me I'll say—"

"Just tell me," T.J. insisted.

"Goodnight."

"Tell me, dammit."

Chance jerked upward, propping himself on one elbow, and glared at her.

"Sue Ann Calder is the wife of Gil Calder, who leads the Calder gang. All right?"

"And?" T.J. urged.

Every line, plane and curve on Chance's face was suddenly etched with rage.

"And they're some of the lowest, filthiest, murdering cutthroats this territory has ever seen. Now, are you satisfied?"

"They're outlaws," T.J. said.

He snorted. "That's a polite way of putting it, lady. And

polite is not what I am when I'm talking about people who ruthlessly kill old men, women, and children." His eyes darkened with rage. "They're murderers, lady. Savage murderers. And as you damned well know, your husband is their leader, and the worst of the bunch."

As he'd been describing the outlaws a thought popped into T.J.'s mind that she found intriguing, even startling, though preposterous. After Jake Calder had killed Lisa, and before the captain had ordered her off the case, T.J. had requisitioned all Jake's records. Included in those records had been a brief history of the man and his ancestors. A frown drew her brow as she tried to remember that sketch. Had there been a Gil Calder? The name bounced around in her head. She could swear there had been—a grandfather, or great grandfather. And Sue Ann. Now that she thought about it in conjunction with Jake, the name did sound familiar, but she wasn't sure.

She looked at Chance. Could it be? If this was 1881, if she truly had traveled back in time, could it be that Gil Calder was Jake Calder's ancestor, maybe his great grandfather? And Sue Ann was his great grandmother?

For the first time since regaining consciousness at the bottom of that cliff, T.J. felt a spurt of hope. Had she been thrown back in time to prevent Jake Calder's existence? She smiled. If Gil and Sue Ann were Jake's ancestors, and if they hadn't already had children, and were caught and imprisoned before they did. . . .

Excitement bubbled in T.J.s chest. If Jake Calder never got born, then Lisa couldn't be murdered by him.

"Who did the Calders kill?" T.J. asked, suddenly certain that the rage she sensed within Chance Burkette when he mentioned the Calder gang was more intense than anyone, even a cop—she corrected her thoughts—even a territory marshal, would feel unless there was something personal involved.

"Don't you know?" Chance drawled cynically.

T.J. forced herself, for the first time since they'd met, to look deep into his eyes. They were narrowed by constantly being exposed to the brilliance of the desert sun, and, though near indigo, they reflected both the pale innocence of the prey within tiny slivers of silver color, and the mysterious, feral instincts of the predator.

Chance lay down, pulled the hat over his eyes, then rolled onto his side and turned his back to her.

The conversation was officially ended.

T.J. stared at Chance's back, the silence of the night broken only by the distant howling of a coyote and the crackling of the campfire's flames. An ache of longing had settled itself deep down inside of her and she was trying desperately to ignore it. She wanted to feel the security of his arms around her again, to immerse herself in the warmth and pleasure the feeling had given her, and to tap into the strength and masculine force she'd felt in him.

At the same time she wanted nothing more than to pick up a rock and bash him over the head with it.

T.J. wrapped her arms around her legs, hugged them to her, propped her chin onto her knees and stared into the orange flames. They danced merrily, licking at the blackness of the night, sending their sparks and smoke up into the dark sky, and casting a golden orange glow onto the immediate surroundings.

Was it really possible? Every thread of logic within her said no, but logic couldn't argue against what she'd experienced since she'd fallen off that cliff. Logic couldn't argue away the fact that Tucson, Arizona of 1996 was gone, that nothing she remembered—the roads, the man-made landmarks—existed anymore. And logic couldn't argue away Chance Burkette. Almost against her will T.J.'s eyes moved from the fire to look at Chance.

His broad shoulders stuck out from the blanket he'd drawn over himself, and the glow of the fire turned the gray of his shirt to the muted hue of a moonlit fog.

Her arms had encircled those shoulders and hugged them to her.

His hair glistened softly in the firelight, creating deep shadows within the hidden depths of each curl.

She had buried her hands within those silken tendrils, and slid her fingers through the thickness of that soft velvety darkness.

Chance rolled over then, resettled himself on his back and reached up to reposition the hat over the upper portion of his face. His black mustache picked up the glow of the flames.

T.J. remembered the feel of his mustache as he'd kissed her, soft, caressing.

"Oh, stop it," she snapped at herself.

Chance bolted upright. His hat tumbled to the ground. His right hand moved with lightning speed, drew the Colt Peacemaker from its sheath and pointed it toward the blackness beyond their campfire. He stared across the fire at her, his finger still ready on the trigger, his eyes narrowed even more, than usual.

"Stop what?"

T.J. started at his sudden movement, and her heart nearly jumped into her throat. Her gaze was glued to the end of the gun, which was now pointed directly at her.

Chance slipped the weapon back into the holster still tied to his thigh.

"Stop what?" he repeated, glaring at her.

"Nothing," T.J. muttered. She silently ordered her heart to stop its slamming beat. "I was just thinking out loud."

The look in his eyes told her that was something she probably shouldn't have admitted to.

He lay back down, picked up his hat and repositioned it over his face, then pulled the blanket back over his legs and folded his arms across his chest. "Try not to think so loud next time," he muttered from beneath the hat.

T.J. stuck her tongue out at him. Ten minutes later she

lay down and covered herself with the blanket he'd given her earlier. She moved several times, first lying on her right side, then her left, then her back, before finally settling down in the exact position she'd first tried, on her right side and facing the fire. The earth was hard and the saddle beneath her head was not exactly the type of pillow she was used to. T.J. closed her eyes and willed herself to go to sleep.

Chance moved his head so that the brim of his hat shifted position and allowed him a view of her across the ebbing campfire. What the hell was he doing out here, in the middle of the desert, with Gil Calder's wife? He'd been asking himself that question ever since he'd kissed her. Hell, if he was honest, he'd been asking himself that question ever since they'd left town. He had to be crazy. Or maybe he had a death wish and just didn't realize it.

She shifted position and Chance stiffened, ready to let the hat fall lower rather than have her catch him watching her.

But her eyes remained closed.

He relaxed again, though there was a thread of tension in his body that was always there, no matter where he was or what he was doing. Some part of Chance Burkette, some sliver of self-preservation, was always taut, alert, and ready for the unexpected. His gaze moved up and down her body. What was there about her that drew him so? She was beautiful, but he'd been around beautiful women before, plenty of them. There was something different about this one, however, something that turned his blood to fire and left him nearly senseless. Whatever it was, the feeling pushed every rational thought from his mind and left him with nothing more than thoughts of her naked body pressed to his, the fires he sensed smoldered beneath that beautiful exterior ignited, hot and burning, and begging for his touch.

Chance felt his body begin to harden at the direction

his thoughts were taking and forced them to turn in a different direction. Reason and bearing, that's what he needed to concentrate on; reason and bearing. The reason part was easy. Gil Calder needed to be stopped, to be caught, and that's exactly what he intended to do.

After he'd killed Chance's family, Calder had disappeared for a while. Rumors had him in Nevada, New Mexico, Texas, and Utah. Chance had followed up on a lot of them, but he'd never caught up with the outlaw. But now Calder was back in Arizona. This was a fact, not a rumor.

As for bearing, he was still having a hard time keeping track of the Calders, even with Morgan and Rick working the inside, but now he could, as long as he didn't let Sue Ann out of his sight. And she was Sue Ann Calder, he was convinced of that. All of her ramblings and denials were not going to change his mind on that point. She obviously wanted to keep him off guard, but that wasn't going to happen. Maybe running into him hadn't been part of their plan, and then maybe it had been. He didn't know. Either way, he was sticking to her like a rattler to a hot rock at midnight.

Why she had jumped or fallen off that cliff he didn't know, and right now he didn't care. What he did care about was where Gil Calder and his boys were hiding, and what their scheme was. And why Sue Ann was pretending not to know who she was, or more to the point, insisting she was someone named T.J. McAllister, a cop, whatever in the hell that was supposed to mean. She'd said it was a police officer, but he'd never heard any police officer being called a cop.

His eyes narrowed in puzzlement. He had a hunch that this charade about her identity, her real identity, was the key to the riddle.

Then a thought struck Chance that chilled his blood. What if her ploy had indeed been designed to get him out of town? He'd thought about that earlier, but had given no credence to it. What if he'd been wrong?

He cursed softly. Maybe it made sense. Elijah Perkins had only been elected sheriff a few months ago, and it had been a default win, since the other candidate had ended up getting himself arrested for rustling just before the election. Perkins hadn't been in office long enough to gain any real experience, and he was young for the job, definitely too young to go up against the Calder gang alone. And Gil Calder would see Perkins as an easy obstacle to rid himself of. Chance sat up and stared at T.J..

No, on second thought, sending her into town to lead him on a wild goose chase didn't really make much sense, unless Calder and some of his men were waiting out here somewhere ready to bushwhack him. Chance was fast with a gun. In a fair fight he knew he could easily take Calder, but Calder didn't fight fair. His gang, which numbered twenty or more, could easily ride into Tucson and over-power Perkins and Chance.

But if Calder had bushwhacking on his mind, it seemed a safe bet that he wouldn't put his own wife in the way of a possible stray bullet. Anyway, Calder knew that all he'd have to do to get Chance out into the open was make it known that he was nearby. Chance had been trying to track Gil Calder on and off for the past three years, and the outlaw knew it. They'd come close to facing each other several times, but Calder had always disappeared just before Chance got to him. If there had been a rumor that Calder was nearby, and moving around, everyone knew Chance would follow it up. And Calder knew that, too.

So maybe she'd just gotten him out here to play a little cat and mouse game, maybe play with his mind a little. Get him worried. Or maybe one of the other members of the gang was in town now, sizing up the bank.

Chance lay down, his nerves soothed by the logic of his reasoning, and the comfort afforded him by the feel of the Peacemaker strapped to his thigh. If they were sizing up the bank today, they'd gotten a surprise, since he knew from Perkins that soldiers from Camp Verde had been due in town this afternoon to protect the army's payroll. He didn't think even Gil Calder would try to hold up an army payroll that was being protected by several dozen soldiers.

T.J. woke with a start. She sat up and looked around. The morning sun was just beginning to make itself visible over the distant horizon, a golden glow dividing the blackness of the earth from the waning blackness of the sky. The tall members of the many saquaro cacti that dotted the landscape created a myriad of black silhouettes against the saffron sunlight, resembling sentinels standing guard against whatever invaders might trespass on their territory. T.J.'s eyes glanced from one object to another: plants, sky, mountains. What the hell was she doing out in the middle of the desert at dawn sleeping on the ground?

Confusion brought panic to her breast. Then her gaze came to rest on Chance lying only a few yards away. He lay on his back, a blanket pulled up over his chest, the black Stetson covering his face.

Everything came flying back to her in a flash. T.J. felt an urge to touch him to make certain he was real, that she wasn't still sleeping and involved in a nightmare of being thrust through time to an era that she knew was past and dead, and yet had unfolded and enveloped her. She wanted to snuggle into his arms, feel the security of his embrace again, the ecstasy of his touch, but knew she couldn't.

Instead, she looked around. The campfire had died down while they'd slept and was now nothing more than a pile of charred, black sticks. Their horses stood quietly a few yards away. T.J. closed her eyes and took a deep breath. It was real then, she was in 1881. She threw the blanket from her legs and stood up. There were Calders in 1881, and they were the ancestors of Jake Calder—that seemed pretty evident. Somehow, for some reason, she had been given a chance to save Lisa, and she was going to make damned sure she did. And the way to do that was to stick as close to Marshal Chance Burkette as she could until he led her to Gil and Sue Ann Calder.

T.J. grabbed the coffee pot and walked to the small stream where Chance had gotten water the night before. Her whole body felt stiff and sore. Sleeping on the ground, especially on limbs that were still bruised and sore from a fall, was not something she was used to. A nice modern, spring mattress was obviously one of the things she was going to miss. She filled the pot and, carrying it back to the cold campfire, set it on the ground.

Coffee. She quietly moved to Chance's saddlebags and pulled out the same little brown cloth sack she'd seen him retrieve the night before. Untying the string that held it closed, T.J. turned back and picked up the coffee pot. A frown creased her brow. She hadn't been paying much attention, but she could swear she'd seen him pour the grinds right into the water. Tilting the bag above the pot, she poured in a third of what grinds were in the bag, set the pot back down next to the campfire site, retied the string on the bag, and returned it to Chance's saddlebags.

Then she busied herself collecting whatever scrub brush twigs she could find that would burn and placed them atop the campfire. It wasn't much considering that the Palo Verde bushes that grew in the area thrived in the desert and didn't die or dry out that often, and the ocotillo didn't grow in as much abundance around Tucson as it did farther south. T.J. stared dumbly at the paltry pile of twigs and a few choice curse words slipped in a breathy whisper from her lips. She didn't have any matches, and she'd flunked the Girl Scout "start a fire by rubbing two

sticks together" training. Anyway, she didn't have two
sticks, all she had was twigs. Frustrated, she looked over
at Chance. How did they start fires in 1881? She didn't
remember him rubbing sticks or hitting stones together
last night.

Then she saw the tiny box lying on the ground next
to Chance's saddle and vest. Her brows rose in surprise.
Matches? Dropping to her knees T.J. leaned past the pile
of twigs and, reaching across the cold campfire, scooped
up the box. Yes, it was matches!

Thank heavens, lifting one of the stick matches from
the box and, seeing there was no strip of sand paper on
the side of the box, she looked around for a rock to strike
the match tip against. Within minutes she had the match
lit, the twigs smoldering and the coffee pot set into the
campfire's center. T.J. tossed the box back across the fire.
It landed on top of Chance's vest and, seeing the thin
brown tip of a cigar poking from an inside pocket, she
frowned. Had he sat up last night, after she'd gone to
sleep, smoking and watching her?

She shrugged. What difference did it make? But the
possibility that he had watched her unsettled her, because
that's exactly what she'd done to him, and she knew where
her thoughts had been. T.J. forced the memory of her
thoughts away, along with the possibility that his had been
similar. There was no time to waste on such nonsense if
Gil and Sue Ann Calder were really Jake's ancestors. Her
gaze moved to rest on Chance again. She had to stay close
to him. He was her best bet at getting Calder, because he
seemed to have a burning need to get the man, too, and
T.J. had a feeling that Chance Burkette was a man who
usually got what he wanted.

T.J.'s gaze remained riveted on Chance as she sat by
the campfire, letting her body soak up the warmth after
enduring the desert's cold darkness. He'd been skeptical
about everything she'd said to him so far, but she couldn't

blame him, not now that she'd finally admitted to herself that she was no longer in 1996 but in 1881. It still seemed unreal.

She inhaled deeply, letting the tangy blend of the brewing coffee and the crisp morning air fill her lungs. She stretched her hands out over the flames. Amnesia. That's what she'd have to do, keep pretending that the fall from the cliff had caused amnesia. That way she couldn't be expected to know anything. That would keep her somewhat safe from his constant barrage of questions. Maybe even stop them.

A rustling sound behind her brought T.J. whirling around and reaching for the gun that wasn't at her waist. Now that she knew there were still Calders to deal with, along with everything else that had happened, her cop instincts were back on edge.

"It's only a ground squirrel," Chance drawled.

Chapter Ten

"Who did the Calders kill?" T.J. asked Chance again as they were riding toward town. It was still quite a few miles away, but clearly visible from the small hill they were traversing. If she'd had any doubt about the situation it was erased now as she looked at the tall mountains in the distance. Directly below the sheer, majestic cliffs of the Santa Catalina Mountains, where the City of Tucson, Arizona, 1996, should sprawl, was cradled instead a town that resembled every old western town she'd ever seen in the movies and history books.

"Can't remember all their names," Chance said.

"Someone related to you?"

He continued to stare straight ahead, but T.J. did not miss the clench of his jaw, the small vein in his neck that seemed to pulse with a life of its own, and the tautness that held his shoulders suddenly stiff. She wanted to wrap her arms about those shoulders and ease away the tension that had so abruptly filled them at her words, but she couldn't, and she couldn't stop asking her question either.

"Someone related to you?" she forced herself to ask again.

The thought that a Calder could have killed someone dear to Chance, as they had to her, sparked an ember of compassion in her toward him. She felt an almost over-whelming urge to tell him she knew all too well how he felt, to offer him what solace and words of comfort she could, even though she knew from experience they would do no good. And he would not believe her.

He pulled up then, a sudden yank of the reins that shocked both his mount and T.J. Diablo pranced in place, his huge hooves pounding the earth in his frustration at being forced to stop so abruptly. "Lady, I've just about had it with your damned prying and pretending you don't know one end of a fig from the other."

Compassion and empathy made a mad dash for cover and T.J. raised her chin in defiance. If she didn't find out as much as she could about the Calders, and Marshal Chance Burkette, including why he was so intent on catch-ing Gil Calder, she would basically be operating in the dark, or at the very least at a disadvantage, and she couldn't afford that. Not now, not in 1881. She already had enough against her just trying to cope with the fact that she was here at all, that there were Calders here, that she was so attracted to Chance Burkette she could hardly keep her mind on anything else.

But that's exactly what she knew she had to do. And she couldn't ask for any help without taking the risk they'd tie her up and ship her off to wherever they put all their crazy people. T.J. summoned every ounce of courage she could muster and looked Chance straight in the eyes. "Then why don't you just answer my question, Marshal?"

Something, a sound resembling the angry snarl of a mountain lion, softly emanated from between Chance's lips. He snapped his heels against Diablo's flanks and the horse bolted forward into an easy lope.

T.J. cursed and kicked her mount. Obviously whatever she was going to learn about Marshal Chance Burkette was not going to come from the man himself. She waited about ten minutes before she tried again.

"How long have you been a marshal?"

"Long enough to know what I'm doing," Chance said, fury still evident in his tone.

"Do you enjoy it?"

"I enjoy seeing a thief behind bars, or a murderer swinging from the end of a rope, if that's what you mean."

"Do you have any family, marshal?"

"Yes."

The answer was more a hiss than a word.

"A wife?" T.J. persisted.

His stony silence went on for several minutes, until T.J. finally decided he wasn't going to answer. Maybe his wife had died. Or perhaps she'd run off with another man. Gil Calder maybe? That could certainly be one reason he seemed to hate Gil Calder so much. T.J. threw a furtive glance at Chance. Whatever it was about his wife that he wasn't saying, she sensed it had hurt him deeply.

The small lines about his eyes and mouth attested to the fact that Chance Burkette was a man who had laughed heartily. Yet there was something about the way he carried himself, the way he held his jaw tight and hard, the steely look in his eyes, that also attested to the fact that it had been a long time since he'd laughed, but perhaps not that long since he'd cried, or raged with anger.

Again a wave of compassion and empathy swept through her, mingling with a surge of desire. T.J. fought all three emotions down and decided to change course. Her mind was telling her to feel nothing toward him, to consider him only as a means to an end. He was an enigma to her, a man out of her time, an antiquated relic. But her body was telling her exactly the opposite. He was real, he was warm, he was flesh and blood, and he was the culmination of all her girlhood fantasies come true. T.J. swallowed the moan that nearly slipped from her throat as an ache of longing lodged deep within her groin.

A few minutes later, after gaining control of both her wayward fantasies and traitorous libido, she tried another question.

"How old is Gil Calder, Marshal?"

"Don't you know?" Chance shot back.

She ignored the sarcastic remark.

"What made him go bad? Do you know?"

Chance shrugged but continued staring straight ahead. "Circumstances, the war, a woman, greed—what difference does it make? The man's a murderer. You'd probably know his reasons better than I do, Sue Ann." He glanced at her quickly. "Excuse me, I meant T.J."

Again she forced herself to grin and bear his sarcasm. "Does he have a family?"

"Wasn't hatched out of an egg, if that's what you mean, though there might be a rattler around here someplace that could correct me on that one." He looked at her again. "Is his tongue forked?"

T.J. felt a distinct urge to slap him and burst out crying at the same time. She had control of her emotions only by the thinnest of threads and the strongest output of will.

"I meant," she said, her tone taut and overly controlled, "does he have any children?"

"Other than by you?"

The hold she had on her temper failed.

"I'm not his wife!" she yelled.

"Yeah, so you've said before," Chance drawled, though the derision in his voice was unmistakable.

T.J. clamped her mouth shut and decided to say nothing else—at least for a while.

Half an hour later they reined up in front of Doc's house, but Chance made no move to dismount.

T.J. swung a leg over the horse's rump and slid to the

ground, then turned a surprised gaze up at Chance who remained mounted.

"I'll take the horses back to the livery," he said, and held out his hands for her reins.

She slapped them into his palm, angry that she'd been unable to get him to talk about himself or the Calders. But she was just as angry with herself as with him. She'd been trained to question people, to get them to open up to her. She had taken special pyschology classes both in college and at the police academy just for that, and she'd gotten good grades, but she was getting about as many answers out of Chance Burkette as she'd get from a brick wall. Every time she'd asked a question about the Calders, or about Chance himself, he'd turned that stony, suspicious glare on her.

T.J. brushed around her horse, slammed through the gate and stalked up the path that led to Doc's front door.

"Hey, calm down, Sue Ann," Chance called after her, and chuckled. "Far as I know, Calder hasn't got any kids at all."

She heard the sound of horses hooves behind her as Chance wheeled the animals around and retreated down the street, but she refused to look back. Fury with him, and with herself, mixed with the relief she felt at his words. Calder had no children.

"Doc?" T.J. called as she entered the foyer. "Doc, are you here?"

The old man shuffled out from his examining room, holding a tiny brown medicine bottle in one hand and a thin, white linen towel in the other. "I'm here, girl, I'm here. No need to shout the roof off."

"Oh, sorry." T.J. exhaled deeply. If she couldn't get answers from Chance, maybe she could get them from Doc. She took a step forward and her legs suddenly felt like rubber. They trembled and threatened to collapse beneath her weight. She grabbed for the wall.

Doc rushed toward her and clasped his hands about her other arm.

"Whoa, I think it's been too long since I've been on a horse," T.J. said.

"Yeah? Well, that bump you got on your head ain't helping things any either," Doc said. "I had a feeling you were one to overdo it too soon. You young'uns never do listen to me on these things." Keeping a tight hold on her arm, he steered her to a chair in the parlor. "Always think you know best, and always find out you don't."

T.J. laughed weakly. "I'm fine, Doc, really. My head is okay, no banging cymbals in there anymore, just a few stray drummers now and then. My problem now, really, is that I just rode all morning with Chance, as well as all yesterday afternoon, and I think my legs are rebelling."

"So sit down and I'll get us both a cup of tea. I was about ready for some anyway."

"Got any coffee, Doc?" T.J. asked as he turned away. She smiled as he looked back at her. "Sorry, I'm really not much of a tea drinker."

"Me neither, but most ladies around here stick up their noses at drinking coffee."

T.J. smiled and remembered her resolution to feign amnesia. "Well," she said slowly, "I'm not from around here, we both know that, and since I can't remember much before Chance found me in that canyon, I'm not really sure I'm a lady. But I do know that I prefer coffee."

Doc frowned, his craggy gray-white brows pulling together to momentarily create one long brow across his forehead.

"You saying you still can't remember nothing?"

"Not much." T.J. tried to look scared and confused. It wasn't too difficult really, since that's exactly how she'd felt on and off for the past day. "I mean, I can remember my name, Theresa Jane McAllister, though somehow I know folks call me T.J. I know I come from around here someplace, Arizona, I mean, but I don't know exactly where.''

"Can't say as I've ever heard of a McAllister family any-where near here."

T.J. raised her left hand toward him, fingers down. "Well, I don't have a wedding ring on," she said merrily, "and there's no white mark on my finger where a ring would have been, so I'd have to guess I'm not married."

"Lucky for Chance."

"Huh," T.J. snorted. "I think the good marshal would just as soon throw me in jail as look at me."

Doc chuckled.

"Maybe so, but that boy's got a lot of feelings inside of him he don't admit to anymore, not even to himself."

T.J. became suddenly serious. "Why?"

Doc shrugged.

"It's a long story, missy, and I figure if he wanted it told, he'd tell it. Ain't my place." The old man turned away and stepped into the foyer. "I'll get that coffee now."

Another stone wall. T.J. felt totally defeated. She stared into the foyer, waiting for the doctor to return. But she wasn't going to give up. Rising, she began to walk around the room, looking at all the bric-a-brac and framed pictures placed here and there. One picture stopped her. She picked it up from the small table it sat on. It was a picture of Chance with two other men.

"Here we go," Doc said. He reentered the parlor car-rying a serving tray laden with two steaming cups of coffee and a small plate of cookies. "I put a little milk and sugar in your coffee. Hope that's how you like it."

"That's perfect, Doc," T.J. lied. Actually she preferred her coffee black, but she didn't want to hurt his feelings. She carried the framed picture back to her seat and held it out so that he could see it. "Who are these men in the picture, Doc? With Chance?"

"Oh, that one on the left is Morgan, Chance's older brother. The other one's Rick, the youngest."

"Brothers," T.J. repeated. She set the picture down on a table beside her chair. "Where are they?"

"California. Left a few months back." He handed her a cup of coffee. "So, you got amnesia, huh?" Doc said, after taking several sips of his coffee. He had settled into a chair opposite her and was looking at her over the rim of his cup, holding it cradled in both hands and just under his nose.

T.J. sighed and tried to look suddenly frightened and confused. "Is that what you call it when someone can't remember things, Doc?"

He nodded his head and took another sip of his coffee.

"Yep. Amnesia. Only seen one other case of it myself, but I read up on it some while you and Chance were gone. Seems a bump on the head like you took can bring it on."

"How long will it last?"

Doc set his coffee cup down on the marble topped table next to his chair.

"No telling. Some cases clear up real quick, within hours or a few days. Some take weeks or months. Others," he paused, eyeing her carefully.

"Others?" T.J. urged.

"Others never get their memory back at all."

"You mean," T.J. called on all her high school drama lessons to bring out a convincing look of shock on her face, "you mean I might never remember anything?"

Doc nodded. "That's a possibility."

Tears were beyond her acting ability. They always had been, so T.J. forced herself to continue to look stricken. "But, what'll I do, Doc? I mean, I can't stay here with you forever. How will I live?"

"Oh, you'll probably remember, honey," Doc said. "That bump you took wasn't all that bad."

T.J. smiled, as if in relief, then changed the subject again.

"Doc, is Chance married?" She could swear the old man's eyes sparkled at her question.

"Nope."

"Was he ever?"

"Missy, you oughta be asking Chance these questions, not me. Ain't my place to go telling a woman about a man's past."

So there had been a wife.

"I did ask him," T.J. countered, "and he wouldn't answer me."

Doc shook his head. "Most likely then, he can't."

"Can't?" That wasn't exactly the explanation she'd expected.

The old man stood.

"There's some things a man can't bring himself to talk about until the time's right. Evidently, the time ain't right yet for Chance to talk about what you're asking."

"Can't you just tell me if he was ever married?"

Doc paused at the door and looked down at her.

"He was married once, a long time ago, but he ain't married now. That's all you need to know, and all I'm going to say on the matter." He stepped into the foyer. "Now, get some rest, missy," he called back.

But instead of heeding the doctor's order, T.J. pushed herself out of the chair and followed him into his examining room.

"Doc, I need to earn my keep. That is, if you're willing to allow me to stay on here for a while."

"You're my patient, missy, of course you'll stay here."

T.J. swallowed hard. Her head had begun to pound again. "Thanks, Doc. You wouldn't happen to have an aspirin, would you?"

"A what?" the old man said.

Mistake. T.J. smiled and forced a weak chuckle.

"Never mind. I don't even know what I meant myself."

She looked at the array of small bottles that cluttered

the examining table. He'd been in the process of cleaning them when she'd interrupted him earlier. "What can I do around here to help?"

"Well, I've got a few calls to make. How about you finish cleaning out these medicine bottles?"

"Done," T.J. said, and took the towel from his hands.

Doc walked past the Red Garter Saloon, stepped from the boardwalk and headed for the jail house across the street. He wanted to talk to Chance, and he wanted to do it where T.J., or whatever her name was, couldn't hear.

The black of his long frock coat soaked in the hot rays of the early afternoon sun, already nearing what he figured had to be one hundred degrees. He looked down at himself. The front edges of his coat were slightly frayed with age, and the knees of his trousers showed a hint of whiteness where the threads were near worn through. It was past time to get a new suit. He pushed the gold-rimmed spectacles higher onto the bridge of his nose, tightened his grip on his medical bag, and continued on across the street.

A heavily loaded dray came rumbling around the corner and straight toward him. Doc hurried his step and just managed to get himself up onto the boardwalk before the massive wagon lumbered past.

"Jones, you old fool," he called after the man and his wagon.

"Sorry, Doc," the man called back.

Doc waved a fist at him and turned back toward the jail house. He could see Chance through the window, sitting behind his desk, both booted feet propped up on its scratched surface, his chair balanced on its two rear legs.

Maybe Chance was right and the woman was Sue Ann Calder. Then again, maybe he was wrong. All Doc knew and he couldn't be one hundred percent certain, was that she didn't have amnesia. In the cases noted in his books, people who had amnesia usually didn't remember their names any more than they remembered anything else. And this woman claimed to remember her name. And she wasn't hysterical as he'd expect a woman to be who couldn't remember her past. No, she remembered, he felt fairly sure, she just didn't want to admit it, that's all, and he had his own theory about that, too. She was running from something, something that scared her, something she felt she had to hide from. Something—or someone.

Doc heard the rattle of another dray rolling down the street behind him. He heard several young boys laughing and calling to one another as they skipped down the middle of the street toward the schoolhouse. He heard Squirrel Toothed Delia, one of the ugliest whores he'd ever seen, yell down a lewd invitation to a passing gent on horseback from her balcony over the Red Garter. He heard it all, but he didn't turn around or pay any attention to it. Instead he continued to stare at Chance.

The boy was his nephew, his younger sister's son, but since Doc had never married, and had helped to raise Chance and his brothers and sister, he looked on them all as if they were his own children. When they hurt, he hurt. Usually he knew what to do about it. This time he didn't.

For three years now, ever since Calder had ripped through the Burkette family, Chance had thought of little else but capturing Gil Calder and bringing him to justice. Unfortunately it hadn't proven easy. Calder was a cagey sort. Part snake, part coyote, and just as ugly as a cross between the two. He only came out of hiding to pull a robbery, then he disappeared back into his hole again, sometimes for months on end. And the man had the uncanny ability to vanish without leaving any tracks behind for the law to follow. Chance was good, Doc knew, but he wasn't that good.

Chapter Eleven

"Okay, Doc, so you have your opinion of the lady, and I have mine," Chance said. He set a cup of coffee down on the corner of his desk for the older man and resumed his seat, settling into the curved back of his chair and propping one foot atop the opposite knee. "This isn't the first time we've disagreed on something."

The roweled silver spur just above the heel of his boot caught the sunlight that shone through one of the two windows framing the entry door and sparkled brilliantly in reflection.

"I'm not saying you're wrong," Doc said. He lifted the tin cup to his lips, blew on the surface of the steaming coffee, and took a careful sip. "But, I don't know, she seems scared to me, not sneaky. I think she's running away from something or someone."

"Yeah, well, Sue Ann Calder is a pretty good actress, Doc. She's fooled quite a lot of people out of their money already. Maybe she's fooled a few out of more than that."

Doc nodded.

"This amnesia thing you were talking about," Chance continued. "She's faking it, right?"

Chance pinned the old man with the same gaze he'd been seen to give an outlaw when demanding the truth.

"That's hard to say, Chance. You've been around me and my practice long enough to know there are some things a doctor can't say for certain, and this is one of them." He took another sip of the coffee and set the cup back down on the desk. "I wish I could."

"So it's possible she's faking," Chance said. It was more a comment than a question.

"It's possible," Doc confirmed. "And it's possible she isn't."

"But you believe she's faking."

"Yes, though I can't be sure. And even if she is, I don't believe she's Sue Ann Calder, though I do believe there's something really wrong."

Chance's instincts shifted into alert again. "Wrong? Like what?"

Doc drained the last of the coffee from his cup and set it back on the desk. "I don't rightly know, Chance, just things. I mean, she seems unfamiliar with things, you know?"

"You mean like all that drivel she was giving us about not remembering why she hurtled off that cliff? Or where she came from?"

"No. I mean she's unfamiliar with simple, everyday things, like not knowing how to operate the cook stove in my kitchen, how to light a lamp, or even get the eggs from the henhouse, things everybody knows." Doc paused as Chance refilled his coffee cup, then continued. "After you left her at my place this morning she got kind of weak and it came out she was hungry, but she wouldn't hear tell of me fixing her anything. Said she could do it herself. Except the fact is, she couldn't. Kept asking me fool questions instead, like where was something called a refrigerator."

Chance chuckled.

"So, maybe it's something rich folks have and she saw it somewhere."

"The Allebees don't have nothing called a refrigerator," Doc countered. "And you know as well as I do that if they don't have it, then nobody does."

Chance didn't want to admit it, but Doc was right. The Allebees were the wealthiest people in Tucson, and prided themselves on having the latest and newest of everything. "Maybe it's something they got back east we haven't heard about yet."

"That would kind of squash your theory that she's Sue Ann Calder then, wouldn't it, Chance?" Doc challenged.

"Maybe. Unless she took a trip back east for something."

"You're reaching, Chance, you're reaching," Doc said. "She ain't Sue Ann, but she is in some kind of trouble. I can feel it in my bones."

Chance stood at the window and watched his uncle as the older man walked across the street. He could be right. The woman might not be Sue Ann Calder, but Chance wasn't ready to believe that yet. Sue Ann reputedly had chestnut colored hair and green eyes. The woman he'd found at the base of the cliff had chestnut colored hair and green eyes. And she was about the right age. Sue Ann was an outlaw's wife. The woman who insisted she be called T.J. had carried a gun, not the habit of too many ladies. Sue Ann had reportedly scouted out the last few towns the outlaws had robbed. T.J. had been alone, and obviously on her way to Tucson when she had fallen, jumped, or been pushed off that cliff.

It all fit. She was Sue Ann Calder, there was no other answer. But even as Chance told himself this, he felt a pang of disappointment in the pit of his stomach. There was no place in his life for a woman, no permanent place anyway, yet he'd found himself more attracted to her than he could remember ever being attracted to any woman, including Caroline.

Guilt washed over him then. He was more attracted to Sue Ann Calder, the wife of the same outlaw who had killed Caroline, Krissy, Morgan's wife, and his mother and father, than he had been to his own wife. His right hand curled into a fist and he slammed it into the unpainted adobe wall before him. Didn't he have enough damned trouble in his life without being betrayed by his own desires?

The door of the jail house suddenly swung open and the sheriff walked in. "You heard the news?" he asked, pausing in the doorway and looking at Chance.

Sunlight shone radiantly at his back, turning his figure into a black silhouette and lent it more menace them Elijah Perkins would be able to purposely produce in any other situation. Chance sighed. Too bad the kid couldn't create that effect every time he walked into a room, especially into the saloons. Maybe then the cowboys and drovers, and every other ruffian that went out on a Saturday night looking for a good time, which ultimately meant a fight, would think twice before challenging him.

"No, what news?" Chance said finally.

"The Earps took over marshaling in Tombstone."

"The Earps, huh?"

Perkins stepped from the doorway into the room and the illusion of menace instantly disappeared.

"Couple of the cowboys are over at the Garter grumbling about it now. That's how I heard." He chuckled. "They're not too happy about it."

Chance felt a flash of alarm. Cowboys. The name Curly Bill Brocious had tagged his gang of cutthroats with. The same ones who also followed Gil Calder when he rode with Curly Bill. They could be trouble, especially if their leaders were around. "Curly Bill's not with them, is he?"

"Brocious? Nah." The young lawman settled be. desk.

"What about Johnny Ringo?"

"Nope, didn't see him either." Perkins settled a hand on the butt of his gun. "I figure they probably know better than to come into my town."

Chance nearly groaned aloud. The kid might be fast with a gun, faster than most Chance had seen, excluding himself, but with that attitude he was going to be filling up a pine box a hell of a lot sooner than he'd planned to.

None of the cowboys had any high regard for the law, just the opposite, and they would have loved an excuse, any excuse, to put a bullet through Perkins' forehead just to give themselves a good laugh.

"Anyway," Perkins continued, "I heard them talking. Virgil's the town marshal now, and I guess Morgan and Wyatt took on as deputies. Sheriff Behan is fit to be tied, or so one of them cowboys said."

Chance nodded as memory came to mind of the enterprising, but suspectedly crooked county official he'd met several times on his way through Tombstone.

"I'll just bet he is." A chuckle of amusement rolled from his lips.

Doc placed his medical bag on a petticoat table in the foyer, where he always kept it, close to the door and ready. The house was quiet. He looked into the parlor, expecting to find it empty as he assumed T.J. was napping, and was surprised to see her sitting in his chair, a book in her lap.

"Whatdya reading, missy?"

He moved into the room and settled onto the settee opposite her.

T.J. looked up, having been so engrossed in the book that she hadn't heard him come in. "A book on Robert E. Lee that was on your shelf, there." She pointed to a shelf full of books beside the fireplace. "You're in it," T.J. added, her tone holding a trace of awe.

A shadow swept over the old man's face.

"Yes, well, that was a long time ago."

"You were a doctor in the Confederacy."

He nodded.

"I don't like to remember those times, much. Too many men died. Senseless."

He smiled in direct contrast to his somber words and slapped his knee.

"How come you aren't taking that nap I told you to take?"

T.J. smiled back.

"Because I'm not sleepy."

She was grateful he hadn't come back twenty minutes sooner. Then he would have discovered her poking through his desk. She had to find out anything and everything she could about this time if she was going to cope with it, but she had to do her research without arousing anyone's suspicion. An excuse of amnesia only went so far, and it didn't include snooping.

"Doc, I was sitting out on the front porch a little while ago, just enjoying some air, and I saw two men ride past. They had bits of red cloth tied to their holsters."

She closed the book and looked up at him.

The old man made no comment, but he had moved one hand to the arm of the settee and his gnarled fingers seemed to be holding it tightly.

"What's the red cloth for, Doc? Are they deputies or something?"

She couldn't quite picture the two men as being Chance's deputies. They'd looked. . . . her mind searched for a way to put her impressions into coherent thought. Mean. It was the only word that came to mind, but T.J. realized it was an apt description of how she'd felt at seeing them. They'd looked mean. Evil, Corrupt. But then this was a different time, a different way of life, and what she perceived wasn't necessarily how it was.

"No," Doc answered, "they're called cowboys."

T.J. brightened and smiled.

"Cowboys, right. But what's the red cloth for? Is it part of an outfit for a particular ranch?"

Doc studied her for several seconds before answering. His gray eyes looked slightly larger than true size as he stared through the thick glass of his spectacles.

"They're not drovers, missy, and they're not wranglers. They're cowboys."

T.J. must have looked puzzled because he went on to explain.

"The cowboys are a gang of men. They kind of rule the southern part of Arizona, especially down Tombstone way. Every cowboy wears a red cloth on his holster."

"They're lawmen?" T.J. said, surprised. She was a cop. How come she'd never heard of these historic red cloth cowboys?

"Outlaws is more like it."

"Oh." Then she brightened again. If those men had been outlaws, then maybe they could lead her to Gil Calder. She certainly wasn't accomplishing anything sitting around here waiting for Chance to do something. T.J. set the book aside and rose.

"Doc, I think I will go take that nap you suggested. Wake me for dinner?"

"You already had dinner, missy, except it was your breakfast." He rose and walked beside her into the foyer. "Unless you're already hungry again, take your nap and I'll wake you up for supper."

T.J. stared up at the old man in confusion. She'd said dinner, not lunch, so why was he . . .? Suddenly she understood. Dinner was lunch. Supper was dinner. T.J. smiled.

"You're right, I wasn't thinking. Most likely my brain is still a little scrambled from this bump." She reached up and gingerly touched her forehead. "I'll rest for the remainder of the day and see you at supper, but tomorrow I start doing more chores for you bright and early. I want to earn my keep until . . . until . . ." Until what? her mind screamed. "Until I get my memory back and know more about who I am, and what I'm doing in Tucson," she finished.

"Fine, fine," Doc said. He patted her shoulder gently with one gnarled old hand. "Been a long time since I had a nurse or a housekeeper. Might be kind of fun."

"Yes, it might be," T.J. agreed.

The old man walked into the examining room, went directly toward the big cabinet that held his medicines, opened it, and retrieved several bottles.

"Think I'll ride out to the Taylor place and check up on Georgeanne. Her baby's just about due."

T.J. slipped into the rear bedroom Doc was letting her use, shut the door and sat on the bed for ten minutes. When she was certain he was gone, she left the house by the back door. The moment she stepped from the porch, T.J. was forced to pause and look around, having momentarily forgotten that she didn't know her way around. But she didn't want to be out on the main street where Doc or Chance could see her if she didn't have to be. She didn't exactly like tromping through folks backyards either. Sighing in frustration she walked between Doc's house and the building next to it and out into the front yard. The street was deserted for the moment. Hurrying through the gate, T.J. made her way to the main street. She paused to get her bearings, not easy considering the situation. She might as well be on an alien planet.

She spotted the jail house almost instantly. It was across the street and half a block down, flanked by a dry goods store, and a leather shop. Was Chance in there? T.J. felt her mouth suddenly go dry and her hands tremble. There were several saloons on both sides of the street.

T.J. cursed softly. The men she'd seen had probably gone into a saloon. That's the first place cowboys went when they hit town. At least, so the movies claimed. But if they had gone into a saloon, which one? She let her gaze roam over the array of horses tied up at hitching racks along the storefronts. They all looked the same: big, brown and saddled. T.J. sighed in frustration and decided to try the nearest saloon. It was the Red Garter, the same one she'd been standing in front of when she'd been shot.

Before stepping from the shadows and onto the boardwalk, she glanced over at the jail house again. If Chance was in there he had a clear view of the street through the front window of the small building. All he'd have to do was glance out at the street and he'd see her, but she had to risk it.

Just as she was about to step up onto the boardwalk, the sound of horses' hooves drew her attention. She glanced over her shoulder and saw five men riding down the street toward her. They reined up in front of the Red Garter, dismounted, and entered the saloon. Each had a piece of red cloth attached to his holster.

More cowboys as Doc had called them. T.J. hurriedly climbed up onto the boardwalk and practically running, she covered the short distance from the corner to the saloon. At least now she knew where she could find them and maybe get a lead on Gil Calder. Maybe Calder was a member of their gang. She could hear the hum of voices, the tinkling of a piano, loud guffaws of laughter, and the clinking of glass gently striking glass. Her attention remained pinioned to the red swinging doors that gave entrance to the saloon, her gaze purposely averted from the jail house across the street.

She took a deep breath and barged through the saloon doors. Everything instantly disappeared from view as she plunged from brilliant sunlight into gloom. The doors crashed loudly against the walls and then swung shut behind her. The raucous sounds she'd heard from within the saloon only seconds before abruptly quieted to a hush of whispers at her entrance. T.J. blinked rapidly. Everyone was staring at her, she could feel it, but she couldn't see a thing except a kaleidoscope of iridescent colors swirling in a haze of blackness. She rubbed her eyes and the room and its occupants came into view, blurry and out of focus. She blinked several more times and her vision cleared.

"May I buy you a drink, ma'am," a deep, velvet smooth voice said at her side.

T.J. turned to look into a pair of the coldest, darkest eyes she'd ever seen in her life. She'd had to stare down a rattlesnake once when she was a kid and had nearly stepped on it while playing in the rocks behind her aunt's house. Her cousin had run for help while she remained as motionless as a statue, caught within the reptile's striking range. She remembered how cold that snake's eyes had looked, but they'd had nothing on the ones the man standing before her possessed.

He held out his arm to her.

T.J.'s gaze moved quickly over the rest of him. His cheekbones protruded like two rock ledges, his nose was short and turned up, and his lips thin beneath a well trimmed mustache. Dark brown hair stuck out from beneath a hat pulled at a haughty angle over one side of his forehead. His body was rangy and lean, and just above the pair of colts he wore low on his hips, T.J. noticed a piece of red cloth tied to his holster. She forced a smile to curve her lips and placed her hand on his offered arm.

"Why, thank you, sir, that would be nice," she said, in her most coquettish voice. She batted her lashes at him a few times for effect, hoping the gesture looked flirtatious and not silly.

His smile widened, though T.J. realized there was no more warmth in it than in his eyes. She wondered if her idea had been such a terrific one. She looked around hastily. Several men were ogling her, their thoughts clearly defined in the lewd grins that split their whisker framed lips.

The piano player had gone back to his tinkling, several men had taken up song, if that's what their croaking sounds could be called, and about a dozen men seated around two tables had resumed their card games. A wheel of fortune spun at the rear of the room. There wasn't one respectable looking person in the room. Of course, as she'd reminded herself earlier, in this era she didn't really know what a respectable person was supposed to look like.

The man led her to a table, pulled a chair out for her. Then he sat in the one next to it, pulling it so close to her she could feel his warm breath on her neck.

"I'm Johnny Ringo." He turned to look at the bar. "Hey, barkeep," he yelled, "bring us a bottle and two glasses."

T.J.'s mouth dropped open at the outlaw's announcement of his name. She clamped it closed just as quickly and tried to ignore the shiver of uneasiness that snaked up her spine. Johnny Ringo. She might not be a history expert, but she knew enough of Arizona's history to recognize the name of one of the state's most infamous outlaws. A sense of both awe and fear blended within her. Accepting the drink Ringo poured for her, T.J. glanced up to meet his gaze and smiled again. If she flattered him she just might get the information she wanted.

"Tell me, sir," T.J. purred and leaned toward him, purposely letting the front of her shirt fall forward just a bit so as to expose a teasing glimpse of her breasts, "are you really Johnny Ringo? I mean, *the* Johnny Ringo?"

"The one and only," he said proudly.

"I've heard you're the fastest draw alive." T.J. settled back in her chair and ran the tip of her tongue over her upper lip.

Ringo slightly shifted position in his chair. "Yeah, and not just with my guns, beautiful."

Careful T.J., she reminded herself silently, you're out of your element and you've got no backup here.

"Faster than Gil Calder?" she asked, her tone both challenging and teasing. "With your guns, I mean."

"Faster than anybody," Ringo answered. "With anything."

Except for Wyatt Earp or Doc Holliday, she thought. She remembered something about Johnny Ringo being killed by one or the other of them.

He scooted his chair closer to hers and wrapped an arm around her shoulders. "Now, what do you want to talk about old Gil for," Ringo said, his tone seductively low and drawling, "when you've got me here, ready to show you a good time?" He lightly pressed the tip of one finger to her bottom lip and traced its outline, then let his finger slide down the curve of her neck.

T.J. swallowed hard, and felt overcome with indecision. One chop with the side of her hand to the guy's throat would send him to the floor and gasping for breath, which was exactly where she'd like to see him. But that kind of reaction to him wouldn't get her the information she needed, yet she wasn't willing to let the guy seduce her clothes off of her either.

"How about it, sweetheart?" Ringo said, his face less than two inches from hers now. "Want to go on upstairs and have us a little party?" His finger slipped between the cleavage of her breasts.

Chapter Twelve

Chance leaned against the bar, one heel hooked over the brass boot railing. His elbows rested on the bar top, and he held a drink in his left hand while his right dangled just inches above the butt of his Peacemaker. He stared at T.J.'s back. He'd seen her enter the saloon a few minutes earlier and, curious, had followed, making no secret of either his entrance or his presence. But she'd sat with her back to both the bar and the door, and was obviously too busy with Ringo to have noticed Chance.

There were two other cowboys standing at the bar, and another sitting at the faro table at the rear of the room. Chance said a small prayer that they weren't a prelude to Curly Bill or Calder and the rest of his gang riding into town. The townspeople didn't need that kind of trouble. He wanted to catch Calder, but on his own terms, and out in the desert, where no innocents could get hurt.

His eyes narrowed as he watched Ringo begin to finger a curl of T.J.'s long chestnut hair. A swell of what he couldn't deny was hot, searing jealousy coursed through

Chance's gut, both surprising and angering him. He didn't
know what she was up to now, and he had a feeling that
even if he did, he wouldn't like it.

Was this meeting with Ringo a planned one? He saw
Ringo's other hand move to T.J.'s neck and the jealousy
smoldering within Chance intensified in spite of his efforts
to douse it.

For some reason, as he continued to watch them, he got
the impression that T.J. was not only nervous, but that she
didn't know Ringo at all. Yet, if she was Sue Ann, she
should. Ringo and Calder were old friends, or at least they
had been. Ringo had ridden with Calder's gang. Then
they'd had some kind of parting of the ways and Ringo
had begun riding with Curly Bill Brocious and the cowboys.

Chance let his gaze move to the twin colts strapped to
Ringo's thighs. The guns had pearl handles and glistening
silver barrels. He'd heard that Ringo polished both of them
every night before retiring.

His thoughts returned to Calder. Obviously the falling
out between the two outlaws hadn't been bad enough for
Gil to draw against Ringo. Not too many men were that
foolish, if they could help it. He'd heard it said there was
only one man who stood a chance in hell of beating Ringo's
draw, Doc Holliday. Chance sighed. He'd seen Doc draw
once, and he'd never forget it. The man was faster than
lightning. Some said Chance was that fast, but he didn't
think he could outdraw Doc, and that meant he wasn't at
all sure he could outdraw Ringo.

An unwelcome thought came to him then. Had Ringo,
Curly Bill, and Calder settled their differences and joined
forces? It was an unsettling prospect.

He turned and set his empty glass on the bar top. The
bartender instantly refilled it. Chance leaned his forearms
on the bar and stared into the mirror on the wall. He had
a clear view of the entire saloon, including T.J. and Ringo.

He saw Ringo's hand moved to the vicinity of T.J.'s breast and Chance felt his stomach tighten into a knot.

T.J. stood abruptly and her chair scooted across the floor noisily as the back of her legs hit it. She slapped Ringo's hand away from her.

"Obviously you need a lesson in manners, Mr. Ringo," T.J. snapped loudly. The heat of anger and outrage laced each word.

Snarling like a wounded bobcat, his eyes flashing black fire, Ringo shot to his feet and grabbed T.J.'s arm with one lean hand. His fingers curled around her flesh and bore down tightly like steel vice grips.

"Maybe you need a lesson in how to treat a man, whore," Ringo growled, and pushed his face nearly into hers.

Chance stared into the mirror, his eyes riveted on Ringo, his shoulders taut with tension. He'd set his glass down and dropped his hand to his side, his fingers only a hairsbreadth from his gun butt, ready to draw it from its sheath if necessary.

T.J. flared at the insult, her cheeks flaming red. "Whore?" she shrieked. "How dare you call me that." She tried to jerk her arm free of his grasp but his fingers tightened their grip.

"I call them like I see them, beautiful," Ringo said. "You've got trousers on like a man and you come sashaying into this saloon in broad daylight. That makes you either a whore or stupid, or both." He laughed at his own words.

T.J. drew one leg back and brought it swinging forward with all the force she could manage. Her bent leg sliced between Ringo's chap covered ones, and her knee crashed cruelly into his groin. Shock instantly widened his features, a rush of air spew from his lips, and his fingers jerked free of their hold on her arm as he clutched at his privates and doubled over in pain. A slew of curses tumbled from his lips.

She backed away from him hastily, knocking over her

chair and sending it tumbling across the floor. All eyes were on her.

Chance kept his back to the room, but his gaze never left the mirror that gave him full view of everything happening behind him. The corners of his mouth twitched upward as he watched Ringo hobble about in a circle, hands cradling his crotch and a steady stream of ribald remarks issuing forth from his lips.

He'd been ready to defend T.J., but obviously the lady could defend herself. He reached up to pull the brim of his hat lower onto his forehead and hunched his shoulders a bit as he saw her turn to leave the saloon. Chance had figured there was a lot of spit and fire hidden behind those fathomless green eyes, he just hadn't expected this much.

He fingered the glass of whiskey that sat on the bar before him. The tense situation, and the prospect of danger and gunplay, had subsided, but it was not altogether eased. Ringo, he knew, was not one to take what had happened lightly. Chance's gaze followed T.J. as she headed for the door. He should follow her, make sure she returned to Doc's and didn't get herself into anymore trouble, but he wanted to keep an eye on Ringo for a while.

Suddenly, out of the corner of his eye, Chance saw T.J. pause, a hand on one of the swinging doors that led to the street. With a frown creasing her brow, she slowly turned back toward the interior of the saloon and stared straight at him.

"Chance?"

Every nerve cell in his body shot to full alert. "Damn," he breathed softly. With the slow, insolent movement of a great cat rising to its feet, Chance straightened and turned toward her.

T.J. strode over to him, her gait purposeful. Slamming clenched fists on her well-rounded hips, she glared up at him, indignation sparking from her eyes.

"Were you standing there the entire time that." She glanced over her shoulder at Ringo. "That man was . . . was—"

"Trying to seduce you?" Chance supplied.

"Rape me is more like it," she snapped.

Chance tried like hell to suppress the chuckle that bubbled up from his throat, but it slipped from his lips in spite of his best effort.

"I'm glad you find the situation amusing, Marshal." T.J. glared at him. "Where I come from that's—" She suddenly clamped her jaws together, almost biting off her tongue in the process.

Chance sobered instantly at her words. Though his gaze was riveted upon T.J., she only had half of his attention. The other half was still on Ringo, who had dropped into a chair and was tossing down shots of whiskey like there was no tomorrow.

"And just where do you come from, Miss T.J. McAllister?" Chance challenged, the words slid slowly off his tongue, each, especially her name, liberally laced with sarcasm.

T.J. paled and forced her eyes downward, away from his gaze. Keeping secrets had never been one of her strong points, but if she didn't keep this one she was going to find herself locked in an insane asylum, which was a bit more than she thought she could handle, not that she was handling this time warp thing all that wonderfully.

"I don't know," she said softly.

"What?"

Her head jerked back up. "I don't know," she retorted loudly, inflicting just as much curtness in her tone as had been in his.

"Or you don't want to tell me," he goaded.

She spun on her heel and marched toward the door. "Even if I could remember," T.J. threw back, holding both swinging doors open and pausing to shoot him a departing glower, "you probably wouldn't believe me anyway." She charged past the doors and disappeared down the board-walk.

"You're right," Chance mumbled.

T.J. stormed back to Doc's house and slammed the door behind her as she entered the foyer. The crash of wood against wood shook the walls and echoed throughout the empty residence, while the glass inset rattled precariously. T.J. cringed, thankful that the glass hadn't shattered. She strode through the foyer, across Doc's examining room, and into the room designated, if temporarily, as hers.

"Damned thoughtless twit," she grumbled angrily, and sat down on the side of the bed. "No self-respecting, law-abiding cop would ignore another's need for backup like that." She rammed a curled fist into the mattress. "He just stood there and watched, the creep." She suddenly realized her head was pounding. No, not pounding, throbbing mercilessly. T.J. squinted, commanding the drummers in her head to cease and desist. They ignored her and continued to bang away against her temple.

Shooting to her feet she walked into Doc's examining room and opened the tall cabinet where she'd seen that he kept his medicine.

"Okay, they don't have aspirins, so what the hell do they take for a headache?"

"Laudanum," Doc said from behind her.

She swung around, startled, losing her grip on the cabinet door and nearly falling to the floor. Only a fast grab at the examining table prevented her collapse.

"Doc," T.J. gasped, "I didn't know you were here."

"I gathered that," he said, chuckling, "from the way you were cussing and carrying on."

T.J. felt embarrassed, remembering that "ladies" of this era most likely didn't use the kind of language she'd been using. Then again, she usually didn't curse either, unless she was angry beyond reason, then it just seemed to pop out.

"Your head hurt?"

"Yes, a little."

Doc crossed the room and took a bottle down from one of the shelves in the cabinet.

"I'll give you some laudanum, but just a bit. Don't like to use this stuff much. Had a woman get addicted to it last year and, well, her husband's raising their three young'uns alone now."

Drug addiction. T.J. felt a start of surprise. She hadn't realized that they'd had to face that in 1881 along with everything else. She'd thought the lack of indoor plumbing, electricity, refrigerators, instant coffee, prepackaged food, telephones and cars was bad enough.

"Never mind, Doc," T.J. said. "My headache's not really that bad."

The old man nodded and returned the bottle to the shelf.

"Good. Don't like giving this stuff to anyone if I don't have to. Try lying down for a while, close your eyes and get some rest. That'll probably do you more good anyway than anything." He smiled. "Come to think of it, I seem to recall telling you to take it easy anyway, which isn't exactly what you've been doing."

T.J. smiled. "I know. But there are some things I just have to see to, that's all."

Doc's bushy gray brows rose as his eyes widened. "Really? You remember something?"

She instantly realized her mistake and hurried to correct it.

"Well, no, not really. I just meant I wanted to do a little more exploring around town, you know? Try and see if anything jogged my memory."

He nodded and turned back toward the foyer. "Well,

I'll be in my office if you need me. Got to go over my books. But if you go out again, young lady, don't overdo it. A bump on the head, especially a nasty one like you took, can be dangerous."

T.J. reentered the bedroom and did as Doc had suggested; she lay down on the bed and closed her eyes. But it wasn't going to be as relaxing an experience as she'd hoped. Pounding the pillow with her fist she rolled over and prayed the movement would divert her mind from the picture it had mutinously conjured up. It didn't. Instead of something peaceful and sleep inducing, like a flower filled meadow or a range of snowcapped mountains, or even a few hundred sheep jumping a fence, she saw Chance Burkette, and with that vision, her body turned to fire.

Yearning filled her veins, flowing hot and swift, sweeping over her like a tidal wave. She had never met a man who had made her feel such instant and strong desire, such deep emotion. And at the same time his attitude frustrated her beyond reason, to say nothing about how easily he could succeed in sparking her anger.

She opened her eyes and stared up at the high ceiling. Why did Chance Burkette, a man born more than a hundred years before her time, a man who, in her world, would be described as antiquated, old fashioned, and chauvinistic, especially chauvinistic, why did a man like that attract her so strongly? She should dislike him, or at the very least find his attitude distasteful. Why, instead, did she find herself daydreaming of having his arms around her, of being cradled in the circle of his strength and virility? Was this some fantasy left over from childhood? T.J. shot upright in frustration with herself, and instantly wished she hadn't. The pounding in her head intensified. She closed her eyes and lay back down.

She was a cop. She was strong, self-sufficient and independent. She was a liberated, free-thinking, free-speaking, free-acting woman of the late twentieth century. She was not some dainty, proper minded, scandal fearing, inhibited little schoolmarm or farm wife of 1881. Neither was she a whore or an outlaw's wife. A sigh slipped from her lips. But how in blazes was she supposed to convince anyone of that when she couldn't tell them the truth?

Somehow God, fate, or destiny had stepped into her life and not only saved her from Jake Calder's bullet, and from being splattered all over that canyon floor like a pancake, but had allowed her to slip through some sort of time barrier. It had sent her traveling back into the past, back to a time before her sister's killer was born, so that she could prevent it happening and save Lisa's life. A swell of emotion caught in her throat and tears filled T.J.'s eyes at the thought of her sister.

She struggled to get her emotions under control, to push the feelings she had begun to experience toward Chance aside, and concentrate on what she was here to do. Chance was the key to her success. She had to get him to talk to her about Gil Calder without constantly insinuating that she should know the answers to her own questions. Somehow, and she wasn't sure how she was going to do it, she had to find a way to stick close to Chance, to go wherever he went, and hope he'd end up leading her to Gil Calder—unless she could get a lead on the outlaw first and find him herself.

A small smile pulled at the corners of T.J.'s full lips. She would work both ends against the middle, keep her eyes on Chance, and try to find Calder on her own at the same time. That seemed the quickest way to get to where she wanted to end up, catching Gil Calder.

A disdainful snort slipped from her lips as thought of what had happened earlier came into her mind.

She'd continue to do a little investigating on her own whenever she could, but she'd try to steer clear of the likes of Johnny Ringo. That was one man she could definitely do without ever seeing again.

She would try to stick close to Chance in case he got a
lead on Calder before she did. Her smile faded. Of course
sticking close to Chance could prove dangerous if she
failed to maintain control over her traitorous emotions
when in his company, but she'd just have to risk it. She
had a second chance to save her sister, and nothing was
going to stop her, not even Chance Burkette.

Chapter Thirteen

T.J. stared up at the ceiling and watched as the light of dawn crept into the room to chase away the blackness of night. Sleep had come only fitfully, snatched in short intervals here and there. But whether asleep or awake, thoughts of Chance haunted her mind. When asleep she had no control over it, but awake she continually tried to turn her mind toward the Calders, toward formulating a plan of action.

T.J. turned to look at the window. She hadn't pulled the shade down last night. The brilliant yellow glow of the sun shone through the glass panes, a bird chirped merrily, and the sounds of a horse drawn wagon rolling past on the street in front of the house echoed faintly on the still air.

T.J. turned her head on the pillow so that she stared, once again, up at the ceiling. The house was deathly quiet. She strained to hear a sound and heard nothing. Obviously neither Doc or Chance were about. T.J. sighed as an image of Marshal Chance Burkette filled her mind again. As attracted to him as she might be, that was not why she was here, and even if it were, and even if, heaven forbid, she were to be stuck in this time forever, he was not the kind of man she wanted in her life. He was strong, virile and devastatingly handsome, yes, and that was wonderful. But he was also ill-tempered, opinionated, bullheaded, stubborn, quick to judge, chauvinistic, and . . . and too blasted old fashioned.

She nearly laughed aloud. Old fashioned? At least he had an excuse for that one. It was 1881, not 1996. Throwing the covers back she sat up and slipped her legs over the side of the bed. Her head felt better. She reached a hand up, touched the bandage, and winced. At least it only hurt when she touched it. She stood and found her limbs had fewer aches, though her derrière was a bit sore. She'd always been a good rider, but it had been awhile since she'd been on a horse, especially for hours on end.

Dressing in the trousers she'd confiscated from Doc the day before, and one of his clean shirts she'd found in the armoire, T.J. quickly ran a brush through her long hair, allowing it to remain free and flowing over her shoulders. T.J. pulled on the rather knotty pair of wool socks Doc had loaned her and realized as she stared down at them that they were handmade. The knitter had missed several loops on one. She reached for her shoes and paused. Beside them was a pair of well-worn cowboy boots that hadn't been there when she'd gone to bed. She picked one up. Stuffed inside was a neatly folded piece of paper. T.J. pulled it out and, still holding the boot in her other hand, flipped the note open.

A wavering script, resembling chicken scratches was scrawled across the paper.

She smiled. Well, he was a doctor.

She struggled over the words.

T.J., try these boots on for size. They belonged to my niece and will do you better if you're going riding again than those little slipper things you call shoes. Went on my rounds. Might be gone most of the day if I decide to ride out to the Carlyle place. Doc

T.J. smiled. The old man really was a dear. She slid her foot into the boot and tugged it on. It fit almost perfectly. She hurriedly pulled on the other and stood. "Now, a cup of coffee and I'm ready to meet the day." She glanced at herself in the wood framed oval mirror that stood, propped up by two curved arms above the bureau that also had held a pitcher of tepid water and the bowl she'd used to wash up in. Her long hair wasn't quite as full and curly as when she used hot rollers, which she couldn't do now since they didn't exist. And she wasn't used to seeing herself without lipstick and mascara, but there was no help for that either. Thankfully her hair had a natural waviness to it, and she had enough color in her face so that she didn't look like a ghost.

T.J. sighed. It was a good thing she was the one who had been tossed for a loop and thrown back in time. She was a cop. Trained for disaster and the unexpected. Trained to take care of herself. She was strong and independent. If it had happened to Lisa instead. . . . T.J. shook her head. Her sister wouldn't have been able to cope. Even when they'd been kids, and playing games amid the cacti and scrub brush, T.J. had been the brazen one, the leader. She had always been the Lone Ranger, Robin Hood, the brave sheriff, or the ruthless bounty hunter. Lisa, on the other hand, had always happily pretended to be a lady in waiting, an opera singer visiting the west, or a wilting southern belle just passing through.

So why was she so scared?

"I'm not!" she snapped at the image in the silver glass.

"And I'd look a lot better without this blasted bandage that looks like an oversized and very ugly sweatband." She stared at her reflection, her forehead completely swathed in the white wrapping that Doc had insisted on replacing. On impulse T.J. reached up and slipped a finger under the bandage, pushed it upward, forward, and off. The wound instantly came into view, swollen and discolored. She grimaced. "Something to remember Jake by," she mumbled sarcastically.

"Who's Jake?" Chance said.

T.J. swung around, startled.

He leaned casually against the doorjamb, one booted foot casually crossed over the other. The Stetson rode low on his forehead, shadowing his eyes but not quite obscuring them from her view. Memory of the mental scolding she'd given herself earlier for thinking about him and not keeping all of her attention on Lisa filled her mind. With it came a wash of guilt that turned her words curt and cutting.

"Do you always sneak up on a lady while she's getting dressed, Marshal Burkette?"

Chance's lips curled into a blatantly impudent smile, and T.J. bristled at the licentious spark that lit his eyes as they slowly and brazenly traversed her body.

"Only occasionally," he drawled, the words and tone just as blatant and brazen as his smile.

T.J. clenched her fists at her sides. Indignation roiled up inside of her at his flagrant assessment. How dare he look at her that way; as if she were nothing more than a piece of meat hung up for inspection. She opened her mouth to retort and instantly snapped it closed again. This was 1881, not 1996. Things were different in 1881, like it or not.

"Who's Jake?" Chance asked again.

"No one you would know," T.J. said. She took a step toward him, intending to leave the room, and realized she would have to brush past him, touch him, to move through the narrow space left between him and the doorjamb. T.J. stopped abruptly. She couldn't to that—she couldn't touch him.

His brow cocked upward as she paused and he looked at her knowingly.

"What's the matter, T.J.?" he drawled, emphasizing her name with a touch of sarcasm.

T.J. took a deep breath and tried to regain control of emotions that were already, at his mere presence, threatening to take off on a course of their own. She was physically attracted to him, she'd admitted that to herself. But she couldn't give into that attraction. She had let him kiss her once; that had been a big mistake. Memory of that kiss, of the way it had made her feel inside, had robbed her of sleep, haunted her nearly all night, invaded her dreams when she had finally fallen asleep. It was taking her mind off of the real reason she was here, the task she had to perform. She raised her eyes and looked directly at him.

"Excuse me, Chance, but I was just on my way to the kitchen to make some coffee."

"Sounds good," he said. "I'll join you."

I didn't invite you. The thought swept through her mind, but she refrained from voicing it.

Chance followed her into the big kitchen at the rear of Doc's house and again lounging in the doorway, he watched her as she filled the coffee pot with water and grinds and sat it on the stove to heat. Doc had left a fire burning in the stove, so at least she didn't have to bother with that. She sat down at the plank table in the middle of the room and stared straight ahead, trying desperately to ignore Chance and focus her thoughts on Gil and Sue Ann Calder and how she was going to find them.

Chance suddenly walked across the kitchen, opened a cupboard and took down a small package and two cups.

He carried them to the table and set the package and one cup before T.J.

She stared at the paper wrapped mound. "What's this?"

"Food," he said. Turning away, Chance walked to the stove and retrieved the now steaming coffee pot. After filling each of their cups he sat down opposite her. "So, eat."

T.J. opened the paper and stared at two hefty, home-made cinnamon rolls.

"How did you know I love cinnamon rolls?"

He shrugged, reached across the table and took one. "I brought them earlier. Figured you might have a sweet tooth."

"Why?" T.J. persisted. "Does Sue Ann Calder have a sweet tooth?"

Chance shrugged again.

"I'm not Sue Ann."

He nodded, and bit down on the cinnamon roll. "So you've said," he mumbled between chews.

"So you've said," T.J. grumbled softly to herself, wrinkling her nose at Chance.

But he wasn't looking. He'd gotten up to pour himself another cup of coffee.

Well, at least he gets his own coffee, T.J. thought. She suddenly pushed away from the table.

"I'm going for a walk." Rising, she headed for the back door.

"I'll go with you."

She paused and looked up at him. "No. I'd rather go alone." Then, remembering her need to keep him friendly, she smiled. "I just have some thinking to do. I'll be all right. I won't go far."

Chance looked at her for several seconds, suspicion evident in the clear blue sparkle of his eyes.

"I promise," T.J. said softly. "Just around the block."

"Chance, help me! Quick!" Doc called from the front of the house.

T.J. hesitated at the back door. Should she offer to help?

Chance whirled around and charged through the foyer. T.J. followed. Doc was helping a young woman walk toward the examining room. She was sweating and in pain. Her free hand cradled her large stomach, as if to stop what was about to happen. Chance swooped down, swung her up into his arms and carried her the rest of the way. An older woman closed the entry door and quickly followed the trio into the doctor's medical room.

"Doc?" T.J. said. "Do you need help?"

The older woman, plump, gray haired, and impressing T.J. as an exact duplicate of Cinderella's fairy godmother, hurried to usher her from the room.

"It's okay, honey," she said, "Doc and I have done this plenty of times before." She reached to close the door after steering T.J. back into the kitchen, then paused and looked at Chance.

"Chance, honey," she said, "Theo rode out to Jesse Wendell's place earlier to buy a cow. Could you please be a dear and ride out to tell him his wife is having their baby now?"

"Sure thing," Chance said. Turning instantly he strode through the foyer and disappeared out the front door.

The woman snapped the door to Doc's examining room closed.

T.J. stood and stared at it for a moment, feeling rejected. Then she gathered herself together. This was her opportunity. She hastened out the back door. It took only a few moments to circle the house, turn the corner, and cross the street. Hopefully the town sheriff wasn't in the office. T.J. paused before the door to the jail house, took a deep breath and gripped the door handle. Before pushing down on it she glanced over her shoulder. Chance was nowhere to be seen. Obviously he'd gone straight to the livery to get his horse and ride out to wherever it was that woman had asked him to go. Relief filled her. So far so good. She pushed down on the handle and swung the door inward, hurrying into the room's shadows.

"Geez, it looks just like in the movies." T.J. stared at her surroundings in surprised amazement.

The floor and walls were made of rough planks. Several wanted posters were tacked to the walls. Excitement coursed through her. This was what she wanted, exactly what she'd come to find, a picture of Gil Calder. She hurried to look over the posters on the walls. There wasn't one of Calder. Turning to the two desks in the small room, T.J. began to rifle through the papers piled on the one nearest her. Halfway through the mound she found what she sought. With nervous fingers she pulled the wanted poster from the pile.

She stared at the black and white drawing of Jake Calder's face. For a second the breath caught in her throat and her heart seemed to stop. Black eyes glared back at her from below an angry slant of dark brows. The nose was hooked, the lips thin and set in a sneer, the jaw pointed. A cold shiver snaked up her spine. She'd seen that face before, it had been seared into her memory and was, in fact, the last thing she remembered seeing before falling from that cliff.

"Jake," T.J. said in a breathless whisper. But even as the word slipped from her lips, she knew she wasn't looking at a drawing of Jake Calder. It was his ancestor, Gil Calder, a man just as mean, just as ruthless, just as murderous as his descendant. She shoved the wanted poster into the pocket of her trousers and hurried toward the door but as she passed the window a movement from outside, on the street, caught her eye. T.J. felt her heart jump into her throat. It was Chance.

Now what was she going to do? She was caught like a thief in the act. T.J.'s head swiveled back and forth as she looked for a place to hide, another door. She saw neither. A clumping sound from outside grabbed her attention, his boot on the boardwalk.

What was he doing here? He was supposed to be gone, riding out after that woman's husband. There was nowhere to hide. She moved quickly across the small room and perched herself on the corner of the desk where she'd found the wanted poster of Gil Calder.

The lever on the door snapped down.

T.J. turned hastily so that her back was to the door and her gaze riveted on the wanted posters on the wall beside the desk.

She heard the door swing open and every nerve in her body tensed. Her back was rigid, her shoulders stiff.

"I thought you were going for a walk," Chance said.

T.J. flinched involuntarily at his accusatory tone. She forced a smile to her lips and bracing herself, turned to face him. "Well, I did, but . . ."

Whatever she'd been about to offer as an excuse for being in his office flitted from her mind as her eyes settled on him and her heart slammed into overdrive. He stood with the door open, his thumbs tucked into the low-slung belt of his holster. With the sun at his back, flowing in around him and filtering into the unlit room, he was a dark silhouette, a menacing specter who's voice was at once deep, sensuous, and challenging.

Grappling to regain both her composure and her wits, T.J. pushed herself up from the desk. Now was not the time to lose it. Better to stand and face your adversary head on, she told herself, a lesson from her training at the police academy, even if you were as nervous as a frightened cat.

"I did go for a walk, but . . ." Think T.J., she ordered herself, Think! "But when I passed here I . . ." I what? her mind screamed. She caught sight of the postered wall out of the corner of her eye. "I saw the wanted posters through the window and I wanted to take a peek."

"Your picture's not there, if that's what you're worried about."

T.J. ground her teeth. Never, not once in all her life, had a man managed to annoy her so thoroughly. And she'd had to travel over a century into the past to find him.

"Well, thank you for informing me of that, Marshal," T.J. said sweetly, in spite of the anger flowing through her veins. "I'd say that was a weight off my mind, except I didn't expect my picture to be up there."

"Didn't you now?"

"No, I didn't," she snapped.

He took several steps into the room, stopping only when he was barely two inches from her. She looked up and found his face so near to hers that she could feel his warm breath flutter across her cheek, like the caressing touch of a butterfly's wing to the wind.

Danger. The warning popped into her mind unbidden, but instantly heeded. T.J. made an attempt to take a step back, to put more space between them, but a desk at her back prevented both retreat and escape. He was too close. She felt the blood in her veins warm; and an overwhelming urge to touch him began to take hold of her. T.J. curled her hands into fists and squeezed them tightly, pushing the tips of her fingernails into her palms in an effort to detour her mind and emotions. Why did she have this reaction to him? No other man had ever affected her this way, why him? What was there about Chance Burkette that threatened to send her senses reeling out of control every time he came near her?

"What's that sticking out of your pocket, T.J.?" Chance asked, breaking into her thoughts and again emphasizing her name with taunting sarcasm.

But the tone of his voice escaped T.J. this time. Only

his words stuck in her mind. Her head snapped downward and she stared at the pocket where she'd shoved the wanted poster of Gil Calder. A corner of white paper protruded from the top of the pocket. She shoved it down with a finger.

"Nothing. Just an article I read in the paper and wanted to save," she said.

"Really? On what?"

T.J. looked frantically toward the door and tried to edge around him.

"I really should be going now," she said, finding her voice had gone near breathless at his nearness. "Doc might need me."

"Everything's fine at Doc's now. I was just there."

"I thought you went to get that woman's husband."

"Didn't have to," Chance said. "Ran into him before I even made it to the livery. He'd bought his cow and was on the way back to the general store to pick Effie up."

"Well, he and Doc might want some coffee."

"Mrs. Reilly is there."

"And I really should get started with my chores for Doc. . . . to pay for my room and board."

She scooted around him, but just when she thought she was home free, when the door seemed only inches away, Chance reached out and ripped the wanted poster from her pocket.

His gaze moved over it with merely a cursory glance, as if he'd already known what it was she'd had, and then he looked back up at her. "Souvenir?"

Chapter Fourteen

T.J. wanted to slap him. She wanted to kiss him. She wanted to pick up a chair and bash him over the head with it, and she wanted to lose herself within the circle of his arms and feel the passion ignite in her body that she knew his mere touch would surely fire.

Chance reached past her and with a flick of one hand, pushed the door shut. It slammed against the doorjamb with a jarring thud.

"I said I had to go," T.J. managed.

"I know." Chance moved to sit behind his desk. "But we need to talk. Where's Gil?"

T.J. sighed in frustration. This was really starting to get annoying. Maybe if she told him the truth, or at least part of it, he would stop with this business of insisting she was Sue Ann Calder. Closing her eyes for the briefest of seconds and taking a deep breath, she met his gaze, trying to instill in her own eyes the same cool, hard, determination she saw in his. "First, as I told you, my name is T.J. McAllister."

"Right." The lone word held enough sarcasm to down a Stealth Fighter.

T.J. felt her temper heating. "Look, I . . ." She stopped. What in heaven's name was she doing? She couldn't tell him the truth, not even a part of it. She couldn't tell him anything. "I know you don't believe me, Chance, but I really remember very little except my name."

"You're right," Chance drawled. He kicked back in his chair, balancing it on its rear two legs and folded his hands behind his head. "I don't believe you."

T.J. shrugged. "Suit yourself." She made for the door again. "I've got better things to do than stand around here trying to convince you that I'm telling the truth." Anyway, T.J. reasoned to herself, even if she did want to tell him the truth, his head was probably as hard as granite and just as tough to crack. He'd never believe her.

"Don't leave town, Sue Ann."

T.J. threw the door open then paused and, turning, glowered back at him.

"Fair warning, Marshal; if you continue to call me Sue Ann, I will not answer."

She stalked over the threshold and slammed the door behind her. It made a resounding crash against the door-jamb. T.J. smiled and stepped from the boardwalk to cross the street. Maybe, if she was lucky, it had shaken the small jail house enough to have thrown Chance from his chair to the floor. She turned toward the corner that would lead her back to Doc's house, then rethought her direction and turned again, toward the Red Garter. Her last excursion into the saloon had brought her only an unpleasant encounter with one of the Old West's most notorious out-laws, and no real information. Maybe this visit would prove more beneficial. And hopefully Johnny Ringo wasn't around.

She put a hand to her hip and stopped dead in the street. Damn Chance Burkette.

Swiveling on her heel, she returned to the jail house, throwing open the door as abruptly, and as loudly, as she had slammed it only moments before.

"I want my gun back," she said.

Chance looked up from the papers he held in his lap.

"I want my gun back," T.J. repeated, and stepped into the room.

"Nope."

Her brows rose in surprise at his answer. This was the Old West. Everyone wore guns. What hope did she have of capturing Gil Calder without her gun? "What do you mean, nope?"

"Just what I said, nope."

Chance tossed the stack of wanted posters he'd been purusing onto his desk and stood up.

"I haven't got you locked up, Sue Ann, but until I know for certain what you're up to, or until you want to leave town, no gun."

"You can't do that," T.J. said.

"I just did." He resumed his seat, picked up the wanted posters again, and began to leaf through them. "Close the door on your way out, would you?"

T.J. spun around.

"A little softer this time?"

She slammed it as hard as she could, and smiled when she saw the plank walls shake and heard the glass panes of the lone window rattle from the impact.

"No gun," T.J. muttered, storming across the street toward the saloon. "Who in the hell does he think he is, Wyatt Earp?"

She pushed through the swinging red doors and paused to let her eyes adjust to the dim interior. Once again the sound of voices, shuffling cards, clinking coins and piano music enveloped her before her eyes could adjust to the lack of sunlight. When they finally did, she walked to stand at the end of the bar and looked over the room's occupants, as they in turn looked over her.

"That the filly you was talking about, Johnny?" a voice called out.

T.J. turned toward it, instinctively knowing whoever it belonged to was referring to her. She caught sight of Johnny Ringo almost immediately. It had been the man sitting beside him who'd called out. She cringed. If the look in Ringo's eyes had been one of ice, this man's was death. Emptiness. That's all she saw there. T.J. hurried out of the saloon. No gun, no backup, and the look in the eyes of those two men had done some severe damage to both her courage level and her determination, at least for the moment. She began to walk toward Doc's again when a stagecoach suddenly barreled its way around the corner in front of her.

Fascinated, T.J. paused and watched it come to a halt in front of the express office just past the saloon. The red coach swayed on the leather straps that kept it elevated above the huge multi-spoked wheels. Quickly wrapping thick leather reins around the break handle, the driver jumped down from his high seat and promptly opened the passenger door, while the shotgun rider began throwing satchels down from the roof.

A young man climbed from the inside of the coach and, in a flourishing sweep of his hand, swept one end of the black cape he wore over his shoulder, revealing its red satin underlining. He then brushed the driver out of the way and turned to extend his hand back toward the open doorway.

A woman appeared and gingerly stepped to the ground.

T.J. stared, slightly mesmerized. In her wanderings about the streets earlier that morning she had seen other women but their gowns had been rather drab and mundane. Utilitarian. This woman looked as if she'd just stepped from the pages of a fashion magazine. Her gown appeared to be made of a soft, lilac silk and was trimmed with a darker hue of velvet at color, cuffs, and hemline. Even the mound of gathered silk that made up her bustle was trimmed with interweavings of the dark velvet. Her neck was encircled by a beautiful ruche of stiff white lace and at her throat was pinned a small cameo, set in gold filigree. She immediately raised a ruffled and lace parasol, opened it, and held it over her head as she paused to look about the streets. Her hair was nearly the same shade as T.J.'s and had been piled atop her crown then allowed to fall loose on one side and drape her shoulder in a cascade of sausage curls.

She met T.J.'s gaze for only a split second, catching and releasing it immediately as if it were inconsequential. Slipping her hand into the crook of the young man's offered arm, she allowed him to escort her toward the hotel down the block.

"So who is that?" T.J. muttered, "the grand duchess of Arizona?"

"Lily Monroe," Chance said from behind her.

T.J. spun around. The man had the uncanny ability to pop up whenever she least expected or wanted him to, and she seemed never to hear his approach. He was leaning against one of the pillars that supported the overhanging roof in front of the saloon. His right hand rested casually, though a bit intimidatingly on the butt of his gun, while his left thumb, hooked within the low slung holster, dangled before him. Thin wisps of white smoke swirled up from the tip of a cheroot he held between two fingers of his left hand.

Something hot, like a little flash of anger or annoyance, swept through T.J. as she saw Chance's gaze move from her to the woman he'd called Lily Monroe. T.J. took a small step sideways, effectively blocking his view of the woman and receiving a small wash of satisfaction at the thought.

"So," she said, one chestnut brow arching slightly, "who is Lily Monroe?"

"Singer. Sam Conners heard she performed in San Francisco a few months back and sold the place out every night. He hired her to come play at the Red Garter."

"Have you seen her perform?" T.J. asked, curious.

"No, but . . ." A small smile curved Chance's lips as he cocked his head to one side in order to see past T.J. and catch one last glimpse of the woman before she disappeared into the hotel. ". . . I certainly intend to."

T.J. felt a flash of temper again. She wasn't jealous. She wasn't. Why should she be jealous? She didn't want Chance Burkette. The mere thought was ridiculous. They had nothing in common, other than both being law officers, albeit over a hundred years apart. It was just irritation at the way he was oogling that woman, that's all she was feeling. It was scandalous. Demeaning. And he ought to be ashamed of himself. She began to walk toward Doc's house again.

Chance's gaze moved from T.J. to the woman who had just entered the hotel, back to T.J., and back to the entrance of the hotel. Chance smiled. He didn't care two figs about Lily Monroe but he had delighted in seeing a spark of jealousy in T.J.'s eyes when she'd thought he was interested in the singer.

Stepping from the boardwalk he slowly walked toward Doc's house. Every instinct within him told him he should stay away from her, watch her, stay on the alert. Everything pointed to her being Sue Ann Calder, which meant trouble, both for the town and for him. So why, for the first time in his life, was he not paying any attention to his instincts? He pushed the question aside, trying to both deny and ignore it.

He'd never wanted for female companionship. It had always been readily available to him, and still was. Before his marriage to Caroline, Chance had shared a bed with a number of females, some ladies, some whores—all beautiful, seductive, and willing. Since Caroline's death, he had restricted himself mainly to the whores, where his heart and his feelings were not in danger of being aroused or hurt. So why now, was he infatuated with a woman who could very well get him killed?

Cursing himself for every kind of a fool, Chance turned abruptly and made his way to the livery stable. Henry Markus was busy repairing a bridle when Chance entered the livery.

"Hey, Chance, what's up?" Henry asked.

"Nothing," Chance grumbled, his thoughts having turned his mood surly. "I need my horse."

"Billy," Henry called out over his shoulder.

The blacksmith's young son appeared from the shadows of a stack of hay. "Yes, sir?"

"Saddle the marshal's horse and bring him out."

"Yes, sir."

"Noticed Curly Bill with Ringo over at the Red Garter this morning," Henry Markus said.

"Yeah." Chance didn't feel much like talking. He especially didn't feel much like talking about Curly Bill and Ringo, or about any of the other cowboys. The saloon operators might figure the cowboys were good for business, but Chance knew they were bad for the town. They were trouble, pure and simple. They brought it, lived it, and caused it, everywhere they went, and Curly Bill and Ringo were the worst—both fast with their mouths, their tempers, and their guns.

Chance sighed. It was probably only a matter of time before he had to face one or the other of them in the street. Then again, he'd heard that the Earps were in Tombstone now, which was the cowboys' favorite haunt. Maybe the Earps would end up solving the problem of Curly Bill and Ringo for him.

Diablo whinnied as Billy brought him out to Chance.

"Here he is, Marshal."

Chance smiled and flipped the kid a coin.

"Thanks, Billy. You brush him down real good when I come back, and give him an extra scoop of oats, and I'll give you another penny. Okay?"

Billy beamed. "Sure thing, Marshal. Sure thing."

Chance settled a foot into the stirrup and swung up onto the saddle. He had no particular destination in mind, he just knew he had to ride awhile. It was the best way he knew to clear his head and make sense of his thoughts when he was troubled. Anyway, he wanted to check on Colossal Cave again. For months he'd had a suspicion that Calder was using the caves as his hideout, but every time Chance had gone there in the past, he'd either found them empty or occupied by a few prospectors or cowboys, but no Calder and none of his gang.

He rode out of town slowly, taking note of each horse hitched to the rails outside the various saloons. Chance calculated there were about six cowboys in town. Curly Bill wouldn't make too much trouble with so few men around him. Feeling a bit more confident about riding out, Chance let Diablo have his head when they reached the outskirts of town. The big stallion broke into a lope, his strides long and easy.

She was Sue Ann Calder. Everything pointed to it. So why did he have a niggling little feeling of doubt? Chance reached up to pull the Stetson farther down on his forehead to block the glare of the afternoon sun. His eyes hardened. He didn't have any doubts. None at all. It was exactly as he'd thought. She had been on her way into Tucson to scout out the town as she usually did for Gil, and somehow she'd fallen or been pushed off that cliff. Now she was just waiting for one of her accomplices to show up in town. Most likely she was scouting it out now, right under Chance's nose.

He remembered her altercation with Ringo. Maybe it hadn't been an altercation at all, but a sly maneuver to pass information without anyone, like a U.S. Marshal, becoming suspicious.

Several hours later Chance was on his way back to Tucson. A search of the caves had once again proven fruitless. There'd been a few cowboys camped out there, a drifter Chance suspected was most likely wanted somewhere else, and a few prospectors. But no Calder.

T.J. watched as Chance rode out of town, torn between the desire to follow him and see where he was going, and the urge to go back to his office and try to get her gun. She decided that retrieving her gun was her first priority. Hunting down an outlaw without a weapon of her own was more than she had courage for. Anyway, why should she? T.J. thought. She might have been tossed back into 1881, but her .38 Special and ammo had been tossed right along with her. She'd be safer if she could just get her hands on them.

As soon as Chance rounded the corner and was out of sight, T.J. hurried across the street and slipped back into his office. The sheriff, she knew, was down the street in the general store. She'd seen him there earlier. T.J. immediately went to Chance's desk. Her gun wasn't in any of the drawers, or in the other desk. She looked at the hooks on the walls. It wasn't there either. Realizing she was being ridiculous, but unwilling not to search everywhere, T.J. walked into the two cells and searched their cots. She went out the back door and looked into the outhouse, the small shed that stood nearby, the grain trough, and even into a pair of old saddlebags lying near the trough.

She went back inside the jail house and searched both desks again and like the first time, did not find her gun. She turned the chairs over to see if it had somehow been secured to the bottom of one, she crawled under the desks to check out the same thing—Nothing. Her gaze jumped about the room in search of another place he could have put her weapon and holster. There wasn't anywhere else. No cabinets, no shelves, nothing.

"Damn the man," T.J. mumbled. "Damn him."

Perspiration covered her forehead in a thin veil. Her shirt clung to her back and breasts and she felt certain her hair had frizzed, but she didn't care. She had to find that gun. Maybe it was at the house. Grabbing the handle of the entry door she swung it open and barreled right into Sheriff Perkins.

"Oh, uh, sorry, ma'am," the young officer stuttered. He stepped back and reached up to snatch a rumpled hat from his head.

T.J. bounced off of him and grabbed the doorjamb in an effort to maintain her balance. She forced a smile to her lips.

"Oh, it was completely my fault, Sheriff, really," she said sweetly.

"Can I help you, ma'am? Is there a problem?"

"Oh, no," T.J. cooed. "I was just looking for the Marshal, that's all."

"Well, he rode out a little while ago, but if you need some law doing, ma'am, I would be glad to help you any way I can."

Lord the man was insistent, T.J. thought. She maintained the smile.

"Oh, that's sweet of you, Sheriff, really it is," she said, "but all I actually wanted was to know if the Marshal planned on being home for dinner tonight."

"Home?" The sheriff echoed.

"Yes." She laughed softly. "Oh, I'm sorry, we haven't met and you haven't the faintest idea what I'm talking about." She stuck a hand out toward him. "I'm T.J. McAllister."

Perkins frowned and stared at her hand, obviously not sure what he was supposed to do.

"I'm staying at the Burkette place for a while," T.J. went on. She let her hand drop back to her side. Evidently men didn't shake hands with a woman in 1881.

The young officer's face lit up in understanding at her words.

"Oh, yeah, Sue Ann—I mean . . ." He blushed. "Yeah, the marshal told me about you. Glad to meet you, ma'am."

"Do you know how long the marshal plans to be gone, Sheriff?"

He shook his head. "No, ma'am. Most'a the afternoon, I'd reckon."

"Thank you." She started to turn away, then paused. "Oh, Sheriff, please excuse my manners. Would you like to come over for dinner?"

"Thanks, ma'am, I'd love to, but I can't. Kinda doubt my wife would understand."

"Well, maybe both you and your wife can come over another time."

He smiled. "I think Dori would like that, ma'am, thank you."

"Good."

T.J. hurried back toward Doc's house, but before she reached it, she found herself waylaid by Mrs. Reilly and drawn into a conversation about making soup. Obviously Doc had told her how much T.J. had raved over her soup.

By the time she made it to Doc's she calculated that Chance had already been gone at least two hours. She prayed that he was going to be gone twice that long. She'd need the time if she had to search Doc's entire house. She entered the foyer and stopped still, listening intently for any sound that would indicate that Doc was in the house. She heard none.

"Doc?" she called out, just to be on the safe side. "Doc, are you here?"

Several seconds passed without an answer.

T.J. peeked into the parlor, kitchen, examining room, and Doc's office. All were empty. Hopefully he wasn't upstairs taking a nap. Since her room was downstairs, she'd have no excuse for being on the second floor where the men's bedrooms were. If her gun wasn't in Chance's office, then it had to be in his room.

The narrow stairs creaked as she made her way toward the landing. Not until she reached it did T.J. realize she'd been holding her breath. She exhaled and clinging to the wall, she peeked around the corner. The short hallway to her right was empty, lit by sunlight shining through a window at its other end. She looked in the opposite direction. Both the hallway and the two doors, one on either side of it, were identical to the ones to her right. T.J. slipped into the first door on her right. The sparse furnishings told her the room wasn't used much. Against one wall was a cot. An old, unadorned and badly scratched armoire stood against the other wall. Next to it was a wooden chair. That was it. She stepped back into the hallway, crossed it, and entered the other room. It was Doc's. She knew immediately from the pipe that sat in a dish on the table next to the bed, the jacket hung on a hook by the door, and the medical text books stacked on table, bureau and floor. Her gun wouldn't be in Doc's room. She felt fairly certain of that.

T.J. stepped back into the hallway, this time walking past the staircase landing and on to the other two doors. The first one she opened was Chance's room. The tangy scent of leather and tobacco lingered in the air, a pair of chaps had been thrown over the back of a chair, and a rifle stood propped up in one corner near the window. But those weren't the only things that identified the room as his. T.J. stepped inside quickly and closed the door behind her. Several shirts were hung on a row of hooks on one wall, along with a hat and what was obviously a dress jacket. A

pair of newly polished boots stood against the wall beside
the bed. She noticed a framed picture on the small table
near the bed. T.J. picked it up. It was a daguerreotype of
a much younger Chance, and at his side stood a beautiful
blonde woman. A toddler sat at their feet.

Chance's wife and child? She stared at the picture and
felt a flash of jealousy, then immediately disregarded it as
foolish. First of all she had no reason to feel jealous. Chance
Burkette meant nothing to her. He couldn't. Second of
all, the woman was most likely Chance's sister. Doc had
said he had a sister, and that was probably her child. If
Chance had a wife and child he obviously wouldn't be
living here with Doc. But it didn't matter to her anyway.

T.J. put the picture down and turned to look at the rest
of the room. Where would he put her gun? Her gaze fell
on the bureau, her attention diverted as she looked not
at the drawers but on the stack of books piled on top of
the bureau. She hadn't pictured Chance as a reader. T.J.
moved closer to read their titles. The Criminal Mind, by
T.J. Taggart. Physical Evidence, by Benjamin Cruen. Crime
and Reason, by Lorne Flint. Tracking the Prey, by K. Prine.
A frown tugged at T.J.'s brow. Chance Burkette obviously
took his job quite seriously.

A door shut downstairs.

T.J. froze. Someone was in the house!

Footsteps sounded on the stairs, hard and solid. Those
weren't Doc's steps. His steps were light and shuffling. She
heard a soft tinkling sound like spurs. Chance! His name
screamed in her brain. Panic clogged T.J.'s throat and
threatened to suffocate her. Think! she ordered her brain.
She ran to the window and looked out. Straight down. No
escape. She could crawl under the bed. Her eyes darted
around the room again.

Chapter Fifteen

Realizing there was nothing else to do, T.J. braced herself for the confrontation and looked directly toward the door.

It opened.

She gulped hard.

Green eyes met blue, hers glistening with fear, his at first startled, then quickly reflecting the question in his mind as to why she was there.

"And to what do I owe this surprise?" Chance drawled. He stood framed within the doorway, making no move or attempt to ease the strained silence that hung between them as he waited for her answer. Quickly fading sunlight streamed through the windows at T.J.'s back and filtered across the room. It settled upon him in a golden haze, but the muted light did little to soften the harsh sarcasm of his words, or the suspicion she saw in his eyes.

Suddenly unable to move or utter a sound in defense of being caught in his room, T.J. stood motionless, frozen to the spot. She found herself powerless to turn away, her gaze pinioned by his, held its helpless prisoner, its victim. His presence seemed to fill the doorway, threatening and dark, in spite of the golden light. Every inch of her body was acutely aware of him, every nerve ready to jump at his slightest movement, every muscle primed to flash into action if he approached. A panic-filled little voice from somewhere in the back of her mind screamed at her to run, to push past him and escape. Instead she remained rooted to the spot, her body incapable of executing the wishes of the faint voice.

He stared at her for a long time, a time that T.J. felt certain, if measured, would prove an eternity.

Finally, Chance stepped into the room and, without taking his eyes off of her, kicked the door shut behind him.

T.J. nearly jumped as it slammed closed. She opened her mouth to voice an excuse for being in his room, but no words uttered forth.

"Cat got your tongue?" Chance asked, finally breaking the silence. A wickedly seductive smile curved his lips and his blue eyes sparkled with sudden mischief as his misgivings about her were momentarily deferred.

T.J. stared at him dumbly. Her mind refused to simulate coherent thought. He had the look of a cat who'd just trapped a mouse in the corner. And that's exactly how she felt: trapped. Totally, irrefutably, unescapably trapped.

He sauntered indolently across the room toward her, the movement an arrogant swagger that should have warned her she was in trouble. But T.J. was too busy staring into those fathomless blue eyes and trying to convince herself that they were having no effect on her whatsoever to bother looking at the way he was walking.

The moment he'd entered the room her pulse rate had gone spiraling out of control like a race car with a little too much horsepower. Her heart had begun a drumroll that was, at least in her ears, loud enough to announce to the world that Elvis was back, and her hands had begun

HERE'S A SPECIAL INVITATION TO ENJOY TODAY'S FINEST HISTORICAL ROMANCES— ABSOLUTELY FREE! *(a $19.96 value)*

Now you can enjoy the latest Zebra Lovegram Historical Romances without even leaving your home with our convenient Zebra Home Subscription Service. Zebra Home Subscription Service offers you the following benefits that you don't want to miss:

- 4 BRAND NEW bestselling Zebra Lovegram Historical Romances delivered to your doorstep each month (usually before they're available in the bookstores!)

  - 20% off each title or a savings of almost $4.00 each month

  - FREE home delivery

  - A FREE monthly newsletter, *Zebra/Pinnacle Romance News* that features author profiles, contests, special member benefits, book previews and more

- No risks or obligations...in other words you can cancel whenever you wish with no questions asked

So join hundreds of thousands of readers who already belong to Zebra Home Subscription Service and enjoy the very best Historical Romances That Burn With The Fire of History!

And remember....there is no minimum purchase required. After you've enjoyed your initial FREE package of 4 books, you'll begin to receive monthly shipments of new Zebra titles. Each shipment will be yours to examine for 10 days and then if you decide to keep the books, you'll pay the preferred subscriber's price of just $4.00 per title. That's $16 for all 4 books with FREE home delivery! And if you want us to stop sending books, just say the word....it's that simple.

It's a no-lose proposition, so send for your 4 FREE books today!

4 FREE BOOKS

These books worth almost $20, are yours without cost or obligation when you fill out and mail this certificate.

(If the certificate is missing below, write to: Zebra Home Subscription Service, Inc., 120 Brighton Road, P.O. Box 5214, Clifton, New Jersey 07015-5214)

Complete and mail this card to receive 4 Free books!

YES! Please send me 4 Zebra Lovegram Historical Romances without cost or obligation. I understand that each month thereafter I will be able to preview 4 new Zebra Lovegram Historical Romances FREE for 10 days. Then if I decide to keep them, I will pay the money-saving preferred publisher's price of just $4.00 each...a total of $16. That's almost $4 less than the regular publisher's price, and there is never any additional charge for shipping and handling. I may return any shipment within 10 days and owe nothing, and I may cancel this subscription at any time. The 4 FREE books will be mine to keep in any case.

Name _____

Address _____ Apt. _____

City _____ State _____ Zip _____

Telephone ( ) _____

Signature _____

(If under 18, parent or guardian must sign.)

LF0996

Terms, offer and prices subject to change without notice. Subscription subject to acceptance by Zebra Home Subscription Service, Inc.. Zebra Home Subscription Service, Inc. reserves the right to reject any order or cancel any subscription.

to tremble like dried leaves in a strong winter gale. She told herself it was fear, panic, dread. That's all.

Sweeping the black Stetson from his head and tossing it onto the bed, Chance halted before her, their bodies only a few inches apart. His gaze moved over her from top to bottom and back up again, flagrantly assessing her, instilling her with yet more unease as it paused upon the rapid rise and fall of her breasts. His eyes taunted her with their insolent appraisal, rose to meet her own, then dropped again to linger upon the full curve of her bottom lip. An imperious little smile tugged at one corner of his mouth as his gaze rose once more to meet hers.

"Why are you in my room?" he asked softly, letting the words roll off of his tongue like smooth, hot, honey.

T.J. had been able to force herself to meet his gaze. She had been able to force herself to remain standing and facing him. But she knew, even without attempting speech, that she couldn't yet manage to speak with the full force of her voice. She swallowed painfully, nearly choking herself in the process, and took a deep breath, hoping it would somehow calm her jangled nerves. She wanted to step back from him, to increase the space between them and couldn't. All she could do was stare up at him mutely.

With his approach toward her he had moved into the light streaming through the windows so that now the pinkish gold beams of sunset wove their way among the curls of his hair, gleaming like precious stones set in ebony. They highlighted the hollows of his cheeks to create canyons out of slopes, kissed the square lines and turned them to strokes of steel, caressed the curves and left them in silver shadow. A shiver rippled over T.J.'s skin as an onslaught of emotion coursed through her, turbulent in its assault, conflicting in its manner. She wanted to flee from him, and she wanted to run to him. T.J. fought to regain control of her emotions. She couldn't get involved with a man who lived in 1881. It was insane.

Chance smiled down at her then, and any hesitation T.J. had about letting herself get emotionally involved with him was instantly and thoroughly banished from her consciousness. Her mind and body were at war, cool logic fighting the stirrings of her heart, of her longings, and cool logic was losing—at least this battle.

Chance stood still, his attention centered solely on her. He knew what he had to do now. He had done a lot of thinking in the last few hours and it was clear now that his approach so far was wrong. To continue acting suspicious of her, to keep challenging her every word and action, was going to get him nowhere. That had been proven already. But if he played along with her game and allowed her to think he believed her about everything— her name, the amnesia, all of it—that might get him exactly what he wanted.

He'd ridden most of the afternoon away searching for Calder's hideout, for some sign of where the cowboys disappeared to when they felt the need to drop from sight, and he'd found nothing. One thing he was convinced of though, they didn't go to the caves. Reports had come to him over the months that the cowboys kept moving, maintaining their camp in one spot only for a few nights, then shifting to another. He was beginning to believe it, but he wasn't about to give up. Though at the moment, like it or not, he had no choice but to admit that it wasn't Gil Calder he wanted, but her, and he was in no mood to argue the point with himself. He wanted her, no matter who she was, no matter why she was in Tucson, no matter what would happen later, he wanted her.

And why shouldn't he have her? Why should he deny himself what he wanted? Gil Calder had killed Caroline, so why shouldn't he at least bed Calder's wife and enjoy her favors for a while? Chance felt a shiver of guilt at his thoughts and callously brushed them aside. Slipping an arm around her waist, he drew T.J. roughly up against him.

"You don't have to explain your little visit to my room, darlin'," Chance said. His deep, slowly drawling voice was like the sweep of a warm summer breeze over her highly sensitized flesh. "I've wanted you since the very first time I laid eyes on you."

T.J. knew she should say something. Anything. But her brain and her bodily functions, especially her mouth, weren't working in unison. Instead of allowing her to pull away from him, her body welcomed the touch of his, actually appeared to reach for it. And her hands, seemingly of their own volition, moved to settle on his forearms, her fingers feeling the steely strength of his muscles beneath their touch. Instead of turning her face away from him, she lifted it toward him, inviting his kiss. She wanted him to trust her, wanted him to accept her so that she could follow him, accompany him when he finally went after Calder, but this was not the way she had planned to achieve that trust.

But this is what you want, a little voice at the back of her mind said softly.

The spontaneous, but involuntary, confession startled T.J. She wanted to deny that there was any truth in it, but she couldn't, not unless she wanted to lie to herself, and there was no point in trying to do that. She let her gaze move upward and join with his.

As always happened when she looked into his eyes when in any mood other than anger, blue blended with green. They were two uniquely different entities drawn together by fortune or destiny, each needing the other to survive in the world that surrounded them.

She sensed that he wanted to kiss her, and she wanted him to. Her hands slid upward, moving over his shoulders, feeling the ropey contours, the iron hardness, the strength. T.J. felt a shiver of desire course through her and, locking her hands behind his neck, she raised up on the tips of her toes to press her lips against his.

Similar to both the gentle swoop of a hawk, and the ferocious pounce of a lion, Chance's lips descended on hers and captured them. Parting her lips in invitation, T.J. felt the hot, moist invasion of his tongue, felt it as a flickering flame filling her mouth. Desire, hot and burning, enveloped her groin and swept through her limbs. It seized her in an ever-tightening grip and turned every cell, every molecule, every fiber of her being into an ache of need.

She should resist him, if for no other reason than the foreboding thought that there could be no lasting relationship between them. It was impossible. Any day, any hour or minute, she could be whisked out of his arms, out of his time, and tumbled back into her own. But resistance to this man, to the emotions, the feelings, the fire that his touch ignited within her body, was not something she could muster.

Compulsively her lips sought his, the yearning within her to be close to him so overpowering that her thoughts were filled with nothing else. His kiss was an intoxicating aphrodisiac that awoke and sparked her body to a sensuality like none she had ever experienced before, and like none, she knew, that she would ever experience with anyone else. It was beautiful, it was captivating, and it was total.

Willingly she gave herself up to the enticement of his mouth, hungrily holding him to her with arms wrapped securely around his neck, her tongue dueling with his: flame against flame.

Chance felt a swelling of satisfaction at her response to his kiss. His arms tightened around her and crushed her to him while his hands began to play upon her back in a stroking series of calculatedly sensual strokes. A soft moan escaped her throat as he tore his lips from hers and pressed them to the hollow of her throat.

"Chance," T.J. whispered, his name a ragged plea upon her lips.

At the unexpected entreaty he heard in her tone, desire fired his blood and turned the need simmering within him to a hungrily devouring inferno. All of the machinations he'd contrived that afternoon, all of the schemes he'd thought up to garner her trust and cooperation, swiftly fled his mind, forgotten as if they'd never existed.

For the first time in his life, Chance's total concentration was centered on a woman, the captivating woman whose body was pressed tightly to his own, whose mouth was ravishing his as thoroughly, as brazenly, as his was hers.

Never before, not in all of his life, had he been filled with such an urgent, desperate need to take a woman to his bed, to conquer her body and soul. It wasn't lust alone that filled him now, it was more, much more, yet the feeling was not only new, it was something he did not want to acknowledge.

She was forbidden to him, yet he had to have her. Tomorrow would bring anguish, he knew. He'd hate himself as well as her, but tonight none of that mattered. Tonight she was the vision his heart had always longed for, the goddess of his fantasies, the woman that could make, if only for a little while, his most secret dreams come true.

He let his hands roam over her back, delighting at the feel of the curving sweep of her spine, the delicate turn of her shoulders, the warmth that emanated from her flesh through the thin fabric of her shirt to penetrate his fingers. Her breasts pushed at his chest, her hips pressed to his hips, and his body continued to harden. Each unconscious movement of her form against his brought a new onslaught of passion that swept through his veins and left him a bit more vulnerable to her and feelings she was arousing deep within him.

Long days in the saddle had turned Chance's body to a sinewy length of hard muscle, used to withstanding the hours of abuse his job created, while his family's murder had hardened his heart. He was used to ignoring even the slightest nuances of feeling, both physical and emotional, but he couldn't ignore what having her in his arms did to him.

Her hands roamed his shoulders and upper arms, slid over the rippling contours, caressed each dip and swell, and glided provocatively up the corded curve of his neck. And as they did, Chance found himself aware of every sensation her touch created, every shiver of pleasure it caused, every ache of need it aroused. He was no longer the dedicated law officer, the avenging widower, or the grieving father, he was a man in desperate need of a woman, this woman.

Downstairs a door slammed.

"Chance? T.J.? You two here?" Doc called.

Silence met his inquiry. Frowning, Doc peeked into several of the downstairs rooms.

"Damned Perkins said Chance came home," Doc mumbled to himself. He began to climb the stairs.

"Chance, you up here boy?" Doc called again as he neared the landing. "Chance?"

The sound of Doc's gravelly voice filtered through the walls of the old house, pierced Chance's consciousness, and rang in his ears. Startled, and abruptly ripped back to the cold world of reality, he tore himself from T.J.'s arms and whirled around to face the door. He stared at it as if it represented the hounds of hell come to get him. "Son of a . . ." he whispered under his breath.

Realization of what had happened to him, of just how completely he had lost control of his emotions, slammed into Chance to further rock his sensibilities and composure. A rapping knock sounded against the door.

"Chance, you in there?" Doc called out again.

T.J.'s gazed darted from the door to Chance and back to the door. He didn't want Doc to see them together in his room, that was evident from the stiffness of his shoulders and the string of curses that flowed from his lips. She felt abashed at having let him kiss her again, but more important, at her response to that kiss. This was 1881, not 1996. She had to keep reminding herself of that. A lady didn't let a man kiss her, not like that. Then of course, a real lady didn't go snooping around in a man's bedroom either. Dashing across the room, T.J. squeezed herself into the small, shadowed bit of space between one end of the armoire and the adjoining wall. She held herself stiff and motionless, hardly daring to breathe and praying that she was not visible to anyone standing at the door.

Chance quickly ran a hand through his hair, tousling it, unbuckled his holster and draped it over the bed's footboard, then walked toward the door.

T.J.'s gaze fell on the small table beside Chance's bed, and directly at the framed daguerreotype sitting there. The woman in the picture stared back at her. T.J. felt her cheeks burn and knew they had turned red. Was the woman Chance's wife? Was the child his child? T.J. felt a sinking feeling in the pit of her stomach.

She heard him open the door and, watching his reflection in the mirror on top of his bureau, saw him yawn exaggeratedly. "Yeah, Doc? What's all the yelling about?"

Doc looked slightly embarrassed. "Oh, Chance, sorry. I didn't expect you to be asleep. It's not exactly late yet."

Chance remained standing in the center of the doorway, one hand holding to the doorknob, the other casually propped on the doorjamb and effectively blocking the older man from entering the bedroom.

"Yeah, well, I rode out to the caves this afternoon, trying to get a lead on Calder. I thought I'd take a nap before dinner."

"Have you seen T.J.?" Doc asked.

"T.J.?" Chance frowned as if he didn't understand who

the old man was referring to, then he suddenly brightened and smiled. "Oh, you mean Sue Ann?"

"I mean our guest," Doc snapped. "And really, Chance, you have no real proof the woman is Sue Ann Calder, absolutely none. And until you do you should call her what she wants to be called, which is T.J."

Chance smiled. "Sounds like you're a bit taken with her, huh, Doc?"

"I like her, if that's what you mean, and I'm a little concerned about her right now. That bump she took on the head might not look that bad, but it was a pretty good one, Chance, and I'm worried she's overdoing it. All this walking around town and riding in the countryside with you." He shook his head. "She's still weak, whether she realizes it or not, and she's going to collapse, Chance. She's overdoing it and she's going to collapse, you mark my words."

T.J. felt both a rush of warmth toward the old man for his concern, and a flash of guilt at causing him to worry. But she couldn't just lie in bed. She had to find Calder before it was too late.

"Now, have you seen her?" Doc asked.

"Yeah, Doc, she was here when I came in, puttering around downstairs. Said something about making muffins. Did you look in the kitchen?"

"Yes. And into every other room downstairs. She's not in any of them."

Chance wrapped an arm around Doc's shoulders and, stepping into the hallway, steered him toward the stairs. "Well, maybe she's sitting out back in your gazebo getting a breath of fresh air," he said loudly, so she'd hear. "Come on, I'll help you look for her."

Chapter Sixteen

T.J. shifted her position on the bed and stared up into the darkness. Dinner with Doc and Chance had been a strained affair. Chance had been cold and surly, a shock after the kiss they'd shared only an hour before. In response she'd found herself unnaturally subdued and quiet. Doc had tried several times to ease the tension that hung over the trio, but to no avail. Finally he'd given up and pretended to rivet his attention solely on his meal, but several times T.J. had caught him throwing furtive glances at either her or Chance and knew he was trying to figure out what, if anything, had happened between them. Most likely he thought they'd argued about Chance calling her Sue Ann Calder. T.J. nearly scoffed aloud. The old man would have been shocked silly to discover that rather than having interrupted an argument earlier, he'd very nearly stumbled upon a seduction.

But it really wasn't funny. There was no longer any way to deny it. She was insanely attracted to Chance Burkette, though every feminine rights instinct within her told her she was crazy. He was about as liberated as Ghengis Khan. Then again, he was one of the strongest, most virile men she'd ever met.

He hadn't really done anything all that chauvinistic. "Except be intolerably stubborn and opinionated," she snapped into the darkness. But he was also tender, sensitive, and caring. She'd seen those traits in him, too, as when he'd carried her all the way back to town, and helped that pregnant woman into Doc's examining room. And he worried over her. Much as he wanted to insist that she was Sue Ann Calder, and try to dislike her, he worried over her, cautioning her not to overdo it, his concern showing in his eyes when she ignored his warnings and did as she pleased.

But she wasn't in 1881 to find the perfect mate or even to merely have an affair. Besides, if that picture on his nightstand was any indication of the truth, Chance probably had a wife and child somewhere.

Throwing the coverlet back, T.J. rose and began to pace the room. She was here to catch Gil Calder and see him put behind bars for such a long time that Jake Calder would never be born. That was the only way she could save Lisa, and she was wasting time. She had to find some way to locate Calder. Chance didn't seem in any hurry to try and track the man down, but that was because he believed that she was Sue Ann Calder, here to check out Tucson so that Gil could ride in and rob it blind.

She'd tried talking to Johnny Ringo on the hopes that one outlaw would know where another was hiding. That hadn't worked. He probably knew where Calder was, but all he'd been interested in talking to her about was getting into bed. And one look at Curly Bill Brocious, with his cold, deathlike eyes, had left her convinced he was one man she didn't want to get near at all, let alone talk to.

T.J. looked out at the moonlit landscape beyond her

window. So how was she going to find Calder? Not pacing this room, that was for sure.

Chance walked down the boardwalk of Dellos Street. The storefronts were all dark now, doors locked, shades pulled against the night. He tried the handle of Brayle's General Store, and satisfied that it was locked, moved on to continue his rounds. When he was in town Chance usually rotated rounds with the sheriff. Tonight hadn't been his turn, but he knew sleep was going to be a long time coming, so he'd told Perkins he would take the first round. The young sheriff had been only too glad to let him do it and spend an uninterrupted evening at home with his new bride.

But it wasn't an attack of mindless insomnia that had Chance walking the dark streets of Tucson, it was the haunting face of the woman he'd held in his arms a few hours earlier, T.J. McAllister, also known as Sue Ann Calder. A fresh sequence of curses spewed from his lips. He wasn't supposed to have felt anything for her. Maybe a little lust, that was natural. But nothing else. Actually, what he should have felt was nothing more than disdain.

When Caroline had decided she didn't want anything further to do with their marital bed, Chance, a virile man with natural hungers, had turned to other women to satisfy his needs. That had been lust. But what had happened to him earlier in his room, with T.J., had not been the same. The hunger, the longing, the need he'd felt for her had all been different, and that's what had him unnerved. He didn't want it to be different. He didn't want to care for her.

"Damn it, she's Calder's wife." The words echoed about him on the night air. But even saying them aloud didn't change the fact that he still wanted her.

Chance turned the corner and began to walk down Main

Street. Music, laughter, and the clink of both coins and glasses seeped from the open doorways of several saloons. He was just about to pass the Silver Palace when a cowboy came tumbling backward through the swinging doors and landed, sprawled on his back, at Chance's feet. The sound of breaking furniture reverberated from within the saloon, along with several shouts and a gunshot. Pulling his own weapon, Chance barged through the swinging doors, his eyes quickly scanning the scene before him. A wrangler stumbled into him, blood gushing from his upper lip where someone's fist had obviously landed. He reeled around and made to jump back into the foray. Chance rapped him on the head with his gun and grabbed him by the collar as he began to slump to the floor. He looked at the bartender.

"What the hell's going on in here, Ed?" he snarled.

"Taggert." He nodded toward the man slumped at Chance's feet. "And his friend, Vermillion. . . ." He glanced toward the doors. "That's the one out there on the boardwalk. They called Fingers a cheat. I told my boys to head them outside but they didn't want to go."

Chance looked at the Palace's resident dealer who was sitting at a table calmly shuffling a deck of cards.

"You dealing square, Fingers?"

The wirey little man nodded, his spectacles picking up the light of the overhead chandelier and reflecting it in a myriad of color. "Yes, sir, Marshal," he said. "You know I always do. The Palace runs an honest game."

"Yeah, okay. I'll let these two be my guests at the jail house for the night, but if I ever do catch you cheating, Fingers . . ." He let the remainder of the warning go unvoiced, knowing that to the little cardsharp the silence made his message all the more threatening.

Ten minutes later Chance had both cowboys locked up and was once again making his way down Main Street. At the hotel he paused and looked in through the lace-cov-

ered window. Lily Monroe was sitting at a table in the
lounge, a small room just off the hotel's lobby. A cup of
coffee sat before her on the table.

Chance smiled to himself. He'd never met an actress
before, but he'd heard some of them could be pretty
accommodating. Maybe that's exactly what he needed to
remind his body that it wasn't really Sue Ann Calder he
wanted. It was just a woman. A nice looking woman. And
Lily Monroe was undoubtedly one hell of a nice looking
woman.

He pushed open the hotel's glass etched entry door
and sauntered inside. The clerk behind the check-in desk
looked up questioningly, then busied himself with some
papers when he saw Chance walk toward the lounge. He
removed his hat as he approached her table. "Miss
Monroe?"

She looked up and smiled. The first thing he noticed
was that her eyes were nearly the same shade as T.J.'s,
though not quite as almond shaped, and her lashes were
not as long or full. The second thing he noticed was that
her hair was nearly the same shade as T.J.'s. However, T.J.
always wore her hair loose and flowing, while Lily Monroe's
hairstyle was one of swirling curls piled atop her head with
a profusion of them draped over one shoulder.

"Yes?" she said finally, after sizing him up as thoroughly
as he had done her. "May I help you, Marshal?"

Chance smiled at the brazen once over. Most women
refrained from such overt gestures, which made his prospects with her look all the better. "Not really," he drawled,
the words insolent and slow. "But you could allow me to
buy you another cup of coffee." He eyed her empty cup.

She laughed. "Yes, I could," she said. "And I think I
will do just that. It's not often that I meet such a handsome
law officer. And with manners, too." She laughed again,
the sound like the hushed tinkling of delicate china bells.
"Most lawmen I've encountered while on tour are pudgy,

old bewhiskered men, or skinny little nothings trying to be bigshots. "But you." She seemed to purr as her eyes roamed over him from head to toe.

Chance slid onto the chair opposite her and motioned to one of the hotel clerks to bring them both coffee. Lily Monroe was obviously not shy, but then she was an actress.

"So," Chance said, "what is a beautiful woman like you doing traveling around the countryside performing in saloons?"

"Having fun."

He laughed. "I saw a young man get off the stage with you this afternoon. Was he part of your company?"

"Oh, yes, Jonathan. A nice boy." She smiled. "He likes to pretend he's my protector when we're not onstage. Actually, he's a magician in the show."

"A magician? That ought to be interesting," Chance said.

Lily sighed. "Well, I hope the audiences here think so more than the last town we played."

"What happened?"

"One of the men in the audience didn't care for magic, I guess, and shot Jonathan's rabbit."

Chance frowned. "Shot his rabbit?"

"Yes. He pulls them magically from a hat he wears on-stage."

"Oh." Chance nodded slowly. "I see." But he didn't see at all. He was too busy trying to figure out how anyone could get a rabbit to sit still long enough to sit on someone's head and then be pulled magically out of their hat. He took a swallow of coffee and looked back at the woman sitting across from him. Her gown was an emerald satin, the same color as her eyes, its sleeves fitted to the curve of her shoulders to leave them bare. The neckline, plunging to a point most women would consider scandalously low but Chance liked, revealed a swell of ivory breasts.

Then again, Chance thought as his gaze lingered upon

her cleavage, who cared how you got a rabbit to remain still long enough to be pulled from a hat. He leaned forward to afford himself a better view of those ivory mountains.

"Would you allow me to escort you to the Garter tomorrow evening for your first performance?" Chance suggested.

She laughed lightly, the spark in her eyes attesting to the fact that she was totally aware of where most of his attention was riveted. "Why, Marshal, I not only would be honored to have you escort me to the Garter tomorrow evening, I would have been wildly disappointed if you hadn't asked."

T.J. stared through the window. She couldn't believe what she was seeing. Then again, she had no choice. They were right there, in front of her. Chance was sitting with the woman who had gotten off the stagecoach that afternoon, and if he wasn't about to do a nose dive into her cleavage, T.J. would eat her hat. Except that she wasn't wearing one. Her gaze settled momentarily on the woman, then jumped back to Chance. He was practically salivating.

Fury roiled in T.J.'s breast, intensifying with each second that passed.

Chance said something and the woman laughed. The sound drifted out through the open doors of the hotel and onto the night air. T.J. cringed. The woman's laugh sounded as fake as a three dollar bill. Fake and oh so sugary. T.J. threw her shoulders back and straightened. Well, if that's the kind of woman he went for, he was welcome to her. Spinning on her heel she stormed back to Doc's house, her intention to poke around and try and get a lead on Calder now driven from her mind by the marshal. What did she care if Chance Burkette was interested in some half-dressed actress? T.J. ground her teeth. He was nothing to her, absolutely nothing. She was attracted to him physically, but that didn't mean anything, or at least not much. She'd be out of here in a little while anyway and he'd be nothing but a bad memory.

So why are you so upset? a little voice in the back of her mind nagged.

"I'm not upset," she snapped aloud.

Yes, you are.

"No, I'm not."

A cowboy staggered out of the Red Garter Saloon and she brushed past him.

"Hey, who're ya talkin' to, lady?" the man called, just before falling off the boardwalk and landing in a sorry heap on the ground.

T.J. ignored him and stormed around the corner. Slamming open the gate in front of Doc's house she stalked toward the porch and entry door, then abruptly changed direction and made for the side of the house. She didn't feel like going inside. What good would it do anyway. She wasn't sleepy.

Moonlight bathed the landscape in a pale glow of silver light, sparkling off of windows, but leaving porches and doorways steeped in dark shadow. T.J. entered the small gazebo that was set just behind Doc's house. Its gingerbread design made it a startling contrast to the rather plane clapboard house. She flopped down on the narrow bench that was built in as part of its interior walls, crossed her arms over her chest and glared out into the night. Why was it that every time she began to care for a man she inevitably discovered he was a jerk? Most of the time they turned into jerks when they discovered she was a cop, but every once in a while they managed to make the transformation before she'd even told them that.

"Maybe it's just a natural chain of events with men," she mused. That made her laugh. "They can't help it."

For over an hour T.J. talked to herself, paced the small confines of the gazebo, stared up at the moon, and worked desperately to convince herself that she didn't care one whit what Chance Burkette did, said, or felt.

Once Doc looked out of his bedroom window and down into the yard. She'd seen him, realized her grumblings must have woken him up, and pressed herself farther back into the shadows of the gazebo. She didn't want company and if he saw her she felt certain he'd come down to make sure she was all right. She glanced up at his window a few minutes later and saw that he was no longer there.

"Well, maybe there's a few exceptions to men naturally turning into Neanderthals," T.J. mumbled.

Just before 2:00 a.m., her temper had cooled somewhat and her energy level had lowered. T.J. lay down on the wooden floor of the gazebo and stared through one of its open sides at the sliver of moon that shone down on the city of Tucson. Within minutes her eyelids drifted closed and she fell asleep.

An hour later, Chance, having left the Red Garter by its back door, started to cut across Doc's property and enter the house by the rear entrance. But as he passed the gazebo a soft mumbling caught his ear and he paused, suddenly alert. It would be just like Calder to sneak into town and ambush him. His hand went to his gun and drew it from its holster quickly, holding it out before him at the ready.

If it was an ambush, he hoped they hadn't already gotten Perkins.

Chance squinted hard and looked around at his surroundings. Nothing seemed out of place. His gaze came to rest on the gazebo and he stared at it long and hard, then moved out of line of its entrance and made his way slowly toward it, listening for the slightest sound.

A soft mumbling came from inside the delicate structure again.

Chance tensed, even though he realized now that the sound did not sound threatening, nor did it sound as if it had come from a male, though it could be a trap.

Crouching low he peered around the side of the entry. Moonlight cut a path through the middle of the gazebo, illuminating its planked floor. T.J. was curled up asleep in the center of the floor, half in, half out, of the moonlight. Chance let out a sigh of relief, straightened, and resheathed his gun. At the same time he found himself surprised to find her there. Stepping softly into the gazebo, he hunkered down beside her. As the first time he'd seen her, also lying on the ground, he marveled at her beauty.

Chance reached out a hand, intending to gently shake her shoulder to wake her, but rather than her shoulder, his hand moved toward her face. His fingers lightly, and gently, brushed several long locks of hair from her cheek, feeling the silk texture of each strand caress his flesh.

Why would such a beautiful woman marry someone like Gil Calder? The thought left Chance cold with contempt, both for her and the way of life she'd chosen. That she might not be Sue Ann Calder, or even if she was that she might not have willingly chosen an outlaw's way of life, were things he refused to consider.

His gaze took in the waves of chestnut hair that cascaded over her shoulder, glistening golden red in the moonlight, the delicate curve of her shoulder, and the saucy turn of her hip beneath the snug fitting trousers. As every other time he had been near her, Chance felt passion sweep through his body, a fiery heat edged with anger, and perhaps just a hint of jealousy.

His touch, tender though it was, startled T.J. into wakefulness. She had been dreaming about Chance, and his image remained in her mind for several seconds, until she looked up to see what had caused her to awaken. A scream caught in her throat as she looked up and saw the dark silhouette of a man hovering over her. She cringed away from him. Fear seized her in its grip and her heart thumped madly in her breast. Then, as her eyes became adjusted to the night, T.J. realized it was Chance kneeling over her.

She stared wordlessly up at him. The sensual dream she'd been having about him was shoved aside and all the anger she'd felt toward him only a few hours before returned twofold. An image of Chance in bed with Lily Monroe filled T.J.'s mind and fed the jealous fury she so wanted to deny existed within her. She pushed up onto her elbows and glared at him. "What are you doing here?" she demanded.

The words hung between them on the still night air, sharp and cold, but T.J. staunchly refused to say anything further to soften them. His presence had reignited not only her jealous fury, but also the guilt she felt over the fact that she'd done nothing since arriving in 1881 but swoon over him, when she should have been chasing down Gil Calder and saving her sister's life.

"That's not exactly the greeting I'd expected to get," Chance drawled, though if truth be told he hadn't truly known what to expect from her. He never did. She was an enigma, warm and seductive one minute, cold as ice and sharp-tongued the next. Why in hell he was so attracted to her was a mystery he doubted he would ever be able to solve.

"Haven't you had enough for one night, Marshal?" T.J. sneered, unable to help herself. "Or didn't your charms work?"

They were not the words she had wanted to say, but they'd sprang from her lips before she could stop them. And it was probably for the best anyway. He was a distraction to her purpose here, a very desirable distraction she'd admit, but a distraction all the same. "Leave me alone," she added, and began to turn away from him.

Instead of heeding her words, Chance jerked her around to face him and swept her into his arms. He wished to God he could leave her alone. It would have been the best thing for both of them, the smart thing, the logical thing. But it was the one thing he found himself no longer able to do. The hunger for her that was ripping at his insides was too much to ignore or deny. She wanted him too, he had seen it in her eyes earlier when he'd kissed her, felt it in her passion, and he'd seen it in her eyes again, just a second ago. If he had not, he would have been able to turn away from her gladly. But her desire was like a beckoning to his, it reached out its invisible tendrils, fanned the flames of passion within him, and teased his senses beyond belief. All of this, and more, her nearness did to him, until he could endure no more, until he could no longer deny his hunger for her, until he no longer wanted to.

"Witch," he breathed softly. His mouth descended on hers, capturing her lips quickly so that she would have no opportunity to utter a protest, but protest was the last thing T.J. wanted to do.

She could feel the hunger of need that held his body taut, and sense the pent-up passion that fired his embrace. His lips parted hers, urgently, hungrily, and his tongue filled her mouth, demanding her acquiescence, commanding a response from her as deep, as driving, as all consuming, as the one that held him within its grip.

Chapter Seventeen

T.J. reveled in the feel of his lips upon hers, of the sensuous caress of his tongue, the pleasure and security of once again being held within the strong, steely embrace of his arms. She felt the hardness of his body, the threatening eruption of his passion, the hunger that had driven him to her, and she rejoiced in it. Every cell in her body yearned to know the exultation of his touch, the ecstasy of his caress.

She had fought against this moment, told herself she couldn't let it happen, that it would only mean anguish for her later. But with one touch of his lips, those thoughts no longer mattered. Destiny had reached out to touch her twice: once when it had gripped her within its folds and transported her back in time, and now again, when it placed her in Chance Burkette's arms. Maybe neither would last forever, but she would deal with all that when it came. For now Chance was all she wanted.

Wrapping her arms around his neck, T.J. gave herself

up to him totally, returning his kiss and telling him with
her body what her lips had been unable to say.

His hands moved slowly, provocatively over her body,
slid along the curve of her waist, the gentle slope of her
hips, and small of her back. She felt one hand cup her
breast, its strong fingers encircling the tender flesh in a
rhythmic caress.

A moan of pleasure escaped her throat. A wave of fire—
intense, hot, and burning—swept through every fiber of
her body. His arm tightened around her, pulling her even
closer and instilling her soul with a hungry, aching longing
that she knew only he could placate.

He kissed her for a long time, and time stopped. The
world as T.J. knew it disappeared, and a new one unfolded
about her—a glorious, brilliantly colored world that was
full of warmth, love, joy, and Chance Burkette.

Slowly, achingly, he pulled his lips from hers and stared
down into her eyes. "I want you," Chance said softly. His
deep, rich voice reached out to wrap around her like a
warm velvet cloak. "I want you more than I've ever wanted
anything in my life."

T.J. reached a hand to the side of his face. "And I want
you," she whispered, "just as much."

A deep growl emanated from his throat and Chance's
lips descended upon hers again. His arms crushed her to
him in an embrace that took her breath away. Hard planes
fitted to soft curves and left not the slightest light of space
between them. His lips were warm and cajoling on hers,
his hands teasing and sensuous as they moved over her
body. Soon she was no longer capable of rational thought,
no longer even desirous of it. His kisses were unhurried,
yet urgent, gentle in their taking of her, yet savage in their
need to conquer, demanding her surrender, and begging
for her willing response.

She savored the warmth of his mouth on hers, the heat
of his hands as they roamed her body, and clung to him,

wanting to give more, wanting him to take from her whatever he needed, whatever he wanted. Her blood seethed with the fires of passion and her flesh rippled in a series of shivers at the euphoric ecstasy his every touch evoked.

His mouth moved to the long column of her throat, skipped in a trail of kisses that left her flesh branded by the fervor of his touch, and pressed the hollow of her throat. She locked her body tighter to his, needing to memorize the feel of him pressed against her, the force of his strength, his passion, his desire, so that she would never forget what it was like to be truly wanted.

His lips continued to tease her skin, the warmth of his breath wafting across her flesh to send a new series of shivers racing through her.

The sweet fragrance of the desert, the faint scent of leather, horseflesh and tobacco that clung to him, the smell and taste of whiskey upon his breath from the drink he'd had before coming to her, all combined to imprint themselves on T.J.'s mind and heart. She drank in the sweetness of his kiss, the rapture of his arms holding her to him, branding every touch, every caress upon her memory.

He slipped one hand up to cup her breast again. His fingers gently began to knead the swollen mound, while his thumb moved in a rhythmic circle over its taut nipple, both teasing and promising.

And then his hand was gone, and T.J. groaned in distress. His fingers adroitly released the buttons that held the front of her shirt closed and, his lips still holding hers his prisoner, he tenderly eased the shirt from her shoulders. The moment her arms were free of the fabric, she raised them to encircle his neck again.

Chance suddenly stiffened and pulled away from her. He stared down at her breasts, and as he did, a deep frown pulled at his brow.

T.J. felt suddenly embarrassed and hurriedly reached for her shirt.

"No," he said softly. He traced the lacy outline of her brassiere with the tip of his fingers.

Realization that women wore camisoles in 1881, not brassieres, suddenly struck her. She smiled. "It's something new," she lied.

Chance smiled. "I like it." He slipped the thin silk straps from her shoulders.

T.J. reached to the thin strap that spanned the width between each breast. "It hooks together here."

He fingered the hook and it snapped apart. "I like it," he said again, his voice husky with the emotion that coursed through him. He brushed aside the lacy contours and covered her breasts with his hands.

Smoldering desire burst into flame and a moan of pleasure slipped from between T.J.'s lips.

His mouth caught hers again, the urgency in his kiss, the need more powerful and evident than ever. One hand wrapped around her waist and pulled her fiercely up against him, while the fingers of his other hand softly caressed the now pebbled nipple of one breast.

His lips moved like a licking tongue of flame over hers, slid to touch her neck and followed the curve of her shoulder. Then, as he gently pushed her back to lie on the floor, his mouth descended upon first one breast and then the other, his lips caressing, his mouth tasting, his tongue teasing.

T.J. knew what it was to be with a man, to make love with him, but never before had she found herself swept into such a whirlwind of emotion, such a cavern of need and longing. Chance Burkette had unlocked a tempest of longing within her that she hadn't even known existed. He was the calm to her storm, the wind to her rain, the sun to her darkness.

All her life had been spent searching, waiting for Chance Burkette. She just hadn't known it.

T.J. felt his hands at her waist releasing the buttons of

her trousers. Placing the heel of one boot atop the toe of the other, she pushed first one, then the other from her feet as she felt the trousers slide down over her hips, then disappear from her legs altogether.

His hands explored her body intimately, thoroughly, leaving no curve untouched, no line uncaressed. They slid down the long arch of her back, traced circles upon her passion tight breasts, and moved with gentle exploration along the rising slope of her hips. Unable to help herself, T.J. moaned in pleasure.

"You're so beautiful," Chance murmured. His fingers teased a path of fire over her thighs, and taunted her with featherlight touches across the taut plane of her stomach.

With each stroke of his hands on her skin, T.J.'s body moved closer and closer to a pinnacle of ecstasy she had never experienced before. A need assailed her to indulge in the same type of exploration of his body as he was performing on hers. Pulling open the front of his shirt, she slipped one hand inside. Her fingers traveled over one smooth, hard pectoral muscle.

"Witch," Chance breathed against her neck. His lips brushed against hers, lightly, and then he pushed himself away from her and rose hastily to his feet.

Alarmed at the abrupt movement and thinking he meant to leave her, T.J. started and looked up at him, an entreaty ready on her lips. She relaxed instantly as she saw him jerk open the front of his shirt and strip it hurriedly from his body. His gaze never left hers.

T.J. watched him in fascination. It wasn't as if she'd never seen a man naked before, but Chance was different, he was special to her. He was beautiful, and there was no shyness in his movements, no modesty, but rather a bold pride and acceptance of who and what he was.

He peeled both vest and shirt from his shoulders and arms at the same time, revealing to her eyes what her hands had already discovered, rippling landscapes of sinewy muscle. His shoulders were broad and sweeping, resembling golden mountains of strength, his bronzed chest a granite wall, his arms well-honed ropes of steel. T.J.'s eyes followed him as one hand deftly released the buckle of his gunbelt while the other tugged loose the thin leather thong that held it bound to his right thigh. Snapping the belt around his body, he caught its ends in one hand, wrapped them around the holster, and laid it gently, almost reverently, on the bench nearby, out of her reach but not his.

He kicked off his boots, the spurs attached just above the wedged heels jingling as he pushed them aside, and then reached to unbutton his trousers.

T.J. felt the pounding of her heartbeat begin to accelerate as her anticipation rose with each movement he made. Nearly hypnotized now by the sight before her, T.J.'s gaze dropped to the tight line of his stomach, and then farther down, to the arousal that was evident beneath the snug fitting fabric. She watched as he pushed the trousers over his hips, let them slide down his long, lean legs and fall to the floor.

He could have looked no more magnificent to her if he were a god. Bathed in the glow of moonlight that shone through the entryway of the gazebo, the soft rays caressed his body and transformed it from mere mortal flesh and bone to that of a bronzed diety. He was an archangel: golden, good, and pure, and he was Lucifer: dark, alluring, and irresistible. Chance Burkette was the fulfillment of her daydreams, and the haunting of her nightmares. He was her fantasy. But now he wasn't a fantasy any longer, he was real.

Chance bent to join her on the floor, stretching out beside her and turning her musings into reality. He gathered her back into his arms.

T.J. snuggled close, content in the world she'd found with him, and never wanting to leave it.

Chance kissed her long and hard then, and as his mouth

ravaged hers, she continued the exploration of his body. Her hands moved over him in fascinated investigation, one finally sliding downward to slip tantalizingly through the patch of dark hair just below his stomach. Her fingers closed around the protruding organ that was hard, swollen and throbbing with his need of her. She felt him start at her touch.

"Sweet God in heaven," Chance swore softly, his hot breath sweeping past her ear.

His arms tightened their grip on her and his body shuddered with the rapture her stroking fingers instilled within him as they moved tauntingly along his length. With a muffled groan he moved so that he lay half on top of her. He kissed her again, his tongue slashing past her lips to fill her mouth and devour whatever sweetness he could find there. He had made love to many women, dozens of women whose names and faces he had long ago forgotten. But none of them had ever ignited the inferno of desire within him that her touch had brought to life. She was like an intoxicant to his blood, a narcotic to his senses, an aphrodisiac to his body.

Unable to wait any longer to know the full depth of her passion, Chance's hand slid between her legs and nudged them apart. His fingers slid through the chestnut triangle of silky hairs that grew at the apex of her thighs.

T.J. moaned at the flash of desire that swept through her as his fingers continued their assault on her, slipping between the sensitive folds of flesh beyond the small thatch of curls, and slowly, tantalizingly, caressing the small nub of sensuality nestled there.

His lips ravaged hers, merciless in their seige of her senses. His mouth swallowed her moans of pleasure as his hands aroused more, drawing out every wave of pleasure and straining to heighten every sweep of rapture.

T.J.'s entire body felt energized by a passionate need more stunning than any she had ever imagined. His caresses were sweet torture, his kisses exquisite torment, the magic he was rendering upon her body almost more than she could bear. Tightening her arms around his neck, her body writhing beneath him with a will of its own, needing to get closer, she drew in the scent of him, the redolence she knew, whatever happened, would always remind her of Chance Burkette.

Sensing she was on the verge of release, and knowing that he, himself, could wait no longer, Chance removed his hand from her. He raised his hips above her and propelled the pulsing organ she had earlier caressed between the thin folds of flesh his fingers had just deserted. His thrusts were urgent and demanding, each carrying him farther into a world of astonishing, all-consuming, passion he had visited with no other woman, a world he had not even been aware existed.

He cupped her buttocks with the broad span of his hand and brought her hips up to meet him as he delved into her again, filling her, teasing her hunger and heightening her need of him. All of his life he had dreamed of a woman like her: smart, strong, independent, and passionate.

"Chance," T.J. breathed, his name spoken as if an oath of love on her lips. "Chance," she whispered again, and arched her body up to meet the thrust of his. "Love me, Chance. Love me." Her fingers dug into his back as a wave of pleasure swept over her.

It was more than Chance could stand. He slammed into her then, pushing harder, deeper. He felt it building within them both. He rose above her, nearly groaned at the surge of desire that swept through him, and thrust back into her, taking them both hurtling over the precipice of ecstasy together, spiraling over the cliffs of fulfillment.

Each clung to the other, the force of their pleasure, the unearthly power of their euphoria, leaving them trembling in each other's arms, limbs entwined, breath ragged.

Long minutes passed as both reluctantly descended back

to earth, their bodies calming, their heartbeats and pulses slowing to a normal pace. Chance lay with his head nestled in the curve of her shoulder, the long tendrils of her red-gold hair a blanket beneath his ebony strands.

T.J. felt the warmth of his breath on her neck and on impulse reached over to trace the outline of his jaw with the tip of her finger.

Chance raised himself from her and rolled to lay on his back. The full impact of what he'd just done, of what he had allowed to happen between them, crashed down on him. He closed his eyes and silently called down a dozen curses on himself. He had known from the moment he'd seen her that he wanted her, but it would not have happened if he had done something to prevent it. He should have locked her up in the jail house, or left her at Doc's and moved himself there. But he hadn't. Instead, he had made love to her and perhaps lost a part of his heart to her forever. This, he thought, was what he deserved. She was Gil Calder's wife, and if for no other reason than that, she was forever forbidden to him.

T.J. lay still, but turned her head to look at Chance. She sensed that he was deep in thought, and the small frown she saw nestled between his brows gave her cause to believe he was troubled. A sense of sadness filled her and she ached to reach out to him, but she knew she shouldn't. She had allowed him to make love to her, and she had made love to him, and in the last few days she had lost a part of her heart to him. But he was a man from another era, and because she believed her stay in his time was only temporary at best, there could be no tomorrow for them, no future.

She had done neither of them a favor by allowing what had just happened between them. Yet she could not find it in herself to be sorry that it had, and if truth be told, she yearned for him to pull her into his arms again, to love her again. This could very well be the only time they had together, and she longed for it not to end.

But because of guilt or pride, she wasn't certain which, T.J. could not bring herself to be the one to prolong their time together.

Finally, after several more long and silent minutes, Chance rose and began to dress. He kept his eyes averted from T.J., his movements methodical and hurried.

She wanted to break the strain of tension that seemed to have settled between them, but she didn't know what to say.

Finally, when he sat on the bench to pull on his boots, he met her gaze. "I've got to make my rounds and then stop in at the hotel." He got up, reached for his holster, and slipped it around his hips.

At mention of the hotel, T.J. suddenly remembered having seen him there earlier with that actress, Lily Monroe. A wave of anger swept over her, as intense and burning as the passion he had aroused within her only moments ago, followed by deep, gnawing humiliation.

"Haven't you had enough for one night, Marshal?" she sneered, her tone cold and dripping with outraged sarcasm. "Or are you totally unsatiable?"

Chance stared down at her as she hurriedly grabbed her shirt and held it over her breasts in an attempt to cover her nakedness from his view.

"Insatiable for what?" he asked in puzzlement.

"I don't know about you," T.J. fumed, "but I don't happen to desire being one third of a *ménage à trois.*"

"A ménage à what?" Chance asked, totally dumbfounded now.

"Not now, in 1881," T.J. continued, not even hearing his interruption, "and not in . . ." She suddenly clamped her mouth shut at realization of what she'd been about to say.

"What the hell is a ménage à whatever you said?" Chance retorted, his own voice laced with impatience.

"A threesome, Mr. Burkette. Or wasn't Lily Monroe receptive to your advances tonight? Did she tell you to come back later?"

She knew the moment she'd said the words that she sounded like a jealous shrew, but it was too late to call them back. And anyway, she didn't want to. The thought of him leaving her to go back to that woman, or any other for that matter, sparked a jealous fire and aching agony within her breast that threatened to consume her.

"What the hell are you talking about?" Chance asked. His tone had taken on a harder edge than he'd intended, but in the few minutes he'd spent dressing, and thinking, he'd done a pretty good job of stoking the anger he felt at himself for what had just happened between them. And now she was babbling in an accusatory tone and he didn't have the faintest idea what the hell she was talking about.

"You," T.J. snapped. "And that actress."

"What?" Comprehension slapped him in the face and he stared down at her as if she'd lost her mind. "Let me get this straight, you think . . ."

T.J. glared up at him. "Don't act so innocent. I saw you with her."

"We had coffee."

"Good for you. Go have some more." T.J. grabbed her trousers and jerked them toward her.

"Thank you," Chance snapped. "Maybe I will." And with that, he turned and stormed into the night.

Chapter Eighteen

Chance walked into the hotel. The lobby was empty and there was no one behind the desk clerk's counter. Great. The way his evening was deteriorating it would be just his luck to find the desk clerk dead behind the counter and everyone else in the hotel murdered in their beds.

He walked to the counter and leaned over to peer behind it. Chance nearly sighed with relief, at no dead desk clerks down there. He slammed a hand down on the counter several times. The check-in registry bounced off the surface with each impact and the loud thuds reverberated through the empty room.

"Okay, okay," the clerk shouted from a back room. "Keep your pants on, I'm coming." He hurried from a rear doorway and into the lobby. Long strands of straight brown hair fell forward and dangled over his nose as he rushed toward the desk. He brushed them back with a bony hand and straightened the little square spectacles that sat perched on his beaklike nose.

"Oh, Marshal, I didn't realize it was you. Sorry." He

hastily straightened his shirt sleeves. "I was just taking inventory of the sheets."

"Find any missing?" Chance drawled.

"Huh?"

Chance cracked a smile he didn't really feel. It disappeared quicker than it had formed.

"You asked me to check back and make sure Curly Bill and Ringo weren't making any trouble."

"Oh, yes, I did, didn't I? Never do know what to expect from those two. Last time they were in town . . ." His eyebrows shot upward and he rolled his already bulging eyes. ". . . well, I only wish you'd been here then rather than up in Prescott. Maybe I wouldn't have had to buy new chairs for the lobby."

"Seems pretty quiet now."

"Yes, well, they haven't returned from the saloon yet. You wait, you just wait. It won't be quiet when those two come back."

Chance sighed. He had no intention of staying up all night waiting for Curly Bill and Ringo to either drink themselves into a peaceful stupor, or stagger back to the hotel to retire for the night. "Okay, well, listen, Jones, if they make any trouble you send someone down to Doc's place to get me and I'll be here in minutes, okay?"

The clerk shook his head. "Oh, no, Marshal, no. I mean, what if . . ." He paused and looked past Chance. His voice dropped to just above a whisper. "Oh, my goodness, here comes Curly Bill now."

Chance glanced over his shoulder. "Well, I'll be damned," he cursed softly under his breath. He turned back to the clerk. "Jones, I'm not here." Chance hurried around the desk and disappeared quickly through the rear door the clerk had appeared from only moments earlier.

Curly Bill, laughing loudly and with Lily Monroe on his arm, swaggered into the hotel. He paused at the desk. "Clerk, keys," he demanded.

Jones quickly handed him both the keys to his own room and those to Lily Monroe's room as well.

Curly Bill turned and handed the actress her room key, then swept a grey slouch hat from his head.

"Miss Monroe," he said, drawing the name out in a mocking tone and bending in a deep bow before her, his movement a deridingly exaggerated flourish of the courtly gesture. "It has been a pleasure meeting you, ma'am." He chuckled softly. "A real pleasure."

"Thank you, Mr. Brocious," Lily said, "for seeing me back to the hotel, and . . ." She smiled. "For being such a gentleman. I had no idea the streets of this little town could be so dangerous at night."

"Yes, terrible isn't it?" He laughed. "Don't know what's the matter with the law around here, letting riffraff like that loiter about and bother fine ladies like yourself."

"Yes, it is terrible. Well, goodnight, Mr. Brocious." She made as if to brush past him and move toward the stairs and, without looking at him, said, "Just remember what you're supposed to do." The words were spoken so softly that Chance nearly missed them.

He frowned and remained still behind the doorway. What was Curly Bill supposed to do for the actress? And what the hell was she doing with Curly Bill anyway? From their words it seemed as if they'd just met, that Curly had discovered her out on the street walking, obviously being bothered by someone, and escorted her back to the hotel. Very gentlemanly thing for Curly to do, very unusual. Gentlemanly was not exactly the word Chance would use to describe the cowboy, or the type of conduct he would expect from him.

Chance stepped from his hiding place as Lily disappeared up the stairs and Curly Bill left the hotel. Chance swore again. He did not need another mystery in his life or another problem. Once he was certain both were out of earshot, he turned back to the clerk, leaned his arms on the desk and glowered. "You hear Curly or Ringo talking about any kind of plans, Jones? Or where they figure on going when they leave Tucson?"

The clerk looked nervous. "Well, I heard them talking about the Earps once."

"Yeah, what'd they say?"

"That they were going to get them, is all."

Mixed emotions swirled Chance's chest. Relief came first. Dread immediately followed, along with anger. If Curly Bill and Ringo were really aiming to get the Earps, and hadn't been just spouting off, then that would mean they were planning on leaving Tucson and riding for Tombstone where the Earp brothers lived. That was good. On the other hand, knowing Curly and Ringo as he did, getting the Earps did not mean standing squared off with the brothers and fighting them fair. That was bad.

Chance was determined to send a message down to Wyatt. If he didn't already know about what Curly and Ringo were supposedly planning, at least he and his brothers would be warned. And Chance had heard Doc Holliday was in Tombstone with them. That put a big plus on the Earps' side of things. Doc was Wyatt's best friend and damned good with a gun, one of the best Chance had ever seen, maybe the best. But more important, he didn't have an ounce of fear in his veins.

Chance turned his attention back to the clerk. "What's Miss Monroe doing with Curly?"

Jones shrugged. "Got me, Marshal. They was talking in here earlier, after you had coffee with the lady, though kind of secret like, you know? Kept their voices low so no one could hear, I guess. They didn't know I saw them, and when they did notice me, they acted as if they were just exchanging the time of day."

Chance chewed on that information, but all it brought forth was the same question he'd started with: what was Lily Monroe doing with Curly Bill Brocious?

"Where's Ringo?" he asked the clerk.

"Hasn't come in."

"You already said that."

The clerk shrugged.

Chance turned to look out the door and across the street at the Red Garter. Ringo had been there earlier. Most likely he still was. The Garter was where most of the cowboys hung out when they were in Tucson, but since they weren't causing any trouble, Chance decided to leave things alone. There was enough trouble for him to take care of without him going in search of more. He looked back at the clerk.

"I'm calling it a night. If you need me for anything, send someone over to Doc's place and I'll come. Got it?"

"But I don't have anyone to send. I mean, I'm on duty tonight alone."

"Then come yourself."

The clerk nodded but didn't look at all reassured.

Chance walked out onto the street and glanced around. The night sky overhead was a blanket of black velvet, fathomless and impenetratable. The stars were like diamonds sprinkled across its dark surface, and the sliver of moon that hung low on the horizon was a crescent of faded silver. He inhaled deeply, filling his lungs with clean night air. Summer days in Tucson were hotter than hot, but at night, when the sun went down, the air cooled, but sometimes took its time doing it.

He glanced down the street toward Doc's house but made no move to step from the boardwalk and cross the street. If he tried to lie down and catch some sleep now all he'd do was stare wide-eyed up at the ceiling. Chance pulled a cheroot from his shirt pocket, along with a box of lucifers and, leaning against a pillar in front of the hotel, slipped one end of the thin cigar between his lips.

Maybe Curly would appear again and he could follow him and get a clue about what the man was up to and whatever it was he was supposed to do for Lily Monroe.

Chance scraped the tip of the lucifer against the pillar and the match burst into flame. Cupping it between his hands, he raised it to the cheroot and puffed several times, drawing flame to tobacco. He flicked the match into the street, watching as it arched upward, then fell toward the earth like a shooting star, its glow dissipating on its downward spiral.

Suddenly a movement across the street, just in front of the window of the Red Garter caught his attention. Chance stiffened, momentarily unable to believe what it was his eyes were seeing. It couldn't be her. She couldn't be that stupid again. He watched as she turned into the alcove that housed the red swinging doors and disappeared through them into the saloon. Or was she being stupid? Maybe she was being crafty.

He threw the cheroot to the ground and stepped from the boardwalk. Maybe that little scene he'd witnessed the day before in the saloon, between her and Ringo had been staged just for his benefit, to throw him off. His temper flared. And that's exactly what it had almost done. He stopped at the swinging doors but didn't push them open to enter. If he did go inside they'd see him, and then would most likely just put on another show for his benefit. Chance quickly stepped back into the shadows and moved to stand beside the window. It didn't afford him the best view of the saloon's interior, but it would have to do.

T.J. met Ringo's gaze and fought to hang on to the cool facade she had assumed at entering the saloon and approaching him.

"I told you what I wanted," she repeated. Hopefully her tone did not reveal the nervousness that was flitting through her veins and turning her stomach into quaking jelly. Just pretend you're undercover, she kept telling herself, at the same time trying to ignore the fact that she had

no weapon and no backup waiting to rescue her if she got
into trouble she couldn't handle.

"Calder," Ringo said. He stared up at her and smiled,
the gesture having the opposite impression on his face
than it should have had. Rather than warmth, it showed
hard, calculated coldness.

T.J. fought not to shiver under his gaze. He was a very
handsome man, but the iciness that shone perpetually
from his eyes, and obviously dwelled within his veins, tar-
nished any attraction his looks might have garnered. "Yes,
Calder," T.J. said again.

"Tell me, Red," Ringo drawled insolently, "why is a
pretty little thing like you . . ." His eyes raked over her
brazenly, stripping off every fold and thread of fabric from
her body as they moved up and down her. "Interested in
finding Gil Calder?"

"Why is an obviously educated man like you running
around being an outlaw and killer?"

The coldness in his eyes hardened further, and T.J. realized, too late, she should not have challenged him.

"You answer me first, Red," Ringo ordered. His gaze
bored mercilessly into hers. "Unless you'd like to trade
me for the information."

His insinuation was blatant and clear. T.J. bristled inside.
Her hand ached to slap his face, but she held herself steady
and calm.

"I told you," she said, "my brother left home several
months ago and said he was going to ride with Calder. I
have to find my brother. It's important. Now." T.J. assumed
an impatient pose and forced herself to ignore his lewd
gaze. "Can you tell me where Gil Calder is or not?"

Ringo's smile widened and turned, if possible, even more
crafty and lewd. "Sure, I can tell you." He smiled. "If I
want to. What's it worth to you, Red?"

"Maybe your life," she snapped.

Ringo started. The smile immediately disappeared from his face as he jerked to his feet and glared down at her.

"I doubt if Gil Calder will take kindly to you, Mr. Ringo," T.J. said, "when he finds out that I had important information for him and he didn't get it because you wouldn't tell me how to find him." She struggled to meet his glare. "Or take me to him," she added. T.J. clenched her hands into fists to hide their trembling. She hadn't done a whole lot of undercover work up to this point, but she was quickly realizing she didn't like it, especially when she wasn't armed and had no one standing by to rescue her if things got ugly.

"Information such as what?" Ringo challenged.

"I can't tell you. It's only for Calder."

Ringo shrugged, pulled his hat down lower on his forehead and resumed his seat. "Then I guess you aren't going to find him, are you, Red?"

"Fine. Have a nice funeral, Mr. Ringo," T.J. snapped. "And the name's not Red." She stalked around him and headed for the door.

"Be back here tomorrow night, Red," Ringo called after her. "Midnight."

She paused and looked back. His hat, a brown Stetson with a hatband of small silver conchos, was pulled down to shade his eyes, but it was not enough to obscure the hatred that blazed from their depths.

T.J. shivered and bolted for the door. Riding out into the desert with him was not something she was looking forward to, but there was no other way. First however, she had to get her hands on her gun.

Chance watched her talking with Ringo, but he had no idea what it was they were discussing. Piano music, clinking glasses, jingling coins and loud conversation and laughter were all he could hear. It was obvious, however, that whatever she was saying to Ringo, he didn't like. Other than being deadly with a gun, the cowboy had a thirst for women and a hot temper. Chance had noticed the lewd expression on Ringo's face when she'd first approached him. He'd watched it just as quickly turn to an angry glare when she'd evidently turned down his advances, and then to a mean glower when he'd bolted to his feet. Whatever she'd said to him, it wasn't an invitation to her room.

He looked about quickly to see if anyone sitting near Ringo was someone he could trust to tell him what the conversation had been. There was no one. Every man close enough to have heard was a cowboy. Then his gaze fell on Perkins. He hadn't expected to see the young sheriff in the saloon, or even out and about town this late, so he hadn't noticed him before. He was leaning over a nearby table, talking earnestly with one of the whores. Chance hurriedly stepped into the alleyway to one side of the Garter when he noticed T.J. storming away from Ringo's table. The darkness quickly swallowed him.

She hurried past. Once certain that she was gone, Chance stepped out of the alley and back onto the board-walk. He looked through the Garter's window again. Perkins was on his way toward the door.

"Eli," Chance called softly, the minute Perkins pushed past the swinging doors.

The young sheriff spun around and crouched low, his hand automatically going for his gun.

"Relax," Chance drawled. "It's just me." He remained in the shadows, preferring not to make a target of himself for anyone else by stepping into the light that streamed from the saloon's window onto the street. Too many law officers got themselves shot by not watching their backs. Someday Eli Perkins would learn to be more cautious. Hopefully before it was too late.

"Oh, sorry." Eli straightened and visibly relaxed, the flash of fear Chance had seen light his eyes subsiding slowly. "Can't be too careful, you know. Especially when someone comes up at your back."

"Yeah. Maybe you ought to think a little more about not showing it around too often."

"Well, I—"

"Listen, Eli," Chance said, cutting off the man's excuses, "you were just in the Garter."

"Yes, I was." Eli's face turned red. "But it's okay, Marshal, I mean my wife, well, she knows. No, I mean, she doesn't know that, I mean there isn't anything like that to know, but—"

"I'm not judging you, Eli. I don't give a damn what you do. I just need to know—"

"But it's not what you think, Marshal," Eli said hurriedly. "Really. I swear. I mean, I wasn't trying to . . . I mean, that girl, she isn't, well, I mean she is but, you see, she's my sister."

Chance frowned, exasperated by the sheriff's rambling conversation and momentarily thrown by Perkins' statement. "Who's your sister?"

"That whore." Perkins shook his head as if in denial of his own words. "No, no, I mean, she's not a whore. I mean, well, she is but, well, you gotta understand, things went bad between her and her husband and, well, she didn't—"

"Perkins," Chance interrupted, in dire jeopardy of losing control of both his patience and his temper.

"I mean, well, what I'm trying to say is that Maggie, that new girl in the saloon, the blonde one, well, she's my sister."

"Right. Good." Chance's attention shifted back to his own problem. "Listen, Eli, you were standing pretty close to Ringo in there."

"Yes, I know. I guess I shouldn't have, him being a cowboy and all. I mean, well—"

"And he was talking with that woman that's staying at Doc's place."

"The one you think is Sue Ann Calder, right?" Eli brightened as the conversation turned away from him. "She sure is pretty, Marshal. Plucky, too. Wonder why she hooked up with someone like Gil Calder?"

"Yeah, who knows. Did you hear what they said? What they were talking about?"

"Well, some," Perkins said. Eagerness lit his face. "I didn't hear it all though cause I was talking with Maggie, my sister, but I think she, that woman, Sue Ann, I mean, not Maggie . . ."

Chance's jaw clenched with the flash of impatience that swept through him but he remained silent. He knew from experience that if he tried to rush Perkins, the young sheriff would just get flustered and take even longer to say what he was trying to spit out.

"Well, I can't be sure, Marshal, I mean I didn't hear everything they said, you know, but it sounded like she mentioned a brother."

"A brother?"

"Or was it mother?" Perkins' entire face screwed into a thoughtful frown, then instantly cleared. "No, I'm almost sure she said brother. And, well, she also said, I mean, it was kind of noisy in there and all, and Maggie and I were talking, too, and I really wasn't listening to her, that woman, but I think she said something about wanting Ringo to take her to wherever Calder is."

"Take her?" Chance repeated, thoroughly puzzled and quickly losing the frail grip he had on his patience. "Take her, or escort her?"

Perkins shrugged.

"Did it sound like she didn't know where Calder was?"

Perkins shrugged again. "Couldn't say, Marshal. I mean, well, sorry."

"Damn it all to hell, Perkins," Chance growled. "Sorry

doesn't do me a cow's tail worth of good." He saw the injured look that immediately swept over the young sheriff's face at his outburst and tried to soften his tone. "Okay. What did Ringo say to her?"

Perkins brightened. "Oh, I heard that real clear. She was walking away, leaving the saloon, I guess, and he called out to her to come back to the Garter tomorrow night. He said for her to come back at midnight."

"Midnight," Chance repeated absently. He felt as if someone had punched him in the gut, and that surprised him almost more than what Perkins had just told him. Somewhere, deep down inside himself, he'd wanted to believe he was wrong about her, that she was telling the truth when she denied being Sue Ann Calder. But now that tiny spark of hope was gone. For some reason she felt she needed Ringo to escort her back to wherever it was Calder was hiding.

An idea came to Chance. Maybe she was afraid he'd follow her and she needed Ringo to help her throw him off—or ambush him. He pulled himself up, visibly drawing back his shoulders, straightening his spine, and resting his right hand on the butt of his gun. "Be here tomorrow night at eleven," he said to Perkins.

"Eleven," the sheriff repeated, and nodded. "What are we gonna do?"

"I'll let you know." Turning on his heel Chance began to walk toward Doc's house.

Chapter Nineteen

Chance stood at the window of Henry Witherspoon's general store and watched the late morning traffic on the town's main street. He'd only caught a few hours sleep on a cot in one of the jail cells, and he felt like hell. But he hadn't wanted to return to Doc's and face her again. Anger, regret, and hurt churned within him. He'd been a fool, a damned, first class fool, but it was too late now to change that, and he had a job to do. Chance cursed softly, gave himself a silent command not to think about her again unless it was in respect to catching Gil Calder, and took a long swallow of coffee from his cup.

It was Saturday, the day most of the ranchers and farmers came into town for supplies, mail, and a little fun. Tonight the town would be wild, not only with the ranchers and farmers, but with wranglers, drovers, and, if luck was running against him, he had no doubt more cowboys would show up in Tucson tonight.

"Need anything else, Marshal?" Henry Witherspoon

said from behind the counter on which he'd just piled the articles Chance had requested.

Chance was just about to turn from the window and answer the store owner when a sight across the street drew and held his attention instead. It had been a reflection of the sun sparking off of her chestnut mane that had drawn his eyes to her, the long, wavy strands cascading down her back gracefully, and bouncing softly as she walked. The trousers she wore, an old pair of Doc's probably, hugged her legs snugly to reveal every curve and line, while a white shirt, tucked into the pants, proved a striking contrast to both the pale golden hue of her skin and the rich strands of her red-gold hair.

His gaze fixed itself to her waist. "Damn it all to hell," he muttered to himself seeing the gunbelt strapped about that narrow breadth.

T.J. walked confidently down the boardwalk. After Doc had left the house earlier that morning, and she'd finished doing a little cleaning for him, she'd decided to search for her gun again. She'd finally found her weapon and holster tucked into the armoire in the spare room, the last place she'd looked. T.J. absently nibbled on her bottom lip. She knew the gun and holster, or rather their modern design, were out of place. They were oddities in this time, but she needed them, and she'd done her best before leaving the house to make her holster look more acceptable. She'd removed the handcuffs, the loop for her club, and the little pocket that a can of red pepper could slip into. She'd thought about cutting off the tiny leather ammunition box too, but realized then she'd have to carry the spare bullets in her pocket, and she didn't want to do that.

The gun itself she could do nothing about. It looked odd, and there was no way to change that. Of course, if she didn't have to draw her gun, no one would see how truly different it was from theirs. That was a big if, however, especially considering whom she was dealing with.

It made T.J. shiver with fear to think of dealing with Curly Bill Brocious and Johnny Ringo, two of the bloodiest outlaws to mar Arizona's history. She cursed herself. If she'd paid more attention in her state history class, particularly to the history of the Old West, she might have a better idea how to proceed now, maybe even where to find Gil Calder. T.J. had never been one to bring home good grades from school, and that included her history grades. But there was no help for it now.

She paused and glanced around. Doc had given her a couple of dollars that morning before he'd left, saying she could pay him back later. Squinting into the glare of the sun, which was almost straight overhead, T.J. looked over the various buildings, reading the names painted on their signs.

Doc had said she could get just about anything she needed at Witherspoon's General Store. She caught sight of it almost directly across the street from where she stood. She also caught sight of something, or rather someone, else. Lily Monroe.

The fires of jealousy sparked to life deep within T.J., as did her curiosity. She knew she should ignore the impulses churning within her, but she couldn't. How many people actually got an opportunity to experience life in another time and meet the people there. When and if she got back to her own time she'd be able to look up Lily Monroe in the history books and know that she had actually met the woman.

She stared long and hard at the actress. If she returned to her own time, and did look in the history books, would she find that Chance had married Lily Monroe? The idea brought a wave of jealousy rushing over her, along with instant dislike of Lily Monroe. She wasn't his type. She was an actress. She couldn't make him happy. She—

"Stop it," T.J., she whispered harshly to herself. "You're being ridiculous."

T.J. forced herself to cross the street and intercept the woman.

"Hello," she called out. "Miss Monroe?"

Lily Monroe paused, turning so that she could peer around the edge of the pale pink lace and ruffled parasol that rested upon her shoulder and shaded her from the morning sun. She looked at T.J. and frowned.

"I'm sorry, do I know you?"

T.J. smiled and held out her hand.

"No, Miss Monroe, you don't. My name's T.J. McAllister, I'm a . . ." A what? She thought frantically. Seeing a reflection of herself in the window of the barbershop they stood in front of, she realized just how out of place she appeared, especially standing beside the ultrafeminine looking actress. "I'm a friend of Marshal Burkette's."

She dropped her hand back to her side when it became obvious Lily was not going to shake it.

"Oh," Lily said, "a friend of Marshal Burkette's." Her gaze swept over T.J. "That's nice."

"Yes." T.J. suddenly felt at a lack for words. She shouldn't have approached her.

"Miss . . . McAllister, is it?"

"Yes, T.J."

"I was just on my way down to Lannie Kay's Restaurant for a bite to eat. Would you care to join me?"

T.J. hesitated only a second. All she needed to do today was buy enough supplies to tide her over for a few days out on the desert, procure a horse and gear, then wait until midnight to meet Ringo. She had only eaten a biscuit spread with jam and a cup of coffee for breakfast. Logic told her to accept the invitation and eat. It could be her last hot meal for a while. She smiled. Then she'd also be able to learn a little more about Lily Monroe. She tamped down the heat of jealousy that still smoldered within her breast. "Yes, thank you, Miss Monroe, I think I'd like very much to join you."

Falling into step beside her, T.J. walked with Lily to the restaurant, then sat across from her at a small table near the window.

"So, Miss McAllister, tell me, what do you do?" Lily asked, once their breakfast of scrambled eggs, sausage and biscuits had arrived.

"Do?" T.J. echoed. The fork she held with a blob of scrambled eggs balanced on its tines stopped midway to her mouth. She stared stupidly at Lily Monroe.

"Yes, you know, for a living: ranch, farm?" Lily laughed lightly. "Rob, rustle?"

"Oh, do," T.J. said. "I, uh, do a lot of, uh, different things." Her mind raced for a more logical answer. "I travel around a lot and do odd jobs here and there, if you know what I mean."

Lily's eyes dropped pointedly toward the gun and holster at T.J.'s waist. "So I gathered." She munched daintily on a piece of butter smeared biscuit, then looked at T.J, her gaze direct. "But you said you were a friend of Marshal Burkette's?"

"Well, yes, but not close."

"Umm," Lily smiled. "He's a very handsome man."

"Yes," T.J. said, her tone cool. "If you like overbearing, extremely stubborn and bull-headed men."

Lily laughed. "Oh, that doesn't sound appealing at all." She took a bite of her biscuit, stared for several seconds out the window and then turned back to T.J. "Does the law ever, umm, interfere with your odd jobs, T.J.?"

"Uh, sometimes." She remembered what had happened just after her sister's murder. Captain Lemke, her supervisor, had ordered her to stay away from her sister's case. She was too emotionally involved, he'd said, and would get the department slapped with a harassment suit before they were ready to arrest Jake Calder. She argued and pleaded with him, but it had done no good.

"Maybe I could help you find a job," Lily offered. "I have a few friends around the countryside who are always looking for a good hand."

"Well, I'm not really looking for a job right now," T.J. said. "I've kind of got someplace I have to go. I'll be leaving town tonight."

"Oh, that's too bad."

"Yes, but I, well, I just wanted to meet you."

"The pleasure is all mine, T.J.," Lily said. A rather sly smile curved her lushiously full pink lips. "But, tell me, where are you headed tonight?"

T.J. and Lily Monroe remained in the restaurant for two more hours, sipping coffee and chatting amiably. To anyone watching it would have seemed as if the two women were very good friends.

Chance stood in the kitchen of Lannie Kay's, making sure to remain well enough away from the door that led into the dining room so that he couldn't be seen. He watched T.J. and Lily Monroe intently.

A scrawny little waitress scurried back into the kitchen after serving a couple of miners sitting at the table next to the women.

"What are they talking about, Celia?" he asked her.

"You."

Chance turned, startled, and stared down at her. Celia was a tiny bird of a woman, with a face to match that description. No one knew where she came from, or who her people were. Some said her husband was an outlaw, others that she was a widow. Still others claimed she was a reformed whore. No one knew for sure and no one really cared. What they did know and care about, was that she was the best waitress Lannie Kay had ever had, and one of, if not the best cooks. She made all the desserts for the restaurant.

"What the hell do you mean, me?" Chance ground out in a low tone. "They've been at it now for over two hours."

Picking up another tray of food, Celia turned her brown eyes on him.

"Well, I can't say they been talking about you all that time, Marshal, 'cause I've got customers to take care of you know, but I mean just what I said. Right now anyways, they're talking about you."

"Me," Chance repeated.

"Well," Celia said, smiling, "I didn't really hear their conversation now, you know. Old Anson there was bending my ear about his new claim, but I did hear them mention your name. Maybe one of them's looking for a husband and they think you're cute."

"Yeah, right," Chance growled. He'd have given just about anything to be able to hear their conversation. He peeked around the doorway. T.J. was sitting with her back to him, but he'd have known that long chestnut mane anywhere. Thoughts of her body pressed to his, naked and hot, her curves perfectly melding to him, filled his mind.

"Damn it all to hell," he murmured.

"Something wrong, Marshal?" Celia asked.

"Huh? No."

He hadn't even been aware he'd spoken aloud. Chance turned his attention back to the two women in the dining room. Last night he'd been a fool, a first-class fool. Hell, he was worse than a first-class fool. They could bronze him and show him off to the world as the number one, all-time champion fool.

From the things he'd heard about Sue Ann Calder, he was probably damned lucky to be alive. He stared at her back. What the hell did Sue Ann Calder and an actress named Lily Monroe have in common anyway? Or was this even the first time they'd met? His mind spun off on a tangent of suspicion. Was Lily Monroe part of the Calders scheme? Another scout perhaps? But, if that were the case, why would both women come to scout out the same town at the same time? Or had Sue Ann been on her way elsewhere when he'd brought her here? Tombstone, maybe?

Chance found his temper heating. He didn't like questions without answers, speculation without explanation.

Thoughts of his brothers, Morgan and Rick, came to his mind then. If something went wrong here in town, if he made a move that wasn't right, especially if that move was with Sue Ann Calder, he could be putting their lives in jeopardy and not even be aware of it.

He turned and walked toward the rear door. "Thanks, Celia, Lannie Kay," Chance threw over his shoulder. "See you later." He hadn't heard from either Morgan or Rick in weeks, and now he had Sue Ann Calder in town, and in his bed, along with the mystery of who the hell Lily Monroe really was. Was she someone other than who she claimed to be? And then there was that little ditty he'd heard the actress say to Curly Bill. It was all turning into one great big puzzle.

Chance swore. He hated puzzles.

He had to rethink his plan now, rework it. Chance made for the livery. If, as Doc had suggested earlier that morning when they'd had coffee together, she was still asking lots of questions about Gil Calder, and now some about Johnny Ringo and Curly Bill, then he could very well be wrong about her. If that were true, it would, on one hand make him feel better. At least he wouldn't have to deal with being attracted to Calder's wife. On the other, it would make him feel worse for the way he'd treated her, and the fact that then he was left nowhere as far as catching the Calders was concerned.

Then again, maybe that's exactly what they'd planned— to confuse him. Maybe the Calders were smarter, cagier, than he'd given them credit for. Could they have already found out about Morgan and Rick? He nearly groaned aloud at that. If Calder had discovered the truth about his brothers, Chance had no doubt the reason he hadn't heard from them was because they were dead.

He walked past the open doors of the livery and into its shaded interior. "Peter," he said to the blacksmith. "I might have to leave town for a while tonight."

The burly man nodded and released the handle of the huge bellows he'd been pulling. Without a glance toward Chance he grabbed an iron pincher, plunged it into the bed of hot coals below the bellows and retrieved a horseshoe.

"Tell Markus to saddle up Diablo after supper, would you, Peter? Along with a couple of blankets, a duster, and extra ammunition. And tell him to pack enough grub in my saddlebags to last me three or four days."

The blacksmith nodded again, pounded a hammer several times atop the horseshoe, then turned and plunged the curved piece of metal into a barrel of cool water. Steam bubbled up from the churning surface.

The man wiped a soot covered wrist over his sweaty forehead and nodded again.

Chance backed away quickly. "Say hi to Billy for me." He turned and left the livery. With that taken care of, there was nothing left to do but wait. He walked back out into the sunlight, then another idea struck him. There was something going on between Sue Ann and that actress, Lily Monroe, and there was something going on between Lily Monroe and Curly Bill. Sue Ann had gone to the Red Garter and approached Ringo twice. Were they all in this together? Whatever this was.

Lifting his hat slightly, Chance ran a hand through his hair, resettled the Stetson, and walked slowly down the street, his spurs tinkling merrily, the sound in direct contrast to his darkening mood.

Several hours later he knew exactly where everyone was. Lily Monroe had returned to her hotel. According to the hotel desk clerk, Ringo hadn't even gotten out of bed for the day yet. And Chance had spotted Curly Bill sitting in Mary Ellen's brothel with a whore propped solidly on his lap.

And then there was Sue Ann. Chance stood across the street from Witherspoon's General Store. As before, his attention was drawn by the golden red color of her hair as the late afternoon sun shone on it. She was near the window, looking at something on the counter. Good. This was the opportunity he'd been waiting most of the afternoon for. Chance walked hurriedly to Doc's house. Maybe there was something more, something that they'd overlooked, hidden in her things, in one of the pockets of that outfit she'd had on when he found her, that would tell him for sure what she was up to.

It only took a few seconds to go through the pockets of her trousers. There was nothing in them. Then he remembered Doc had said they were dirty and torn when Chance brought her in and he'd had Mrs. Reilly wash and sew them. He grabbed the trouser's matching shirt off another hook.

"Just what do you think you're doing?"

Chance spun around to face her. His eyes went directly to the gun she held in her right hand, and pointed at him. Gold pink rays from the setting sun streamed through the room's lone window and cast her in a soft haze of light. Desire instantly fought to overtake him, but he immediately and coldly squelched it. This was definitely not the time for such ridiculous emotions. Fury at himself for being caught off guard, for not sensing her approach at his back, burned within him instead. He'd been careless and that could get him killed.

"My job," he growled. "Now either put that damned thing away or go ahead and kill me."

"Don't be in such a hurry," T.J. retorted, "I haven't decided which to do yet."

He threw her shirt onto the bed.

"Why are you here?"

His gaze bore into hers, and his tone, hard and accusatory, held none of the gentle drawl, the deep seduction it had possessed when he'd made love to her.

Her brows arched upward and her own tone turned haughty.

"I believe this is my room."

"You know what I mean," Chance snapped. "Why are you in Tucson? What do you want?"

"You brought me here, remember?"

He didn't answer, but merely scowled at her, waiting for a better answer.

T.J. sighed. "You wouldn't believe the truth even if I told it to you."

"Try me," Chance challenged.

T.J. considered it for one brief flash of a second, then just as quickly discounted the idea. He wouldn't believe her, she didn't doubt that for a second. And it would most likely only make matters worse. Though she wasn't sure how much worse they could get unless she got herself locked up as a crazy person, which was probably exactly what would happen if she tried to convince Chance she came from over a century in the future.

All she'd managed to accomplish so far was to antagonize Chance and then idiotically fall into his arms, and get Johnny Ringo, whom she thought of as Mr. Sleaze, to agree to take her to see Calder. Of course, she wasn't sure she could trust Ringo. For all she knew he could be planning to guide her just far enough out of town to rape and kill her without anyone knowing. But she had to go through with this. She had to get to Calder. It was her only chance to save Lisa, and since Chance didn't seem to be preparing to go after Calder any time soon, Ringo looked like her best and only—bet.

She reholstered her gun. "If you've finished going through my things, Marshal, I think I'd like to lie down for a while before I prepare Doc's dinner. Uh, supper," she corrected herself, remembering that lunch was called dinner and dinner was called supper. The word lunch didn't seem to exist in 1881. She stood to one side of the doorway to allow him to leave her room.

"Now, if you'll please excuse me?"

Chance started to brush past her. He'd found nothing among her things to tell him one way or the other if his suspicions about her were right.

If he was lucky, later this evening Lily Monroe would be out and about town and he could search her room. The desk clerk could stall her in the lobby if she came back before he finished. Chance paused before T.J. as she stepped to one side of the open doorway to allow him to pass. He looked down at her. "Sorry," he mumbled, not even sure why he said it.

Her eyes rose to meet his. In direct contrast to the stony set of her features, the bravado and confidence he'd heard in her tone, he recognized softness, warmth, and fear in the deep green pools, and found himself unable to move away from her. Suddenly he saw in her eyes that her thoughts were speeding along the same path as his, remembering what had happened between them only a few short hours before, wanting it to happen again and afraid that it would.

"Tell me where he is," Chance said, his voice husky with the raw emotion that churned through his veins. "Turn him in, and you can go your own way, Sue Ann. Lead me to him, or lead him to me, and you can go free. I promise."

The words slipped from his tongue almost without his awareness. He had never made a deal with an outlaw before, and he'd never wanted to, never even been tempted to. But an image of Yuma Prison formed in his mind: ugly brown adobe walls and barred windows, tiny cells and a barren yard. Its walls imprisoned several dozen robbers, rustlers, and murderers who would just as soon kill a man as look at him.

What would they do to a woman locked in their midst?

Chance didn't want to know. The idea of her ending up there, of knowing that she was wasting away behind those adobe walls, and that he was the one who had sent her there, was more than he could bear to dwell on.

T.J. returned his penetrating gaze.

"I can't tell you what I don't know, Marshal."

"Damn it, Sue Ann, you'll end up in prison," Chance snarled.

He knew he shouldn't care one way or the other where she ended up, but he did, damn it. He grabbed her arm, his fingers curling about it like steel claws. "You'll spend the rest of your life in Yuma Prison, behind brick walls and windows with iron bars on them. Is that what you want?"

She jerked free of him, angered and hurt that he still thought of her as Sue Ann Calder.

"Leave me alone, Chance," T.J. said. She turned to move away from him and into the room but he stepped to block her path.

Lisa. She had to do this for Lisa. Calder, that's all she could think about, getting to Calder. There was no room in this situation for anything more between her and Chance.

Against her will she felt the sensual sparks igniting between them again, became conscious of the irresistible attraction he held for her. She was hypersensitive to his lean, hard body, so close she could feel its warmth.

Memory assailed her of what it had felt like to be loved by him, to have his strong hands on her breasts, his long legs entwined with hers, his need buried deep within her. She knew that the same thoughts that had suddenly assaulted her had also surfaced in his mind. It was evident in the darkening of his eyes, sky blue turning to deep indigo as they continued to stare down at her from beneath the black Stetson. She saw it in the slant of his mouth, the slight twitch that pulled at the vein in the side of his neck, and the tiny frown that burrowed itself upon his forehead, pulling the black brows closer together.

T.J. fought against the feelings swelling to life within her. This was wrong. She hadn't been sent back here for him, or for anything to happen between them. It was for Lisa. She was here so that she could save her sister. But she couldn't deny what she felt for Chance Burkette anymore than she could deny herself breath.

She stared up at him, wanting to run, to flee from him, but unable to move. The soft sunbeams that shone, filtered, through the window's lace curtain turned the hollows of his cheeks to slopes of shadow, the rigid curve of his cheekbones to inclines of bronze, the black mustache to a shield of ebony that shadowed and partially hid the lips that, with one touch to hers, had the power to instill her body with flame.

Another time, another place, and things could have been so different for them. Why did it have to be like this? Why had they been born to two such different worlds? The anguish of longing and regret filled her. She could, at any time, be pulled back to her own world, to her own time. And he would remain here, only a memory to her, and maybe a few small lines in a history book somewhere. Would it be so terrible to love him just once more? To feel the rapture his kisses brought her, the ecstasy she might never feel again once they were forever separated?

Chance was conscious of the exact moment her defenses against him began to crumble. He knew he should retreat, knew he should get away from her as fast as he could and stay away. He should merely watch her, and once she met with Ringo, he should follow them. They'd lead him to

Calder, and then he'd have the revenge he had sought for so long. But he didn't want it to happen that way. Not any longer. He didn't want to follow her, to remain in the shadows and sneak after her. He wanted her to help him, willingly. He wanted her to save herself. Yet she had spurned his offer of help. That was all he could offer. And more than he should have.

His gaze dropped momentarily to the shirt that fit snugly about her breasts, his mind and body more conscious of her nearness, of her tantalizing curves, than of the danger he might be counting. He had slept little in the past three years since Gil Calder had killed his parents, wife, and child. He had slept even less since she had appeared only a few days ago.

Long lashes fluttered down quickly over her eyes, obscuring them momentarily from his view. He felt a flash of searing heat invade his groin. She looked up at him again, and Chance found himself near mesmerized by the deep, forest green eyes that had haunted his every waking and sleeping moment since the day he'd found her on the canyon floor. That she held him in some kind of spell, that she had the power to ignite his desires almost beyond his control, enraged him. That she was Gil Calder's wife incensed him.

She obviously embraced everything and everyone he hated. Fury erupted deep within him, but it was a fury tinged with jealousy, jealousy of the man who had committed almost every despicable act of inhumanity known to man against the people of the Arizona Territory; a man who was crude, lawless, and cruel, and who had not only this woman's loyalty, but also her love.

Grabbing her arm, Chance hauled her fiercely up against him. His other arm encircled her and crushed her to him.

"Tell me where he is, Sue Ann."

Chapter Twenty

It had been a mistake to touch her. Chance realized it instantly, but even then it was too late. Her lips were too close to his, their pink softness a teasing lure to his senses. He felt her breasts crushed tantalizing against his chest, felt her hips pressed into his. The soft, silken tangles of her hair covered the arm he held at her back, and the fresh scent of her filled his nostrils.

Desire swept through his body like a prairie fire, moving through his veins with the same hungry rapidity, the same urgent sweep. It shook him to the core to realize the physical power she held over him. His hunger to take her again was nearly devastating, his need to feel her supple body writhing beneath the caress of his hands, to taste the sweetness of her passion, the honey of her lips, brought a hardening to his body he could not ignore.

It was insane to still want her, he knew. She had rejected his offer of help, in essence telling him that Gil Calder was more important to her than even her freedom, and undeniably more important to her than whatever Chance could offer her, including himself. But at the moment none of that mattered. His pride and reasoning were gone. He wanted her. That was all he knew. All he was aware of.

He knew he should push her away from him, should deny the hunger she stirred within his body, yet he also knew he was unable and unwilling to do either.

"You're a witch, Sue Ann," he swore savagely. "A damned, spellbinding, witch." His mouth ground down hard on hers.

Held prisoner in the strong circle of his arms, secure against the wall of his body, T.J. had little opportunity to resist him. She tried to twist away, to jerk free, but his hungrily seeking mouth effectively held hers captive, exploring her lips, his tongue filling her mouth, probing, caressing, inflaming her own passions even as she fought against him. But she was fighting as much against herself, and the overwhelming desire to remain in his arms and forget the rest of the world with all its troubles and ugliness.

She tried to raise her arms in resistance against him, to pound at his chest with her fists, but both were pinioned between their bodies, rendering her helpless. And the will to defy him, to break his hold on her, was quickly ebbing away.

"Sue Ann," Chance murmured against her lips. "You can't leave."

T.J. tensed, her entire body turning stiff. He knew she was planning on leaving town? But how? She silently cursed herself. He'd been watching her, following her. He had seen her with Ringo. Most likely someone he knew had been near enough to hear their conversation and reported it back to Chance. Furious with herself for being so careless and with him for insisting she was the wife of the outlaw he hated, and the one she had been sent back here to get, T.J. tore her mouth from his.

"Let me go," she demanded.

Chance dropped his arms from around her, his ardor

instantly cooled by her rejection. He drew his emotions back under control quicker than even he had thought possible.

"Or what?" he drawled indolently. His eyes sparked with challenge. "Your husband will come into town and kill me?"

"He's not—"

T.J. clamped her lips together. If she convinced him she wasn't Sue Ann Calder, then he'd want to know who she was, and she had nothing to tell him that he'd believe. T.J. felt a shudder of desire rock her body and drew in a shaky breath as it was replaced by frustration. How could she explain to him, to anyone, that she had traveled through time, that she was from the future? How could she tell him that she was a police officer just like him, that she was after Gil Calder, just like him, only that she was from 1996, not 1881? He wouldn't believe that. And she couldn't expect him to. She had a hard time believing it herself, and she was living it!

Chance smiled, though it was not a gesture of friendly warmth, but of shrewd calculation. "Maybe that's the only way to get this whole thing over with, huh, Sue Ann? Get your husband to come into town after you? Rescue you from my clutches, so to speak?"

"What are you talking about?" T.J. asked, suddenly alarmed. "That's ridiculous."

He took hold of her arm in a grip that left little room for resistance.

"I think we should adjourn to the jail house for the night, and wait for Gil."

"What?" T.J. couldn't believe what she'd just heard. She stared up at him, maintaining control over her panic only by the tighest of wills. "No. You can't do that. I haven't done anything wrong."

"I'm the marshal, remember Sue Ann?" Chance looked down at her coldly. "I can lock up whoever I want, when-

ever I want, at least for a while. And I want to lock up
you.''

T.J. tried to jerk away from him.

She had to meet Ringo. It was the only way. If she was
right, Calder would know immediately it wasn't Sue Ann
that Chance had in jail. But he'd know Chance was setting
a trap for him and he'd most likely head elsewhere for a
while. If that happened, she'd miss her opportunity to
catch him and make sure he spent the rest of his life
behind bars. Or, remembering the era she was in, met his
maker at the end of a rope. She wouldn't be able to save
Lisa. She twisted violently, trying desperately to pull away
from him. This couldn't happen. It couldn't. She had to
get away, get Calder, for Lisa.

''Stop it, Sue Ann. It's no good.''

''Let me go, damn it,'' T.J. cried. ''You don't understand,
Chance, please. I'm not Sue Ann.'' She tried to jerk away
from him again. ''I'm not her, can't you understand that.
I'm T.J., not Sue Ann.''

Chance's grip tightened about her arm, and his fingers
pressed down cruelly on the soft flesh. ''I understand that
Gil will come looking to rescue you when he finds out
you're in my jail, Sue Ann. And then he'll pay for all the
lives he's taken. Whether you like that idea or not.'' Chance
jerked her around toward the foyer.

T.J. staggered after him. ''Damn it, Chance, listen to
me!'' she screamed. ''Please!''

He slammed a chair out of his way, not bothering to
slow his pace or glance back at her as he dragged her
behind him. He seethed with anger, she could sense it,
feel it, see it in the hard line of his jaw, the stiff posture
of his shoulders and back. Chance Burkette looked suddenly as if he were made from hard, cold iron and granite,
rather than flesh and bone.

T.J. had to skip to keep up with him as he stormed
through the house and out the front door. Several people

passing by stared as she and Chance made their way around the corner and down the street toward the jail house.

"Damn it, Chance, listen to me," T.J. said again. "Please, this isn't right. You've got to listen to me. I'm not Sue Ann, I swear."

He stopped abruptly and whirled to face her, dragging her up against his chest. "Then who the hell are you?" he demanded.

T.J. gulped hard. "I told you, I'm. . . ."

"Yeah, T.J. McAllister. Which means what?"

She stared up at him. "You wouldn't believe me if I tried to—"

"It won't work, Sue Ann." He spun on his heel and charged forward again, jerking her behind him and forcing her to follow. Being this cold, this hard toward a woman wasn't easy, but he forced himself to do it. She had made her choice and given him none. "So do us both a favor and stop trying."

"Of all the stupid, bull-headed men I've ever met, you are the most idiotic, the most obstinate. . . ."

The names didn't seem to faze him either. He crashed a hand against the door to the jail house, throwing it open, and half led, half dragged her across the small office space, not pausing until they stood directly before one of the cells. Maintaining a grip on her arm with one hand, he unlocked and swung the cell door open with the other.

T.J. stared into the cell, unable to believe he was really going to lock her in it.

"Your new home." He pushed her inside and released her arm.

T.J. swung around instantly to face him. She had no choice now but to tell him what she suspected.

"Lily Monroe is Sue Ann, Chance, I'm almost sure." T.J. looked at him in desperation, her eyes wide, her breath ragged. "I talked to her this morning for over two hours, and she's no actress, Chance, believe me, not a professional one anyway. She knows very little about the stage and performing. And she's no lady.''

"And you are?" Chance challenged. He slammed the cell door and turned the key.

T.J. shot forward and grabbed the bars, pressing her face between them. "No, at least not the kind you're used to. Will you just listen to me?''

He tossed the keys on his desk and sat down, his back to her.

"Would Sue Ann Calder stay in Doc's house with you, the marshal, living there?" T.J. asked. "Would she go riding out into the desert with you, and not try to kill you? Would she kiss you, and make love with you?''

She saw his back stiffen again, saw his hand clench into a fist as her words reminded him of their night together. Hope flared within T.J.'s breast and she hurriedly continued.

"She's Sue Ann, Chance, not me. You've got to believe me. She might not look like what you'd expect Gil Calder's wife to look like, wearing those fancy clothes, but that's the point. She's here in disguise, Chance. Would Sue Ann Calder, an outlaw's wife, come into town any other way? She has to disguise herself so that no one will know her.''

Chance remained motionless and rigid.

T.J. stared at his back. Lily Monroe was Sue Ann Calder. She would stake her reputation on it, except that here in 1881 she didn't have a reputation to stake it on.

Chance didn't move, didn't speak, and T.J. felt the small spark of hope that had flared within her begin to fade. Fear held her tightly. If he kept her locked up there was no hope for Lisa. Or Chance, she thought suddenly. The already rapid beat of her heart accelerated. The Calders were going to hit Tucson. That's why Sue Ann was here. And Chance knew it. That's why he'd suspected that she was Sue Ann. He knew she was most likely coming into town to scout it out and size up the authorities. Chance would be killed. He was only one against all of Calder's gang, all of the cowboys, including Curly Bill and Johnny Ringo. A cold chill of panic swept through her.

"Please, Chance, listen to me," she pleaded frantically. Of course he could have backup of his own. Maybe there were some other marshals or deputies on their way to Tucson right now. But that would just end this whole mess in a bloodbath, and there was no guarantee that Calder would be caught or killed and that Chance would survive.

"Don't you think that's a little low?" Chance growled, his back still to her, "trying to pin this on another woman?"

"You big idiot!" T.J. shrieked, momentarily losing control of her temper. "She's Sue Ann, and I think she's leaving town tonight with Curly Bill. If my guess is right they were going to meet up with me and Ringo out on the trail somewhere. Maybe kill me out there, or maybe Ringo believed me when I told him I had information for Calder, I don't know. That doesn't matter now.

"She's sized you up, Chance, she knows it's only you and Perkins against all of them." T.J. felt a catch in her throat and swallowed it. "Chance, they're going to come back, and they'll kill you, and maybe a lot of other people, innocent people. You can't let that happen, Chance. You can't."

He turned to look at her then, his features still hard, but his eyes not quite as cold as they had been moments earlier. He wanted to believe her. Damn it. What she said sounded possible. He shook the thought off. No, she was trying to trick him into releasing her.

At that moment Perkins walked into the jail house.

"Chance, if you don't believe me, go and check it out. She's probably preparing to leave with Curly Bill right now." T.J. urged. "Leave me here with the sheriff, but go check it out. Please."

"So Curly Bill can come in here when I'm gone and kill him, and then break you out?"

"Chance, damn it," T.J. said, "I'm telling the truth." She dropped her voice to a soft, pleading tone and fixed him with a pointed gaze. "If last night meant anything at all to you, if I mean anything at all to you, please, just do as I ask and go check her out."

"Check her out," he repeated.

"Yes. Go to the hotel and watch her. Maybe go through her room. Her things. See if I'm right." T.J. straightened. "Or are you afraid you'll be wrong?"

"She told you she was leaving town tonight with Curly Bill?" he asked, sneeringly, his tone making it evident he didn't believe her.

"No. I told her I was leaving town tonight. Later, she said that she might be seeing me again. On the road, she said."

"And that leads you to believe she's meeting Curly Bill and she's Sue Ann Calder?"

"No, there was more. Lots more, but we don't have time to discuss it all now. And anyway, it was just little things she said, insinuated really. Please, Chance, go to the hotel. You have me locked up here like you want, you have nothing to lose if I'm wrong."

He rose to his feet. "Perkins," Chance yelled.

The young sheriff, having been leaning back in his chair, bolted forward as if startled, the chairs front two legs crashing to the floor at his movement. "Yeah?"

"Load a rifle and keep it on your desk. Take out your six gun, cock the hammer, and put it within easy reach. Then lock the shutters over the window and bolt the door behind me when I leave."

Eli stood up and grabbed a rifle from the gun rack on the wall near his desk. "What's going on?"

"I want to make sure you two are still here, and alive, when I get back. I'm going over to the hotel." Chance jerked the door to the street open then paused and looked pointedly back at the sheriff. "Don't open this damned door for anyone but me, Eli. Understand?"

"Yes, sir. No one but you." Eli looked a bit confused. "How will I know it's you?"

Chance nearly sighed and asked himself for the hundredth time how in tarnation Eli Perkins had ever been elected sheriff. Pulling the brim of his Stetson lower onto his forehead, Chance turned to go. "I'll yell." He slammed the door, waited until he heard Eli bolt it, and then began to walk toward the hotel. Halfway there he ran into Doc.

"Chance," Doc hurried toward him. "I'm glad I ran into you."

Chance noticed instantly that the older man looked slightly disheveled, a rarity for Doc, and he wasn't carrying his medical bag. That fact alarmed Chance more than Doc's slightly mussed appearance. He grabbed his arm. "Doc, what's wrong?"

"T.J. Have you seen her?" the old man asked. "I'm concerned about her, Chance. I found her wardrobe open and her clothes strewn all over the bed."

Chance nearly sagged in relief. For one horrible second he'd thought Doc was bringing him bad news about Morgan and Nick. "She's in jail, Doc."

"Jail?" The old man's bushy gray brows soared upward. "Jail?" he repeated. "But why?"

"Because I think she's Sue Ann Calder, Doc, and unless I miss my guess, Gil will come to get her when she doesn't go back to their hideout. Or when Ringo or Curly Bill ride out to tell him I've got her locked up."

"Chance—"

"Doc, stay out of this," Chance growled. "I know what I'm doing."

"I certainly hope so, Chance," Doc said softly. "I certainly hope so." He turned and shuffled back toward his house, shaking his head as he went.

Chance continued on his way, grumbling with each step

at being a fool, first for rescuing her, then getting involved with her, and now for giving even the slightest hint of credence to the fact that she might be telling the truth. He couldn't have acted the simpleton more if he'd planned it himself. Chance slammed a hand against the hotel's entry door. It flew open and crashed against the adjoining wall, the loud impact bringing the clerk up from behind the desk with a startled leap.

"Mar . . . Marshal Burkette," he stuttered nervously, "is something wrong?"

"Is Miss Monroe in her room?"

The clerk turned to look at the key boxes built into the wall behind him.

"Yes, I believe so. She came in awhile ago and went upstairs. Said she wanted to take a bath before going out tonight. She hasn't rung for anyone to go back up and get the tub and water, so I guess she's still up there."

"Good. Which room?"

The clerk looked shocked. "Pardon me, Marshal?"

"You heard me, dammit. Which room?"

"Well, uh, nine."

Chance took the stairs two at a time then paused at the second floor landing. A candle set into a sconce attached to the wall near the stairs illuminated the hall. There was another at the opposite end. Both threw a flickering, yellow glow over the long, narrow passageway. Room number nine was halfway down the hallway, the highly polished brass number clearly visible on the door panel. Chance stood in front of her door, his back pressed up against the wall opposite it. Curly Bill and Ringo were also staying at the hotel, and he didn't want a bullet finding its way into his back.

He leaned over and rapped his knuckles on the door.

It swung open almost immediately. Lily smiled up at him.

"Why, Marshal Burkette, what a very pleasant surprise."

She stepped back and opened the door wider, inviting him to enter.

He did, and closed the door behind him. His eyes darted to the corners of the room hastily, his hand poised just above his gun, ready to draw it if necessary. Only when seeing she was the room's only occupant did he relax somewhat. He turned his full attention to her then, realizing for the first time that she was dressed in only a sheer, white, batiste nightgown, her curves fully visible with the light of a lamp at her back.

"I . . . I'm sorry to bother you." He cleared his throat. "But, I need to talk with you, Miss Monroe."

"Talk?" She smiled sweetly, then picked up a fan from the table, snapped it open, and began to flutter it back and forth in front of her face. "Well, I guess we could do that, Marshal." She glanced at him coyly. "First."

"Where's the last town you played, Miss Monroe?" he asked, forcing himself to ignore the blatant suggestion.

"Last town I . . . ?"

"The last town you played," Chance repeated. "Where was that?"

"Why, San Francisco." She passed in front of him to stand near the window, giving him a saucy smile as she did. "Why, Marshal?"

"Not Denver?"

She looked suddenly flustered.

"No. Well, I mean yes, we did play Denver, but it was only a short engagement, really, not one even worth counting, let alone mentioning. But why do you ask? Is something wrong?"

For the first time since she'd come to town Chance looked long and hard at her hair. It was down now, falling loosely over her shoulders, rather than pinned up as every other time he'd seen her. Chestnut. His eyes moved hurriedly over her from head to foot, and he remembered the woman he had made love to the night before, the woman who now sat in a jail cell. They were nearly the same build. Was it possible she had been telling him the truth? That this was actually Sue Ann Calder, and he'd made a mistake? But if so, then why wouldn't she tell him who she really was? And why she was in Tucson? "When do you start your engagement at the Red Garter, Miss Monroe?"

"Oh, well," she smiled, "in a few more nights." She fluttered her eyelashes in a flirtatious manner. "Why, Marshal? Getting anxious to see me perform?"

"Yeah, you saw right through me."

"I'd like to see a lot more of you," she cooed, and moved to stand before the lamp again.

"Listen, Miss Monroe, I have to leave town tonight for a few days and, well, I—"

"Need a little loving to tide you over on the trail," she suggested. Her smile widened and she moved to stand before him, her hands pressed to his chest.

"Well, no," Chance said awkwardly. "Actually, I doubt my fiancée would understand that."

Lily laughed. "Oh, you naughty boy. You didn't tell me you had a fiancée. But, it really doesn't matter, does it?"

"Well, I was really looking forward to hearing you sing, Miss Monroe, and . . ." He raised one side of his mouth in a suggestive grin. "Well . . ." He shrugged, as if embarrassed. "Do you think you could sing a little song for me now, just in case I don't make it back before you leave town?"

She looked suddenly aghast. "Sing? Now?"

"Yeah, just a bit. I'd really appreciate it."

"Well, I . . ." She cleared her throat and hummed. Her voice broke. She smiled weakly at Chance. "I don't really think I can right now, Marshal. My throat's been a bit sore the last few days, you know, and my doctor told me I must rest it for as long as possible. That's one reason my engagement at the Garter doesn't start for a few days."

The sheepish, shy look on Chance's face suddenly turned to one of stone and his eyes took on a purposeful glare. "Miss Monroe, I know this is going to upset you, but I'm going to have to give you a choice here. Either you sing for me now, loud and clear like you plan to do on the stage, or you take a little walk with me to the jail house."

"Come with you to the jail house?" A look of panic lit her eyes, like that of a trapped animal. "You can't do that. I mean—"

"Sing," Chance ordered.

"I most certainly will not."

He grabbed her arm, his patience having already been strained to the breaking point earlier when he'd felt forced to throw T.J. in a cell. "Fine, then you can visit my jail." He snatched her cloak up into his hand, swirled it out to land on her shoulders, and forcibly urged her toward the door. "After you," he said.

"Humph. Such a gentleman."

"Yeah, that's me."

She swept gracefully down the street, staying a step in front of him, her head held high, one hand holding the cloak closed at her throat. Only when they approached the Red Garter and saw Curly Bill lounging on a chair beside its front door, did she pause.

Chance was immediately at her heels. "Something wrong, Miss Monroe?" he asked, leaning over her shoulder and eyeing Curly Bill suspiciously. There was something between these two, he could feel it. But was it merely an actress's flirtation with an outlaw, or something more?

"Only that you're taking me to jail," she said, throwing a glance at Curly Bill.

The outlaw tipped his head toward her, then turned a sneering gaze on Chance.

"Why, Marshal, you arresting ladies now?"

Chapter Twenty-One

Chance stared at the two women. His mood turned even blacker. They could be sisters. Not that they really looked that much alike. They were the same build, same height, and both were beautiful, there was no denying that. But that was the extent of it. Lily's nose was aquiline in shape, whereas Sue Ann's—or perhaps T.J.'s—was turned up at the end, making it appear pert and sassy. Lily's eyes were hazel rather than green, and now that he saw the two women standing only a few feet apart from one another, he realized that Lily's hair was a shade lighter. But that didn't make her Sue Ann Calder.

Neither of the two women was answering his questions. He felt ready to erupt he was so furious. Sue Ann, T.J., or whatever the hell her name was, had, for some unknown reason, suddenly clammed up when he'd brought Lily Monroe back to the jail house.

Before he'd left for the hotel he couldn't shut her up with her accusations and pleadings, and now she wouldn't talk at all. She just glared at him and whispered to Lily

Monroe when he wasn't within earshot. But he wasn't so convinced anymore of Lily Monroe's innocence either. She might not be Sue Ann, but her silence and refusal to cooperate indicated that she sure as hell was involved in whatever was going on, right up to her pretty little neck.

"Eli," Chance bellowed suddenly, ramming his desk drawer closed and bolting to his feet.

The sheriff's eyes shot open and he jerked forward in his chair. His hat fell to the floor and one hand grappled awkwardly on his desk for his gun.

"Yes, sir? Got it, sir, where are they?" He pointed the gun toward the door and stared at it through bloodshot eyes.

"I'm going out. Stay here and guard these two. And lock the damned door after I leave."

Eli slunk back in his chair and let out a long sigh. "Yes, sir," he said weakly, only a second before Chance slammed the door shut and disappeared.

He walked directly to Doc's. It was late, but the old man was still up.

"Doc?" Chance called, closing the entry door and walking into the parlor.

Doc looked up from his book. "Chance. You had supper, boy?"

Chance sighed, took off his hat, and sunk down into a chair opposite the older man. "Yeah. Lannie Kay sent something over to the jail house."

"Good." Doc set his book on a nearby table. "So, what's going on, Chance? Why do you still have T.J. locked up in that jail cell?"

Chance looked at him long and hard before answering. "Because . . . ah, hell." He shrugged, got to his feet, and began to pace the room. "I was sure she was Sue Ann, Doc. I was sure, you know? Then she started babbling about Lily Monroe being Sue Ann and how I was stupid if I didn't at least look into it. So I did."

A smile tugged at the corners of Doc's mouth. "And now you're not so sure anymore," he said.

"No."

"So what are you going to do? You can't keep her locked up in there forever?"

"I've got them both locked up."

"Both?" Doc looked at him incredulously. "You've got T.J. and Lily Monroe in jail?"

"Yeah. She couldn't sing."

"Couldn't sing?"

"Yeah. Lily Monroe. I went to her hotel and gave her a line about having to leave town and how much I'd appreciate it if she'd sing me a song 'cause I wouldn't be around to hear her show. I figured that was the best way to tell if she was who she said she was. But she couldn't do it."

Doc sat back in his chair. A deep frown appeared on his brow as he began to stroke his chin with his index finger and thumb, a habit he had when he was thinking.

"I guess it doesn't really matter which one of them is Sue Ann though," Chance said, "Calder will come to break his wife out and as long as both women are in jail . . ." He shrugged again without finishing the sentence.

"What about that wallet we found in T.J.'s trousers the day you brought her here? And that badge she was wearing?"

"They were fakes. I sent out a couple of wires. No one's heard of her."

"What about the Pinkertons?"

"Haven't heard from them yet, and they're so damned secretive they might not tell me the truth even if she is one of theirs, which I doubt." Chance rose and went to stand before one of the windows. He looked out at the street. "Anyway, that card she had on her didn't say anything about her being a Pinkerton agent."

"It said she was a police officer."

He turned back to face the old man. "And I haven't

heard back from anyone who's heard of her. Nobody. The dates were wrong on the card too, Doc. And even if that was some kind of printing mistake, her picture was colored. Someone touched it up with paint or something."

"Maybe they do that back east."

"It said she was a police officer in Arizona, remember? Specifically Tucson."

Doc nodded. "Yes, there seems no explanation for that." He frowned thoughtfully. "But, well, what if she's with some secret government agency?"

Chance looked at him as if he were crazy. "There's no secret government agency like that."

"If it's secret, Chance, how would you know?"

"I'm a U.S. Marshal."

"Still, U.S. Marshals don't know everything. Remember that money in her pocket? You didn't know about that."

"It's fake," Chance said. "It has to be. Or experimental or something."

"I'll admit, it's strange looking, but it did have the same year on it that the identification card had, and, well, she did have that badge—"

"What are you trying to say, Doc? That she's a deputy here and I didn't even know it? That Perkins didn't know it? That no one in town knew it?"

"No, of course not."

"Then what? That she came here from another time?" Chance laughed derisively. "Hell, why stop there, Doc? How about we figure she came from another world?"

Doc folded his hands across his midriff and looked up at Chance. "I didn't say that. Anyway what's your theory?"

"She was sent here by Calder."

"I thought you just said—"

"She may not be Sue Ann Calder," Chance continued, talking over Doc's interruption, "but I still think she could have been sent here by the cowboys, or even Calder himself. Maybe to send me off on some wild goose chase."

Chance moved across the room and stood before the cold grate of the fireplace. "They probably never figured I'd lock up a woman."

Gunshots suddenly filled the air, echoing on the night's stillness and sending a chill of alarm up Chance's spine. He grabbed his Stetson, rammed it onto his head and made for the door.

"Be careful," Doc called after him.

Intuitively Chance knew what had happened. He ran for the jail house. The door was standing wide open. "Eli?" he called, as he ran into the small room.

Eli Perkins was hanging onto one corner of his desk with both hands and trying to pull himself to his feet.

Chance glanced quickly at the jail cells. Both doors stood wide open, and both cells were empty. He hurried to help Eli into a chair.

"Are you hurt?" He looked the young sheriff over quickly and determined there was no blood, so he wasn't shot. Worry gave way to anger. "What the hell happened?"

Eli gulped hard. "They, I mean, he kicked the door in. Scared the hell out of me."

"You're lucky he didn't shoot the life out of you. Now, who's *he*?"

"Ringo. I think. I mean, I thought I heard someone outside by the door, and I walked over to it. I kept it locked, like you said, but I, uh, called out and asked who was there." He shook his head gently and placed a hand over his eyes. "Next thing I knew the danged door flew at me. It hit me and knocked me halfway across the room."

"You're lucky it knocked you out. Most likely that's the only reason he didn't kill you. Ringo likes to see his victims squirm. Did he take the woman?"

"Yes." Eli dropped the hand from his eyes and blinked rapidly several times. "I mean, uh, I think it was Ringo. My head was spinning after that door slammed into my forehead and I was trying not to black out, you know."

Chance moved to the rack of rifles on the wall and took one down. From his desk drawer he grabbed a box of bullets and shoved it into the pocket of his vest.

"Was Curly Bill with him? Or Diamond Jack?"

"I, well, I, uh, don't know. Really. I mean, I heard voices and tried to open my eyes, but, well, it hurt like heck. Could have been the two women talking with him." Eli blinked rapidly again, tried to stand, teetered, and sunk back into the chair. "I think, I mean, I'm pretty sure, I heard one of them, one of the women, I mean, call Ringo by name."

"I'm going after them."

"Uh? But, you can't, I mean, you shouldn't go alone."

Chance paused at the door and looked back at him. "You're in no condition to go with me, Eli. And anyway, someone needs to stay here and keep order in town. That's your job, Eli. Mine is out there. Yesterday I wired the governor for help. When his men get here, send them after me."

Eli nodded and dropped his head into his hands again.

"Oh, and Eli," Chance said, pausing at the door on his way out, "deputize a few men, just in case."

Chance tightened the cinch on Diablo's saddle and checked his gear. He had enough grub for a week on the trail. If that wasn't enough he'd hunt whatever he needed. He rechecked the ammunition he'd packed into his saddlebags; enough to take on half the Mexican army. His nerves were on edge and he itched to get on the trail.

He glanced outside again. Darkness enveloped the landscape and the moon was such a thin sliver of silver, its light dissipated before ever reaching the earth. It would be impossible to follow their trail now. He had no choice but to wait until dawn, unless he wanted to risk being gunned down in an ambush. And getting himself killed sure as hell wouldn't do Morgan and Rick much good, assuming they were still around to do much good for. Chance knew waiting to set out after them until first light was the only logical thing to do. Even so, his gut churned with anger and frustration at the delay.

He slapped a hand on the horse's long, sleek neck. "Rest while you can, boy," he said to the animal, "we've got a damned hard ride ahead of us in a few hours."

The horse whinnied softly, as if in understanding and lowered his head to the pile of hay Chance had thrown on the floor before him. Chance walked out of the livery and paused just beyond its huge doors. His eyes surveyed the street. Five saloons were within his range of vision, one being the Red Garter. Each was packed, each boisterous with noise and music. More than a dozen saddle horses were tied here and there to hitching racks. A few wagons and buckboards were also parked along the street.

It had been more than three hours since Ringo broke the women out of jail. Chance had gone to the hotel and confirmed that Ringo wasn't there. And he wasn't at any of the saloons. His horse and gear were gone too.

"But Curly Bill's still here," Chance mumbled to himself. He'd seen the man passed out cold at Mary Ellen's place, and that worried him.

His gaze moved slowly over the scene before him and his eyes narrowed as he thought of the outlaw who he suspected was not only cunning and mean, but half crazy. He glanced over his shoulder and back into the livery at the horses stabled there. Curly Bill's painted mare stood in a center stall, but Ringo's mustang was gone. "Why?" The word hung on the night air, taunting him. Curly Bill and Ringo usually rode together. "Why is Ringo gone, and Curly still here?" he said to himself.

When the first feeble rays of dawn crept over the horizon, muted golden streams of light that barely cut through the blackness of the receding night and did little to warm either the cold earth or the air, Chance swung up into the saddle and rode out of town.

T.J. reined in beside the woman the good people of Tucson knew as Lily Monroe, and she knew as Sue Ann Calder. "How much farther?" she asked.

The woman turned toward her, but rather than the friendly warmth she'd seen in her eyes earlier, now there was nothing but contempt.

"Why? Afraid the marshal is too far behind us to rescue you if we decide to kill you?"

T.J. forced a laugh from her lips and struggled to look incredulous while she fought down the panic that had erupted in her breast at the woman's words. "What are you talking about? Why would the marshal want to rescue me? And why would you want to kill me?"

"Because you told the marshal I was Sue Ann Calder."

T.J. shook her head. "No, no, I didn't." Nothing was working out the way she'd planned. When Ringo had burst in to break Sue Ann out of jail, T.J. had screamed at her to take her with them, that she wanted to join Calder's gang. And they had. That part of her impulsive plan had worked fine. This part was not in her script.

"Look honey, Ringo had you pretty well figured out before you went back to him the second time. He had you watched, you know."

T.J. frowned. "Then why did you befriend me?"

A sly spark beamed from Sue Ann's hazel eyes. "It seemed a good idea at the time."

"But it's not true. I'm not working with the marshal. I didn't tell him anything. I didn't even know him before a few days ago."

"You live with the man, honey," Sue Ann said, her tone both accusatory and sultry, "and you let him have his way with you. Ringo said you enjoyed it, too." She laughed.

T.J. stared at her, shocked speechless. Ringo had watched them make love? Her gaze jumped to meet his and a shiver of revulsion swept over her.

"I figure you can share a little of that fire with me, too, beautiful, when we get to camp." Ringo said. He leaned forward in his saddle to peer around Sue Ann at T.J. A smug smile curved his lips.

T.J. looked back at Sue Ann. "Listen, it's not what you think, really. I was using him. That's all. I had an accident a few days ago and he took me to the doc's. It's his uncle. They share the house. I didn't tell the marshal anything," T.J. babbled. "Especially not that you were Sue Ann Calder. How could I? I've never met you before. I wouldn't have known Sue Ann Calder from Mary Todd Lincoln."

Sue Ann turned to Ringo. "Do you think he would have tried following us in the dark?"

He shook his head. "No. Burkette's too smart for that. He'd be afraid we'd set up an ambush. Ringo looked up at the sky with its first faint traces of dawn breaking its blackness. "I'd say he's starting out just about now."

T.J.'s heart sank. The woman didn't believe her.

"And we left a good enough trail for him to follow?"

Ringo laughed. "Hell, Sue Ann, we left a trail a damned blind man could follow."

Sue Ann smiled. "Good. We wouldn't want the marshal to get lost while trying to find our hideout, now would we?" She laughed, the sound wafting across the still desert.

T.J. shuddered at the implications of the woman's words, and the heartless tone of her laughter. She'd seen a number of female criminals in the span of her short career as a police officer, but she'd never seen one whose smile brought as much cunning coldness to her eyes as Sue Ann Calder's did at that moment. Fear for Chance filled her. "You want him to follow you?" she said finally.

Sue Ann looked back at her then, her hazel eyes holding a glimmer of amusement within their icy depths. "Well, of course, honey. That way we'll finally be able to get rid of Marshal Chance Burkette once and for all without anyone being able to blame us for it.''

A trap. T.J.'s heart fluttered with fear and panic. They were leading Chance into a trap. He'd be murdered, cut down in cold blood, and it would be all her fault. She felt tears sting the back of her eyes. It would be all her fault. Despair swelled within her breast and she fought to ignore it and blink back the tears threatening to fall from her lashes. This wasn't the time to give into tears or give up. Maybe she could find a way to escape, or at least a way to warn Chance that he was riding into an ambush. But how? How?

Ringo sneered. ''Once Burkette's out of the way, then all we have to take care of is the Earps, and things will go back to the way they used to be.''

''That's right,'' Sue Ann said merrily.

T.J. gasped and leaned forward to stare at Ringo. ''You mean, Wyatt Earp?''

His lips tightened into a thin line of hatred as his cold, dark eyes bore into hers. ''You know the Earps?''

T.J. straightened instantly, taking herself out of his sight, and he out of hers. ''No,'' she said quickly. ''I mean, just by reputation.''

Sue Ann smiled. ''Honey, somebody should have told you before this, but, you don't lie too good.''

''I'm not lying,'' T.J. said.

She kept her gaze on T.J., but said to Ringo, ''You know, Johnny, I think our little Miss McAllister just might be more valuable than we thought. Maybe we shouldn't kill her until after we take care of our business down in Tombstone.'' She laughed lightly and turned to Ringo. ''Wyatt and those self-righteous brothers of his might just like the opportunity to rescue a friend from our midst.'' She looked back at T.J. ''Especially a female friend.''

Chapter Twenty-Two

T.J. looked around, paying more attention to her surroundings as daylight broke over the land and allowed her to see more clearly. They were heading southwest, into the Tucson-Santa Rita mountain range. Her heart sank just a little. She had hoped they'd go near enough to the mission so that she could somehow summon help from the padres, but they were heading too far west to pass anywhere close to the mission.

She twisted about to look over her shoulder. The movement pulled on the leather binding that kept her hands bound together and imprisoned to the horn of her saddle. It cut into her wrists and she winced. Her shoulders sagged, but whether from relief or disappointment she wasn't sure. All she could see behind them was the same as before them, and to each side, scrub brush, cacti, and craggy plateaus of dry, red earth. There was no rider on horseback charging to her rescue.

T.J. straightened and tried to concentrate on some way to get herself out of this situation, some way to prevent

Chance from riding into a trap. But her mind wasn't cooperating. Instead of schemes of rescue and daring, her mind dwelt only on the man whom she was afraid was going to die now because of her dogged determination to get to Gil Calder no matter what.

She closed her eyes and tried to clear her thoughts of him. This was the time for cold, hard logic, for determining a way to escape her captors, for preventing Chance's death. This was not the time for memories of a man who had made love to her, who had held her in his arms and, through the tormentingly sweet language of his body, through the silent caresses and strokes, transported her to a world of ecstasy. But those thoughts refused to be banished.

She had spent the major portion of her life acting independent, totally self-sufficient, and resourceful. Only Lisa had seen beyond the cool exterior she had built around herself, only Lisa knew that behind it, well hidden, T.J. had barricaded her heart against the hurt and pain of rejection. She had loved once, and been spurned because of what she was. That would not happen again. She would not let it.

T.J. opened her eyes and looked out at the awakening desert, but it was Chance that she saw, his image in her mind, filling it, the invisible presence of him embracing her, protecting her, loving her. She remembered his smile, an expression that was all too infrequent on his handsome face, but one that transformed those rigid lines to planes of warmth and tenderness. His eyes, that night in the gazebo, had shown her a man who had been hurt deeply by love, and because of that had built a barrier around his heart and emotions. But she had seen past that barrier, to the love that he had to give, the love that he wanted desperately to give, but was afraid to offer, especially to her.

A tug of emotion caught at her throat. The scent of him

still filled her nostrils, the feel of his arms around her still tingled beneath her skin, and the memory of their lovemaking instilled her with a yearning ache.

T.J. turned her gaze skyward. They had ridden long and hard for several hours. Southwest, but that's all she could tell, and she wasn't even certain about that. All of her landmarks, the streets, the buildings, the roads, didn't exist here, and it was only occasionally that she could tell where they were by looking at the landscape. Her body was sore and exhausted, yet there didn't seem an end in sight.

The sun had risen over the mountains and turned the lower part of the sky, the portion that hugged the horizon, to a sweeping vista of pink gold, while above it a blue sky stretched endlessly. Was this her destiny? T.J. wondered. To be swept back to 1881, and fall hopelessly in love with a man out of her time, then to lose him, and finally, to die?

Love. The thought, the word, struck her like an electrical shock. She was in love with Chance Burkette. A wave of melancholy swept over her. She was in love with Chance Burkette, a man from a different time, a different way of life to hers. He was a man she could not have. A long sigh slipped softly from between her lips. She had vowed never to give her heart to a man again, and now she found she had broken that vow without even being aware of it until it was too late.

T.J. had faced the prospect of dying. In her chosen occupation it was not something she could ignore. But falling in love again, and losing again, that was something she had forced herself not to consider a possibility, not even for a moment.

Straightening her shoulders T.J. knew what she had to do. Fate had swept her back to 1881 so that she could save Lisa. And she believed that once that was accomplished, if it was accomplished, she would be swept back to 1996, and out of Chance's life. But she couldn't let him die. Not now, not because of her. She had to find a way to thwart Sue Ann's plans.

She looked about. They were climbing the mountains now. She twisted in her seat to look back. Far off on the horizon she could see the mountains across the valley floor, the mountains that made up the northern boundary of the City of Tucson. She settled forward in her saddle and glanced around her again, realizing that they were nearing the spot where she had encountered Jake Calder in 1996 and fallen off the cliff. A shiver of recognition tickled its way up her spine. She had come here, to the cliff, with Chance just after he'd rescued her, and nothing had happened. She tensed against the continuing sensation. Nothing could happen now. She couldn't be swept back to her own time now, not now, not when she hadn't saved Lisa, not when Chance might be killed because of her. Not now.

But the farther up the mountainside they traveled, the stronger the sensation became, and the harder she fought against it. T.J. looked around frantically and her eyes finally settled on a sharp peak of red rock. She recognized it instantly. When she'd been climbing up the sheer mountain face after Jake, when she'd been clinging to the rocks and had looked up at him, confronting his taunting, that same red peak had been the backdrop for his face. T.J. wrapped her hands around the saddle horn and, closing her eyes against the scene, squeezed the hard leather between her fingers.

"Please, no," she whispered softly. "Not yet, please. Please. Not yet."

Suddenly, as quickly as the sensation had assailed her, it disappeared.

T.J. sighed in relief, but she had only a moments peace. Then she started thinking maybe it was the wrong emotion. Maybe she should have wanted to go back. At least she would be alive and in her own time. But Jake Calder would still be alive. Lisa would still be dead. And Chance would . . .

Once again she felt the burning sensation of tears at the back of her eyes and blinked rapidly to stem their tide. Chance would be dead. Yes, he would be dead, but from natural causes? Or murdered by Johnny Ringo and the Calders?

"Make sure the lookout recognizes you Ringo," Sue Ann said, breaking the long silence that had surrounded the three for the past several hours.

He pushed the brim of his hat back with his thumb. "They usually do," he said easily. In spite of his casual words, he took out a red silk scarf from his saddlebag and wrapped one end of it around his hand, leaving the other end trailing so that he could wave it in the air to the lookout.

"Yeah, well, just make sure. I don't want to get shot at on my way home."

Ringo looked back at T.J. "Ready to have a little party tonight, sweetheart?"

T.J. knew, no matter how long she lived past this moment, whether only a few hours, a few years, or decades, she would never forget the cold, dark, lifelessness she saw reflected in Johnny Ringo's eyes. For a moment, a fleeting timeless moment, she felt an overwhelming surge of pity for the man.

The lewd smile on his face died away and the handsome features once again turned unyielding and stony. His hand snaked out and slapped her cheek. Her head jerked to one side at the impact.

"Don't look at me like that," he said.

T.J.'s cheek burned and tears filled her eyes. She'd been unaware that her face had revealed to him what she'd been feeling. She looked away and blinked rapidly. If she'd had her baton she would have been more than happy to give Johnny Ringo a taste of his own medicine.

"That wasn't nice, Johnny," Sue Ann purred.

He laughed. "Who the hell ever said I was nice?"

They rode over a ridge and riding around several rock outcroppings, moved through a narrow alleyway of earth that eventually opened onto a wide canyon. It became deeper the farther they rode. Half an hour later T.J. could see that the cliffs before her signaled the end of the canyon. It was a dead end.

A sudden spark of light caught her eye and she looked up. A man stood on a rock ledge halfway up the cliff wall. The metal barrel of his rifle caught the sun and reflected it in small bursts of brilliant light. The lookout.

As if to confirm her thought, Ringo reined in and waved his hand at the man. The red scarf trailed behind his arm like a brilliantly colored snake as it swung back and forth over his head.

The man waved back and they passed safely.

T.J. checked the area for other lookouts. She saw no one else, but had no doubt they were there, somewhere. Minutes later they rode into a small valley set within the canyon walls. T.J. experienced a shudder of apprehension.

Several cowboys were gathered around a corral off to her left, watching another cowboy as he attempted to break a young stallion. They all turned and grew silent as she and the others passed. With a sense of dread that left her skin cold and her heart in her throat, T.J. had to admit to herself that escape looked just about impossible. She forced herself to defiantly meet the cold stares of the cowboys as she rode past them. Still more cowboys lounged lazily on a group of crudely fashioned wooden tables and chairs set around a large campfire. She met their stares, too, but nothing had prepared her for this, not even her training as a cop. These men were terrifying. They were hard, unfeeling, and merciless. She was more frightened than she'd ever been in her life.

"Hey, Ringo, you gonna share that one?" one of the older cowboys called out.

Ringo grinned. "Maybe when I'm done with her."

T.J. shuddered.

Several of the cowboys laughed and made a few lewd, cat calls toward her, some calling out promises that she'd enjoy them the best.

They rode on. Two cowboys were brushing down their horses, two more were just saddling up. Several tents had been set up to one side of the small valley, almost against the foot of one of the sheer cliff walls.

They reined in near one of the tents and Sue Ann began to dismount. A cowboy took her horse.

"Gil, honey," she called out, looking toward one of the tents. "Gil, honey, where are you?"

Its front flap flew opened and Gil Calder stepped into the sunlight.

T.J. gasped. If she hadn't known better, she could have sworn it was Jake Calder she was looking at. Their appearances were nearly identical. Gil had the same massively built body, the same straight black hair, and the same cold dark eyes as those that had looked at her when she'd fallen from the cliff.

"Gil, Ringo and I brought you a present," Sue Ann said. She hugged her husband, who towered over her, then turned toward T.J., pointed and laughed.

"You brought me another woman, Sue Ann?" Gil said, the sarcasm in his tone making it evident he knew full well that was not the case.

Once again T.J. shivered. Even their voices were alike.

"Yes, to use as bait."

"Bait?" He stared at her, then turned his gaze to Ringo. "What's she talking about?"

"Burkette had her in a jail cell, along with Sue Ann," Ringo said. "But we think he's kind of sweet on this one and he'll come after her. And us." Ringo laughed that same sardonically dark laugh T.J. knew she could never get used to, and would never forget. "He's been living with her."

"And when he does come," Sue Ann said, "we'll kill him and be rid of Marshal Chance Burkette once and for all."

Gil smiled, a wily grin that split his face and did nothing to soften the harsh, rigid lines and pockmarked skin.

"That's good, Sue Ann," he said. "That's real good." He looked up at T.J. "I can see why Burkette's sweet on her."

Sue Ann tugged on his arm and the smile on her face instantly disappeared.

"Yeah? Well, you just never mind that, Gilman Calder," she snapped, throwing T.J. a murderous glare.

He laughed and wrapped a husky arm around her waist, then yanked her roughly up against him.

"Hell, sugar, you're all the woman I need, you know that." His lips descended on hers in a possessive kiss.

A minute later Gil looked back up at Ringo. "Do something with her," he said, and nodded toward T.J.

Ringo smiled and looked over at T.J. "Oh, I intended to." Leaning over, Ringo jerked the reins of T.J.'s horse out of the hands of the cowboy who had been holding them. "I'll see to her, Sid," he snarled, then smiled down at the man, "unless you want to take exception to that?"

It was a threat, not a question, and it was obvious the young cowboy knew it. He shook his head and hurriedly backed away.

Ringo laughed and jerked on the reins of T.J.'s mount. The horse immediately turned to follow Ringo's lead.

"Treat her good, Ringo," Gil yelled out, and laughed. "We wouldn't want the marshal to get upset with us 'cause we didn't treat his lady friend right."

Ringo led the horses toward another tent. Swinging a

leg over the front of his saddle, he slid to the ground, then moved to stand beside T.J.

"I can get down on my own," she said.

He grinned. "Maybe you can, beautiful, but then you'd deprive me of the pleasure of helping you." He started to reach up, as if to take hold of her waist. "I think we're going to have us a real good time tonight," he said. But instead of her waist, his hand dropped to her thigh and slowly slid up and down its length before finally moving up to her waist. "Yes, a real good time."

T.J. tried to jerk away from him but, sitting astride the horse with her hands still bound left her limited movement.

He seized her waist and dragged her roughly to the ground, then held her before him, her arms grasped tightly in his grip, his face barely an inch from hers. His hot breath wafted across her cheeks, and the stale smell of cheap whiskey that was on his breath met her nostrils and turned her stomach. She felt his warmth, his strength, his cruelty, and she tried not to shudder again.

He dropped one hand to hers, wrapping his fingers around the leather thong that held her wrists securely bound together and left her helpless. His other hand moved to her breasts. She tried to pull away. Ringo laughed, yanked her toward him, closing the space between them even more, and jerked at the front of her blouse. The small buttons tore off as the shirt front was ripped open.

T.J. gasped her outrage and tried to twist away from him again.

Ringo grabbed at her breast. His fingers dug into the soft, sensitive flesh hidden only by the lacy covering of her brassiere. He stared down at her, waiting, watching for a reaction.

T.J. forced herself not to wince, not to show any emotion, even pain. That's what he wanted, what he was waiting for, her response to his lusty, animalistic behavior, and she'd be damned if she would appease him.

Ringo jerked her around and dragged her to a small table set beside a cold campfire. He pushed down on the leather thong, forcing her to drop to her knees on the ground. "Stay here," he ordered.

"No." T.J. struggled to her feet and tried to run. Maybe she could get to her horse.

Ringo caught her easily by the long tendrils of her hair and swung her around to face him. His other hand arched through the air and the back of his knuckles connected with her cheek. T.J. reeled, nearly falling to her feet from the impact. She felt as if her cheekbone had just exploded. Pain shot through her temple and filled her head.

"I said stay there," he ordered again. "Or do you like it rough? Is that it?" He pushed her back to her knees. T.J. glared up at him through her tears. Even as he snickered in satisfaction at her cowering, her mind was flailing about, searching for a way, a plan, to outwit him, to save herself and Chance.

Chapter Twenty-Three

They had ridden easily. Even so, they had a lot of distance on him. Chance hunkered down on his haunches and ran the tip of one gloved finger over the imprint of a horse's hoof in the dry desert floor. It was a good enough track to follow, yet it was not cut deeply into the earth, attesting to the fact that they were moving at a steady, but not necessarily hurried pace and were making no effort to cover their trail.

This bothered him. They had to know he'd follow, that he'd be after them. So why weren't they moving more rapidly? And why were they making no effort at all to cover their trail?

A series of soft curses slipped from his lips as he straightened. He was an expert tracker, even so, the night had given them a head start, and the pale light of the morning had slowed his efforts.

They had at least seven hours on him, and he could only travel so fast without taking the risk of losing the trail.

In direct contrast to all previous hopes, Chance prayed

that Calder's camp wasn't too far away from Tucson. If it was. He thought of T.J. then. He had no doubt now that she'd been telling him the truth. She wasn't Sue Ann Calder. That didn't tell him who or what she was, but he felt certain now that Lily Monroe was Sue Ann, and she had forced T.J. to go with them when Ringo busted her out of jail.

Chance looked around, his eyes scanning the desert floor, the plateaus in the distance, the subtle shifting heights of the earth, giving witness to crevices, creekbeds, and canyons. There had been no sign of Apaches, although that didn't mean they weren't there. But that was a worry he didn't have time for. Moving up beside Diablo, Chance took the canteen from his saddle and, uncorking its top, allowed himself a swallow of water. He recorked it and looped its strap back over the saddle horn. A long sigh slipped from his lips. He reached up to lift the Stetson from his head, ran a hand through his hair, brushing off the perspiration already forming on his brow from the warming morning sun, then resettled the hat and mounted Diablo.

"Come on, boy," he said to the big stallion. "My guess is we've still got a long ways to go, but they've left us a good trail." He looked down at the imprints in the hard earth. "Maybe too good."

He had a hunch, and his hunches were usually right. Except maybe the one about T.J. being Sue Ann. He'd been dead wrong on that one.

As he rode, hour after hour, stopping only long enough to stretch his legs, take a swallow of water, a bite of jerky, and a closer look at the trail, he pondered everything that had happened in the past few days. Did Johnny Ringo and Sue Ann know, somehow, about what had happened between him and T.J.?

He smiled despite his worry. It made him feel a little better to think of her as T.J., as if it confirmed that she'd been telling him the truth. A frown returned to his brow. Did they know he cared for her? Is that why they'd taken her, why they'd forced her to leave the jail with them, so that he would follow?

It made sense. Which meant he was riding into a trap, and that was what he'd suspected all along. He nudged Diablo with the tip of his spurs and the large horse picked up his pace. Chance pulled the brim of his Stetson lower onto his forehead. There was no emotion etched in his features now, no warmth or compassion. Only a spark of worry in his eyes gave evidence that any feeling stirred within his blood at all. He still didn't know who she was, which meant he wasn't sure he could trust her, but he couldn't deny what he felt for her any longer. Every time he thought about her he was filled with a yearning ache of desire.

And every time he thought about her with Ringo, forced to do only heaven knew what, he was filled with a burning hatred. No other woman had even come close to breaking through the barrier he'd erected around his feelings in the past three years. And no other woman had ever touched his emotions in such depth, or aroused such strong feelings within him, as he had to admit, T.J. did. Not even Caroline had made him care so much. He remembered the soft sparkle in T.J.'s eyes when she laughed, the delicate curve of her lips when she smiled, and the silky feel of the long chestnut curls as he'd allowed them to slip slowly through his fingers the night they'd made love. She had touched his soul, made him feel what he'd never felt before, and he had to find her.

The Tucson-Santa Rita mountain range loomed up before him. Chance reined in and looked around. The trail definitely led into the mountains. He sighed and shifted his weight in the saddle. It was going to be a long day. Maybe only one of many. Riding into the mountains meant he could be bushwhacked at almost any time. They were filled

with canyons, crevices, and passes: a hundred places a man
could hide, a hundred places a man could be killed, his
body never found.

Tall saquaro cacti grew everywhere, protruding up from
the earth like giant fingers pointing toward the sky, some
with projecting arms that also pointed upward.

A jackrabbit scurried into view from behind one of the
nearby saquaros, froze when he spotted Chance, then dived
into a hole.

Many of the saquaros were tall and fat enough for a man
to hide behind and pick Chance off with one well-aimed
bullet.

A humorless smile tugged at his lips. Ambushing wasn't
Ringo's style. He liked to face a man down, instill him with
fear. Ringo was like a leech. He took nourishment off of
instilling fear into people. It thrilled him. No, he wouldn't
ambush Chance. Johnny Ringo was too egotistical for
that—and too good with his guns. He would want to face
him, so that he could boast to the world that he'd outdrawn
and killed U.S. Marshal Chance Burkette.

The rich green of the saquaros made him think of T.J.'s
eyes, so mesmerizing and full of life. Thoughts of her were
rarely out of his mind now. They haunted him constantly,
hovering just at the periphery of his consciousness, teasing
him. He struggled now to keep them at bay and forced
himself instead to concentrate on tracking them, on what
he would do to Johnny Ringo, or any other cowboy, if they
had so much as laid a hand on her before Chance could
get to them.

Nothing else mattered to him anymore, not even getting
Gil Calder and salving the need for revenge that had dwelt
in his heart since the massacre of his family. Nothing mattered but getting T.J. back. If he was wrong about her now,
if she had gone willingly and was part of their scheme,
then he would face that. And he would probably die, just

as they wanted. But if he wasn't wrong . . . he didn't want to think about what they might do to her.

Chance reined in and looked around. He'd been riding all day with little rest. They'd taken him in circles, obviously purposely, before leading him to the mountains. Why? To give Curly Bill time to get ahead of them? For Calder to ride into town and rob it while Chance was riding around in the middle of the desert? It didn't matter. He had to find T.J., and following their trail was the only way.

The sun was quickly sinking behind the mountains. It would be only a matter of minutes before it was gone and the landscape plunged into darkness. If the moon was visible as it had been for the past few nights, there would be enough light to see his way through the thick growing cacti and mountainous terrain, but not enough to see a trail of hoof prints on the ground from Diablo's back.

An inferno of rage roiled about in his chest as he realized that he would have to make camp and wait for the darkness to pass before he could go on. They could travel at night, they knew where they were going. He didn't.

"Damn," he cursed, looking up at the sky. If there truly was a God, why had He put T.J. in this danger? Calder and Ringo, and most likely every other cowboy in their camp, were after him. It was Chance they wanted, not her. But they'd taken her to get him. He had no doubt of that now.

An hour later it was too dark to go any farther. Not only did he risk losing the trail altogether, but he risked injury to Diablo. In the dark one misstep could result in the horse falling or breaking a leg. In a small clearing, Chance begrudgingly dismounted. He uncinched the saddle from around Diablo's belly and tossed it to the ground, then pulled a blanket around his shoulders, settled himself on a rock, and stared out into the black night. Sleep and a fire were two things he couldn't afford. Sleep would leave him vulnerable to anyone sneaking up on him; a fire would pinpoint his location not only to the outlaws, but also to the Apaches. He'd faced the prospect of dying many times in his life already, but if he had a choice about it, he'd rather be killed with a swift bullet and be buried with his scalp intact.

Diablo whinnied softly and Chance whirled around on the rock. He whipped the Peacemaker from his holster as he spun. A small lizard skittered across a rock near the horse. Chance smiled and breathed a sigh of relief. "Take it easy, boy," he said softly. "We'll be okay."

The night passed slowly, and each hour gave Chance a lot of time to think: some of his thoughts pleasant, some he would have rather not have had come to mind at all. He shifted position and his gaze swept over the dark horizon. Searching for movement within the ebony shadows and finding none, he relaxed somewhat. The sky was a pristine panorama of blackness, its vistas broken only by a slivered crescent of moon nestled just above the horizon, while scores of tiny, diamond like stars glistened from within the dark, endless abyss. Thoughts of T.J. filled his mind.

How could a woman he didn't really know, a woman who had come out of nowhere and wouldn't, or couldn't, tell him about her past, about herself, come to mean so much to him in such a short time—more than his own wife had ever meant to him? He'd loved Caroline in the beginning, but with the passing of their years together, their love had passed away also, until they had been only friends. Chance brought a foot up to rest on the rock, then draped one arm over the bent knee and dropped his head onto it. He let his eyelids flutter closed.

Gil Calder had killed Chance's family. He had savagely murdered them in cold blood, yet the desperately driving need for revenge that had kept Chance going since that day, the thirst for vengeance, was no longer the force driving him. Now it was the living that needed him, and he could only pray that he would succeed. T.J. needed him. Morgan and Rick needed him. He had to find a way to get to them, to save them before it was too late.

T.J. remained on the ground where she'd fallen after Ringo slapped her and pushed her to her knees. Hours had passed since that moment, but she hadn't moved away from the spot. Not because she was frightened, but because moving might draw attention to herself, and until she found a way to escape, she had decided to draw as little attention to herself as possible. At the moment she was just thankful that Ringo hadn't returned for her. After hitting her he'd marched into a nearby tent and reappeared a second later with two bottles of whiskey, one in each hand. Evidently sex wasn't a driving force in Ringo's mind when he was mad.

"Thank heaven for little favors," she'd whispered as he stalked past.

He'd stopped beside her and she feared he had heard her words.

"Just going drinking for a while, beautiful," he'd said. "Don't go away. Cause I'll just have to come after you, and that might make me mad." She remembered the ugly laugh that had rolled from his throat then. "And Sue Ann tells me I'm not too nice when I get mad."

T.J. shivered just remembering the look that had come into Ringo's eyes when he'd threatened her. She'd gotten the feeling he would almost have been glad if he returned and found her gone, so he could go after her. But she wasn't going to try to escape unless she was sure she could succeed. There was no point in getting Ringo any more vicious than he already was.

They'd entered the canyon valley and the outlaws' hideout just before sundown. That had been hours ago. The sky was now pitch black, the only light filtering her way was that reflecting from the moon.

A loud hum of talk and laughter hung over the small clearing. T.J. leaned forward, peering around the table toward the other grouping of table and chairs where most of the cowboys, including Ringo, had gathered. Empty whiskey bottles littered the ground around them. A half dozen women—white, Mexican, and at least one Indian or half-breed—were in the crowd, their bodies draped over those of the cowboys they were with at the moment. Obviously they weren't with any one cowboy in particular. T.J. had watched two of the women move from one cowboy to another, flirting, laughing, sliding their hands provocatively over the men's bodies.

Maybe, if she was lucky, Ringo would forget about her. She watched him take a long swig of whiskey directly from a bottle. A thin river of it escaped the corner of his mouth and trickled down the side of his neck. T.J. shivered in disgust.

Suddenly two men stepped from Gil Calder's tent. The camp fire set up only a few yards away cast the immediate area in a blaze of golden light nearly as bright as that from the morning sun. T.J. felt herself start in surprise.

"It can't be," she muttered to herself. "It can't be." But it was. She gawked openly, her eyes wide with disbelief, her jaw hanging agape at the shock that had filled her at first sight of them.

Gil Calder left the tent to stand beside Morgan and Rick Burkette. Morgan, the taller of the two brothers, had removed his hat, the only reason T.J. recognized him. His hair was dark brown, rather than the deep black of Chance's, and his features were different. Where Chance's face was square, his features hard cut, almost chiseled, the lines of Morgan's features were smoother and not quite as severe. T.J.'s gaze moved to rest on the youngest brother, Rick.

She knew from talking with Doc that Morgan was thirty-two, and Chance a year and a half younger. Rick was twenty-four, a year older than Lisa. She quickly pushed the thought of her sister from her mind and turned her attention back to Chance's younger brother. He wore a thick mustache like Chance. Morgan's face was clean shaven. She couldn't see his hair for the Stetson he wore, but the ragged ends at the collar of his shirt attested to the fact that it, too, was dark like his brother's. Firelight danced off of the curving line of his cheekbones, testifying to their height and prominent shape, as well as from the nose that was straight but slightly flared at the end.

They looked exactly as they had in the picture hanging in Doc's parlor.

But what were Chance's brothers doing here with Gil Calder? Were they outlaws? She immediately dismissed that idea as ridiculous. Chance's brothers couldn't be outlaws. She would have heard. Someone in town would have spoken about it and she'd have heard. Doc would have said something. But Doc had said they were in California.

Her gaze moved to Ringo. He was still sitting on a bench in the midst of twenty or so other cowboys, the whiskey bottle he held in his hand nearly empty now. Or would Doc have kept silent about it if Morgan and Rick had turned bad? Would he have lied about where they were? Maybe so as not to embarrass Chance?

She heard the men laugh then, and felt another start of surprise that Chance's brothers would find anything to laugh at with Gil Calder.

As if he had just remembered her presence, Ringo turned and caught T.J.'s gaze. His eyes grew wide as a lewd, lascivious grin curved his lips and, without taking his gaze from hers, he lifted the bottle to his lips. Firelight reflected off of the liquor that swirled around in the bottle, turning it to an inviting golden amber.

T.J. shuddered and momentarily forgot about the presence of Chance's brothers as she was held spellbound by the look she saw in Ringo's eyes. Insanity was the only word she could find to describe it. Cold, senseless, souless, insanity.

He rose and threw the empty bottle to the ground and it crashed against several others.

T.J. started, fearing the worst.

At the same time one of the women pushed a rather rotund, grizzled old man away from her. He fell on his face in the dirt, the clinking sound of glass breaking against glass lost in a roar of laughter from the surrounding cowboys.

Ringo staggered toward T.J., several dark curls of hair falling over his forehead and giving him an even more sinister appearance.

T.J. cringed.

"Hey, beautiful," Ringo said, slurring his words so that they were almost incoherent. He reached down and grabbed her arm, then jerked her up.

T.J. scrambled to her feet and tried to pull away from him.

"Ah, ah, ah," Ringo muttered, as if scolding a small child for misbehaving. He laughed and jerked her toward him. His fingers tightened cruelly on her arm, squeezing the tender flesh and nearly crushing her bone.

A small shriek of pain flew from T.J.'s lips and she tried to twist away from him, yanking on her arm and lashing out at him with one foot.

Ringo stumbled, but maintained his grip on her with one hand. His other swung out wildly, as quickly as the strike of a snake, and struck her cheek.

T.J.'s head snapped back at the powerful and surprising impact.

"I told you before, beautiful," Ringo said, "that kind of stuff can get you in a lot of trouble." He laughed again and staggered, nearly tripping over her. "Come on," he snarled, and jerked her toward his tent. "You and me's going to have a little fun now."

"Over my dead body," T.J. snapped. She dug her heels into the ground and twisted her body.

Ringo hauled her up against him and glowered down at her. He reeked of stale whiskey and cheap cigars, and when he talked into her face, his own barely an inch away from hers, the smells were so powerful, T.J. recoiled in disgust.

"That could be arranged, beautiful," Ringo said, "later." He laughed lewdly.

"I like my women with a bit of fire in them, and dead women ain't got no fire. Now get the hell in there and take your clothes off."

He put a hand on her back and pushed her savagely toward the tent, then staggered in after her.

T.J. stumbled forward and into the tent's canvas flap. She fell to her knees. The slap of the thick fabric struck her cheeks and brought tears to her eyes. She tried to push back to her feet but before she could, Ringo's boot pressed against her rear end. He shoved sadistically and sent her sprawling onto the floor inside the tent. As her chest smashed against the ground T.J. felt the air being forced from her lungs. She gasped for breath. Her lungs burned, her throat ached, and she was blinded by a haze of stinging tears in her eyes.

Ringo threw himself down on a cot beside her. "Take your clothes off," he ordered, the words all running together.

T.J. turned to look at him, unsure of what he'd said. He sat up and stared down at her.

"Off!" he yelled. One hand shot toward her and grabbed at the shirt front he'd ripped open earlier. His fingers curled around the collar and pulled at it.

T.J. heard the fabric tear and felt a rush of cool air on her shoulder. She jerked away from him.

"Off!" He reached out to grab at her a second time.

"No," she screamed, scurrying away from him. Her

hands clutched at the front of her shirt. "I'll do it myself." She stared at him defiantly, daring him to grab her again.

He smiled wickedly. "Me first." He flopped down on the cot and threw his limbs out in a spread eagle position.

T.J. frowned at his words but tried to tell herself he couldn't possibly mean what she thought he meant.

"What do you mean?"

He raised himself halfway up, pulled the gun from his holster and put it on the cot beside him, then lay down and looked up at her expectantly. "Undress me first."

"Undress you?" T.J. repeated, stalling for time, though she didn't know what she expected to happen. There was no one here to rescue her, no back up to come barging into the room. He remained silent but his fingers curled around the gun at his side.

"Now, beautiful," he said softly. His tone, in spite of the exaggerated slurring of words, was more threatening than any she'd heard him use so far.

Rising to her knees T.J. unbuckled the holster, slid it from beneath his hips and placed it on a saddlebag that lay nearby. If she got the slightest chance, just the slightest, she'd find a way to bash his head in. He kicked off his own boots. T.J.'s hands moved to the buttons of his shirt. She made to open one and her fingers hesitated as they felt hot flesh beneath their touch. Her eyes darted to his and he grinned. T.J. shuddered, but held her body taut so that he could not see the involuntary ripple of abhorrence that shook her.

"Keep going, beautiful." He sighed.

She unbuttoned his shirt and pushed it from his shoulders. Ringo did little to help. He merely watched her and kept the gun securely clasped in his hand. Even when she went to slip the shirtsleeves from his arms, he transferred the gun from one hand to the other rather than let go of it altogether.

T.J. looked at his bare chest. It was as bronze as the

desert floor under a hot, summer sun. Johnny Ringo could not be called a muscular or powerfully built man. He was tall and sinewy, his limbs lanky, but strong. A small sprinkling of curly brown hairs nestled in the center of his chest.

She glanced toward his face and saw that his eyes had rolled upward and his lids were drooping and almost closed.

At her hesitation to continue, Ringo's bloodshot eyes shot open and he reached up, clasped his fingers about her arm and shoved it toward his groin. Blushing, and angrier than she'd ever been in her life, T.J. grabbed at his belt buckle and yanked it loose, then tore open his pants, uncaring whether the buttons were ripped off or not. Another sprinkling of dark hairs covered his stomach and descended in a line downward, disappearing below the edge of the long johns he wore beneath his trousers. Steeling herself against him, and struggling to maintain the fury building within her, T.J. pulled both the trousers and long johns over his hips and down his legs. She kept her eyes purposely averted from the turgid evidence of his lust that came into view as she undressed him. Ringo was not quite as near passing out as she'd hoped.

She tossed the trousers to the floor.

"Now yours," Ringo ordered. He pushed up on one elbow and looked at her. His eyelids dropped dramatically.

T.J. swallowed hard. If she didn't think of something soon . . . She left the thought unfinished, not wanting to think about what would happen here if she wasn't presented with an opportunity to escape him. Taking a deep breath she reached up to take the front of her blouse in her hands. She pulled it back and over her shoulders. T.J. glared at the outlaw with each movement, trying not to look anywhere but at his face, at those cruel, inhuman eyes that were the essence of Johnny Ringo.

But Ringo didn't meet her gaze. His eyes were too busy watching the soft, smooth, golden flesh that was slowly

being revealed to him by her movements. She saw the
animal hunger in his eyes, sensed the carnal lust that
heated his body, and shuddered with revulsion. She
removed her boots, then stood up.

Ringo started, and his fingers tightened around the gun
still held in his hand. "What are you doing?" he
demanded.

T.J. battled the fear that had sharpened at his grabbing
of the gun, and smiled. His eyes were getting glassier looking, and his words were so slurred as to be little more than
murmurs.

"I can't take my pants off if I'm sitting down," she said
sweetly. She tried to look coy. "You do want me to take
them off, don't you, Ringo?"

He grinned and ran his tongue over the length of his
bottom lip. His hand slackened its hold on the gun as his
eyes moved over her body.

T.J. unbuttoned the trousers and pushed them from her
hips. Her pulse was racing and her heart was hammering
wildly within her breast. If he didn't pass out soon, it might
be too late, and she had yet to see a way to overpower him
and get away. The man might be drunk, but he was still a
lot stronger than she was. The trousers dropped to the
floor.

Ringo dropped back on the cot and stared up at her.

T.J. paused.

"Keep going," he ordered gruffly.

But instead of unhooking her brassiere, or removing
the bikini underpants she wore, T.J. sat down on the side
of the cot and smiled down at him. "Well, I thought you
might like to take some of it off," she said teasingly. "Isn't
that part of the fun, Ringo?"

His face split in a wide, hungry smile. "Changed your
mind about things, huh, beautiful?" He laughed softly and
reached up to grab her arms. His fingers closed like steel
claws around the tender flesh.

T.J. stiffened, unable to help herself. But his hold on her and the look in his eyes gave her hope. His grip was still strong, but she could see now that his movements were slowing, as if his limbs were becoming heavy, and the glassy look in his eyes was worsening. His lids began to droop.

He jerked her down toward him and, before she knew what he'd intended, he twisted, threw her body down to the cot, and rolled half on top of her. One of his legs pinned hers to the cot and he lay with his chest half over her, one breast crushed beneath his weight. She could feel the hardness of his hunger pressing against her thigh, hot and swollen.

"Show me some fire, bitch," Ringo commanded. His lips crashed down on hers, his mouth wet and hungry, his tongue forcing its way between her lips, between her teeth.

T.J.'s stomach churned with nausea stirred by her repugnance to his touch. For one fleeting second she thought about biting down on his tongue, but she refrained. He would most likely kill her if she did, and she didn't want to die, not yet. If she died now Chance would most likely be killed, too, and she couldn't bear to let that happen. She prayed that the liquor Ringo had consumed would soon plunge him into an unconscious stupor, while at the same time she tried to push him away and found that one of her arms was imprisoned beneath his weight. She smashed her free hand against his shoulder and raised it to strike at him again.

Ringo grabbed her arm and jerked it up and over her head. His fingers curled around her wrist, a bone-crushing vice that brought a groan of pain from her lips.

Holding her his helpless captive, Ringo's mouth maliciously raped hers.

His weight shifted slightly, not enough to set her free, and she felt his other hand grappling with her brassiere, tugging at it. Then suddenly, his mouth left hers and he lay still, his breath coming in ragged gasps. He lay with his head beside hers, the putrid odor of his whiskey and tobacco tainted breath wafting over her.

T.J. swallowed hard, and forced herself to breathe through her mouth so that the horrid smell would not intensify her nausea. She needed all her strength to get through this, and getting sick would only rob her of a good deal of it.

Chapter Twenty-Four

Chance stood and whipping the blanket from his shoulders, stretched his arms wide. It had been a long night, one of the longest he'd ever known. But at least it had passed peacefully, with no Apaches or cowboys trying to sneak up on him. He yawned, resettled the weight of his gun and holster on his hips, and bent to pick up Diablo's saddle blanket.

There was no telling how much farther he had to ride. He had no doubt now that there was no way he could lose the trail, even if the terrain turned rockier than it was now. It had become obvious that Ringo and Sue Ann were making certain that they left enough of a trail for him to follow, which meant he had to be more cautious than ever. They were definitely setting a trap for him. The question was when did they plan to spring it?

Normally such an obvious trap wouldn't have bothered him, but this time he had T.J. to think about, as well as Morgan and Rick, if they weren't dead already. The possibility weighed on his heart.

Thoughts of T.J. had tormented him all night. The memory of how it felt to hold her in his arms, to kiss her, he now knew was branded on his soul. He had vowed, when his marriage to Caroline had begun to crumble and the hurt of that dying love had ripped open his heart, that he would never allow himself to be put in a position to feel that way again. And he had succeeded, until now.

Somehow, even when he had been thoroughly convinced that she was Sue Ann Calder, an outlaw's wife, T.J. had managed to penetrate the cold, hard barrier he had built up around his emotions. Without his realizing it was happening, she had managed to slip past his anger, past his suspicions, his resolve, and his fear, and touch a part of his heart that had never been touched before.

And now, because he hadn't listened to her sooner, he had put them both in a position to be killed.

"Damn." The lone curse slipped from his lips and hung on the quiet dawn air.

Diablo whinnied softly behind him, then lowered his head and continued to munch on a small patch of wild grass.

Chance threw the saddle blanket onto the stallion's back, then settled his saddle on top of it and reached to fasten the cinch. He would follow their trail only until he confirmed their direction and felt it unsafe to go any farther, then he would veer off and parallel it as best he could.

If Calder had a hideout in this mountain range, which obviously he did, then Chance was pretty sure he could travel a coinciding trail to that of Ringo and Sue Ann, and eventually find the hideout on his own. At the same time he'd avoid whatever trap Ringo and Sue Ann had set up for him.

He rolled the blanket he'd used to cover his shoulders all night, tied it behind his saddle, and mounted. Coffee was something he was going to have to go without this morning. Smoke from a camp fire would only alert anyone

watching for him of his exact whereabouts. Chance too
a long swallow of water from his canteen, then softly
touched his spurs to Diablo's flanks to urge him forward.

T.J. sat on Ringo's saddlebags, her shoulders slumped
in depression. At the moment it would be easy to kill him.
He was unconscious and had been for hours. But that
wouldn't get her out of this mess. There were at least three
or four dozen more outlaws outside, and as far as she knew
there was only one way out of this canyon, the same way
they'd come in.

T.J. turned her thoughts to Chance's brothers. She still
wasn't sure what they were doing here, but she had nearly
convinced herself that they couldn't be outlaws. They had
to be here undercover. It was the only answer that made
any sense. Chance was a marshal. Calder and his men
were outlaws. Chance's brothers must also be marshals, or
deputies. If she could just get a message to them, they
could help each other.

Ringo snorted and rolled over.

T.J. jumped, glared, then seeing that he was still asleep,
screwed her face into a grimace at him. It would truly be
nice if he died in his sleep, but she was pretty sure that
wasn't going to happen. She wasn't positive, but it seemed
she'd read in a history book that Johnny Ringo had been
killed by the Earps, or Doc Holliday after the gunfight at
the O.K. Corral in Tombstone.

Several times, after Ringo had passed out in a drunken
stupor, T.J. had poked her head out of the tent in the
hopes of seeing a means of escape, but her hopes had
been dashed every time. Cowboys stood on guard everywhere. Then the sun had risen, but Ringo slept on. Now
it was midafternoon and she was beginning to wonder if
he was ever going to wake up. Not that she really cared,
except with him seemed to be the only way she was going

to get out of this tent, and getting out of this tent was the only way she was going to be able to reach Chance's brothers. She took a deep breath, her lungs filling with the hot, dry air in the tent. It was near suffocating. Feeling the need to stand up and stretch, T.J. rose to her feet. A shimmering veil of perspiration covered her breasts and caused her shirt to cling to her back.

The tangy aroma of a pot of freshly brewing coffee wafted into the tent and teased her nostrils, as it had several times over the past few hours. Maybe a good, strong, hot cup of coffee would get her brain cells working again. She turned to step from the tent.

T.J.'s hand froze on the tent flap as a rustling sounded behind her.

"Where do you think you're going, beautiful?" Ringo growled.

T.J. stopped and turned back, gritting her teeth.

He had risen up on one elbow.

She forced a seductive smile to her face and a purr to her voice. "Why, to get you some coffee, sweetheart." She made her eyes move slowly and suggestively up and down his body. "I thought after last night, and all the energy you expended, you might need a little nourishment. Especially since you've nearly slept the day away."

"Last night?" Ringo echoed. His eyes shone with blank confusion.

T.J. compelled stiff legs to move toward him, then knelt to bring her face level with his. The game she was playing was a dangerous game, she knew, but he'd left her no choice. She raised a hand to his cheek and caressed it with the back of her fingers.

"You were really wonderful last night, Ringo," she whispered, and brushed her lips across his. "Absolutely wonderful."

"Yeah?"

She smiled coyly.

"Better than your marshal?" His eyes held hers and he moved one hand to her breast. He cupped it within his hand, then his fingers moved to her nipple and he squeezed it hard.

T.J. clenched a fist against the pain his cruel act brought. If she could only have one more thing out of life, it would be that Chance be saved. If she could have two things, she would wish she could dig her fingernails into Ringo's eyes and rip them from their sockets. She smiled instead.

"Umm, much better than the marshal, handsome," she said, hoping the words had the ego stroking effect she desired. She laughed softly and arched her back toward him, thrusting her breast farther into his hand. "Much, much better."

Ringo smiled like a cat who'd just swallowed a prize mouse, and stretched his arms wide. The thin blanket she draped over the bottom half of his body to obscure its nakedness from her sight, fell from his legs. She looked away quickly, but not fast enough to obliterate a view of the small, shrunken organ that had so terrified her last night with its swollenness.

"Get me some coffee," he said, and closed his eyes against the sunlight that filtered through the thin canvas and lit the tent's interior. "My head's killing me."

"Certainly, sweetheart," T.J. cooed. She pushed back to her feet and walked from the tent. The moment she stepped into the crisp morning air and out of Ringo's sight she wiped a hand over her lips, as if to eradicate the lingering feel of his mouth on hers. She straightened her shirt as best she could. Only one button was left intact to hold it closed so she'd been forced to tie its ends just beneath her breasts rather than tuck it in. T.J. looked around at the camp. A group of about ten of the outlaws were standing around a camp fire drinking coffee.

"I need a cup of coffee for Ringo," she said, approaching them.

Several dark eyes met hers.

"Give him a good time last night, honey?" one cowboy asked. He leered at her knowingly.

"Maybe you could visit some of us tonight?" another suggested.

"Or even this morning?" yet another said.

They all laughed.

T.J. pushed past them and grabbing a cup from the ground, reached for the tin coffee pot set on the smoldering fire. Rising, she looked at the faces that surrounded her. Neither of Chance's brothers was there. With her heart just about in her toes, T.J. started on her way back to the tent; then she caught sight of Rick Burkette near the horses. He was brushing one down. She walked toward him.

"Rick?" she whispered. "Rick Burkette?"

His fingers tightening their grip on the horse brush he held, he turned slowly to face her.

"I'm T.J. McAllister."

"You must have the wrong guy, lady. My name's Burgess, not Burkette."

She looked over her shoulder to make certain no one else was nearby, then turned back to him.

"I was with Chance yesterday," she whispered. "Ringo and Sue Ann made me come here with them. They figure Chance will follow to rescue me and they can ambush him. Please, Rick, he's your brother. You've got to help me save him."

He turned away from the horse, looked in both directions, and hurried to stand before her. He pushed his hat from his forehead and stared down at her, the slant of his mouth leaving no doubt that he was angry. His features resembled Morgan's much more than Chance's did. Except for his eyes. They were near identical to Chance's, the same clear, but sometimes fathomless dark blue. "Who the hell are you, lady?"

"That doesn't matter," T.J. said. "What matters now is that they're going to kill Chance if we don't do something to stop them."

"How do I know this isn't a trick? Why should I believe anything you say?"

She had no answer for that, and shrugged. "I can't prove it, Rick, but—"

"Who are you?" he insisted.

"T.J. McAllister. I was hurt, and Chance saved me, took me to Doc's."

"So why would they think he'd come rescue you?"

T.J. felt her cheeks warm. "Because they found out I'm in love with him."

"And he loves you?" Rick asked.

A sad smile curved her lips. "I think so. But that doesn't matter now. What does is that he'll come and they're going to kill him."

Rick looked around again. "So, how'd you recognize me? How did you know who I was?"

"I was staying at Doc's house and saw your picture. He talked a lot about you and Morgan and Chance. But he didn't tell me you were here with Calder."

"He doesn't know. No one does, except Chance, and if we blow our cover now, Calder might never be caught and this damned band of outlaws put behind bars."

"If you and Morgan don't help me, they're going to ambush Chance and kill him."

"Son of a b . . ." Rick slammed a fist against one of the rough hewn beams of wood erected as part of the horse corral. "Lady, if you're lying—"

"I'm not."

"Then I guess I'd better find Morgan."

"He's right here, Rick," Ringo said.

Rick Burkette swung around, his hand automatically

reaching for his gun. T.J., instantly recognizing Ringo's voice and grabbed Rick's arm to prevent his draw. From what she'd overheard, and what little she knew of him from history, there was no way Rick could outdraw Ringo.

Morgan and Ringo walked out from among some of the other horses. T.J. gasped softly as she saw Ringo's gun pressed to the small of Morgan's back.

Ringo laughed. "That was a damned good game you tried to play, beautiful," he said, "damned good. But not quite good enough. I never forget when I sample a lady's favors." He laughed again, the sound tinged with an ugly ring of smugness. "Or when I don't sample them."

T.J. burned with anger and humiliation. She had made a fool of herself, and he had let her and obviously enjoyed it. Every curse she had ever heard ran through her mind, and all were directed at herself. She had caused all of this with her stubbornness and stupidity.

Ringo pushed Morgan forward and then waved his gun toward the camp fire several yards away where the other outlaws stood congregated. "Move it."

They began to walk toward the camp fire.

"Sorry," T.J. mumbled to Rick and Morgan.

"Yeah," Rick grumbled. "Great."

Morgan remained silent.

T.J.'s temper flared. How could she, a well-educated, well-trained cop from 1996, blunder so badly while in a primitive Old West town? She should have been able to outwit them all so easily. Instead she'd botched everything, and now she was responsible for the fact that they were all about to get killed—including Chance.

And she hadn't even saved Lisa.

Chance crawled on his belly toward the precipice of the mountain top. He'd left Diablo in a narrow canyon a half mile back, not wanting to risk the stallion scenting a mare in heat, whinnying his fool head off, and giving Chance's position away. He had also left both his Stetson and his rifle there. One glint of the late afternoon sun off either the Winchester's barrel or the silver conchos on his hatband would also alert the outlaws to his presence. Slowly, carefully, he inched himself forward. Fast movement could draw the attention of a lookout. Sweat trickled from his forehead, caused from both his nervousness and the stifling heat of the day.

God, what he wouldn't give for a drink.

He raised his head and looked over the curving crown of the mountain. His gaze moved first over the range of raised earth that lined the opposite side of the canyon below. It was nearly the same height as the peak he was on. There was a lookout positioned on it.

Chance swore under his breath. As long as he stayed hidden by the tall saguaro he lay behind, he wouldn't be visible to the lookout. But if he made a wrong move, he'd be easily spotted. His gaze moved slowly over the remaining hilltops. There were two other lookouts stationed at the mouth of the canyon. Chance turned his gaze skyward. It would be several more hours before dark.

He was just about to push his way back down the slope of earth when a shout from below caused him to pause.

"Hey, Gil, I've got a surprise for you," Ringo called out. He laughed loudly. "One helluva surprise."

Chance felt his gut twist into a knot as he peered down into the canyon.

"Hey, Gil," Ringo called again. He raised a gun in the air and pulled the trigger.

Gil Calder stepped from one of the tents, his shirt hanging open and revealing a brawny, hairy chest.

"Damn it, Ringo, what are you trying to do firing your gun like that, tell every lawman in the country where we are?"

Ringo laughed.

"This better be good, Ringo," Calder said. "Me and Sue Ann was having ourselves a little supper party." He laughed. "If you know what I mean."

Their voices drifted clearly up to Chance, each word as concise and distinct as if he were standing right next to them. His fingers dug into the hot earth as his heart contracted with fear.

"How about a couple of spies? That good enough for you?" Ringo said. He shoved his gun into Morgan's back again and roughly pushed him forward.

"Spies? What in the hell are you talking about Ringo?" Calder growled. "That's Morgan and Rick Burgess. They been riding with us for months now."

Ringo laughed. "No, they're Morgan and Rick Burkette, Gil. Burkette."

"Burkette?" Calder thundered, his rage turning his face purple. He grabbed Morgan's shirtfront and yanked him forward so that their faces were barely an inch apart. "You a brother to that son of a bitch marshal, Chance Burkette?"

Morgan remained silent and merely glared at Calder, who shoved him back and turned his attention on Rick. He smashed Rick's face with the back of his hand. Rick spun away but kept his feet. He straightened.

"What about it, sonny?" Calder demanded when Rick faced him again. "Are you two Burkette's brothers?"

Rick didn't answer.

"They're his brothers all right," Ringo said. "And she's his woman."

Calder smiled, an ugly, lewd, evil curve of his lips. He turned to look at T.J. "Yeah, that's what Sue Ann said. When I gave her time to talk." His eyes moved over T.J. with blatant hunger. "Was she any good, Ringo?"

The outlaw laughed. "Can't tell you, Gil. I had a little too much to drink last night and passed out. But I'll let you know in the morning."

"Stake them two out," Gil said, motioning toward Rick and Morgan.

Ringo called to several of the other outlaws, then looked back at Calder. "Why not just kill them now and be done with it?"

"Because I want to kill all three of them Burkettes together. So they can watch each other die." A wide grin split his face. "Real slow like."

Ringo smiled. "Sounds kind of fun."

"Yeah."

Chance watched, enraged. He saw T.J. reach to one shoulder and pull at her sleeve. For the first time he noticed that it was ripped from its seam. His fury intensified, its flames licking at the taut rein of self-control, which was the only thing that kept him still.

He felt his muscles tense for action. His finger ached to curl around the thin curve of his gun's metal trigger and blow Calder and Ringo to kingdom come. Instead, he remained still, watching, hardly daring to breathe lest someone discover him there, knowing that if his brothers and T.J. were to escape certain death, he was their only hope.

A rush of anguish filled him. He couldn't lose her now. Fate couldn't be so cruel—as to wrench another woman from him like this, a woman who had made him believe again in the possibility of love. Chance felt tears fill his eyes at the thought of T.J. being murdered, and his being unable to save her. He looked down into the canyon through the mist that covered his eyes and a steely determination stole over him.

Chance slowly pushed himself back down the slope of earth, exerting extreme caution, not wanting to disturb one rock that might alert anyone to his presence. Once back to the spot where he'd left Diablo, Chance checked his guns and the ammunition he'd brought, taking the bullets from their small boxes and shoving them into his pockets.

He knew what he had to do, and how he was going to do it. When he went in, he hoped he wouldn't need to fire a shot. If he did, his fragile plan could go up in smoke. He scoffed at the wording of his own thoughts. More likely if he had to fire, his plan would go up in a barrage of returned gunfire and he'd end up looking more like a piece of Swiss cheese than a man. But then, a man didn't need to care what he looked like when he was dead.

He turned back to his horse, and removed both bridle and saddle. If he didn't come back he'd rather have Diablo running wild and free on the range, than captured by Gil Calder or any of his gang.

A single shot suddenly broke the still twilight air echoing through the canyons, over the mountains, and down into the valley far below.

Chance froze, terror turning his blood to ice.

Chapter Twenty-Five

Ringo and another cowboy shoved Morgan and Rick toward one side of the canyon.

"No, here, tie 'em up next to my tent," Gil called to them. "If they try to escape, or Burkette tries to come in for them, I want to know about it."

The two men steered Morgan and Rick toward the side of Calder's tent. One viciously pushed Morgan's back and sent him staggering forward. The other cowboy rapped the butt of his gun against Rick's head. He fell, unconscious, to the ground.

T.J. stood rooted to the spot, unsure of what was happening, and knowing, with a feeling of despair, that there was nothing she could do to help them. Another cowboy walked past at that moment, and she considered, for one fleeting millisecond of time, grabbing the gun that hung sheathed in his low-slung holster. The sure knowledge that Ringo would then kill all three of them stopped her.

The two cowboys who'd taken over guard of Morgan and Rick pounded wooden stakes into the ground while

Ringo smugly stood over the brothers, ready to kill either
of them if they made one wrong move. Morgan glared up
at Ringo. Rick was regaining consciousness. One of the
cowboys took some leather thongs from his pocket.

"Spread 'em out," he growled, and shoved Morgan
down onto his back between the stakes.

He tied a thong around one of Morgan's wrists and its
other end to one of the stakes. He repeated the gesture
with Morgan's other hand and his ankles. When he'd finished, and Morgan was spread-eagled, his limbs spread and
held so tight T.J. knew he had to be in pain, he turned to
Rick and repeated the process.

T.J. nearly groaned in despair. She had been sent back
here by some quirk of fate, some second chance at destiny,
to save Lisa. Instead she was going to get not only herself
killed but three men. Unable to help herself she lunged
at Ringo. Her hands grasped his gun hand and jerked it
upward.

"No," she screamed. "No, you can't do this."

He tried to jerk his gun hand free of her. "Damned
whore, get off." He tried to slap her with his free hand,
but T.J.'s fingernails dug into his arm.

The gun roared in an explosion of sound. Ringo jerked
free of her hold on him. His hand connected with her
jaw and sent her flying backward and sprawling onto the
ground. A kaleidoscope of stars swirled around her head.
Then blackness loomed up to overtake her. T.J. struggled
against it, knowing that to give in to it meant unconsciousness, and that meant helplessness. She struggled to her
knees.

"Try that again," Ringo snarled, "and I'll have you tied
down too. Then each of the boys can take a turn at you."
He placed a boot against her arm and shoved hard.

T.J. flew sideways, her hands flailing outward to break
her fall. She felt the heel of one hand slam into the earth,
the palm of the other crash down on something hard and

jagged. Blood spurted from her palm. Dazed, she wiped it hurriedly on her pants, then pushed herself to her feet. If Ringo wanted to kill her, she was at least going to be standing and facing him when he did it.

But Ringo wasn't interested in killing her at the moment. His cold, snake-like eyes met hers.

"Joe," he yelled to one of the other men. "Tie her to that table. I want to get some dinner."

"Just let the boys have her," Sue Ann said. She stepped forward and looped an arm around one of Gil's. "They need a little fun."

"Not yet," Ringo growled. "When I'm done with her, then they can have her all they want." He looked at T.J. and smiled. "But not before."

Sue Ann shrugged and turned back to her own tent. She glanced over her shoulder and toward her husband. "You coming, Gil?"

He turned. "Yeah, baby. Yeah."

The cowboy Ringo had called Joe grabbed T.J.'s arm and shoved her to the same crudely made wooden table she'd sat at the evening before. "Sit there," he commanded and walked away. A moment later he returned, a length of rope dangling from one hand. Grabbing both her wrists, he tied the rope around them and then, shoving her to the ground, tied it around one of the table legs. "That ought to keep you till Ringo's ready."

T.J. glared up at him. Were these men all animals? She jerked at the ropes as the outlaw turned his back on her and walked away. The rough twine scratched against her skin and scraped some of it off, which brought tears to her eyes. Her gaze moved to the table's leg. Maybe she could lift the table with her back and slip her arms free. She bent to look at the table. It was massive, solid, and there was no way she could lift it, let alone slip her arms out from under its leg while she held it up with her back. Paul Bunyan she was not.

Obviously there were no weapons lying around, like a knife or a razor to use on the rope. And all the broken glass from the previous nights whiskey bottles lie several yards away, surrounding another table, but not this one.

T.J. dropped her head to her arms. She had to think of something. She had to.

When he heard the lone shot, Chance bolted up the hillside, his rifle clutched tightly in one hand. Fear shoved his heart into his throat and nearly robbed him of breath. His imagination ran wild and he tried to ignore the horrible pictures it conjured up. The fingers of his free hand scratched at the dry earth as he scrambled over its steeply sloping surface. He threw himself flat to the ground and peered into the canyon below. Night had fallen over the desert quickly but there was enough moonlight so that he could still see.

He immediately spotted his brothers. They were staked out Apache style to the ground, near what he had ascertained earlier was Gil Calder's tent. Their arms and wrists were bound to small stakes that had been pounded deep into the earth, their limbs stretched nearly beyond their full length and held taut by their bindings. Chance knew this was an Apache method. Most likely the leather strips had been soaked in water. When the sun came up in the morning, they'd begin to dry and shrink.

His eyes searched frantically for T.J. He didn't see her anywhere. Terror seized his heart. "T.J.," he whispered, her name an agonized plea on his lips. "T.J., dammit woman, where are you?"

Rage, fear and a deep, searing anguish tore at his insides, and left him feeling weak and helpless. His finger rested on the trigger of his rifle and curled around the thin curve of metal. If they'd hurt her, if anything had happened to her, he would kill them—all of them.

A movement several yards away from where his brothers lay, and nearly obscured from his sight by a lacework of both moonlight and shadow, drew his attention. Chance squinted, trying to pierce the blackness of the night and bring into focus whatever it was that had drawn his eyes.

T.J. jerked away from the table at that moment, pulling on her rope binding and inadvertently throwing herself into a pale stream of moonlight.

Chance saw the glistening reflection of chestnut hair, the white shirt, and knew immediately it was T.J. His fear abated slightly and he was at least able to breathe. She was sitting on the ground, half under, half beside the table. Chance frowned in puzzlement, then watched as she again jerked her arm away from the table. As he watched he realized she was tied to one of the table legs.

His gaze moved back to his brothers. A cowboy stood nearby, obviously guarding them, though it seemed highly unlikely that they could escape. Obviously Gil Calder wasn't taking any chances. There was at least twenty yards between where his brothers lay staked to the ground and where T.J. sat bound. There was no guard on her, though Chance had no doubt that oversight would be corrected momentarily, unless Ringo or Calder had other plans for her.

He cursed and again mentally measured the distance between her and his brothers. Impossible. Even if he could manage to sneak down into Calder's camp undetected, there was no way he would be able to release his brothers and T.J. before he was spotted, especially since, only a few yards from where T.J. sat, was another table and a roaring camp fire. Gathered around both were at least a dozen more outlaws; most of them were drinking.

What the hell was he going to do now? He had thought to sneak in and somehow get T.J. out without anyone being aware until it was too late. That was out of the question now. The moment she disappeared from beside that table, someone would notice. And he couldn't leave his brothers in there now that they'd been found out.

He looked back at his brothers. Somehow Calder had discovered Morgan and Rick's true identities. Chance's gaze traveled the twenty or so yards that separated his brothers from T.J., then moved to the mouth of the canyon. Impossible. They'd never make it.

A wave of frustration swept over him. Chance closed his eyes and dropped his head so that his forehead rested on the back of the hand clutching the rifle. He had to think of something, and it had to be soon.

For the next few hours Chance remained atop the mountain peak, watching every movement in the canyon. The cowboys gathered around the camp fire continued to drink and their boisterous, drunken laughter filled the air. Calder and Sue Ann had disappeared within their tent and Ringo was busy being fawned over by several women near another camp fire set toward the mouth of the canyon.

T.J. pulled on the rope binding again. The skin under the rough twine had been scraped raw by her twisting movements, but she wouldn't give up. She could feel that the binding had loosened—not much, and certainly not enough to slip one of her hands out, but a little, and that was enough to keep her trying to work herself free and ignore the burning pain her efforts caused her.

Breathless from several straight minutes of yanking, jerking, twisting, and pulling on the rope, T.J. paused to rest. She looked over at Morgan and Rick Burkette, then turned to glance at the outlaws gathered around the camp fire several yards away. They were all too busy drinking and boasting about their adventures and conquests to pay any attention to her. She looked back at Chance's brothers.

Earlier, one of the outlaws brought a bottle of whiskey over to the guard that was watching the bound men. He had guzzled it down and now sat, his back against a small outcropping of rocks, in a deep sleep.

"Morgan, Rick," she called out softly.

Neither man responded.

"I'm sorry," T.J. said. "I never meant for this to happen." She sighed, and waited, but again, neither man spoke. "I'm sorry."

"Why did they bring you here?"

"Rick?" T.J. brightened, just a little.

"Morgan."

She nodded. "Sue Ann saw me with Chance and assumed we . . . I mean, that there was a rela . . . I mean, Ringo saw us together and knew—"

"Do you love him?"

The question was blunt, to the point, and it caused T.J. a moment's start. Did she love him? How could she answer that? She and Chance were from two different times, two different cultures, two different worlds.

Tears suddenly filled her eyes. For years she had dreamed about meeting a man like Chance Burkette, a man so strong in his own right, so sure of himself, so confident in his own abilities and beliefs, that hers were no threat to him. Chance had that strength and much more. He also had warmth, sensitivity, honesty, and passion.

A wave of heat rolled over her skin as the fleeting memory of their lovemaking flashed through her mind and filled her with an ache of longing.

Yes, she loved him. She loved Chance Burkette more than life, but what did it matter? Whether she died here at the hands of some filthy, demented outlaw, or was whisked back to her own time, there was no hope for them. At least not together.

"Do you love him?" Morgan repeated, his tone a little sterner now.

"Yes," T.J. said, the word spoken so softly as to be little

more than a whisper on the still night air. A tear slipped from the long, red gold ruche of lashes where it had hovered and dropped onto her cheek. She glanced up at the sky, as if to ask the heavens how they could be so cruel, and moonlight turned the tiny river of tears to a glistening trail of sparkling silver.

"Do you love him?" Morgan said again. This time his tone was hard, demanding.

"Yes," T.J. repeated, loud enough now so that he heard. "Yes."

"Does he love you?"

"I . . . I don't know."

T.J. blinked away the threatening tears. She had to remain strong. This was no time to fall apart. If there was any chance of getting away at all, she'd have to remain strong.

"He never told me you were with Calder," she said, purposely changing the subject. She couldn't talk about Chance anymore, couldn't think about him, or she knew she'd be unable to stem the tide of tears just waiting to flow out of control. She took in a deep breath and fought to get her emotions under control.

"He wasn't supposed to tell anyone. Only he and the territorial governor know we're here."

"Why?" T.J. asked.

She heard Morgan sigh.

"We've been after Calder for a long time," he said, keeping his voice low, "but we could never get him for anything and make it stick. Too many judges around here are afraid of him, afraid to put him in jail for fear of what he'd have done to them or their families. We thought this was the best, maybe the only way to get him."

"We figured if we set a trap he couldn't squirm out of and caught him in the act, that would be that," Rick added.

Morgan let loose with a scoffing laugh. "But it didn't work. And since getting rescued by the cavalry is pretty much out, and there doesn't seem to be any angels floating down from the sky to untie these ropes, I'd have to say it isn't going to work."

T.J. looked at the two men.

"They left a trail for Chance to follow."

"It's a trap," they both said in unison.

"Will he know that?" T.J. asked. "Will he be able to get around it and get in here to us without getting caught?"

"He'll know it's a trap, and he'll get around it," Morgan said. "But he won't get in here without getting caught. Look around, there's only one way in and out."

"But he'll try anyway," Rick added. "Nothing will stop Chance from going after Calder. Nothing."

"He hates him that much?" T.J. said. "He'd purposely walk into a trap?"

"Yes."

T.J. felt her heart sink. She didn't want to know the answer to the question that filled her mind now, but she had to ask it. She had to know. "Why?"

"Calder killed our parents," Morgan said. "Shot them down in cold blood."

"And Chance's wife and little girl," Rick added softly.

"We were with the posse that was chasing them," Morgan continued, "but we were about four hours behind them. They stopped at our father's ranch and wanted fresh horses. Pa said no, and they shot him. Then they shot everyone else and took the horses. Pa was still alive when we rode up. He lived just long enough to tell us what happened."

"I'll never forget the look on Chance's face when he saw Caroline and Krissy," Rick said.

T.J. sat frozen beside the table as Morgan and Rick's words rang in her ears.

Chapter Twenty-Six

Chance knew what he had to do and had finally figured out a way to do it. He sighed heavily. It was the only way, but the success of his plan depended on Sue Ann Calder, and that was the part he hated. It was also the part he had absolutely no control over. If she didn't give him the opportunity he needed, he'd end up with very little time to get the hell back out of their camp without being shot. And if that happened, his brothers and T.J. would most certainly be lost too.

Leaving his rifle on the ground, Chance pushed himself up. He crouched low as he began to make his way down the mountainside and into the canyon. Night was quickly becoming his only protection, as the saguaros and scrub brush became sparser on the canyon's sloping walls. He found himself forced to move slowly, the pale moonlight of very little help in guiding his steps. One rock nudged out of place, one slip of his foot resulting in a shower of dirt, and every cowboy in the camp below would be alerted to his approach. He moved around several huge boulders, past cavities that resembled natural tunnels, always careful to stay clear of the saguaros and smaller barrel cacti with their sharp thick needles.

Halfway down the mountainside, Chance paused beside a large rock and stood within the blackness of its shadow. The sound of his own ragged breathing and his thudding heartbeat filled his ears. He looked down into the canyon, his eyes moving to the camp fire, then to Calder's tent, and finally in the direction where he'd last seen Ringo. Everything was quiet enough, maybe too quiet.

Chance caught himself, he couldn't think that way. If he did, he might procrastinate the night away, and he couldn't afford to do that.

Only two cowboys still sat talking and drinking next to the camp fire. The rest had either staggered off to find their bedrolls, or passed out on the spot. Ringo and his whores, bedded down near the canyon entrance, had quieted down a while ago and remained so. Calder and Sue Ann were still in their tent, obviously making up for their little separation.

Chance sighed and looked up at the sky. Once he made it to the Calders' tent, he'd give her half an hour. If she didn't come out, he'd have to go in after her. That was dangerous. He needed Calder alive for his plan to succeed and once he went into the tent, there was no guarantee he could get back out without killing him.

He glanced in T.J.'s direction. She was sitting still now, resting her head on her bent arms. Her legs were pulled up tight beside her. A cowboy sat on the table above her smoking a cheroot, obviously her guard. Chance's gaze moved toward his brothers. They, too, were quiet, and their guard still appeared to be passed out.

Chance began his journey the remainder of the way down the mountainside. It sloped more steeply the farther he went. Halfway down he stepped on a rock and the wedged heel of his boot twisted beneath him. Pain shot through his ankle. He fell to one knee. He grabbed for something, anything, to prevent him from careening down the mountainside and creating a shower of dirt, dust, and pebbles. His hand smashed down in the middle of a hedgehog cactus. Chance clamped his jaws together forcibly to stop a shriek of agony from bursting out of his throat.

Gritting his teeth, he jerked his hand back from within the depths of the spiny little plant. Its long needles ripped his shirt sleeve as he pulled away. A stream of curses raced through his head as he cradled his hand to his chest and stared down at it. At least a dozen of the small needles were stuck in his hand and forearm, their rapier sharp points embedded in his flesh. Blood began to ooze from each puncture wound. Why in the hell hadn't he worn his gloves?

His hand began to throb. Scooting quickly behind a short, fat saguaro so as not to be seen, Chance pulled the needles from his flesh as best he could. He yanked his neckerchief off and wiped the blood from his hand. Ten minutes later his hand and arm still hurt like hell, but at least he no longer looked like a porcupine.

Chance began to descend the mountainside again, throwing a parting glare to the hedgehog cactus that resembled a couple of dozen fingers pointing to the sky, each covered with a profusion of spiny white needles.

Once on the canyon floor, he stealthily made his way toward Calder's tent, then stopped about ten feet from it and squatted behind a scrub brush to wait. He released a long sigh of pent-up breath that he did not even realize he had been holding until just that moment. Chance stared at Calder's tent, taking note of its size, its position, and its flap. His eyes bore into the flap that was its only entry. Half an hour passed. Chance felt his stomach churn. If he had to go into that tent, things could get real ugly real quick, the least of which would be Calder waking up.

Chance stood. His hand moved to the Peacemaker settled on his thigh, pulled it halfway out of its sheath, then dropped it back in. He repeated the movement several times, a habit he always followed whenever it looked as if he might have to draw the weapon quickly. His right hand was still sore from its encounter with the cactus, but not sore enough to prevent him using his gun if the need arose. Taking a deep breath, Chance took a step toward the tent.

Its flap suddenly flew open and Sue Ann Calder stepped out.

Chance stopped. This was exactly what he'd been waiting for. Maybe the heavens had decided to grant him a little good luck for a change.

"Where're you going, Sue Ann?" Gil Calder called from within the tent.

Chance froze.

She bent and looked back in at him. "To go," she said. "You want to come watch?"

Gil laughed and Sue Ann turned away from the tent. "Back in a minute, sugar." She began to walk in the direction where Chance stood hidden.

He couldn't believe his luck. Now if it just continued to hold, they might have a chance.

Sue Ann hesitated halfway between the tent and the saguaro Chance stood behind. A frown pulled at her brow and she looked around, as if sensing something was wrong and not quite certain what it was. She peered long and hard into the surrounding darkness, turned and looked back at the tent, but after a few seconds, she shrugged and continued on.

When she was within a few feet of him Chance tensed, his fingers flexing in readiness. She walked past and he pounced on her.

Sue Ann tried to scream, but Chance was ready for that. One hand clamped down on her mouth and tucked her head into his shoulder while the other circled her midriff and held her to him. She reached for the gun tucked into the waistband of her trousers, but Chance caught it first. He jerked it loose and shoved it into his own waistband then stopped the flailing of her arms as his arm again held her in his vicelike grip. She struggled fiercely, throwing her body this way and that, twisting and jerking about and trying to free her face from beneath his hand.

He pushed her first to her knees, then flat to the ground and held her down with one knee. With one hand still clamped tightly over her mouth, he grabbed the neckerchief from his pocket with the other and shoved it, wadded up, into her mouth.

She tried to scream, but the sound came out more a muffled groan.

Chance grabbed her wrists and jerked them behind her. He quickly tied them together, then hauled her to her feet. "Relax, Sue Ann, dammit."

She twisted around to face him, hatred burning bright within her eyes.

"Stay calm, Sue Ann," Chance whispered. "I'm not going to hurt you, unless you force me to. And you don't want to do that, do you?"

Her leg shot upward, but Chance had anticipated her move. He turned and, rather than her knee slamming between his legs, as she'd intended, it rammed into the front of his thigh.

"Dammit," he swore under his breath as he cringed from the blow.

She tried to jerk free of the hold he had on her arm. Chance straightened instantly and tightened his grip, his fingers pressing down into her flesh until she winced and cringed in pain.

"Don't make me do that again, Sue Ann," Chance ordered in a hushed and threatening tone. "Normally I wouldn't hurt a woman, but . . ." He left the sentence unfinished, the rage she heard in his voice, the fury she saw in his moonlit eyes more than enough to tell her exactly what he meant. If she did it again, he'd hurt her.

"Now, we're going up that mountain, and I don't want you to try anything, understand?"

She remained stoic, her eyes averted from his, her body stiff. Her stance told him that, whether she understood or not, she had no plans for making this easy on him.

He jerked on her arm and forced her to look at him. "Listen to me, Sue Ann," he whispered harshly. "If my plan doesn't work I've got nothing to lose here. Understand? So I suggest you cooperate, unless you want to die, 'cause that's exactly what will happen if you try anything."

She tried to jerk away and he tightened his grip on her arm.

"I might die if you manage to call attention to us, Sue Ann, but before I do, I'll make sure you go with me. And I'll get Gil too. My first bullet will be for you, the second for Gil. After that, it doesn't matter." He jerked her toward him. "Got it?"

Chance saw in her eyes that she understood. But more important, he saw a small spark of fear.

Holding tightly to her arm, he looked out at the camp again. No one had stirred. He pulled her down to a crouching position and then shoved her in front of him. "Start moving, Sue Ann," he whispered, "and stay down."

He nudged her forward. Chance had meant what he said about dying and taking her with him. He just hoped to blazes she believed him, that way maybe they'd both live to see another sunset.

It was a lot rougher getting back up the mountainside than it had been coming down. But Chance wasn't sure if that was merely because it was uphill or because he had Sue Ann with him. She wasn't exactly in a hurry to get to the top.

Several times she stumbled and fell, and each time he'd yanked her roughly back to her feet and warned her that if she was trying to call attention to them from below, she was just hurrying her own death.

It took well over an hour and was nearly sunrise by the time they reached the small clearing where he'd left Diablo. Chance forced Sue Ann to sit on the ground. He retrieved a wanted poster and a piece of charcoal from one of his saddlebags and began to write his note to Gil Calder on the back of the poster. Minutes later he folded the note and slipping Diablo's bridle back on him, he tucked the note under one of its leather straps.

He turned back to look at Sue Ann. He had to go back up on the mountaintop, but if he left her here he had no doubt she'd run off. Cutting a piece of rope from the lariat tied to his saddle, Chance hunkered down before Sue Ann and tied her ankles together, then, forcing her to lie on her stomach, he looped that rope around the one that held her hands behind her.

She glared up at him.

"I'll be right back." He turned and climbed to the same spot he'd occupied only hours before while he had watched the outlaw camp below. Pulling Sue Ann's gun from his waistband he set it down on the rocks with its barrel protruding out. When the sun came up, it would glint off the gun barrel. That way, just in case they started looking for him before he was ready, they'd look in the wrong direction. He hurried back to where he'd left Sue Ann, quickly untied her legs and helped her to her feet.

"Okay, Sue Ann, we're going to take us a little walk."

She mumbled angrily through the cloth still tucked into her mouth and tried to jerk away from him. Chance yanked her back and thrust his face into hers. "Don't make this any harder on me than it already is, lady," he growled. "We can either both get out of this alive, or we can both die. Remember, if I die, you die."

Grabbing Diablo's reins, he turned the horse back in

the direction they'd come the day before and steered Sue Ann before him. "All right, let's go."

It took an hour to reach the mouth of the canyon, and by the time they did, the sun had risen over the horizon. Its golden pink rays once again turned the desert to a landscape of both primitive beauty and harsh wasteland, but at the moment, appreciating the sights was not on Chance's agenda. All he wanted to do was get to where he was going.

Sue Ann looked at him curiously, the puzzlement she felt reflecting from her eyes.

Chance smiled. "I assume your husband loves you."

The frown on her brow deepened, testifying that she did not understand his comment.

Chance turned to Diablo. "Find Morgan," he said to the horse. "Find Morgan." He raised his hand and slapped the animal's rump.

Diablo whinnied loudly and bolted forward in a full gallop.

Chance turned to Sue Ann. "Okay, now we go." He took hold of her arm and led her away from the mouth of the canyon, in the opposite direction from which they'd come. They began to climb the steep slope of the mountain again, but this time toward the plateau that overlooked the canyon from the opposite side than that which Chance had sat the night before.

He remembered the lookout he'd spotted and moved cautiously. This was not the time to get careless. Half an hour later he spotted the man.

Sue Ann made a sound in her throat. Chance stopped and grabbed her jaw with one hand. He held it tightly between his fingers and thumbs, pressing down hard as he forced her to look up at him.

"Don't," was all he said, but the guttural sound, muttered more like a growling whisper from deep within him, was enough to still her resistance and renew her fear of him.

Shoving her to the ground, and onto her stomach, he wound a length of rope around her ankles and tied it to the rope that bound her wrists.

"I'll be right back."

She grunted and wiggled about on the ground.

Chance hunkered down beside her.

"Sue Ann," he whispered, "I really don't want to hurt you. I've never hurt a woman in my life, but there's a first time for everything."

She grew still and looked up at him.

"They can't get to you before a bullet can. Remember that." He rose and moved away from her. Several minutes later he was in position.

Chance crept up behind the lookout, praying with each step that the man didn't sense him. One shot would bring everyone in the camp looking up in his direction. The man whirled just as Chance stepped up behind him, but it was too late. The butt of his Peacemaker cracked against the man's skull, and he sagged to the ground instantly. Chance grabbed the rifle that fell from the outlaw's hand before it hit the ground, then turned and hurried back to get Sue Ann. Once he had her on the plateau with him, he rolled the man onto his stomach and tied his hands and legs together as he had hers only moments before.

There was already a lot of shouting and movement in the canyon below. He glanced at Sue Ann. "I think they got my note."

She glowered at him.

Chance peered around a large rock that hid them from view of those below. He looked down into the canyon. Diablo stood near where Morgan and Rick were spread-eagled on the ground. Calder stood in front of his tent. Ringo and Curly Bill were with him. Chance's brows rose. So, Curly Bill had finally shown up.

Others were scurrying everywhere. One outlaw was untying T.J.'s hands.

Gil Calder threw a wad of paper down on the ground and stepped away from Curly Bill and Ringo. He looked up at the surrounding canyon walls.

"Burkette," he called out suddenly. "Burkette, can you hear me, you lowlife, son of a—"

Without showing himself, Chance answered, "Yeah, I hear you, Calder."

"How do I know you really got Sue Ann, Burkette?" Calder bellowed. "How do I know she ain't dead?"

Chance took Sue Ann's arm and forced her out into the open so that Calder could see her. The morning sun was just beginning to peek over the far off horizon. "That satisfy you, Calder?" Chance yelled. He let her stand there just long enough for the outlaw to spot and recognize her, then jerked Sue Ann back behind the rock.

"Yeah, but I got your woman, too, Burkette." Calder laughed. "And I also got your brothers."

Chance forced Sue Ann out into the open again, but this time he accompanied her, his gun drawn and pointed to her temple.

"That's not my woman, Calder," Chance said. "You murdered my wife a few years ago, remember? That woman you've got is just some two-bit pickpocket that was in my jail."

"That ain't the way I heard it."

"Then you heard wrong."

"But I still got your brothers," Calder roared. "And your damned horse. And I'll kill all three of them right now if you don't let Sue Ann go."

"I don't think so, Calder," Chance challenged.

"Curly, Ringo," Gil yelled, "get those two bastards over here."

The two outlaws immediately moved to cut Morgan and Rick's bindings, then hauled them to their feet and shoved them before Calder. Rick stumbled and fell to one knee. Morgan grabbed his brother's arm and helped him up to his feet.

"Wanna watch them die, Burkette?" Calder yelled up to Chance. "I'll give you a chance to reconsider. I'll kill your horse first."

He pulled his gun and lifted it to Diablo's head. His thumb pulled back on the hammer.

Chance aimed his rifle and pulled down on the trigger. An explosion of sound filled the canyon, echoing off of its sheer walls. Gil Calder's gun flew from his hand as the bullet from Chance's rifle struck its barrel.

Calder, thrown sideways by the impact, screamed and jerked his arm back.

"Send the horse out now, Calder," Chance yelled, "then my brothers and the woman. When they're out, I'll release your wife."

"No way," Calder called back, cradling his gun hand to his belly.

"Now, Calder," Chance roared. "Or your wife dies."

"No."

Chance ripped the gag from Sue Ann's mouth. "I don't think he believes me, Sue Ann," he said softly. "Unless he just doesn't love you." He glanced back at Calder. "Maybe that's it, huh? He doesn't love you?"

"He loves me," she said defiantly.

"Yeah? Then unless you want to die, you'd better convince him I mean what I say."

She stared into his eyes for several long seconds, then jerked her head around and screamed at her husband.

"Gil, do what he says. He's crazy and he means it; he'll kill me."

Calder's lips curved in a viciously ugly grin and he turned to Ringo.

Chapter Twenty-Seven

Ringo released Diablo's reins and slapped his rump. The horse instantly charged forward and ran for the mouth of the canyon.

"Now my brothers and the woman," Chance called down. "And I don't want to see you, Curly, or Ringo move until they're out, you understand?"

"This ain't fair bargaining," Calder called up. "Trading four for one."

"Yeah, but she's your wife, Calder," Chance shot back. "And she says you love her."

"Take them to the mouth of the canyon and let them go," Gil ordered one of his men.

The man motioned with his drawn gun for Morgan, Rick and T.J. to begin walking toward the opening.

Calder turned to Ringo. "You know what to do?"

Ringo nodded. "Yeah. They're not going anywhere. The minute they step out of the canyon my boys will be on their heels and follow them to Burkette." He grinned.

"But you don't kill them until I get there."

"What if he fires on us?"

"You don't kill him until I get there," Calder snarled.

Chance watched as his brothers and T.J. were escorted to the mouth of the canyon. Damn. He should have told Calder to send them out on horseback.

Sue Ann struggled against him and he jerked her back.

He'd just have to tell Calder to send out some horses, but he'd wait until his brothers and T.J. were out.

His gaze roamed over the entire camp. Something was wrong. There weren't as many cowboys milling about as there should be. He frowned, narrowing his eyes against the sun, and let his eyes roam over the scene again, more slowly this time, pausing at each tent, each shrub and bush. But he came up with the same number. Last night he'd figured there were three dozen or so in the canyon. This morning the number was less than two dozen. Twelve men were missing.

Calder was trying a double cross. He looked at Sue Ann. "You sure your husband loves you, lady?"

She glared hatefully at him.

Chance took Sue Ann's arm and forced her back over the ledge of the mountain.

"Where are we going?" she demanded. "You're supposed to let me go now."

"I'll let you go when we're safely out of here."

"That wasn't the deal," Sue Ann snapped. She stopped and whirled about to face Chance, fury etched in every line of her face. "You told Gil you'd let me go when he released your brothers and that woman."

"I lied," Chance snapped.

Sue Ann shrieked with anger and rushed at him. Her shoulder plowed into his stomach. Chance went down and she tumbled on top of him. He scrambled to his feet instantly and retrieved the rifle that had flown from his hand and fallen against a nearby cactus. Then he turned to Sue Ann and hauled her back to her feet. "I already fell into one damned cactus today, lady," he growled, his own anger near to boiling over. Chance shoved her in front of him. "Now, move, and don't try that again."

Halfway down the mountainside he saw Morgan, Rick, and T.J. walking toward him. Diablo was right behind them.

"So far so good," he muttered.

As they neared, Chance tossed Morgan the rifle.

Morgan caught it easily. "Good to see you, Chance," he said.

"Yeah, I thought we were goners for sure," Rick added.

"Don't breathe too easy yet."

T.J., unable to restrain herself, ran to Chance and threw her arms around his neck. "Oh, Chance, I'm sorry. I didn't mean for this to happen, I was just trying to . . ."

He wrapped an arm around her waist and held her to him tightly, reveling, if only momentarily, in the feel of her body pressed to his, in the relief that, for now, she was safe. "It wasn't your fault, darlin'," he said. "We've been coming toward this for a long time."

She looked up at him with understanding in her eyes.

"I just wish the odds were a little more in our favor," he added.

"My gun," T.J. said. "Did you bring my gun?"

He smiled and freeing himself from her embrace, he reached down and pulled up both the leather legging that covered his trouser leg, and the trouser itself. Chance reached into his boot and pulled out her gun.

"I don't know why I brought it, exactly." He shrugged and handed it to her. "Guess I just figured if you were still alive when I got to you, you'd want it."

She smiled. "You figured right." T.J. slipped the gun into her waistband.

"Guess you kind of lied back there about who she is,

huh, little brother?'' Morgan drawled easily, a teasing lilt
to his voice.

"Yeah. Just a little.'' He looked down at T.J. "You all
right?'' he said, his voice husky with the emotion and worry
that had been roiling in him ever since discovering that
she'd been taken.

"Yes,'' she said, and slipped an arm around his waist.
"I am now that you're here. But how are we going to get
out of this place?'' She looked pointedly at Diablo. "We
can't all ride one horse.''

"I know. But that might be the least of our worries.''

"So what's your plan?'' Rick asked.

Chance smiled, but it was more a sickly grimace than a
smile. "Well, truthfully, Rick, my plan just ran out.''

"Ran out,'' Rick repeated. He stared at his brother stupidly.

Sue Ann laughed. "You're dead now, Burkette.'' She
glared at each of them. "You're all dead.''

"Then so are you, lady,'' Morgan said.

Sue Ann paled at his words.

Chance turned to T.J. "You take Diablo and try to make
it back to town. Go to Sheriff Perkins and get us some
help and some horses. We'll start walking and hopefully
meet you on the trail.''

She shook her head. "But he'll kill you the minute you
let her go.''

Chance looked at Sue Ann. "I know. That's why I have
no intention of letting her go.''

"No,'' T.J. said. She shook her head. "I'm not leaving
you. Let Rick or Morgan go.''

Taking her by the arm Chance gently steered her away
from the others. "Darlin', listen,'' he began, "I don't
want—''

"I'm not leaving you, Chance.''

He sighed. "I don't think I told you this before,'' he
said, his voice soft, "but you're the stubbornest, orneriest,

most troublesome, bull-headed vixen I've ever met. You infuriate me. And I love you."

T.J. smiled, suddenly realizing how desperately she had wanted to hear those words from him. She looked deep and hard into his eyes and knew she would never again be able to love a man as deeply, as thoroughly, as she loved Chance Burkette. "I love you, too, Chance," she whispered, and raised a hand to gently touch his cheek. "With all my heart."

"Uh, I hate to break this up," Morgan said, "but I think we've got company."

Chance whirled to look toward his brother. Instead his eyes caught sight of half a dozen men bearing down on them from the direction of the canyon mouth.

"Son of a . . ." Chance pushed T.J. behind him. Calder had double crossed him and sent some of his men after them.

"Hit the rocks," Morgan yelled. He turned and ran, shoving Rick before him.

"Give me a damned gun," Rick called to Chance.

"I don't have another one."

"Great."

The four dived behind a cluster of boulders. The outlaws instantly spread out. Two ran to the right, two to the left. One hunkered down behind a small ledge of rocks, another stood behind a tall saguaro. But no one fired.

"What the are they waiting for?" T.J. asked. She knelt beside Chance, the .38 held tight within her grip, her finger ready on the trigger.

"I don't know, but I don't think we should wait here to find out." Chance looked toward the rock cliffs at his right and began to move away from the others. He took only a few steps, paused, and looked back. "Come on."

"Where?" Morgan asked.

"Away from here," Chance said. "If we stay in this spot," he glanced upward, toward the top of the mountain from which he'd just descended, "they can work their way around behind us. "And if we go up, we're trapped. Our only choice is to see if we can find a safer position."

"With the amount of ammunition we've got, I don't think it really matters," Morgan drawled. "Do you?"

Chance looked hard at his brother. "We've been in tough situations before, Morg, and we've survived. I'm not about to give up on this one until I have to."

Morgan nodded. "Let's go."

They began to climb the rocky crevice in the direction that Chance indicated, moving parallel to where they'd been.

Suddenly Sue Ann, her hands still tied behind her back, broke away from between Morgan and Rick and made a dash in the opposite direction.

"Get her," Chance shouted.

Rick, startled by Sue Ann's action, and propelled into his own by his brother's shout, lunged for her. His arms encircled her waist, his shoulder rammed against her spine, and his bulk and the impacting force of his body smashing against hers, brought her crashing to the ground. Rick landed on top of her.

The air left her lungs in a loud whoosh and Sue Ann immediately began to gasp for more.

"Rick, get down," Morgan yelled. "You're in the open."

Grabbing Sue Ann's arm, Rick dragged her back to the rocks, then crumbled down himself and pulled in several deep gulps of air.

"You all right?" Chance asked.

Rick nodded.

Chance turned his eyes to Sue Ann. Never before in his entire life had he wanted to even so much as raise a hand to a woman, but now, as he glared down at Gil Calder's wife, he knew why some men did. Hatred turned his features as hard as the surrounding desert rocks, and his eyes dark and fathomless. He grabbed Sue Ann's chin between his fingers, and squeezing roughly, forced her to look up at him. "Lady, you pull some stunt like that again, and it'll be the last thing you ever do. You understand?"

"He'll kill you for this," Sue Ann snarled.

"Then you'll go with us."

He felt her hatred, but the fear he'd seen in her eyes earlier was still there.

"Don't push it, Sue Ann," Chance said. "If I feel I'm going, you'd better believe I'm taking you with me." He turned back to the others. "Come on. As long as we have her, Calder's not going to fire on us unless he can get real close for fear she'll take a bullet. And we're not going to give him that opportunity."

Moving in a single line, with Chance leading the way, T.J. directly behind him, and Morgan bringing up the rear, they began making their way through the rocks, squeezing through narrow crevices, jagged natural passageways, and over and around huge boulders. Several times Morgan called up to Chance that someone was behind them.

"Burkette."

The lone word echoed over the silent desert mountain range.

Chance stopped dead in his tracks, his hand automatically moving to rest on the butt of the Peacemaker strapped to his thigh.

"Burkette?"

"That's Calder," he said softly to the others.

"You can't make it across the flatlands," Calder called out. An ugly laugh followed the threatening words.

Chance walked back to where Sue Ann stood, grabbed her arm and half dragged, half shoved, her up and onto a rocky ledge that he knew put both of them in clear view of Calder and his men.

"Chance," T.J. said. She and the others stood in the shadow of the ledge. Terror filled her heart. "You're a clear target up there."

"Trust me." He held onto Sue Ann and looked out at the deceivingly peaceful looking desert. No one was within sight. "Calder," he called loudly. "You make one move toward any of us, take one shot, and Sue Ann dies. You got that? Your wife will be the first to go."

A single rifle shot suddenly rent the air.

A soft shriek spew from Sue Ann's lips as the bullet struck her chest and she sagged to the ground.

"Chance!" T.J. screamed.

He jumped immediately to the ground.

"I don't believe it," he muttered, staring up at the dead woman. "I don't believe it." Her red-gold hair cascaded over the edge of the rock precipice and glistened beneath the morning sun. One delicate ivory hand was outstretched and half hidden beneath the tangle of silken strands. "The son of a bitch murdered his own wife."

"Yeah, and now he's coming after us," Morgan yelled, his words drawing Chance's attention to the outlaws now making their way up the mountainside toward them.

Several more shots split the air. T.J. turned and fired at one of the outlaws who was running from the cover of one saguaro to another, his six gun spitting bullets as he moved.

He fell just before reaching his destination.

Chance shot surely and slowly, squeezing down on the trigger of the Peacemaker only when he had a man definitely within his sights. He fired three bullets in little more than one minute and took out three outlaws.

Morgan did the same with the rifle.

"I feel helpless as hell," Rick yelled.

Another two minutes, another round of shots, and T.J., after taking out five of the outlaws, found herself out of bullets. She tossed the gun down and knelt beside Chance, holding on to him and saying a prayer, the first she'd said in she couldn't remember how long.

She started as Chance's gun fired again and she felt the small tremor in his arm at the weapon's kick.

"I'm out of ammo," Morgan called, and tossed the rifle down.

T.J. glanced at him, and tightened her grip around Chance's waist. He'd already reloaded once. He had enough bullets left on his holster for once more, but T.J. knew that wasn't enough to get them out of this situation alive.

Chance fired until his gun was empty, quickly reloaded, and then slipped it into his holster. He grabbed T.J.'s hand.

"Let's move," he ordered gruffly, "but stay low."

Morgan and Rick nodded and got to their feet.

Bullets whizzed all around them, ricocheting off of the rocks they were crouched behind.

Chance held tightly to T.J.'s hand as they hurried over the rocky terrain.

"Where are we going?" she asked, gulping for breath, as he momentarily paused.

Morgan and Rick moved up behind her.

"I don't know," Chance said, "but moving is better than sitting still and waiting for them to pick us off."

The gunfire that had been ripping the terrain around them ceased.

"What happened?" T.J. asked. "Why did they stop?"

"They're probably moving in closer. We're hidden behind these boulders for the moment."

He drew her into his arms and held her tightly against his chest.

"I'm sorry, darlin'," he whispered, and pressed his lips against her forehead. "I thought as long as we had Sue Ann, we had a pretty good chance of getting out of this."

T.J. looked up at him, the love she felt for Chance Burkette shining in her eyes.

"If this is anyone's fault, Chance, it's mine." She reached up to touch a caressing hand to his cheek. "I should never have tried to fool her."

He opened his mouth to speak again, but T.J. pressed her finger to his lips to silence him.

"I love you, Chance Burkette," she whispered. "And that's all that matters."

Chance lowered his head and brushed his lips lightly across hers, the touch of her mouth bringing a groan to his throat. But it was a groan not only of passion and desire for the woman he held in his arms, but also of regret for all of the days they would never spend together, at least not on this earth.

"Chance, move it," Morgan suddenly bellowed.

Several shots broke the quiet air and slammed into the hillside just above Chance's head.

He grabbed T.J.'s hand and lunged forward, then suddenly stopped.

T.J. rammed into his back and bounced off of him. She looked up at him, momentarily dazed.

"Damn," Chance swore. He looked back at the others, then turned and drew T.J. into his arms. "This is it, guys," he said to his brothers, over her head. "I think our luck just ran out."

T.J. pulled away from him and looked around. There was nowhere else to go. The hillside dropped off into nothingness several feet away, sloped down on one side, offering no cover whatsoever and ascended steeply on the other side, lending little hope of being climbed. She turned and looked back in the direction they'd come. Gil Calder and his men were scrambling over the rocks toward them.

She slipped her hand into Chance's and watched the Calder gang approach.

"You got any bullets left?" Morgan asked softly.

"Yeah," Chance answered. "But not enough to do us any good."

"At least take out Calder," Morgan said.

Chance drew the Peacemaker from his holster and, his finger ready on the trigger, the hammer already drawn back, he aimed and waited. If he was going to shoot Calder, he was going to make sure he killed him.

Chapter Twenty-Eight

T.J. held tightly to Chance's hand, her fingers entwined with his. As was her heart, she thought, as she watched Gil Calder and his men draw nearer. It can't end like this, her mind screamed over and over.

She could feel the tension that emanated from the men standing on either side of her. Chance's hand was hard and strong, his grip on her solid, offering her the strength she needed to face what was about to happen. Morgan, on her left, and Rick on the other side of him, stood rigid and unmoving, willing to meet their fates with dignity and pride.

No, T.J. thought. This is wrong.

Then she felt it. An insane, but unresistible urge to look around, to look at the mountain's edge behind her, at the sheer drop it undoubtedly led to. A sense of dèjá vu swept over her and caused shivers to snake their way up her spine. She took a step back, trying to see over the edge.

Maybe she'd been wrong she thought suddenly. Maybe she hadn't been hurtled back through time to prevent

Jake Calder's birth and save Lisa's life. Maybe she'd been sent to save Chance. Her fingers tightened around his. She took another step back and strained to see over her shoulder.

"What are you doing?" Chance whispered.

She glanced up at him quickly. His eyes remained riveted on Gil Calder.

"Step back," she said. It was their only hope. "Please. Trust me," she implored, echoing the words he had spoken to her only a short while before.

He threw her a puzzled look but nodded and did as she asked. The spurs on his boots jingled as he moved.

"Chance?" Morgan said.

"Step back," Chance ordered.

"We'll go over the edge," Rick snapped.

"What the hell difference does it make, Rick?" Chance growled. "We're going to die anyway."

The two brothers did as he requested.

T.J. felt a spark of hope burst to life in her heart. It was the same place. "Oh, God," she breathed. She looked up at Chance.

"Well, ain't this a real pretty picture," Gil Calder said. His voice was laced with contempt for the group that stood before him.

T.J. whirled around and stared at the outlaw. Hatred, regret, sorrow, and searing fury swelled within her breast. Because of him Lisa had died. And now he was threatening to kill her, Chance, Morgan, and Rick.

She looked back at the cliff. What if . . . ? Her mind spun with questions and fears. There was no guarantee it would work. It had been a freak happening. A quirk of time. She looked back at Calder who was still gloating and taunting Chance and his brothers. But what did they have to lose? She straightened, lifting her chin defiantly, and looked directly at Gil Calder. "Mr. Calder," she said loudly.

Interrupted in the tirade of obscenities he had been

spewing at Chance and his brothers, Gil started at her outburst. He turned hate-filled eyes on her. "What?" An evil grin pulled at his lips. "You want to make a little deal with me, honey?"

"What I want is a favor."

"A favor?" He roared with laughter. So did the men standing beside and behind him.

"I would like a minute to say good-bye to my friends in private."

"You want us to leave?" Gil asked, snickering in disbelief.

"No. Just let us talk together for a minute." She shrugged. "Unless you're afraid we can overpower you somehow. Are you afraid?" She hoped goading him would get her what she desperately needed.

"Tell Burkette to drop the gun," Gil ordered.

She turned to Chance. "Holster it," she said softly. Her eyes were full of pleading. "Please?" she added, at his hesitancy.

Chance returned the Peacemaker to his holster. "What are you doing?" he asked, his deep voice barely above a whisper. "If we're going to die, I want him to die too."

She looked at Calder. "Is it okay? Can we have a minute?"

"Yeah, sure," he growled. "Why not."

T.J. motioned for Morgan and Rick to come near. They leaned down slightly, bending their heads toward her.

"You got a plan?" Rick asked anxiously.

"Yes, but you may not like it," T.J. said.

They looked at her curiously.

"What have we got to lose?" Chance asked, looking first at one brother, then the other.

They both shrugged.

"I want us to hold hands, tightly, and step backward off the cliff."

"What?" they all said in unison.

If the situation hadn't been so desperate, T.J. would

have laughed at the startled look that came to each hand-some face as they stared at her.

"Please. I can't guarantee anything, but. ..." She looked at Chance, her hand already holding his. "It's the only chance we've got."

"I don't call that much of a chance," Morgan said.

"Then as you all said before, what have we got to lose?" T.J. asked.

"I think I'd rather just let Calder shoot me," Rick said. "Jumping off a cliff just isn't natural."

"Neither is standing still and letting a bullet pierce your heart," T.J. countered. "Anyway, do you really want to give Gil Calder the satisfaction of killing you?"

They all answered the same. "No."

"Good. Then trust me." She looked at each of them in turn. "I don't want to die," she said softly, turning her gaze to Chance. "Not when I've just found something wonderful to live for."

He smiled and squeezed her hand.

"Please." She looked at each of them again. "I know it sounds crazy, but do it."

They all nodded.

"Okay." T.J. straightened and turned back to Calder. "Thank you," she said politely. She reached out and took Morgan's hand in her free one. "Take Rick's hand," she told Morgan, and waited until he did, then she looked back at Calder. "And now, Mr. Calder." They all took a step back, and T.J. smiled. "Good-bye."

Another step and T.J. felt them plummet over the edge of the cliff. They fell swiftly, their bodies plunging toward the canyon floor. She held tightly to Chance and Morgan's hands, her fingers pressing into their flesh, between the bones of their knuckles, a desperate clasp to keep them together—through time, or to death.

"Burkette!" Gil Calder yelled after them, and ran forward.

As if what was happening were in slow motion, T.J. looked up at the cliff's promontory and saw Gil Calder looking down after them, an expression of mingled shock and fury etched on his face. She felt a smile of satisfaction form on her own.

"Burkette!" he called again.

Then suddenly, Gil Calder was gone. The vast blue sky and blazing sun were the only things visible to T.J. as she continued to fall, and fall, and fall.

T.J. opened her eyes and looked up at the sky. It was black. She bolted upright, the fingers of her right hand still entwined tightly about Chance's, those of her left holding to Morgan. She jerked around and stared at Chance. He lay on his back, the Peacemaker still securely sheathed within his holster, his hat lying on the ground beside him.

She whirled around to look at his brothers. Morgan and Rick lay in similar positions to her left. T.J. looked up at the sky again. Now she saw the stars, hundreds of them. And the moon hung over the horizon, shining brightly. A soft roar suddenly filled the otherwise still night air. T.J. cocked her head and listened. A car. It was the sound of a car.

"T.J.," Chance muttered softly. His fingers moved on hers, pressing down slightly.

Her heart nearly jumped into her throat. She felt like screaming with joy. "Chance, Chance," T.J. cried. She shook his shoulder. "Wake up, Chance, wake up. It worked! Oh, my God, it worked." She shivered with excitement. "I can't believe it. It worked!"

Chance roused himself to a sitting position and looked at her, total confusion in his eyes. "Damn, what happened? Are we in heaven?"

"No," T.J. said, holding tightly to his arm. She was afraid if she let go of him, he might disappear.

"Then we're in hell."

He reached up and touched the back of his head gingerly. "That must be why I've got a headache."

"No," T.J. said, and laughed softly. "We're okay. We're not in heaven or hell. We're not dead."

"We're not?" His brow furrowed in a deep frown. "How could we not be dead?" He looked up at the cliff, its ridge a good seven or eight hundred feet above them. "Impossible." He nodded, as if in confirmation of his own thoughts. "We're dead."

"No." T.J. threw her arms around his shoulders and hugged him. "We're not, I swear." She laughed again, then turned to rouse his brothers. "Morgan, Rick, wake up."

Morgan's eyes opened first, then Rick's. Both men sat up and looked around in confusion. "Where the hell are we? Or was that a bad choice of words?" Morgan asked.

They all looked at T.J.

"We're at the bottom of the cliff," she said simply. "The one we jumped off of."

"That's impossible. Unless we're dead," Rick said. He slapped his hands together. "I don't feel dead. I mean, I felt the sting."

"I think I need to explain a few things to you," T.J. said, "while we walk to town."

"Walk?" Morgan said. "You mean we can't just float?"

She reached over and pinched his arm.

"Ouch!" He jerked away from her.

"You're alive, silly," she said. "Now get up and start walking."

Chance stood up and brushed himself off, then stiffened and reached for his Peacemaker. "Is Calder still up there?" he asked, and glanced up at the mountaintop.

"No," T.J. said. "He's gone, and we're safe." She slipped an arm around his, and then looked at Morgan and Rick. "We're safe," she repeated.

"You're sure?" Chance asked.

She smiled. "I'm sure." T.J. turned toward Morgan and Rick who were still staring up at the cliff top. "Come on you guys. Start walking, and I'll explain what happened as best as I can."

Fifteen minutes later they arrived at the top of a hill. T.J. looked down into the valley where she knew the Old Tucson Studios were located. Except for what she knew were the security lights of the studio, blackness hung over the valley floor. Obviously no movies were being shot that night.

They continued to walk.

"Believe me, guys," T.J. said again, for the hundredth time, "I know it sounds like something out of a sci-fi movie, but—"

"A what?" Chance said.

"Sorry, I'll explain that one another time. Anyway, it happened. I'm telling the truth. I traveled through time to your world, and now you've traveled to mine. You're not in 1881 anymore. It's 1996."

"Yeah. And I'm Billy the Kid," Morgan said.

"I think you're too old for that one, Morg," Rick teased.

They walked over another small hill and came to Speedway Road.

The three men stared at its surface. "What's that?" Chance said.

T.J. frowned. "What's what?"

"That stuff, on top of the road."

"Asphalt." She chuckled softly.

"Asphalt," Chance repeated, and looked at her skeptically.

"Come on, it won't swallow you up." She pulled them onto the edge of the road. "Town's this way."

They followed her hesitantly.

"Now, there are a lot of changes since your time. And I do mean a lot. It'll take some getting used to."

"You sure this whole thing isn't just a joke?" Morgan asked. "Or a dream?"

A car suddenly appeared at the crest of Gates Pass and bore down on them.

Morgan nearly jumped out of his boots.

Rick let out a startled shriek.

Chance pushed T.J. behind him and, crouching low, whipped the Peacemaker from his holster.

"No!" T.J. screamed, lunging for his arm.

The car sped past.

Chance resheathed the gun and stared after it. "What was that thing?" he said, voicing the same question that he knew was running through both of his brothers' minds.

"A car."

"A car," he repeated, and looked at her. "So what the hell is a car?"

"A horseless carriage."

"Yeah. A carriage that speeds down the road all by itself. With lights on it."

"Yes," T.J. said. "Exactly. Except not quite by itself. People drive them."

His brows rose. "You mean there was somebody in that thing?"

"Yes."

Chance shook his head. "Not for me," he mumbled.

T.J. laughed again. "You'll want one."

Chance shook his head again. "Uh-uh, not me. I'll stick with a horse."

They came to the crest of Gates Pass.

"What the hell?" Morgan muttered, and stopped cold.

They all paused to stare down at the city of Tucson.

"What in blazes is that?" Rick asked, his voice filled with awe.

"Tucson," T.J. said.

"Tucson? That's not Tucson," Rick argued.

"Not the one you knew, but it's the one I know." She chuckled at their startled expressions. "Remember guys, it's 1996. The world's grown a lot since 1881."

"Maybe too much," Chance said.

T.J. turned to him, her excitement at the fact that they'd made it safely to 1996 rather than being killed by Gil Calder suddenly paled. Had she made a mistake in bringing him with her? She had saved his life, but what if he couldn't get used to life in 1996? What if he didn't like it?

Chance turned to her then, as if able to read her thoughts. He wrapped an arm around her shoulders and drew her to him. "It's all right, darlin'," he said softly. "As long as we're together everything will be all right."

Three hours later they stood in front of the house T.J. had grown up in, and which her parents still lived in. She turned to the three men.

"I don't know how this is going to go, guys," she said. "I mean, this is going to be a big shock for them too."

Chance took her hand and held it tightly in his. "We're with you," he drawled softly.

"But Lisa died before I was thrown back to your time. If . . ." Her voice threatened to break. She cleared her throat and tried again. "If Sue Ann's dying didn't prevent . . . if Gil had children by another woman, then Lisa might still be—"

"Let's go find out," Chance urged.

Morgan and Rick nodded their support.

"They might not understand about you guys," T.J. added. "They may not believe what happened."

Chance smiled. "You're their daughter," he said simply, "they'll believe you."

T.J. inhaled deeply and walked up the path that led to her parents' front door. The house was exactly as it had always been; a low, rambling adobe ranch house set in the middle of twenty-five acres of natural desert. Light streamed out from the windows of the kitchen and family rooms. T.J. reached for the keys that usually dangled from a clasp on her police holster and realized she didn't have them. She knocked on the door.

"Mom?" she called out. "Dad?"

The door opened almost instantly. "T.J., where have you been?" Stella McAllister asked, an anxious tone to her voice. "We were worried sick over you, disappearing for several days like that."

T.J. smiled. "Sorry, Mom. May we come in?"

Stella looked at the three men standing behind T.J., her green eyes taking in their clothes, and looking for several seconds at the gun strapped to Chance's thigh.

"It's okay, Mom," T.J. said, seeing her mother's apprehension. "He's a very special friend." She smiled. "They all are."

Stella nodded and stepped back to allow them into the house.

"Of course, honey, I'm sorry," she said, and smiled. "Please, come in, all of you."

"Stella, who's there?" Ken McAllister called to his wife from the family room.

"Your other daughter," Stella called back.

T.J.'s heart leapt with a spurt of hope at her mother's words.

Ken and Lisa appeared in the archway that led to the family room.

"Lisa?" T.J. said, both shocked and thrilled.

"T.J.," Lisa said breathlessly. "Where've you been?" She ran to T.J. and threw her arms around her neck. "We were all so worried about you."

T.J.'s eyes brimmed over with tears. "About me?" She hugged Lisa to her.

Lisa released her hold on T.J. and stepped back so that Ken could kiss his daughter.

"When you disappeared like that, T.J., we didn't know what to think." He held her hand tightly. "Everybody's been worried sick, honey. The department even put an all points out for you."

"The department?" Chance asked.

T.J. looked up at him. "The police department. I'm a cop. . . ." She smiled at his frown of confusion. "A police officer, like you, remember?"

He nodded. "Oh, yeah."

T.J. turned to look at Lisa again. "You're all right. I mean, you're really all right?"

"Me?" Lisa said. "Of course I'm all right, why wouldn't I be? I'm just a plain old working girl, remember? Not a cop."

T.J. shook her head. So her sojourn back in time had worked, but obviously she was the only one, other than Chance and his brothers, who knew it now.

She turned back to her parents and Lisa, then looped her arm through Chance's. "Mom, Dad, Lisa, let me introduce some very special friends to you, and then, if you'll fix us some coffee, Mom, I'll try to explain where I've been."

Epilogue

"Everyone want Cokes?" Lisa called out through the open patio door.

"Beer," Chance called back. He turned to T.J., who sat next to him on the picnic bench at the rear of her parents' home. "Coke." He shook his head as if in puzzlement. "Why'd they stop calling it sarsaparilla?"

T.J. smiled and shrugged. "I don't know. I think there's a difference though, between Coke and sarsaparilla."

"Not that I can tell," Chance countered.

Rick bounded away from the table to help Lisa carry the tray of drinks outside.

Morgan stood at the other end of the table, one foot propped on the bench, one arm leaning on his knee as he stared down at the newspapers that they'd spread all over the table.

Behind them, at the rock barbeque pit her father had built when T.J. was ten years old, Ken McAllister stood keeping watch over the steaks sizzling on the grill. Stella was busy setting up another table with plates and napkins.

"It's still hard to believe," Morgan said.

"You've only been here a month," T.J. answered. "Give it time."

Chance shook his head. "I just wish they hadn't come to that assumption."

T.J.'s gaze followed his to the article he was staring at. Chance had the *Tucson Extra* spread out before him, the edition's date of publication, August 1, 1881 was printed under the paper's name. Directly beneath the date large headlines proclaimed Marshal Chance Burkette and his brothers had disappeared and authorities presumed they had been killed by Gil Calder and his gang of cowboys. She'd read the story several times, but her eyes moved over the words again.

MARSHAL CHANCE BURKETTE AND
BROTHERS KILLED

Several days ago Marshal Chance Burkette rode out of Tucson in pursuit of Gil Calder and his gang, who had kidnapped a young woman from the city jail. It was learned from Doctor Zachary Burkette, that he suspected the Marshal's brothers, Deputies Morgan and Rick Burkette, were working undercover in the Calder gang to lure the outlaw into a trap and apprehend him. It has been several weeks now since the Marshal rode out, and not a word has been heard from him, but the Calder gang has been seen in town several times. Sadly, we have heard rumors, from some of the gang members, that the Marshal and his brothers, as well as the young lady the Marshal was trying to rescue, were killed and are buried somewhere out in the desert. The gang members will not say where, as obviously it is somewhere near their hideout.

"Yes," T.J. said, "but it could have been worse."

Chance turned and met her gaze.

"It could have been true."

He smiled. "Except for you," he said, and leaned over to touch the tip of her nose with his lips. "You were our miracle."

T.J. laughed. "I'm the one who got you into that mess."

Chance's expression turned serious. "No, darlin'. We were after the Calders long before you showed up. We would have ended up on that mountain even if you hadn't come." He leaned forward and touched his lips lightly to hers. "But you got us out."

T.J. felt so much love for him that she thought she'd burst.

"I'm just glad Calder got what he had coming to him," Morgan said.

T.J. and Chance both turned to look at the newspaper Morgan stared down at. It was another issue of the *Tucson Extra*. This one dated March 5, 1884.

Jake Calder dies in gunfight.

That satisfied the Burkette brothers. What satisfied T.J. was one little sentence halfway down the article.

Jake Calder, whose wife mysteriously vanished around the same time the Calders presumedly killed Marshal Chance Burkette and his brothers, Morgan and Rick, in 1881, left no heirs or other family.

She smiled as Morgan flipped to another paper, dated the spring of 1882.

Earp posse in shootout with cowboys. Curly Bill killed.

And then yet another.

The body of John Ringo, renowned outlaw and partner of the late Curly Bill Brocious and Gil Calder, was found dead at Turkey Creek. Assailant unknown. Some suspect

*the Earp posse killed Ringo. Others swear it was Wyatt
Earp's friend, Doc Holliday.*

Morgan began to fold up the old newspapers.

"Those are all great," T.J. said. "But I'm kind of partial
to this article." She pointed to a newspaper only two days
old.

*August 5, 1996. Retired Police Officer Theresa Jane
"T.J." McAllister was married today to Chance Burkette,
also in law enforcement, and a newcomer to the city of
Tucson. Her bridesmaid was her sister, Lisa McAllister.
The groom's two brothers, Morgan and Rick Burkette, shared
the duties of best man.*

At that moment the doorbell rang.

"I'll get it," Lisa called, and disappeared into the house,
with Rick right behind her.

"Umm, those steaks sure do smell good," Morgan said,
glancing over at Ken McAllister.

"You boys just hang onto your appetites," Stella said.
"And we'll eat in a few minutes." She set a huge bowl of
potato salad in the center of the table she'd just set.

T.J. looked lovingly at her parents. It had been a shock,
when she'd told them what happened, and they'd found
it almost incompehensible, but one thing they had always
taught their daughters to do was to tell the truth, so they
believed her.

And they'd welcomed Chance, Morgan, and Rick into
the family with open arms.

Lisa had especially welcomed Rick.

"Hey, look what's here," Lisa called, reappearing at the
patio door. She stepped aside to reveal Rick carrying a
large box. He walked to the table where his two brothers
and T.J. still sat.

"It's the brochures," T.J. said. She stood and pulled the

lid off of the box. Chance rose and slipped an arm around her waist. T.J. lifted one of the brochures from the box and held it up so everyone could see.

The Burkette Agency, Private Investigations
Chance, T.J., Morgan, and Rick Burkette, owners.

A picture of the four of them standing together appeared under the heading.

T.J. pulled Chance away from the others as they each took a brochure from the box and began to look it over, commenting excitedly about the prospects of what was yet to come from their new venture.

She looked up at him, concern evident in her eyes. "Are you all right, Chance?" she asked softly. "Here, I mean, in this time? Are you happy?"

He slipped his arms around her waist and pulled her close to him. A crooked smile curved his lips and lifted one side of his dark mustache. "I'll always be all right, darlin'," he said easily, "as long as I'm with you." His head lowered toward her. "Anywhere, anytime." His lips covered hers then, and T.J. felt his love flow through her body, entwining their souls together, forever.

Author Note

I have borrowed many historical facts for the background of this story and of course fabricated a few. The Calders, as well as T.J., Chance and their families were born in my mind. However, Curly Bill Brocious and Johnny Ringo, two of the most notorious outlaws of Arizona history, were quite real and did lead a gang called the Cowboys, all of whom wore red sashes to distinguish themselves as gang members, and terrorized the countryside in the late 1870's and early 1880's . . . until Wyatt Earp, his brothers, and Doc Holliday brought their own brand of law to Tombstone, Arizona.

Several months after the famous gunfight at the O.K. Corral, and in retaliation for killing several members of the Clanton and McLowry families, Curly Bill Brocious ambushed the Earps and Doc Holliday. It was the last thing Curly Bill ever did.

Johnny Ringo met his end at Turkey Creek, Arizona in 1882. Though the killing is credited by many to Wyatt Earp or Doc Holliday, who had formed a posse and were scouring the land for the remainder of the Cowboys at this time, my research showed that there is no real proof of this. Only Ringo, Doc, and Wyatt know for sure what happened that day, and they're not talking anymore.

I have tried to make the geographical locales for my story as authentic as possible, though with the Tucson of 1881 I have taken a few liberties with the names of streets and saloons. Otherwise, the landscape of both 1881 and 1996 I believe to be accurate.

About the Author

Cheryln Jac is the pseudonym for award-winning Zebra author Cheryl Biggs. Cheryl lives in Concord, California, at the foot of Mt. Diablo, with her husband Jack, who is more supportive of her writing (and her quirks) than any woman could ever ask for, and their menagerie of five cats and one new little dog. When she's not writing, reading, traveling, shopping, she's watching television, preferably mysteries, and whenever possible, a good cowboy or detective movie. Under her psuedonym of Cheryln Jac she has written *Shadows in Time, Night's Immortal Kiss, Night's Immortal Touch*. As Cheryl Biggs, she writes historical romances for Zebra; *Mississippi Flame, Across a Rebel Sea,* and the Braggette Brothers stories; *Hearts Deceived, Hearts Denied, Hearts Defiant,* and *Hearts Divided.*

She also writes contemporary romance under the names Cheryl Biggs and Cheryln Biggs. If you would like promotional materials, or to be included on Cheryl's mailing list, please send a SASE to Cheryl Biggs, P.O.B. 6557, Concord, Ca. 94520.